Never
Cry Wolf

Never Cry Wolf

CYNTHIA EDEN

BRAVA

KENSINGTON PUBLISHING CORP.
www.kensingtonbooks.com

BRAVA BOOKS are published by

Kensington Publishing Corp.
119 West 40th Street
New York, NY 10018

All Kensington titles, imprints and distributed lines are available at special quantity discounts for bulk purchases for sales promotion, premiums, fund-raising, educational or institutional use.

Special book excerpts or customized printings can also be created to fit specific needs. For details, write or phone the office of the Kensington Special Sales Manager: Kensington Publishing Corp., 119 West 40th Street, New York, NY 10018. Attn. Special Sales Department. Phone: 1-800-221-2647.

Brava and the B logo are Reg. U.S. Pat. & TM Off.

ISBN-13: 978-0-7582-4215-0
ISBN-10: 0-7582-4215-8

First Kensington Trade Paperback Printing: July 2011

10 9 8 7 6 5 4 3 2 1

Printed in the United States of America

*This book is for all of the readers who wrote to me
and asked, "What about Lucas? Will he get a book?"
He has one now, and I hope you enjoy it.
Long live those wolves!*

Chapter 1

Lucas Simone paced the confines of the eight-by-twelve foot jail cell, a snarl on his lips. The wolf within howled with rage, and the man that the world generally saw, well, he felt more than a little pissed, too.

Collared for a murder he hadn't committed. Talk about shit-luck. Yeah, Lucas had played on the wild side, he'd even killed before, and the bastards had more than deserved the death he'd given them.

But this time, for this crime, he was innocent. Right. Like the cops would buy that story.

His hands tightened around the bars. If he wanted, he could rip those bars apart, and if they didn't let him out soon, he would. "I want my lawyer! Now!" His pack had to know where he was. A leader didn't just vanish, and if he didn't make contact with them soon, Lucas wasn't exactly sure what would happen.

Probably hell on earth . . . or wolves running wild in LA, which, yeah, that equaled hell on earth. Especially if he wasn't there to keep the wilder wolves on their leashes.

Everyone already knew that wolf shifters had a tendency to dance on the edge of sanity. Once those leashes were gone . . . *hello, hell.*

The bars beneath his fingers began to bend as the rage swelled inside him.

A human was dead. Tossed on his doorstep like garbage.

Not my kill.

Because Lucas had a rule. Just one. *Don't attack the weak.*

As far as he was concerned, there wasn't any being weaker than a human.

"Guard!" His teeth burned as they lengthened in his mouth. No more fucking nice wolf. He was getting out, one way or another. The metal bars groaned within his grasp.

"Simone!" Not the guard's voice. The dumbass detective who'd brought him in for "questioning." Only he hadn't been questioned. The cop had just thrown his ass into a cage.

Lucas's kind didn't do so well with cages.

He'd make sure the detective didn't make the same mistake again.

His eyes lifted, tracked to the left to meet that beady gray stare—

And instead got caught by a pair of green eyes.

His nostrils flared. The woman stood behind the detective, a slight frown between her brows. She was tall, curved just the way he wanted a woman to be, with sensual, full breasts and hips that would let a guy hold on tight for a wild ride.

Pretty face. Straight nose, tilted just a bit on the end— kinda cute. A light spray of freckles across her high cheekbones. Sexy red lips. Jaw that was a bit stubborn.

And gorgeous hair. A thick mane of dark, dark brown hair that curled around her face.

Her stare widened as he gazed at her. She licked her lips, a quick swipe of her tongue.

His cock began to swell, an immediate and instinctive response, even as suspicion rose within him. What was the sexy little human doing at his cell? Was she another cop? A lawyer?

Her eyes—the greenest he'd ever seen—stayed locked on his. That emerald stare didn't waver at all. Not even to glance toward the right, to lock on the jagged remains of his ear.

Most women looked. Like they couldn't help it. Looked, flinched. So did the men.

Lucas had never really given a damn. The top of his ear had been ripped off years ago in the worst fight of his life. He'd been ten at the time.

But she didn't look.

A guard came scurrying into the holding area, keys loose and jingling in his right hand.

"Get him out." The order came from Detective Dickhead.

Lucas let go of the bars, even as he tried to chain the beast that demanded he lunge for the ass's throat.

Playing it civilized sucked.

The door opened seconds later with a harsh moan.

The woman smiled—with her lips, not her eyes. "Lover . . ." A sexy purr of sound.

He felt that purr run the length of his body, even as the lie burned in his mind. He knew he'd never been *this* lady's lover.

Not yet, anyway.

"You're free to go, Romeo," Detective Dickhead drawled. "Your lady gave you an alibi for last night, one that we were able to back up with accounts from three other witnesses."

Bullshit.

Last night, he'd gone running solo. He'd let the wolf out so that he could howl and hunt as much as he wanted.

He'd come home with the taste of blood on his tongue, and then he'd found blood staining his front steps.

Lucas rolled his shoulders, trying to force the tension back, and stalked out of the cage. Then she was in his arms. Throwing herself against him. Wrapping slender arms around his neck and pressing her mouth to his.

Lucas wasn't a stupid man. If a sexy woman wanted to plaster her curves against him, he wasn't gonna argue.

But he was most certainly gonna take.

His hands lifted, caught her, locked right around the firm flare of her ass, and he pressed her closer. His mouth took hers, his tongue plunged deep.

Oh, but she tasted sweet.

Not the wild tang of his kind. Women who could shift into the powerful form of a beast usually tasted like aged wine.

She tasted like candy.

He'd always had a sweet tooth.

Her tongue moved against his, soft strokes, like a kitten, licking. A moan trembled in her throat.

His cock strained against the front of his jeans. Okay, so he didn't know who she was. Not gonna stop him. Because he'd sure like to screw h—

"Ahem." Dickhead again.

The woman in his arms stiffened.

For show. He knew she hadn't forgotten the detective's presence. And neither had he. Lucas just hadn't given a damn that they were being observed.

"Sorry I wasn't here sooner." Her voice was husky, sexual. Like a silken stroke right over his groin.

"No problem, babe." He curved his fingers under her chin. Two could play. He saw the small tremor that shook her, and he smiled. Deliberately, he let her see the sharp edge of his teeth. Way sharper than a human's.

But no fear flashed in her eyes.

Interesting.

The lady knew the score, he'd stake his pack's reputation on that fact. She knew he wasn't human. Probably knew exactly *what* he was.

And she was still coming to his aid.

Now, as a rule, Lucas didn't believe that people were good. No, he knew they were more apt to be influenced by the devil than any pure motivation, so he figured the lady had an angle.

"The Los Angeles police department apologizes for any inconvenience," the nasal voice of Dickhead told him.

Lucas released the woman. Gently, he pushed her to the side. His eyes narrowed as he cocked his head and waited for Dickhead to finish.

"Of course, you have a known history of affiliation with certain—"

He moved in one quick lunge. Lucas grabbed the detective, lifted the jerk by his too-thick throat, and slammed him against the bars.

The guard stepped forward.

Lucas's head snapped to the right. "Don't even think about it." Guttural. Because really, a guy's patience could only last so long.

The guard's Adam's apple bobbed.

"Good." He glanced back at the detective. "Bruce, I think you and I need to clear the air." So others were there watching—big deal. He wouldn't play subtle. "You've got a hard-on for me. You been dodging my feet for the last two months." He let the beast show in his eyes. Lucas knew the glow of the wolf would burn from his blue stare. "You stay out of my way from now on or you'll find out just what I do to bastards who piss me off."

The detective's skin bleached. "You—you can't threaten a cop—"

He let his claws dig into Bruce's flapping flesh. "I just did."

"*What are you?*" A whisper.

His smile faded. "Someone"—*something*—"you don't want to have as an enemy." His fingers loosened. The detective slid from his grip. Dropped to the floor. Probably pissed himself.

Lucas glared down at the man. He let Bruce see the intent in his eyes. Then he caught the woman's hand. "Let's get the hell out of here."

Sarah King let the tall, dark wolf shifter drag her down the twisting hallways of the police station. Her heart slammed into her chest with every step and her palms slickened with sweat. And her knees—it was a good thing he was doing all the dragging, because they were shaking so hard she might not have been able to walk so well on her own.

Lucas Simone. The badass of the LA wolf pack.

She wondered if the detective knew just how close he'd come to serious injury.

You didn't mess with a wolf. Shifters, in general, were considered wild because of the beasts they carried inside. Unpredictable. Five times stronger than humans. Senses—hearing, sight—more like an animal's than a man's.

Because *they* were more animal than man.

Shifters were part of the *Other*. Humans didn't know it, but they were living in a nightmare. A world inhabited by vampires, demons, djinn—every creature imaginable and some that folks didn't *want* to imagine.

The wolf shifters were said to be the worst. Too powerful. And quite often . . . insane. A not-so-nice little side perk of their genetics.

Oh, yeah, the detective had come close to—

Lucas shoved open the glass door at the entrance of the station. Nobody made the mistake of getting in his way.

Evening sunlight hit her hard. Sarah blinked, trying to adjust her eyes, but Lucas didn't pause. The wolf just kept dragging her. Down the stone steps. Across the street, into the park that was overgrown with weeds, then back into the stretching shadows of the trees.

Uh, oh. Time to stop. Sarah wrenched her hand free.

The shifter turned on her with narrowed blue eyes.

All the moisture in her mouth dried up in an instant.

Lucas Simone was dangerous. One glance at his stony expression could tell any fool that.

The guy was big, towering well over six feet, muscled, with wide shoulders. Freaking linebacker shoulders.

No way was he handsome. His face was all angles. His cheekbones were too sharp. His jaw too square, too hard. His lips were too thin, a little too cruel.

And his eyes were too hard, that fierce gaze saw too much. *Dangerous. Wild.*

No, Lucas Simone definitely wouldn't classify as handsome, but Sarah really wasn't the type to be swayed by a pretty face.

She was much more the I-need-a-freaking-badass-to-save-my-ass right-now type.

"I should explain . . ." She began, clearing her throat.

"Yeah, you should." An order.

Her own eyes narrowed. "Uh, I think it's important to note that I saved your hide back there." Very, very important to note. In fact, she was wagering on the old wolf pack code to help her out. The *I-Scratch-Your-Back, You-Protect-Mine* code.

He grunted. "I didn't need saving, babe."

"Yes, you did." The wolf would still be caged if it hadn't been for her—and the folks she'd bribed. *Using the last of my cash.*

She needed shelter. Her growling stomach reminded her that she also needed food.

And she desperately needed some serious muscle.

Her gaze dropped down to his chest.

Muscle, check.

"We haven't had sex, *lover.*" He drew the last out, more like a growl instead of a word.

Sarah couldn't help it, she flushed. She felt her face heat and knew she had to be beet red. The curse of her fair skin. She always blushed too fast. "You were in *jail.* They were pinning a murder rap on you." Facts that really shouldn't have to be pointed out to the ungrateful wolf. Come on. Where was her thank you?

"I remember every woman I've had sex with," he continued as if she hadn't spoken. His eyes, hooded, swept over her, making her cheeks burn all the more. She'd dressed, deliberately chosen the sexy attire, before going down to the station. Her red blouse plunged to reveal the swell of her breasts. The short, black skirt revealed a long expanse of leg. Her sandals were small, curved, and designed more to be sexy than serviceable.

He whistled slowly. "I don't remember you."

Right, and she didn't buy for a minute that the guy remembered every woman he'd—

"Some women like to take things slow. They like to kiss,

they like to stroke. Others like to strip, to fuck, as fast as possible." A pause as his eyes rose back to hers. "They like it rough because they like the rush of being with a monster."

She swallowed and took a quick step back, unable to help herself because Lucas looked very, very threatening.

"Are you one of those women?" He moved forward, closing that distance. His hand lifted and traced her cheek. "Do you like the thrill of walking on the wild side?"

Her heart was racing. Her knees were knocking again—well, okay, they'd never stopped. She licked her lips and managed, "No."

His nostrils flared, and the grin that curved his lips was grim. "Liar."

Oh, hell. *Shifter senses.* Some said their senses were acute enough to catch a lie. Not to actually smell a lie, but to hear the jerk of an increased heartbeat or to scent the sweat that broke through the skin at a lie.

"You're turned on right now," he told her, voice so rough that she almost shivered, "just like you were when we kissed outside that damn cage."

Now what was she supposed to say to that? Especially since the guy was right?

His hand slid down her face and his fingers curled over her throat. His palm pushed against her pulse. He didn't hurt her, not like he'd hurt the cop, but Sarah tensed, knowing just how dangerous he could be.

I saw the photos. He's killed before. Without remorse. Fast, brutal. I know what he can do.

That's why she had come to him.

When a girl was caught between hell and a hard place, she needed the devil to help her out.

"Who are you?" He breathed the words against her. "Not some angel come to save me in my dark hour of need . . ."

Hardly. She managed to lift her chin. "Let go of me and I'll tell you everything." Almost everything. Okay, not even almost, but at least the important parts.

A deep laugh rumbled from him. "Think you're tough, do you?" But his hand fell away.

She sucked in a sharp breath. *Tough?* Not anymore. "Sarah. I'm Sarah King." Her name would tell him nothing. It wasn't who she was that mattered. No, it was *what* she was.

"And what brought you to my cell, sweet Sarah?"

Now this was the tricky part. "I saw your story on the news."

"And you decided to run down to the station and give a killer an alibi?" One brow rose. "What a good Samaritan you are." The sarcasm dripped all over her.

Her hands clenched into fists. "You didn't kill John."

Now he was the one to tense. "John," he repeated the name softly. "You knew him."

"I—"

"Don't lie." The words snapped like a whip. "You might think you know about the supernaturals in this world, but you don't. We've got secrets—secrets humans can't even begin to guess." His lips twisted. "I heard the way you said his name. You *knew* him."

Yes, and she didn't like thinking about John's death. "You didn't kill him," she repeated.

"And how do you know that?" He looked around them, his gaze sweeping to the left and the right.

They probably shouldn't stay out in the open much longer. She knew she had to make this quick. She had to get Lucas to take her with him and to *keep* her by his side. Day and night.

Sarah exhaled slowly. "John was at your house because he wanted protection." True.

"What?"

"He was being hunted and he knew that you could keep him safe." Knew, hoped, same thing.

If only Lucas had been home in those early hours before dawn. Then her friend wouldn't be dead, dammit, and she wouldn't be on her own again.

Life sucks. Deal with it—and try to keep living. Her mantra since she was seventeen.

"Keep him safe . . . from what?"

A twig snapped. Sarah jumped but Lucas didn't move.

"Squirrel," he said softly, without even looking.

She was nervous as all hell. It was starting to get dark, and she knew exactly what kinds of creatures came out once the darkness trickled across the sky. "We should go . . . get out of the open."

He didn't move. "I'm not the running type."

If you were one of the baddest of the bad, you didn't have to run. You could stay and fight and kick some good old ass.

But, if you were human or . . . a weaker supernatural, you learned early that it paid to run. And run fast.

"Tell me what's going on," Lucas demanded. "Why was that guy—John—coming to me for protection?" A line pulled down his brows and his right hand rose to rub along the jagged edge of his ear. "Pack protects pack, but that wasn't shifter blood dripping down my steps."

She flinched. *Be strong. Life sucks, just like vampires.* Yeah vamps were real, too. All the monsters that people feared—they existed.

Lucas's hand dropped. "He was human."

"No, he wasn't." Time for her big confession. "And neither am I." Okay, just say it. "Lucas, I need you to—"

His nostrils flared. Then he jerked her behind him in a move she barely felt, much less saw. "Lucas? What—"

"We're not alone."

She heard the growl then. The hair-raising sound came from the thicket of trees that Lucas faced, hands loose at his sides, his body still.

The dark hadn't fallen yet.

But it looked like the monsters had decided it was time to come out and play.

Chapter 2

They sprang from the bushes, bodies tense, fur up, snarls on their lips. Two coyotes with muddy brown coats and red-rimmed eyes. Saliva dripped off their teeth. Their bushy tails brushed the ground as they crouched, preparing to attack.

Oh, damn, damn, damn.

Sarah grabbed the back of Lucas's shirt. Her nails ripped through the fabric. "You need to shift!" What was the guy waiting for? Two against one! Not the best odds. They didn't have time to waste. The change from man to beast wasn't instantaneous and those coyotes were less than ten feet away and—

They attacked.

Sarah didn't bother screaming. She bent low, her fingers automatically going for her ankle sheath. The knife might not be much, but it was all she had. And the weapon had saved her ass more than a few times.

Lucas grunted when the first beast came at him. He didn't retreat, didn't so much as stumble. He just lifted his arm, caught the coyote around the neck, and threw him against a tree.

"Come on," he said, and Sarah blinked, realizing he wasn't talking to her. He was inviting the second shifter—because Sarah knew they weren't being attacked by simple animals, no, these creatures had the minds of men—to attack.

Inviting the attack? Maybe the wolf shifter was psychotic, after all. Figured. That would be her luck.

The beast's pointed ears twitched. He let out a loud barking cry, then he sprang forward.

Lucas raised his hand and his claws—claws that Sarah had hoped never to see so close to her—sank into the coyote's body.

The creature fell, hard, his body thumping into the ground as blood darkened his brown fur.

Color her impressed. Sarah pushed her knife back into the sheath and rose quickly. "Nice job."

Lucas glanced back at her and growled.

The wolf was in his eyes, glowing brightly. Lucas might not have shifted fully, but he'd definitely let his beast off the leash a bit.

The bloody coyote pushed to his feet with a whimper.

"What the hell is going on?" Lucas demanded as his gaze flew back to the other shifter. "You bastards *know* who I am and you know you're damn well supposed to stay out of *my* territory."

"Uh, Lucas . . ." Her eyes searched the thick brush. They only had about thirty minutes of sunlight left, if that much. "Can we please get out of here?"

"No, these assholes are gonna shift and explain exactly why they attacked—" He took a step forward, turning slightly as he held up his hands, and Sarah saw the waning light glint off the claws extending from his fingertips. "Or I'm gonna skin 'em."

As far as threats went, Sarah thought that one was pretty good. Mostly because she knew that Lucas meant exactly what he'd said.

The coyote shifters must have known it, too. The creature who'd been tossed against the tree gave a half-hearted howl, and, as Sarah watched, fascinated and horrified at the same time, his body began to change. No matter how many times she saw a shift, she'd never get used to the brutal transformation. Bones snapped. Fur disappeared. His muzzle shortened. His ears flattened.

In moments, a man stood before her. Tall, thin, skin tanned a deep brown, and, of course, naked.

His head was bowed. Shaggy brown locks of hair covered his face. The pose was one of submission—like Lucas was gonna buy that. She inched to his side. The better to watch.

"Why did you attack me?" Fury vibrated in Lucas's voice.

"Not you." One long, bony finger lifted and pointed toward her. "The woman."

Goosebumps rose along her arms. "We really need to get out of here." *So the bastard had followed through on his threat.* He'd put a price on her.

Lucas's blue eyes focused on Sarah. "Why are you after her?"

She held his stare. She'd explain everything to him when they were somewhere nice and safe and out of the *open*.

The coyote shifter said, "There's two hundred grand being offered for her."

No, being offered for her *dead body*. But, of course, the jerk coyote wasn't going to admit that part. Surely Lucas understood though, he knew these games.

"Lucas . . ." His name slipped past her lips. She couldn't look away from his eyes. Okay, this wasn't his fight, so maybe he probably should just turn his back on her and walk away.

But if he did that, she might as well just jump into a grave. Without a pack to aid her in this mess, she wouldn't survive. All her allies had vanished. Or been killed.

"I saved you at that jail," she reminded him, and dammit, that was partly true. "Pack law says you owe me now." She licked her lips and tasted her fear. "Help me." She wouldn't beg. Not yet, anyway. But maybe in about five more minutes, if more of those smelly coyotes burst from the bushes and came at her with claws and teeth.

Lucas stared down at her. Watching. Weighing. After one very long moment, his gaze tracked down her body. No expression passed across his face.

"Help me."

When his gaze rose again, he inclined his head in the faintest of moves, then he turned his attention back to the coyote.

Oh, Christ, please let that have been a yes.

Lucas crossed his arms over his chest and glared at the trembling man. "You caught my scent the minute you crept into the park."

The shifter glanced up at him from beneath thick clumps of hair.

"You knew I was a wolf." Lucas's lips curled down in a hard frown. "And I'd bet that you knew *exactly* who I was." A pause. "But you attacked anyway."

"Her! Not you—her!"

The snarl that burst from Lucas had the guy stumbling back. "She was with me, and you attacked." Lucas shook his head. "Wrong move, asshole."

Sarah straightened her shoulders.

"You don't ever, *ever* come at me again with bloodlust in your eyes and teeth bared, you understand?" The words vibrated with rage. "If you do, I guarantee it will be the last fucking mistake you ever make."

The shifter gave a quick nod.

"Get out of here, and take your dog," *Ooh, big insult that, the coyotes hated being called 'dogs',* "with you."

The guy scrambled. He grabbed the bleeding coyote and tossed the "dog" over his shoulders. That second shifter had to be injured pretty badly if he hadn't been able to transform back to human form.

Lucas waited for the man to turn away with his bleeding buddy before saying, "I've got *your* scents now. You'll have two hours to get out of town. If I see you after that—you're both dead."

The shifter broke into a run.

"And you . . ." He slanted a dark glance her way. "Pack protection doesn't come as cheaply as you seem to think. I don't give a shit about the old laws."

Her stomach dropped. "If you don't help me, then *I'm* the dead one."

A shrug.

What? "You can't be that cold of a bastard. I *need* your help, and I've traveled over seventeen hundred miles to find you." Just like John had. Hopefully, her quest wouldn't end the same way.

She wasn't ready to die.

Sarah sucked in a deep breath. "I know who set you up for murder. If you give me protection, I'll give *him* to you."

Both brows rose. "Oh, you'll most definitely give him to me, one way or another."

Her back teeth clenched. "I could have left you in jail," she gritted.

A hard smile. "And I could have let the coyotes have you."

She flinched. Okay, he had a point there. A rather nasty, cold-hearted one, but . . .

"You must have done something pretty bad to get a price on your head."

Not really. She'd actually tried to do something good. That just hadn't worked out so well.

"Sarah King . . ." He drew out her name, as if tasting it. "Are you a bad woman?"

Yes. Don't trust me. She bit back the words. Now really wasn't the time for that much honesty between them. So she didn't speak but she managed to hold his stare.

After a moment, he lifted his hand and offered it, palm-up, to her. "Once you come with me, there's no going back."

The heated look in his eyes told her he wasn't just talking about a few days of protection.

But right then, she would have traded what was left of her soul to walk away with Lucas Simone.

"I don't want to go back." The rumors she'd heard over the years, about humans being absorbed into the packs—women, mostly, who disappeared after they were linked with male shifters—those stories drifted through her mind once more.

Some wolf shifters roamed on their own. The Lones. Some Lones existed in society, blending almost seamlessly with the humans. But *most* of the Lones didn't blend so well. They had breakdowns. They'd been known to go on killing rampages. Often, they were tagged as serial killers and put down.

The rest of the wolves . . . they were pack. Pack was sacred. Pack was strong.

What would she have to do in order to belong? What would she have to sacrifice?

And did it matter?

Sarah took Lucas's hand and kissed her old life good-bye.

Lucas didn't take the woman back to his house on Bryton Road. The place was probably still crawling with cops and reporters, and he didn't feel like dealing with all that crap.

He called his first in command, Piers Stratus, to let him know that he was out of jail and to tell him that there were two unwanted coyotes in town.

The woman—Sarah—didn't speak while he drove. He could feel the waves of tension rolling off her, shaking her body.

She was scared. She'd done a fair job of hiding her fear back at the police station and then at the park, at first anyway. But as the darkness had fallen, he'd seen the fear. Smelled it.

Sarah had known she was being hunted.

He pushed a button on his remote. The wrought-iron gates before him opened and revealed the curving drive that led to his second LA home. In the hills, it gave him a great view of the city below, and that view let him know when company was coming, long before any unexpected guests arrived.

When the gate shut behind him, he saw Sarah sag slightly, settling back into her seat. The scent of her fear finally eased.

Like most of his kind, he usually enjoyed the smell of fear. But he didn't . . . like the scent on her.

He much preferred the softer scent, like vanilla cream, that he could all but taste as it clung to her skin. Perhaps he would get a taste, later.

With a flick of his wrist, he killed the ignition. The house was right in front of them. Two stories. Long, tall windows.

And, hopefully, no more dead bodies waited on the steps here.

He eased out of the car, stretching slowly. Then he walked around and opened the door for Sarah. As any man would, Lucas admired the pale flash of thigh when her skirt crept up. And he wondered just what secrets the lovely lady was keeping from him.

"We're going in to talk." An order. He wanted to know everything, starting with why the dead human had been at *his place*.

She gave a quick nod. "Okay, I—"

A wolf bounded out of the house. A flash of black fur. Golden eyes. Teeth.

Shit. It wasn't safe for the kid. Not until he found out what was going on—

The wolf ran to him. Tossed back his head and howled.

Sarah laughed softly.

Laughed.

His stare shot to her just in time to catch the smile on her lips. His hand lifted, and almost helplessly, he traced that smile with his fingertips.

Her breath caught.

Lucas ignored the tightening in his gut. "Shouldn't you be afraid?" After the coyotes, he'd expected her to flinch away from any other shifters. And Jordan was one big wolf, with claws and teeth that could easily rip a woman like Sarah apart.

She looked back at the wolf who watched them. "He's so young, little more than a kid. One who is glad you're—"

No.

Understanding dawned, fast and brutal in his mind. *I'm more than human.* She'd told him that, he just hadn't understood exactly *what* she was. Until now.

His hands locked around her arms and Lucas pulled her up against him. Nose to nose, close enough so that he could see the dark gold glimmering in the depths of her green eyes. "Jordan, get the hell out of here." He gave the order to his brother without ever looking away from her.

The wolf growled.

"Go!"

The young wolf pushed against his leg—*letting me know he's pissed, 'cause Jordan hates when I boss his ass*—and then the wolf backed away.

"Now for you, sweetheart." His fingers tightened. "Why don't we just go back to that part about you not being human?"

Her lips parted. She had nice lips—sexy and plump. He shouldn't be noticing them, not then, but he couldn't help himself. He noticed everything about her. The gold hoops in her dainty ears. The streaks of gold buried deep in her dark hair. The lotion she'd rubbed on her body—that vanilla scent was driving him wild.

He was turned on, achingly hard, for a woman he barely knew. Not normally a big deal. He had a more than healthy sex drive. Most shifters did. The animal inside liked to play.

But Sarah . . . he didn't *trust* her, not for a minute, and he didn't usually have sex with women he didn't trust. A man could be vulnerable to attack when he was fucking.

"You know what I am, Lucas," she said and shrugged, the move both careless and fake because he knew that she cared, too much.

"*Tell me.*" Her mouth was so close. He could still taste her. That kiss earlier had just been a tease. *Want more.*

"I'm a charmer," she whispered.

A charmer. The weakest of the paranormals, and, in his mind, the damn sneakiest. Charmers blended the best with the humans. They got to live in the bright, fake world of date nights and football games. They passed as humans all the time, had all the perks of human life, but charmers had magic inside, weak, but still there.

Charmers were able to communicate telepathically with animals. To "talk" with them. Each charmer had one type of animal that she or he could talk with—some spoke to bears, tigers, hell, he'd even known one lady down in the South who could talk snake to a Burmese python.

"Who do you talk to?" Because his suspicion couldn't be right. No way. *It was impossible.*

She bit her lower lip. That sexy, red lip—

Shit.

He kissed her. Lucas crushed his mouth against hers and let the hunger take over—the hunger that had been building the whole time he'd been trapped beside her in that SUV, trapped with her soft flesh so close and her sexy scent surrounding him.

He'd had a piss-poor day. Time to stop playing nice and get back to doing things *his* way.

Hard and dirty.

Her mouth opened, lips quivering. *Perfect.* His tongue swept inside, driving deep. Her kiss wouldn't be as good as before. Couldn't be. He'd imagined that lick of fire, that wild arousal, that—

His cock jerked. *Dammit.*

Her breasts pushed against him, nipples tight and pebbled. The scent of her arousal teased his nostrils, and Lucas realized he was in serious trouble.

Just as bad as before. No, just as good, and that equaled one big-ass problem.

Growling, he pulled back. "Who . . ." He swallowed, and tried to sound more like a man than a beast as he demanded, "Who do you talk with?" Who, what—same thing in his world.

Her lips were red, swollen, and her eyes were so wide. "Wolves." Her voice was husky, tinged with the same need that had him aching.

Hell.

A new worry shot through him. "My kind . . . can you—" He wanted her mouth again. *Soon.* "Can you read us when we're in human form?"

A slow shake of her head. "No. Only when you're the wolf."

He wasn't sure he believed her.

But he still freed her and stepped back. Because if he didn't,

Lucas knew he would have taken those lips again, and he wouldn't have stopped with such a simple taste.

"Go inside. There's a room on the second floor, to the right of the stairs—you can use it, for now." Until he figured out exactly what was happening and how to get the price off her head.

Why do I care?

Because she *had* saved him at the jail. While he'd denied it to her, he did follow pack law. Up to a point.

Lucas turned away from her. He'd need to send Jordan someplace safe. Until this shit was smoothed over, he wasn't going to risk his brother.

He'd almost lost him before. No way was he going to put his brother in harm's way again.

"Is having sex with you the price of protection?"

Her voice froze him. Then anger ripped through his gut. He glanced back at her, frowning. "If it is?"

The wind tossed her hair. The moonlight glittered in her eyes. "I didn't realize you were that hard up, wolf."

He almost smiled. *Nice bite.* He loved women who knew how to fight. "You're not gonna have sex with me because you want a safe place to hide." And hiding, yeah, he knew that was what his little charmer was doing. Hiding with the big, bad wolf.

"Good to know, I—"

"You're gonna have sex with me because you want me, just as badly as I want you." Immediate attraction. Animal lust—that's what his kind called it. Sometimes, the beast inside just recognized a perfect sensual partner.

In bed, he bet they'd be great. He couldn't wait to have her, naked and hungry, in a big, soft bed. Or maybe out in the open, beneath his glowing moon. Either way, he *would* have her.

He paused, waited for her denial.

Sarah headed for the house. "Keep hoping, wolf."

Her arousal, the rich scent of woman, teased his nose. He smiled. "I will, babe, I will."

Chapter 3

Waking up to find yourself in a wolf's den wasn't the best experience, but, hey, it was better than being dead.

The next day, Sarah crept down the stairs, all too aware of the silence in the house. After he'd dropped his little sexual bombshell, she hadn't spoken to Lucas again last night. She'd kept silent because, mostly, because he was right.

She did want him. Arrogant bastard.

She'd been thinking about him for months. Ever since she'd first seen his picture and heard the tales of the LA alpha.

His father had been slaughtered when Lucas was ten. Killed by the leader of a rival pack who'd wanted to claim the LA territory.

If the tales were true, and, after meeting the man, Sarah figured they had to be, Lucas had gone after his father's killer. He'd attacked a full-grown wolf shifter, in human form—and the form of a ten-year-old boy really wasn't that tough. Lucas had somehow survived that fight. He'd escaped death and disappeared from LA for six years.

At sixteen, he'd come back, and the shifter who'd murdered his father had been dead within an hour of his return. In the seventeen years since, he'd been the wolf running these streets.

So, okay, she had more than a little crush on the guy. A crush that had caused her to risk her ass when she found out he was in danger. She still couldn't believe she'd driven all the way from Arizona to try and save him.

Well, *his* life—and her own skin.

Sarah reached the bottom of the stairs. "Hello! Lucas?" He'd better not have gone hunting without her.

"You're pretty in the morning." His voice came from the right. He stepped from the kitchen, crossed his arms, and studied her. "But I think I liked the other outfit better."

She'd tossed on the jeans and t-shirt she'd stuffed into her travel bag. Since her goal today wasn't seduction—not her main goal, anyway—she'd been glad to get back into her casual clothes.

Her hands dug into her back pockets. "I—um, thought you had already left."

His lips curled. "I'll be hunting soon enough."

Sarah didn't doubt it.

"Confession time, huh, sweet Sarah?"

She nodded. They needed to talk today, to plan and to attack. Because, once night fell, she knew more coyotes would be coming after her.

And him.

So where should she start?

"Tell me about the dead man." He leaned back against the doorframe.

All right. That was one place to start. She cleared her throat. Took a nice slow breath. *He'll know when I lie.* Well, he'd know, unless she was very, very careful. "John Turner was . . . like me."

"A wolf charmer?"

"He was a charmer, yes, but the coyote was his linked animal. He worked with them." Because every charmer she'd met had a primary link. Some could pick up thoughts from a few other beasts, but one animal was always primary, with a link so strong it took no effort to form the connection.

"Worked with?" Lucas repeated carefully.

Ah, now she had to be very careful because "worked with" was actually a nice euphemism for John's spy work.

When the coyotes got together for their hunts with other factions, John had always been there. Pretending to be a guard, but secretly picking up the thoughts of all the coyote shifters there and reporting back to his coyote leader.

Charmer spies were valuable commodities in the shifter world. Because when the beasts roamed free, it was so easy to discover what lies the men had been keeping.

"The dead guy was spying on coyote packs?"

Lucas obviously knew the score. She nodded.

"While he was . . . working, John got word of a planned attack in LA." No sense sugar-coating. If she hadn't been so tired lasted night, she would have gotten all this crap out into the open then. But she'd been running on fumes and the minute she'd found the bed, one that held John's wild scent, she'd crashed.

It had been the first time she'd slept in the last thirty-six hours.

"John picked up the thoughts of a coyote named Hayden. The guy wanted more power." Hayden. She'd met the jerk a few times. Squinty eyes. Handsome face. Evil grin. "He thought if he pulled off a coup here, he could start his own faction." And then the coyotes could take back the power they'd lost to the wolves in LA.

"I've got a pact with the coyotes. They stay out of my space and I stay out of theirs." Hard. Angry. He wasn't slumping against the wooden frame any longer. His body stood at full attention, his broad shoulders filling the doorway.

"I hate to tell you," she murmured, "but that truce is pretty much worthless." To Hayden, anyway. "Hayden found out that John was onto his plans and he put a price on his head."

"Like the price that's on yours?"

Unfortunately, yes. That was the way the coyotes liked to play. A price would be put on prey. Then the hunt would begin.

She took a quick breath. "John thought his best chance of survival was coming here, telling you what was happening . . ."

"And getting my pack to watch his ass."

The way she hoped they'd watch hers. "Yes."

He strode toward her. "And where do you fit into all this? Why are they after *you?*"

"Because I know the attack isn't just coming from the coyotes." Bad enough, but . . . "Hayden is working with wolves—they are coming for you, too." Wolves she knew. Wolves she'd trusted, once.

Then she'd seen their true nature.

"A war is coming to this town, Lucas. You're going to get slammed from both sides." This time, she sucked in a deep, gulping breath. *Confession.* "I know the wolf who's leading the charge."

"Know him?"

Not going to lie. A lie wouldn't work with him. She stepped away from the stairs and headed closer to him. "He was my lover." He'd also used her to spy. At first, she hadn't minded. Not like spying was new for her. Besides, she'd been so happy to find someone who didn't think she was some kind of freak.

And he'd been a wolf. It had seemed so perfect. As if he were made for her.

Then the killings had started.

She'd realized he wasn't so perfect after all.

Sarah had gotten away from him, barely, but he was out there, and closing in—on her and Lucas.

"*Your lover.*" A growl. "You like to play with wolves, do you?"

Sarah kept her chin up even as her hands clenched into fists. "John died trying to save your ass."

Black brows rose. "Sounds like he died trying to save his own ass." He walked around her, circling like the wolf he was as he closed in on his prey. His gaze raked her, head to toe, lingering a bit too long on her breasts and hips.

Sarah was all too aware that they were alone and that Lucas could rip her apart with one swipe of his claws. She knew first-hand just how strong a wolf shifter's claws could be. The mark on her back had only healed a few weeks ago.

He circled her once more, then stopped just behind her. His breath stirred the hair near her ear as he said, "Tell me the wolf's name."

Not yet. Because wolves had a tendency to stick together, and she didn't want to find herself on the outside, with two packs sizing her up. "Do you believe me?"

"I believe you've managed to piss off the coyotes."

Not close to being good enough. She turned her head a bit and met his stare. "I'm a charmer. I can read the minds of wolves."

"Then read my mind." A taunt, one laced with sensual menace.

Her eyes narrowed. "I can't read you when you're in human form, you have to *shift* first."

"I've heard there are only a handful of charmers in the world who can read a shifter's mind." The doubt was obvious. "Most charmers stick to *real* animals."

"Shifters *are* real animals." The insult burst out automatically, but she'd seen too much to think otherwise.

His lips curled, revealing the sharp tips of his canines. "That we are." He leaned closer and she caught the soft inhale as he scented her hair.

Sarah held her body very, very still as his mouth came close to her throat. His lips feathered over her, pressing lightly against the side of her neck.

If he wanted, he could rip her throat open. But she knew what this move was about. Damn pack rules.

Dominance. Submission. Lucas was the freaking alpha, her only hope for living out the next forty-eight hours. So she had to play the game.

Sarah tipped back her head, baring her throat in a gesture she knew he'd understand.

A rumble slipped from his mouth and seemed to vibrate on her skin. She felt the light nip of his teeth, and, damn it all, a shot of heat streaked through her body. *Can't want him. Can't trust him. Can only use him and walk away.*

His tongue swiped over her throat, licking the small wound. "His scent's not on you."

It took a second for his words to register, a second too long, because Lucas caught her arms and yanked her around to face him.

He bent toward her, bringing his eyes close to hers. "Babe, I know wolf shifters. If we're fucking, we're marking our partners. If you had a wolf lover, his scent would be all over you."

Bastard. "Only if we'd been together in the last month. It's been four months since I got the hell away from him." Partial truth.

His nostrils flared. *Smell a lie . . .*

"I'm telling you the truth." If she said it, maybe he'd buy it. "You're in danger, your pack's in danger and—"

"We'll see." His hand lowered and snagged her wrist. "I think a little test is in order." He pulled her with him.

What? A test? "Lucas—"

But he didn't stop. His grip was freaking unbreakable, because she really did try every way possible to break it. He led her through the house, dragged her outside, hauled her down the hill—and ignored her shouts to explain *what the hell he was doing.*

When they burst through the brush and into the small clearing and four wolves—huge, furry beasts with saliva dripping from their teeth—lunged toward them, Sarah finally understood her little "test."

The wolves circled them. She couldn't help it. Sarah inched closer to Lucas. Two of the wolves were black. Two were solid white. All looked like they'd been taking some kind of shifter steroids. Way too large for normal wolves. She swallowed.

"Let's see what part of your story was true," Lucas said, "and what part was bullshit."

He freed her wrist. Then the guy stepped away from her. Far away. He left her in the middle of that circle of wolves and the animals closed in.

"The bitch made contact with Simone."

The coyote leader lifted his brows at that. "So she's dead?" Good. One less worry for him. Of course, picking up the bounty on her head would have been a nice bonus, and killing her would have given them a good in with the other wolves but . . .

The coyote shifter in front of him raised his head, and the guy's thick, dirty brown hair scraped across his shoulders. "Simone didn't kill her," Marcus DePaul confessed.

Very, very slowly, Jess Ortez lowered the shot glass he'd lifted to his mouth. "He didn't kill her," he repeated softly. "You didn't kill her . . . so what the fuck happened to Sarah King?"

"Sh-she's under his protection. They were together. I-I followed 'em to the park, tried to get her—"

Oh, shit. His head began to throb. "You weren't stupid enough to attack when Lucas Simone was there."

But the idiot's trembling lips told him that, yes, he had been. Fuck. The glass started to crack. "We've got a truce with him!" He threw the glass back over the bar.

"But Alpha, I thought you wanted—"

Jess lunged forward and caught the shifter's head in his hands. He stared into Marcus's eyes. "Don't think." One twist, that's all it would take and he'd snap the wiry bastard's neck. "You're not supposed to think. You're just supposed to do whatever the hell I tell you."

That was the whole point in being the coyote alpha, right? He gave the orders, all the other bastards rushed to obey, and if they didn't rush fast enough, he killed them.

Sweat trickled down the dumb bastard's face. "P-please . . ."

"Does Lucas know I'm here?"

"I don't th-think—"

His fingers tightened.

"No! He just—he must have figured we were just hunting! Said if he saw me or Grimes again, we were dead."

Not as bad as it could be, but still . . . now the wolf would be on guard and if that bitch managed to get him to believe *her* story . . .

Screwed.

He drew in a long, slow breath. "Guess what?" he murmured.

Marcus blinked his watery eyes. "Wh-what?"

"You *are* dead." His hands yanked hard to the right.

Snap.

Lucas watched the wolves close in on her, and he crossed his arms over his chest. And waited.

Sarah stood in the middle of that tight circle, her body tense, her hands fisted at her sides. Her gaze darted from wolf to wolf, and the scent of sweat and fear teased his nose.

Again, the smell of fear didn't tempt his wolf. But, it did have the beast inside snarling . . . and damn if he didn't want to go back to her. *Protect.*

"This should be easy for you," he called out, deliberately keeping his voice cool and expressionless. "You're the charmer. Just tell me what they're thinking."

Her lips pressed together. So he wouldn't see the tremble? Too late, he'd already seen. Sarah was scared. Charmers didn't usually fear their linked animals, but then wolf shifters weren't your typical beasts.

"I've already played this game," she gritted. "You were there, you saw me with the boy."

The boy. Jordan. "All you did was guess that he was a young wolf. Not a very impressive guess." He shrugged. "This time, I want details." Proof. *"Tell me what they're thinking."*

Because if she really was what she claimed to be . . .

Her right hand lifted and her index finger pointed to the white wolf that stood less than a foot away from her. "Piers here thinks this test is a damn waste of time, and he wants to go for my th-throat."

The drumbeat of Lucas's heart echoed in his ears. *Could be a guess. Everyone knows my first-in-command is Piers.*

Lucas lifted a brow. "You've got three other wolves still waiting," he said.

But she wasn't looking away from Piers. "Tell him to stand down. I don't want this jerk taking a swipe at me." She backed up a step. Not the brightest move. You didn't show weakness to a wolf. Wolves liked weakness too much.

Lucas dropped his hands and rolled his shoulders. "Ease back, Piers."

The white wolf immediately backed off.

Sarah's green gaze rose to meet his. "Thank you." No mistaking the fear in those eyes.

He inclined his head. "Three more."

"You really are a bastard, aren't you?"

"That's what they say."

Her eyes narrowed. "Right, you're—" Her gaze shot to the left. To the big, black wolf with night-black eyes. "He says you're a bastard, but you're a *fair* bastard."

"He?"

"Michael." Her breath heaved out. "He says I shouldn't worry, that you don't usually eat women."

Then her face flushed. A dark, fiery red. Her gaze darted to the other white wolf, Caleb McKenzie. He was a little smaller than Piers. Just a little. "*He* says you—ah—in bed . . ." Her hand lifted and shoved back a heavy mass of her hair. "I *don't* need to know this."

Lucas never looked away from her. "One wolf to go."

She swallowed. "Dane knows I'm telling the truth, so he's trying to keep his mind blank now so I can't see inside." A brittle laugh. "No dice, Dane, and yes, I do think more coyotes will be after me. I think they'll be here by nightfall and we need to stop screwing around with these stupid tests and get ready for them."

"Shift," Lucas ordered.

Sarah threw up her hands. "Wait!"

Too late. The snap and crunch of shifting bones filled the air. Fur melted away from the bodies of the wolves as dark, golden flesh appeared. Hands formed from paws. Muzzles slid back into the curved features of men.

Didn't take long. Just a few minutes, and the wolves were gone. Naked men stood surrounding Sarah. Lucas bent toward the bag Piers had brought out earlier. He pulled out the jeans and tossed them to his men. Then he marched to Sarah's side. The pulse at the base of her throat beat far too fast.

"You play with us," he murmured as the men dressed, "but we scare the hell out of you."

"Trust me on this, Lucas," she said, voice quiet, "if I could have chosen, wolves would have been the last animals I would have linked with."

But charmers didn't have a choice. Their gift just kicked in when the right animal was around.

His gaze was on the faint mark on her throat, his mark, when he asked, "Was she telling the truth?"

"I wanted to rip her throat out," Piers admitted. "Yeah, she knew."

"She plucked the exact words from my mind," Michael Montoya said. "We all know what a *fair* bastard you are."

A snort from Piers.

Dane Gentry edged closer. "She can link with us." He whistled. "Who the hell would have thought the stories were true? A charmer who can link with shifted wolves—that's fucking rare."

Her shoulders were so straight they had to hurt. "So I guess this means I passed your test? You believe me now?"

"I believe you're a charmer." His hand lifted and brushed against her back. "I believe that—"

But Sarah had leapt away from him. When his fingers touched the base of her back, she yelped and shot forward, running and slamming right into Dane's outstretched and scarred arms.

"Whoa, sweetheart," Dane murmured, "there ain't no cause for you to—"

She kneed him in the groin. Dane immediately dropped his hold and stumbled back, swearing.

Sarah whirled back around to face Lucas. He raised his hand, a command for the others to stand down. *Don't touch.* He knew terror when he smelled it. They all did.

"Are all wolves the same?" she asked, voice tight. "Sure, I know most folks say you're all psychotic killers, but, hell, *some* of you have to be normal, right? Some of you have to have consciences?"

He caught the faint tightening of Piers's eyes. Years ago, they'd had to put down Piers's father when the guy went Lone—and went on a five-state killing spree.

"We're not all fucking psychos," Piers snarled.

"Really?" And one brow arched. "Then why were you so worried a minute ago that you'd be crossing the line and killing? Why are you afraid that you'll like the taste of human blood too much and—"

Piers lunged toward her.

Lucas stepped in front of Sarah. "You don't touch her." Guttural. Suddenly, the tension was so thick he could feel the beast stretching beneath his skin.

Piers glared at him, his light green eyes a mix of fury . . . and fear. The guy wasn't afraid of Lucas. No, Piers was afraid of what he might become.

"If you didn't want me looking," Sarah's voice came from behind him, quavering just a little, but still with a fuck-you air that he liked, "then you shouldn't have been one of the guinea pigs who tested *me.*"

Lucas didn't glance back at her, not yet. He kept his gaze on Piers. "You back in control?"

A grim nod.

"Good. Stay that way." Then he turned to Sarah. "I want the wolf's name."

Her lips parted, but she shook her head.

"*His name.* If the bastard is gunning for me, I'm taking him out."

"I need assurance first." She rocked back on her heels. "I need to know that you won't throw me to the—"

"Wolves?" He finished, and let his mouth curl. "Can't promise you that, babe." The wolves already had her.

"Promise me . . . promise me that you'll keep me safe. You'll keep the coyotes and the wolves off my back."

"Can't imagine why they want to tear into you," Dane muttered, and from the corner of his eye, Lucas saw the guy wince. Yeah, a sore cock could make any guy wince.

"The name," Lucas said again, not about to be distracted.

But Sarah actually shook her head, *at him.* "Your promise first. I want you to vow right in front of your pack."

Oh, she was pushing him. He leaned in close, towering over her. He let the tips of his claws burst through his finger-tips, then those claws scraped lightly over the flesh of her arms. Not cutting the skin, but the threat was there. "I could always make you tell me."

"No," she said quietly, "you can't. You're not the first wolf who's thought he could break me."

Now what the fuck was that about? "*The name.*" He wanted to know the bastard who'd hurt her, who'd—

"I'll tell you the wolf after you—"

Was it the same asshole who'd hurt her? Her lover? Talk about piss-poor taste in men.

"—once you make the vow."

He dropped his hands, not even leaving a scratch on her. "I give my word that you have my protection."

He was aware of Piers and Dane both tensing at that.

Sarah studied him silently for a moment, then said, "Not that I don't think you're the big, bad asshole who can claw his way through just about anything and anyone, but . . . I want your whole pack's protection, not just yours."

Pushing . . .

"Because if you happen to eat a silver bullet, I want to know that my ass is still covered."

"Fine," he bit out. "Give me the name, and you have the pack's protection."

"For how long?" she asked, nibbling a bit at her lower lip. "This could go on for—"

"*Forever!*"

"Shit," Piers muttered. "No, he damn well didn't just say—"

But Sarah was smiling now. A real, wide flash of her lips that made the corners of her eyes crinkle and for an instant, she went from pretty to full-on gorgeous. "Then we've got a deal." She offered her hand to him.

What? Now she wanted a fucking handshake?

He grabbed her hand. Curled his fingers around her delicate bones. Stared at her mouth as she breathed the words, "Rafael Santiago. Rafe."

He knew the wolf. His fingers tightened around Sarah's and he pulled her in even closer. "Time to seal our deal." Then he put his mouth on hers. Sarah's lips were open, parted just right, and his tongue plunged inside. Her mouth was as soft as before, as lush, and her taste—

Still just as fucking sweet.

With every lick, every stroke of his tongue, he wanted more. The woman was meeting him head-on for the kiss. No shy backing away. Need and lust. Just what he wanted.

His cock shoved against the front of his jeans. If they hadn't been surrounded by an avid audience, he would have pushed the kiss farther and taken so much more. But . . . they *did* have an audience, and he'd never been the sharing kind. Just a little longer and he'd—

She tore her mouth from his. Her breath panted in ragged puffs and her eyes met his.

He almost smiled at her. "Now, we have a deal." One he would have preferred to seal while they were naked in bed, but they'd get around to that part. He just had to stir Sarah's need enough, then she'd come to him.

Her gaze darted to the other wolves. "What do we—what happens now?"

"Now I get ready to hunt." He inclined his head toward Michael. "Take her back inside."

Michael nodded and stepped forward.

Sarah's gaze searched his. "They'll be coming for me soon."

Sooner than she realized. "Then they'll have to get through me if they want you."

Those eyes of hers were so deep. The greenest he'd ever seen.

She nodded. "Thank you."

Don't thank me yet. She didn't realize how she fit into his plan. She would. Soon enough.

Sarah turned away and followed Michael back down the worn path. He watched them for a while, no, watched her, until she was out of sight.

Piers opened his mouth to speak—and Lucas raised his hand, quieting him.

Sarah's hearing wouldn't be as good as a wolf's, but he wasn't taking chances.

He waited a minute. Two. Then he nodded for Piers to speak.

"What the hell are you thinking?" Piers demanded. "We can't trust her, not for a damn minute."

Lucas stared at him. "Watch the tone, Piers."

Piers inhaled and his hands unclenched. "What do you know about her? We can't—"

"We know she's a charmer who can read the minds of shifted wolves," Dane interrupted. "And that's a real rare talent."

"A talent that could be very useful to us," Caleb added, the drawl of his native Texas sliding in and out of his voice.

"Or very dangerous." Piers yanked a hand through his hair. "Any time we're in wolf form, she'll be able to get in our heads, to find our secrets."

"There are no secrets in a pack," Lucas told him quietly watching his first closely. "Or are you worried she'll discover something I don't know?"

A muscle jumped in Piers's jaw.

"Every time we meet with the other wolves, she'll be able to tell us what they think." Caleb smiled, showing off his still-sharp teeth. "Hell, yeah, we'll watch her back forever, because we can keep her *forever*—"

"You really think the woman is gonna be 'kept'?" Dane interrupted, then whistled. "My aching cock says, uh, hell, *no*, that lady ain't doin' nothin' she don't want to do."

No, she wouldn't. Too much fire to be controlled. But then, he'd never cared about controlling his lovers. Not his style. He just went for the passion and the pleasure.

"I want a full check done on Rafe Santiago," he said, bringing the pack back to the issue that mattered most. "I want to know where the asshole is," real doubtful the guy was out of state, like he *should be,* "and I want to know who the hell is supporting him."

Piers and Dane nodded.

Lucas stabbed a finger at Caleb. "You still got a source at the ME's office?"

"Um, if you mean am I still sleeping with the night clerk? Then no, Kelly and I broke up."

Lucas kept staring at him.

"But she has hooked up with Michael," Caleb said quickly. "And I'm sure he can use the . . . uh . . . connection to get us in."

"Good. Because I want to see that human's body. I want to know if wolves got him or if the coyotes tore him up and left him on my doorstep." Either way, there'd be payback. The painful kind that left a trail of blood for miles.

"She thinks the coyotes are gonna be coming after her." Caleb scratched his chin. "But they won't be dumb enough to come right on your turf—"

Lucas's nostrils flared as he turned his head and looked out over the city. "Oh, yeah, those assholes will be dumb enough to come." Because they wanted the woman too much to let her go. He glanced at the dark shifter near his side. "Dane, one more thing . . ."

His brows lifted.

"Find out just how much of a bounty is really on her head." Had to be high, high enough for the coyotes to risk death. He exhaled, "And make sure word gets spread that anyone coming after her will find the LA wolf pack standing in the way."

Because he'd made a deal with sexy Sarah, and he'd hold up that deal . . . for now.

But not forever.

Because he knew a lie when he scented one, and Sarah had smelled of deception.

Chapter 4

"*Stay inside.*"

Sarah whirled around at the snarl and found Lucas in the doorway. His claws were out and the sharp edges of his teeth peeked behind his lips. Uh, oh. Not a good sign. "What's happening?"

His nostrils flared. "Coyotes."

The glass slipped from her hand and crashed on the kitchen floor. It shattered at her feet. "Al-already?" She shot a glance to the window. Oh, damn, the sky was turning red. Bloody, with the setting sun.

Lucas crossed the room with a long, gliding stride. He caught her arms and lifted her up, holding her close against his chest.

"Lucas?"

"The glass . . ."

She glanced down. The glass hadn't hit her feet. Like the wound would have bothered her. What was a little scratch compared to the hell she'd been through?

No. Can't tell him that. Can't let him see . . .

She wrapped her arms around his neck and kept her lashes low, the better to shield her gaze. "Thank you." She breathed the word against his neck and felt the hard stiffening of his body against hers.

He carried her over the glass. Held her lightly, moved easily. And she was no lightweight. But then, the guy did have shifter strength.

He put her down just outside the kitchen. "Go upstairs." Her body brushed against his. His pupils flared, but he said, "Whatever you hear, whatever you see . . . just stay inside, understand?"

She wasn't an idiot. If coyotes were outside, um, yeah, she'd be staying *inside*. But she didn't rush up the stairs, not yet. "Be careful."

He laughed at that. "I'm not the one you need to worry about."

Right. Big, tough badass. "They'll . . . lie to you. They'll tell you stories about me, about the things I've done." Some of those stories would be true, but Lucas wouldn't know that. No way could he know that.

But he just shook his head and eased away from her. "Babe, they're coyotes. That means they were born to lie."

Most *Other* said that about all the shifters. The shifters were the ones born with two faces, some even thought two souls. Born to deceive.

"You won't turn me over to them?" The question slipped out.

His eyes burned a bit, the blue heating with the fire of the beast. "Don't worry, I've got plans for you."

Not the giant reassurance she was hoping for. "You think you can use me, too, don't you?" Now why did that bother her?

"You mean like you're using me?"

Hit. Damn the wolf.

"I think we can use each other."

The words should have been cold, hard, and they should *not* have sent a shiver of sexual awareness over her. But they did.

"Sure you can't read my mind?" he murmured and that bright stare slipped down her body.

Didn't have to be a mindreader to know what he was

thinking. "Not in human form." She'd never been able to read a wolf shifter while he was human. If she had, she wouldn't have been in this current mess.

A howl echoed outside. His lips firmed. "Go upstairs."

"Can't I get a weapon? I mean, you've got guns some-where in this place, right?" Even he would know that some-times claws and teeth weren't enough.

"I'm not giving you a weapon." He turned away and strode quickly toward the foyer.

"Why the hell not?" she called after him.

He fired a quick glance over his shoulder. "Because I don't trust you. You might use it to shoot me in the back."

Pretty good reason.

He reached for the doorknob. She ran for the stairs.

The leader of the Mexico coyote pack was a tall, wiry bas-tard named Jess Ortez. They'd tangled a few times in the past, managed to reach a truce, a rocky one, but usually they stayed out of each other's way.

Since Jess was on his doorstep, the coyote was doing a real piss-poor job of staying out of Lucas's way then. Of course, Lucas had known that the coyote would be coming—he'd even left orders for the coyote and his men to be allowed past the gate.

Jess raised his hands when Lucas walked down the main steps. "*Amigo!*"

"Save the bullshit." Dane and Piers appeared at Lucas's sides. Other wolves were in the shadows, waiting. "Just tell me why your ass isn't below the border like it should be."

Jess's wide smiled dimmed a bit. He glanced back at the two pickup trucks behind him and straightened his shoul-ders. *Always had to put on a big front when pack was watch-ing.* "I came to pay you my respects."

"Your respects?" He stalked forward, aware that Piers and Dane had his back. Always. "Two of your men attacked me last night."

"No, no!" Jess lifted his hands, palms out. Probably trying to look defenseless. Failing because the tips of his claws had already broken through the flesh. "They didn't attack you."

"Could have fooled me," Lucas drawled.

Jess's dark eyes narrowed. "They just wanted the woman." The coyote made a real bad mistake then. He glanced up, his gaze zeroing in on the third upstairs window. The window that was in Sarah's room. He'd caught her scent.

Lucas lunged forward and grabbed the bastard around the throat. He lifted Jess up, letting the shorter man's feet dangle above the ground. "They're not getting her."

The coyotes in the pickup trucks growled.

Jess's hands flew up and his claws sliced into the flesh on Lucas's forearm. Lucas didn't let him go. His blood splattered to the ground.

The coyote's face began to turn purple. Easy to see that change, even in the waning light. Lucas tightened his hold on Jess's neck, letting the coyote know he didn't have control here.

Jess's eyes burned into his.

Slowly, taking his sweet time, Lucas released the coyote.

Jess sucked in deep gulps of air. "B-bring 'em!"

He tensed at that, knowing this wasn't gonna be pretty. He wanted to glance up at that third window. To see if Sarah was there. She'd be watching, peeking through the curtains, and he didn't want her to witness this.

Michael had damn well better be doing his job.

Two coyotes jumped from the back of the first gleaming pickup. They were carrying a long tarp. A tarp that had been rolled up, tight.

Two more coyote climbed from the second pickup. They had a tarp, too.

Jess watched him, those black eyes studying Lucas closely. "My pack owed you an apology."

"Yeah, you did. That's why I let you past my gates."

Jess grunted, and motioned with his right hand. The tarps were both tossed at Lucas's feet.

What was happening? Sarah squinted through the crack in the curtain, trying to see below. Some coyotes had jumped out of the trucks. Were they going to attack Lucas? Were they pissed that he'd choked their leader?

"You need to come away from the window."

She jumped at the voice and spun around. *Michael.* His long, black hair brushed the collar of his shirt and his dark eyes bore into her.

"What are you doing here?" Sarah asked. "Shouldn't you be outside?" *Protecting Lucas's back.* Too many coyotes were out there. They way outnumbered the wolves she'd seen.

"I'm where I'm supposed to be." He filled her doorway. "You're not. Step away from the window."

A chill skated down her spine. Her fingers slid over the soft edge of the curtain.

"The coyote alpha already has your scent. He knows exactly where you are." Michael's brows rose. "And just in case one of those dogs out there has a gun, you need to move away from that glass."

Right. Gun. The weapon she'd wanted. She hurried forward. But still wondered . . . *what had been in those tarps?*

Jess's claws cut through the ropes that bound the tarps. "They were hunting the woman. She's got one real high price on her head." He glanced back at Lucas. "You've come into my territory following a hunt, and I never stopped you."

Right. "I never attacked *you* during the hunt."

Jess's lips twisted. "True." He sliced through the tarps. "And that's why I brought you a little present."

Lucas's gaze dipped to the open tarps—to the two dead men who'd been gift-wrapped for him.

"I didn't give the order for them to come at you," Jess

spoke quietly. "They broke the pact we had. The punishment for that was their lives." He shrugged. "I knew you'd be coming for 'em anyway, so I figured I'd just save you the trouble."

The men's faces had already taken on the stark white of death. From what Lucas could see, their bodies had stiffened with rigor. They'd died hours ago. Then been hauled out to him.

"Our pact stands." Jess stepped over the bodies. Offered his hand.

Lucas didn't take it. "You know, I'm getting tired of bodies being dumped on my doorstep."

Jess kept his hand up. "We'll take the bodies with us." And the coyotes hurried forward to drag them away. "I just wanted to give you proof, wolf. All my pack understands, you're not to be touched."

But Sarah was fair game?

Lucas smiled and reached for the coyote's hand.

"Can you—can you hear what they're saying?" Sarah asked because the curiosity was killing her.

Michael's brows rose. "You think my hearing is that good?"

Maybe.

Michael shrugged and walked back toward the window.

"Wait! What are you doing?"

But he didn't wait. He brushed back the curtain and stared down below.

"Bullets, man, bullets!" Why should she need to give him the reminder?

He grunted and lifted one strong shoulder. "The glass is bulletproof."

What? "Then why the scare tactics?" She inched closer. "Why make me pull back?"

He didn't look at her. Just gazed below. "Because I knew Lucas wouldn't want you seeing the bodies."

The bodies. Her breath caught in her throat. She'd seen

her share of the dead over the years. But . . . "He's—he's killing them, now?"

"No." Michael's dark head cocked to the right. "Now . . . now he's shaking the coyote alpha's hand."

She rushed forward and shoved the wolf out of her way. *I'll be damned.* They *were* shaking hands. Her own fist slammed into the glass. Of course, it didn't break—not the glass anyway. But her hand started throbbing like a bitch.

"Glad that's settled," Jess murmured. "No sense in bloodshed between our packs."

Not when my wolves can kick your ass so easily.

"Now, about the woman . . ."

Lucas tightened his hold on the coyote's hand. "What about her?"

The faint smile faded from Jess's lips. He tried to pull his hand back. No dice. When it came to physical strength, Lucas could take the coyote any damn day. But when it came to underhanded backstabbing, no one beat Jess.

Well, usually no one did.

Jess stopped tugging his hand and his eyes began to glow with the light of the coyote. "I want her."

"Um, do you?"

Those glowing eyes rose and locked on window number three. "Just have your man send her down. We'll be even."

"Even?" He yanked the coyote closer. "Not even fucking close," he growled in Jess's ear. Then he let the shifter go.

Jess stumbled back.

"You'll have her, and you'll have the bounty on her head." Lucas shook his head. "Why should you get all that cash?"

But Jess locked his muscles and stood his ground, and, once more, his gaze drifted to the window. "It's not just about the money. The bitch owes me, and she *will* bleed for me."

The hell she would. "Pretty soon someone will be bleeding," Lucas murmured, "but it won't be her." In one move, he could slice open the coyote's throat. One fast move. Then his men could take out the others.

"Why'd you take her in?"

Behind Jess, the coyotes tossed the bodies back into the pickups.

He shrugged. "Maybe I was in the mood for a fuck."

"Bullshit. You think you can use her." Jess laughed at that and spat on the ground. "She'll be the one doing the using. And she'll turn on you, just like she turned on her last lover."

"Rafe?"

His eyelids flickered. "Know that, do you?"

Lucas didn't speak.

"She shoved a silver knife into his chest. Another inch and she would have taken his heart."

Interesting. Not quite the delicate little flower she appeared to be. Good.

"She also killed a coyote." Jess pointed to the window. This time, Lucas glanced up, too. He saw Sarah, her palm pressed against the glass. "She and that charmer lover of hers—they set him up and they *fucking killed him.*"

Sarah's stare met Lucas's.

After a moment, he turned back to Jess. But Jess was still looking up at her, and pointing with his claws out. "I owe her payback. That bitch is *mine.*"

"No," he said softly, "she's mine."

"The fuck you say! You can't—"

"You took care of the men who attacked me." He smiled and let his fangs flash. "I'll take care of the one who murdered your man."

Jess's eyes narrowed. "You'll kill her?"

"Sometimes death is the easy part," he murmured.

Jess laughed at that, a low, rumbling laugh that groaned in his throat. "Damn straight. Make her suffer."

So it really wasn't about money for the coyote. It was about pain. Interesting.

"Now, Jess, I hope you don't mind . . ." *Actually, I don't give a shit if you do.* "But get the fuck off my land."

Jess jerked his head, but didn't move. "I'll want proof."

The guy just kept pushing. "You'll have it."

"By tomorrow?"

"That's hardly enough time to play."

Jess locked his teeth and gritted, "Tomorrow night."

Lucas inclined his head. "Deal." So this was what it felt like when you bargained with the devil.

Jess spun away and headed for the first truck. Giving his back as a target really wasn't his brightest move. But then, Jess had never claimed to be a genius, just a tough coyote who'd once sold out his own brother so he could take the position of pack alpha.

Loyalty. Didn't it matter anymore?

Jess climbed into the passenger side of the truck. Raised his hand. The trucks roared to life and the tires spun on the gravel drive. Lucas was aware of Dane moving toward the trees. Moving fast.

Good. Dane would follow the coyotes. He'd watch them, and he'd see just who the bastards were aligning with in this town.

When the dust cleared, he turned back to face the house. Piers stood a few feet behind him.

"You believe anything he said was true?" He jerked his thumb back toward the house. "Did she really kill a coyote?"

"Maybe." Not like he could judge. He'd killed a coyote, too. And so had Jess . . . funny that the bastard was demanding vengeance when he'd just killed two of his own men.

Of course, Sarah was human. Pack took care of pack, but when humans tried to hunt . . .

"And what about Rafe?" Piers whistled. "You buy that she went after him with a silver knife?"

Now that gave him pause. "We didn't search her when she came in." The woman had looked so defenseless. Fucking mistake on his part.

"Shit." Piers's eyes widened. "You think she's still got the knife."

"I think I'm not going to be taking any more chances with

our charmer." He glanced back up at that window and found her gaze on him. "No chances at all."

"The coyotes left." And there hadn't been a giant, all-out brawl below her. She exhaled on a hard breath that fogged the glass. "That's great, right?"

Michael didn't answer.

She turned and elbowed him. "Right?"

"Dane's following them."

She glanced back through the window, squinting. Night was falling so fast now, she could barely see anything. "Why?"

"Because I want to see if the coyotes really are teaming up with Rafe." Lucas's deep voice filled the room.

Sarah whirled around. "You shook his hand." She'd seen that part clearly, and she'd taken the punch right in her gut. "I *told* you that the coyotes wanted to take you out and you stood there and shook a coyote alpha's hand?" She marched toward him, anger humming through her. "I didn't think you'd be such an easy mark."

"I'm not." Deadly quiet.

Wait—was that some kind of warning about the coyotes or was he saying—

"Get out, Michael. Get to work with Piers."

Michael nearly ran out of the room. *When the alpha says jump . . . You say how fucking high.* Rafe's words drifted through her mind as goosebumps rose on her arms. "What happened to the bodies?"

His eyes widened, just the tiniest bit. "You shouldn't have seen—"

"I didn't." Michael had made sure of that. Did they really think she was that fragile? If they only knew. "Did you kill them?"

He leaned in close and his breath feathered over her cheek as he said, "You tell me. Am I a killer?"

Yes. That's why she wanted him. No, why she needed him. He laughed, and the husky rumble just made the goosebumps worse. "This time, I didn't have to lift a hand. The coyote alpha—"

Jess Ortez. Yeah, she knew the lying asshole.

"—he wanted to make up for . . . offending me. To show that our deal was still in place, he killed the two coyotes who came after me."

"Your deal?" And the two coyotes from the park were dead? She swallowed. *Don't think about it, don't! They would have killed you in a heartbeat.* Hell, they *would* have, if Lucas hadn't been there.

"I stay in California. He stays in Mexico." A pause. "For the most part. We stay behind our boundary lines and no one gets ripped apart." His fingers lifted and brushed down her cheek. "When shifters tangle, the blood flows fast."

Every part of him seemed to surround her then. His body was too big. His eyes too intense. The wild, woodsy scent that clung to his skin filled her nostrils.

Lucas.

"Jess had a few stories to tell about you." His finger slid under the curve of her chin, forcing her to keep looking into those bright eyes. "And now I've got some more questions for you, Sarah."

Oh, she just bet he did. But he wouldn't be able to spot a lie now. Her heartbeat was already racing hard enough to shake her chest.

"Did you kill one of Jess's men?"

"What?" Not the first question she'd anticipated.

His fingers trailed down her neck. He leaned in close and his lips pressed lightly against the base of her throat. "Did you kill a coyote on your way to find me?"

The tip of his tongue lapped her skin. Her hands flew up and caught his shoulders. Held tight. "No."

His fingers eased down her shirt, pausing in the hollow between her breasts. "You sure about that? Jess seemed pretty certain you and your charmer lover murdered his coyote."

Her charmer lover? "John wasn't . . ."

The back of his hand brushed her breast. She sucked in a

sharp breath and realized she had a death grip on his shoulders. Sarah forced her hands to ease their tight hold. "He wasn't my lover." Her voice came out too husky and soft.

"But Rafe was?"

"Yes." So she had a weakness for bad boys. A weakness that was lifting its head again. *Didn't you learn anything before?* Bad boys were fun for a while, until they turned on you.

His hands were on her body, steady, strong. He eased her back, walking slowly, until her legs bumped against the bed.

"Your lover put a bounty on your head."

"He didn't take rejection well." True, but he also hadn't wanted her to get away from him, not when she knew so much.

"Um . . ." That growling rumble vibrated from deep in his chest. "How much are you worth to him?"

His fingers skated down her bare arms. The flesh seemed hypersensitive to his touch. "Two hundred grand."

One brow rose.

"Th-that's what the coyotes said, you heard them in the park—"

"Coyotes lie." His lips brushed the hollow of her throat. "And I think you do, too, babe."

True. But was lying to protect yourself so wrong? "Three hundred grand." That really was the truth.

"Dead?" He asked quietly, the whisper at her throat. "Or alive?"

She flinched. "Does it matter?"

"To me, it matters one hell of a lot." Then he moved, fast, pushing her down and Sarah's back hit the soft mattress. She didn't have time to twist or jump out of the way because he was on her instantly, covering her with his body and trapping her on the bed.

"Playtime's over," he told her, no sensual heat in his eyes. Just hard, cold wolf.

His voice might have been arctic, but the body pressing

against hers seemed to burn with fever, and there was no mistaking the fierce bulge of his cock as it pressed against her.

Sarah's hands shoved at his shoulders. "I don't know what you—"

He caught her wrists, held them tight in one hand, then he twisted and his right hand shot down to the bottom of her jeans. Oh, shit, no, he *knew.*

It only took about two seconds for his fingers to find the ankle sheath. His eyes glittered down at her.

Fear dried her mouth. "L-Lucas . . ." *I can explain* stuck in her throat.

He pulled out her knife. The light glinted off its sharpened edge. "I'm guessing the blade is made out of silver." He turned the knife a bit, inspecting it. Then he stretched over her again. The strong hand that held her wrists jerked high, forcing her hands over her head.

And he brought the knife in close. "It *is* silver, right?"

Not the handle, or his flesh would be burning, but . . . "Yes, the blade is silver." The knife was way too close to her throat for comfort.

What do you know about him? The voice of doubt she'd heard all during that long drive to LA.

What did she know?

That he was a killer.

That he led the most vicious wolf pack on the West Coast.

That he'd fought a band of vampires to free his brother. *Loyal.* He might be a walking nightmare to some, but Lucas had protected Jordan. She'd heard that story about him, managed to steal that tale from the minds of the wolves. Lucas had attacked a Born Master Vampire—and Born Masters were the strongest of those blood-sucking vamps—for his brother. He'd risked his life to save Jordan's.

A guy who did that couldn't be all bad. Right?

But that blade was *so* close to her throat.

"Have you ever used this knife on anyone?"

He already knew the answer. He'd known that she had the

knife, so that meant the coyotes had told him about her and Rafe. "Yes."

"On your lover?" He shook his head. "Tell me, did Rafe put the bounty on your head before or *after* you tried to take his heart?"

This wasn't looking good. She sucked in a breath, tried to exhale, and realized her breasts were crushed against his chest.

"Before . . . or after, Sarah?" Harder now, angrier.

"After." Dammit.

His gaze seemed to bore into hers. "So you come here, you tell me that a rival wolf is out to kill me, that he's put a bounty on *your* head, but you neglect to mention that you drove a silver knife into the guy's chest?" He rose above her and his fingers tightened around the knife. "Is this some damn setup? Do you get off on pitting two wolves against each other?"

Oh, hell. "Lucas!"

He threw the knife. It flew, end-over-end, and embedded hilt-deep in the far wall.

"Why did you attack him, Sarah?"

"Because he was trying to kill me," she snarled because she was afraid and she was tired and she was angry. *Why? Why'd* this hell happen to her? "When a six-foot-four asshole comes at me with claws and fangs, I'm going to fight back."

"And you just happened to have a silver knife? Handy, having that."

"John gave me the knife."

"He told you to use it on Rafe?"

And on you, if it comes to that. She nodded.

"The coyotes just swore they had my back," he told her. "The alpha killed the two men who attacked you—he wanted to make amends for their actions."

Death was the way to make amends? A shiver worked over her flesh.

"Rafe has never come at me," Lucas said, "Never attacked. I haven't even heard a whisper that he's eyeing my territory."

She couldn't see anything but him. He was all around her. Hard muscles. Angry eyes. Dark, rumbling voice.

The faint lines around his eyes deepened. "But you come here, and you sneak in a *silver* knife. What were you planning to do? Wait for a moment when I'm weak? Maybe try to stab me when I sleep so you can take me out?"

No.

His head lowered and his mouth feathered over hers in the lightest of kisses. She hadn't expected the sensual touch and heat flooded through her. *Even now . . . want him.*

The adrenaline in her blood was spiking. The anger and fear mixed with the need the man could stir too easily. His mouth . . .

Sarah tried to pull back.

His tongue licked her lip. "Tell me . . . did you think you'd fuck me and slip past my guard?"

Her head lifted. She caught his lower lip with her teeth. Nipped him. Hard. Time for him to see that she could bite, too. "*No, dammit.*" The driving need trembled in her voice.

His tongue swiped over his lip, as if tasting her mark. "Then tell me what the fuck is really happening."

"I have! Rafe is coming after you. He's coming after me. He won't stop until we're both dead." The hard length of his aroused flesh pressed against her sex, and Sarah couldn't control the small arch she made against him.

His gaze searched hers, probably saw too much. Then he nodded, the move quick and grim.

Oh, great, now what—

"I guess we'll just have to make sure we kill him first," Lucas said, and then he gave her what she'd wanted—he pressed his mouth to hers. A hard, hot kiss.

Chapter 5

It wouldn't be the first time that a woman had set him up to die. Pretty women were used as bait by all sorts of paranormals and even by humans.

So maybe Sarah was screwing him over. Maybe he'd be a fool to trust her, but right then, one thing was clear to Lucas.

He fucking wanted her.

Her scent filled his head. Drove him crazy. She was all curves and silken flesh beneath him. Her hands were on him, holding tight to his shoulders as she urged him closer.

Sarah wasn't shoving him away because she was afraid of the beast he carried. She knew just how deadly he could be, and the woman still wanted him.

He could smell her arousal in the air.

She twisted beneath him, her hips pushing against his aroused flesh.

Fuck.

Was this the kind of response she'd given to that bastard Rafe? His hands flew away from her. He grabbed the bedcovers, and his claws sliced right through the fabric.

But he kept kissing her because he couldn't let her mouth go. The woman's taste was addictive.

She moaned low in her throat and the sound vibrated in his mouth. Her breasts stabbed at his chest, the nipples tight and tempting.

Sarah turned her head, tearing her lips from his. "I shouldn't . . . want you." The words were gasped out.

And they really pissed him off. "Because of what I am?" Maybe it was there, after all. Hiding beneath her surface. *Fuck a monster, but fear him.*

But she shook her head, sending those thick locks of hair sliding back over her cheeks. "Because this isn't me." Whispered now. "I don't . . . I don't respond this way normally."

Were her cheeks red? Her heartbeat drummed so fast it shook her chest. He stared down at her, claws still in the bed, and wondered what the hell he was supposed to do with her.

Take her.

Protect her.

Both were instincts from the beast. The same instincts he'd had from the beginning. Those instincts made him nervous. Humans were supposed to be prey to him. Easy pickings. He wasn't supposed to care what happened to them.

But he cared about her.

Protect her.

Even from himself?

Lucas sucked in a deep breath. He caught her scent— wanted more. *Not now. Can't.* Time was running out.

He shoved away from her and managed to rise to his feet. Her breath came too fast, making her chest heave as she stared up at him. "I told you we'd have sex," he said because they needed to be clear about this.

Her chin lifted. "And I told you sex wasn't part of our deal." Her lips were red, swollen from his mouth.

"No, it's not." His cock was so heavy and hard that the damn thing ached. *For her.* "But you want me, I want you, and even the monsters at the gate aren't going to stop me from taking you soon."

"Lust is fleeting." Her gaze seemed to look far away. Not even seeing him. "It's just a need, just a—"

"*Sarah.*"

She blinked. Her gaze sharpened on him. Good. He spoke

deliberately, wanting her to know what would come. "I don't know what sex was like for you before, but I can tell you this . . . it won't be fleeting with me. The need will be so strong it will feel like it's ripping you apart, and when you think you can't stand it anymore . . . that's when the pleasure will come, and it'll make your whole body burn."

The rasp of her breath seemed loud in the room. Or, shit, maybe that was *his* breath. What was she doing to him?

Take her. The beast was growling in his head again. But Sarah rose from the bed. She crossed her arms over her chest, staring at him a bit nervously. Did she think he was about to pounce? Again? Tempting.

"Next time, you come to me," he said. "Come to me, and I'll give you all the pleasure you can handle. And it won't have a damn thing to do with our deal." The attraction between them was a bonus, or maybe a deadly temptation. He really wasn't sure which yet. Time would tell.

He turned away from her and headed for the door.

"I don't sleep with every wolf I meet."

That froze him. He looked back at her, aware that his jaw had tightened. "Good to know."

"I've only been with one wolf. Just Rafe."

And me, babe. You'll be with me, but we'll get to that soon enough.

"That didn't end so well," she murmured and he saw her blink quickly. Wait—was she blinking back tears? *Tears?*

His gut clenched.

But she spun toward the window, her shoulders straight and tense. "What kind of deal did you work out with the coyotes?"

Not the question he'd expected right then. Lucas didn't answer because, really, there wasn't an easy way to put this.

"Lucas?" She waited a moment, then, when he didn't answer, she turned back to him. No tears were in her eyes. Just determination. "I know they didn't just bow their heads and leave. They knew I was here—"

"Yes."

"So what deal did you make with them? How did you get them to walk away?"

He exhaled on a hard sigh. "You're worth a lot of money, lady."

Her lips curled in a humorless smile. "Too much for them to walk away."

True. So why lie? "We reached a deal." How would she take this?

A faint line appeared between her brows. "What did you promise?"

Not much, just . . . "To kill you."

The scent of death surrounded her. Sarah stood in the medical examiner's office, eyeing the closed metal lockers. Bodies were in there. A body was on the table next to her, the toe tagged and a sheet tossed over the victim's face and chest.

"I don't think we should be here," she managed quietly, but what she really wanted to say was *This is stupid! The cops are close! We need to get the hell out of here!*

But after telling her that he was planning to kill her—*um, what?*—Lucas had pulled her down the stairs, shoved her into an SUV, and driven her back to the city. One of his shifters had been waiting for them at the door. Michael, the tall, dark shifter who seemed to follow Lucas's orders so very well.

"No one will be back here for another hour." Michael went to the metal locker on the right and jerked it open. Cold air wafted to them, and he yanked out a slab. "Kelly gave me the schedule and the key—we're clear."

Lucas stalked to that slab and the dead body on it.

"That's John, isn't it?" Sarah forced herself to speak and was rather impressed by the even tone of her voice. Sure, her nails were digging so hard into her palms that she was pretty sure she'd draw blood soon, but she sounded normal.

Michael grunted and pulled back the sheet.

Sarah stumbled and her elbow slammed into an instrument tray. Scalpels and tweezers and she didn't even want to *know* what else clattered to the floor.

"First dead body?" Michael drawled.

No. About the twentieth. Was she supposed to get numb to them? "A dead *friend*," she snapped back and whirled away from him. She hadn't realized the attack had been so . . . brutal. John's throat had been ripped wide open. No, not ripped. Clawed.

And Michael was going to mock her? *Asshole*. How would he react if he were looking at one of his shifter buddies? Oh, wait, if he was anything like the coyotes, he'd be the one doing the killing, so he probably wouldn't give a shit if a packmate died.

Her shoe kicked against the scalpel. She bent and began picking up the surgical instruments. She crouched low, and slid the scalpel up her sleeve, securing it with the band of her watch.

"Sarah?" Lucas's quiet whisper.

She rose quickly, and dumped the other items back on the tray.

His fingers wrapped around her shoulder. "You okay?"

"No, I'm *not*." She faced him. "I don't like seeing my friend sliced open, okay? It's not one of the highlights of my night."

"While the coyotes are in the city, you go where I go." His lips tightened. "And I need to check this body, so I know it sucks, but you have to stay here."

She inclined her head in a brief nod. She understood all this, it just didn't mean she had to like the situation. And that thick smell of disinfectant was making her sick.

He caught her chin and tipped her head back. "You hurt for him and you're furious that this happened to him. Right now, there's no time for the hurt. Just focus on the fury, and it'll get you through this." His hand fell away.

She blinked. *Focus on the fury.* Interesting. It almost

seemed like the wolf cared how she felt. *No, don't fall into that trap. He sees you as a tool he can use, just like Rafe.*

"Claws ripped his throat open, no doubt." Michael's voice. Her gaze shot to the left. He was leaning over John's body, his eyes slitting as he studied the wounds on John's neck. "No knife did this." He glanced at Lucas, nodding. "Definitely shifter."

Lucas stepped closer to the body. "Wolf or coyote?"

Sarah's breath froze in her throat. She couldn't help it, she had to look at John's face. Still handsome in death with his strong nose, high cheekbones, and that stubborn jaw. But his blue eyes were closed, no longer snapping out energy. The bronzed skin was too pale.

I'll meet you in LA. Simone is the one we need. We can end this thing. He just has to help us. Then the road ahead is free.

She brushed past Lucas. Ran her hand over the too-icy flesh of John's cheek. This wasn't the kind of freedom he'd been talking about.

"I smell coyote all over the poor bastard," Michael said.

"So do I," Lucas agreed. "But the guy was a charmer, he worked with the coyotes."

So their smell *would* be on him.

Sarah felt the stare on her and she looked to the left, meeting Michael's assessing brown gaze. "He worked with them . . . like she worked with the wolves." Not a question from the dark wolf.

But, yeah, they'd both been spies of a sort.

I'm sorry, John. If she'd gotten to LA sooner, would she have been able to stop this?

Michael pulled back the sheet and studied John's arms. "No defensive wounds."

"Because he didn't have time to fight," Lucas said and she knew he was right. "Probably never saw the guy coming."

No, because if he had, John would've fought.

She pulled her hand away from John. Her fingers balled

into a fist. She could still feel the cold touch of his flesh. "If it was fast, then he didn't suffer much." Shouldn't that have been comforting? Why wasn't it?

Michael exhaled. "There's no wolf scent on this guy, and those marks on his neck . . ." He scratched his chin. "Not quite as big as a wolf's . . ."

Coyote.

"Then we know what got him." Lucas yanked the sheet back over John's body. "Close him up, Michael." He caught Sarah's arm. "Let's get the hell out of here."

Finally. This time, she was the one to pull him along as she hurried outside. She wanted air. Her cheeks felt too chilled, almost as cold as John's. Her feet thudded down the hallway. The tiles gleamed up at her and the fluorescent lights dimmed a bit overhead.

Her left hand slammed against the exit door. She sucked in a deep breath of fresh air. *Not death.* She tried to rush forward—

But Lucas's hold stopped her.

"What—"

He yanked her back, pulling her into the shadows and caging her body between his and the hard brick building. He still had her right hand, his fingers holding it tightly. "Did you think I didn't notice?"

"Notice what?"

He shoved back her sleeve and the scalpel glinted.

The wolf saw too much. She'd remember that. Now she just snapped, "If you hadn't taken my knife, I wouldn't have needed a backup weapon."

He slipped the scalpel free and tossed it on the ground.

Great. "You told me you were going to *kill* me," she reminded him. *Don't think about John. Not yet, don't.* "So, yes, I took the chance to grab a weapon—"

"Is that what I said?" His thumb brushed over her wrist. Her pulse pounded quickly beneath that light touch. And since when was the alpha wolf given to light touches?

"Y-yes . . ." The heat from his body was slowly banishing the cold. "You made a deal with the coyotes. You said—"

"You really think I haven't lied to them before?" He smiled at her then, flashing those sharp teeth. "You and I already have a deal, don't we? And it's a deal that doesn't involve your death."

But if he'd lied to the coyotes, how did she know he wasn't lying to her? *Especially since I'm lying to him.*

"You're gonna have to trust me for this to work," he told her and his breath feathered over her cheek.

"Trust isn't exactly easy for me."

"Do you have a choice now?"

No.

"I'm not going to kill you to satisfy those bastards." Flat. "And I'm not turning you over to them."

She swallowed.

"Trust me."

There was no one else she could trust. If he turned on her, she was dead. *But if he wanted me dead, I would have been dead last night. A shifter is always armed. One slice of his claws, and I would have been on a slab next to John.*

"Now what thought just ran through your mind?" He asked, his lips coming close to hers. "What made fear flash in your eyes?"

She took a breath and tasted him. "I want my knife back."

Lucas shook his head. "That's not what caused the fear."

He was very good at reading her. "You want me to trust you. I want *you* to trust *me*." She licked her lips and watched the dip of his gaze as he followed the movement. "You don't attack me, I don't attack you, but I want that knife. I'm not going to be defenseless." And she wasn't, not really, but he didn't know that. A woman had to keep some secrets in this world.

His lips pressed against hers and he stole her breath. Then his tongue slipped into her mouth, bringing his wild taste, and Sarah's heart raced even faster.

The door squeaked open. "Lucas?"

He raised his head. "You're not defenseless." Then he eased away and called, "We're here, Michael."

Her gaze darted to the scalpel. It wouldn't be hard to pick it up . . .

"It looks like a coyote hit," Lucas said, "but I want to see the house again. There was no time yesterday. As soon as I got out of the car, the cops swarmed me."

Ahem. Ah, yes, that had actually been *her* fault. Should she mention that part of the story now?

"Your house is still a crime scene, man." Worry hardened Michael's face. "It's taped off and the cops are probably patrolling the area."

Lucas laughed softly. "Like a few human cops are going to stop me."

Like *anything* would stop him.

Dane had to keep his distance from the coyotes. If he came within a mile of them, they'd catch his scent. So he pulled his motorcycle to the curb, hid in the shadows, and used his night-vision binoculars to watch the bastards.

He counted ten of them. The youngest was a kid, barely looked eighteen. The oldest seemed to be skating close to forty. Two women were in the group—but he couldn't tell if they were coyote shifters or humans.

Their base was a ranch-style house, one that was fairly secluded in a patch of woods. Nothing fancy, because the coyotes wouldn't have wanted to draw attention to themselves. It wasn't as easy to kill when attention was on you.

After a few moments, all of the coyotes went in the house. He lowered the binoculars and pulled out his phone. Three seconds later, he had Lucas on the line. "2408 Wyler Road."

"Any signs of Rafe?"

Lucas had briefed them all on Sarah's story, and Dane knew Rafael Santiago. Their paths had crossed once in Chicago. "No. No signs . . ." He inhaled, caught only the scent of coyote, "of any other shifter."

"Keep your eyes on 'em. If you see *any* sign of a wolf . . ."

"I'll report right away."

"Do that. And watch your back."

He always did. Dane tucked the phone into his pocket. It was going to be one damn long night. But maybe the coyotes would oblige him and produce the wolves—then he could have some ass-kicking fun with his pack.

A twig snapped behind him. Dane didn't glance back. He kept his gaze on the house. *Ass-kicking fun.* Looked like he'd get that good time sooner than he'd thought. His claws pushed through the tops of his fingertips. The wild scent of shifter filled his nose.

So did the lush scent of woman.

"It's really not my style to attack from behind." Her voice floated to him. Soft, sexy.

Interesting.

He spun around. She smiled at him, a flash of white teeth and sexy red lips. Small, curved, and tempting, the pretty redhead stood just in front of a line of thick trees. The moon shone down on her, illuminating her pale skin.

"It's not *my* style," she said again, and her gaze darted just over Dane's shoulders. "But it is his."

And a freight train slammed into him.

To appease Michael, Lucas waited until the patrol car's tail-lights disappeared around the corner, then he jumped out of the SUV and headed for his house. Sarah moved just as quickly, hurrying out and sticking to the shadows as she headed for the house on Bryton Road.

The scents of the night hit him. Gasoline. Alcohol. Stale cigarettes. And blood. Lots of blood.

He slipped under the yellow police tape and stalked toward the porch steps. With his enhanced vision, he could still see the giant bloodstain that marred the wood. The poor bastard had bled out fast.

Guess that was a good thing.

Some prey deserved to suffer, some didn't.

"I'm still not scenting wolf," Michael muttered from behind them. "Least not any wolves that don't belong here."

'Cause he let some of his pack visit—very rarely, but sometimes.

"Maybe . . . maybe the attacker blocked his scent," Sarah said quietly, near the porch but with her face carefully averted from the steps. "It is possible, you know."

Yeah, he knew. He'd blocked his scent with herbs a few times when he didn't want the coyotes to know that he was hunting. But . . .

He closed his eyes and inhaled deeper. So many scents. Some old, some faint. Others fresher, stronger.

Sweeter.

His eyes opened and, very slowly, Lucas turned his head to stare at Sarah. She'd wrapped her arms around her body, as if to keep warm. But it wasn't a cold night. Far from it.

"Looks like the crime-scene guys from the LAPD did a good sweep of this place," Michael said, not seeming to pay them any attention. "Can't even find cigarette butts on the ground."

"John didn't smoke," she said at once.

Lucas's nostrils flared. "Someone did. I can still smell the ash." But the evidence had been removed.

Because he was watching her so closely, Lucas saw her flinch. Interesting.

"Time to pay a visit to Marley," he said.

"*What?*" Michael spun around. "Aw, hell, you still got that demon playing watchdog for you?"

Sarah's brows pulled low. "Marley?"

He caught her hand. "Come on." No sense going inside. The dead guy had never made it past the porch.

They'd parked the SUV down the deserted street, but he didn't head back to it. Instead, he cut through the thin line of trees and snaked to the left, toward the old, rundown house that bordered his strip of property. That place was his, too, though no one would ever be able to find a record that said so.

He'd bought both places because he liked his privacy and they were the only two houses on the street. Yeah, he liked privacy, but he also liked protection. That was where Marley came in.

He didn't bother knocking when he bounded onto the sagging porch, he just kicked the door in.

"Lucas!" Sarah's horrified whisper.

An old woman spun to face him, her hair stark white and her face etched with deep lines. She shuffled toward them, her steps small and mincing. "What do you—why are you here?" Beady eyes swept the group.

He growled. "Cut the damn act, Marley."

The old woman vanished in an instant. Demons and their glamour. Those skilled at cloaking magic could project any image they wanted to the world. Marley transformed in front of them, the white hair darkening to black, the deep wrinkles slipping away until smooth skin remained. Another mask? Probably, but it was the one Marley liked to use the most.

"Why are you here?" She asked again, glaring. "You said I'd be left alone, Lucas. I did my part. I burned those bastards to ash, but *you said I'd be left alone.*"

Ah, another deal. A demon who'd been desperate to slip away from the world and a wolf who'd needed vengeance. Their agreement had been fairly satisfactory.

"There a particular reason you let those assholes haul me away, huh, Marley?" He stepped closer and the demon didn't back up. Surprising. For a while, Marley had backed up when anyone came close. *That's why she'd wanted to hide in the woods. To stay far away from everyone and everything.*

Since he'd needed a guard on his house who didn't smell of wolf, he'd humored her. Humor time was over.

Her lips lifted in a taunting half-smile. "I knew the cops wouldn't keep you for long."

"You saw the attack." Not a question. He heard footsteps behind him as Michael and Sarah came inside the cabin.

Marley's blue gaze—another lie, a demon's real eyes were black—lowered a bit, then flickered to Michael. "I . . . I didn't see the kill." Quiet. "By the time I caught the scent of blood on the wind . . ."

A demon's sense of smell was nowhere near as powerful as a shifter's.

". . . it was too late. The human was dead."

Great. "I let you stay here because you said you'd guard the house." His one retreat. The place away from the pack. Now the place was stained with blood. Hell, wasn't everything he touched stained with blood?

"I *have* been guarding it, okay? I went out—I do that sometimes, you know. If you want full-time surveillance, get a freaking video camera."

Right. Because he wanted footage of himself shifting into a wolf. That would be great when it fell into the wrong hands and got blasted all over fucking kingdom-come.

"I didn't see the kill." Marley tossed back her hair and lifted her hand. Her finger pointed straight at Sarah. "But I did see her."

Sarah didn't gasp in shock. Didn't start yelling that the demon was lying. He glanced at her from the corner of his eye. Her face appeared totally blank.

"Something you need to tell me, Sarah?" he asked softly but Marley's words weren't a surprise. Just confirmation. He'd caught Sarah's scent near the porch. Fainter, but still sweet vanilla.

Her gaze tracked to his. "I was supposed to be with John. We were supposed to meet at your place—"

"How did you even know about his place?" Michael interrupted, his voice rough as the wolf began to near the surface. "You and the dead human shouldn't have—"

"Rafe knew about the place, so that meant I knew."

He was getting real sick of old Rafe.

Sarah held Lucas's stare. "I was late. I should have been here sooner, *but I was late.*"

If she hadn't been late, would he have come back and found her dead body on his doorstep, too? And would he even have cared?

Wouldn't have known her. Wouldn't have kissed her.
A dead human.
Would he have cared?
His claws broke through his fingertips. "Why didn't you tell me sooner?" *Can't trust her.* He knew that. The woman wore secrets like other women wore perfume.

"What was the point? When I got here, he was already dead." She stared down at her hands. She turned them over, staring at the palms. Lucas thought of the pool of blood that had surrounded the body.

Did it stain your hands, Sarah?
"You weren't there," she told him. "*No one* was there. So I ran."

"Then the cops came," Marley muttered, watching Sarah closely, "right after your girl vanished." She shrugged. "So I had to vanish for a time, too. Until those jerks stopped searching the property."

"No wonder you gave me an alibi." Lucas cocked his head as his gaze slid back to Sarah. She was still staring at her hands. Still seeing blood? "You're the reason the cops tossed my ass in jail."

She dropped her hands, and her gaze lifted to his. "No. You got tossed in jail because you've got a history with the cops. It's not my fault you and that detective—detective—"

"Bruce Langston." Dickhead.

"—have some kind of war going on." She straightened her shoulders. "I wasn't just going to leave John's body out here to rot. He deserved better than that."

"Most folks don't deserve the way they die."

Michael crowded in close to her. "And some folks do." His eyes had narrowed with suspicion. "Some folks deserve exactly what they get."

Her small jaw clenched. "Back off, wolf," she gritted.

Lucas slanted a hard glance at Michael.

The wolf eased back a step, but he glared at Lucas. "Don't let your dick lead you, man. The woman lied to you!"

"He never asked me if I was here!"

"What the fuck? *You never said!*" Michael snarled right back.

Lucas's gaze darted back to Marley. She was watching Michael and Sarah, a faint gleam in her eyes.

Marley. The bloody and beaten demon who'd come to him six months ago. She'd begged for his pack's aid, saying she only wanted a safe place to stay, and in return, she'd given them her fire. Demons were so good at controlling fire.

And there had been some murdering assholes who deserved those flames.

As far as Lucas knew, Marley had never left the house since they'd made their agreement. Food and supplies were brought to her. So after six months, suddenly, she decided to take a stroll . . .

He moved quickly, catching both of her arms and pinning them behind her back.

"Lucas!" Her scream of shock.

Sarah and Michael both froze.

"Where'd you go, Marley?"

She twisted against him. "Let me go!" Fire began to lick across the floor.

"*Where'd you go?*"

The fire flared higher—then it shot straight for Sarah. "Get her out of here!" Lucas ordered because no way was he letting the demon go then.

Michael grabbed Sarah's arm and hauled her toward the door. They'd taken about three steps when the door slammed closed, trapping them inside. Damn demon power.

Lucas brought his hand to Marley's throat. "Let's try this again," he whispered and he let her feel the sting of his claws on her flesh. "I *know* you didn't go any damn place. I *know* you're lying. So who the hell did you see slice that human?"

The flames circled Sarah and Michael. The fire burned higher.

His claws pressed deeper. "If the flames don't die, you do." His gaze darted to Sarah.

Her eyes met his through the flames. He knew she'd see

the beast shining in his stare. See the claws, see the teeth.
Here's the monster, never really hidden by the man.

The fire was so close to her skin. Charmers were weak
when it came to magic. The fire would hurt her, kill her—

A growl worked in his throat as he turned his fury back on
Marley. If this was the way it would end . . .

The flames died. Smoke drifted in the air. "Jess . . ." The
name was a sigh that broke from Marley's lips. "He and the
coyotes . . . they killed him."

"And what?" he whispered in her ear, not wanting Sarah
to hear. "You just stood back and fucking watched?"

A tremble shook her. "It was watch or die myself."

He knew Sarah heard the words because her eyes widened.

"They were going to wait for her," Marley said, and Lucas
kept his claws near her throat. "But it took too long. You
were due back . . ." She swallowed, and he felt the gulp
against his hand.

He dropped his hold but didn't step back. "Was it all a
setup?" Fuck, how long had this plan been in motion? "They
sent you in . . . just to set me up?"

Her chin lifted as blood dripped down her throat. "I'm a
low-level demon. Barely a three on the power scale. All I can
do is use the glamour. Cloak. Hide." Her brittle laugh filled
the air. "I might as well be human. A freaking rag doll for the
paranormals out there."

She'd looked like a rag doll the first time he'd seen her. A
broken, bloody doll that had been thrown away. "They beat
you, then they sent you to me?"

He caught the sad whisper of Sarah's gasp.

"No." Marley's lips tightened. "They didn't want their
scents on me." Her gaze darted to Michael. "They had the
demons beat me, *then* they sent me to you."

He knew she hadn't lied about her attack when she'd first
come to him. And he'd wanted her fire. Seemed like a fair ex-
change at the time.

His eyes collided with Sarah's. Was any deal really fair
these days?

"Why did you help them?" Because Marley had helped. Not just watched. *Helped*. Dammit. "*Why?*"

"Because they would have killed me if I didn't!" Marley's words came out, fast, tumbling. "And all I did was let them know when the charmer came. That's all they wanted. I haven't told them anything else, I swear."

Because there'd been nothing else to tell. He'd never let Marley in on pack secrets.

Silence.

Then, "John was a good man," Sarah's voice drifted through the cabin. "Did you care about that at all? Did it matter to you who died?"

"No." Marley's voice was much softer. "Didn't matter at all . . . as long as I was the one who got to keep breathing."

She would have stood back and watched Sarah die, too.

"Did you tell them we were here tonight?" Lucas asked but he already knew the answer.

"S-sorry . . ." She whispered and her head fell forward, the long locks of her hair dropped to cover her face. "And they know it's just you and Michael. That you don't have the full strength of your pack." A weak, bitter laugh. "Or even the strength of your four horsemen."

Caleb. Dane. Piers. Michael. His own apocalypse that sent death to his enemies.

Her shoulders dipped. "Th-they'll be here soon."

To kill you. To take the girl.

"Oh, shit," from Michael.

"I would have protected you," Lucas said quietly as rage pumped through him. The change was coming. There would be no way to hold back the shift. The beast's rage was too strong.

Her head whipped up, and she stared at him with wide eyes.

"Now, I'll have to kill you."

She stumbled away. "Lucas—"

A howl split the night. Not the harder, longer cry of a

wolf. Shorter, higher. A coyote. But that howl was immediately followed by another. Another, another.

"Fuck." He spun around. A trap. One he'd walked right into. He yanked out his cell. Piers answered on the second ring. "Get to Bryton Road. The dogs are out." But he wasn't going to wait for backup to arrive. That was time they didn't have to waste.

"Where are they?" Sarah was at the window, peeking through the old blinds. "I can hear them, but I can't see them."

"They're all around us." Michael stood right behind her, his body a long, lethal shadow. His gaze shot to Lucas. "I see at least ten."

Freaking coyotes.

The floorboard squeaked behind them. "Going somewhere?" he asked Marley quietly. It was a shame. Marley had always been weak, not just in terms of power scale, but—

"They know *your* weakness, wolf." Marley's words came out with more heat than he'd expected from her. "Why do you think they sent me?"

He glanced back at her. At the tilt of his head, Michael closed in on her. Sarah followed him.

Marley's gaze jumped to Sarah. "They understand how to get beneath your skin. Know what makes you weak. Before you even realize it, you'll—"

Sarah lunged forward and drove her fist right into the demon's face. Marley went down, and she didn't get up.

"Dammit!" Sarah shook her hand, and flexed her fingers. "That hurt!"

Probably hurt Marley more.

"I was scared she'd start another fire," Sarah told him, turning her eyes to his. "We've got enough trouble without—"

More howls. So close. Those dogs would be on them soon.

"Not the worst odds we've ever faced," Michael said, even as his bones began to snap and pop. He dropped to the floor, bracing his hands as his body stretched and his clothes ripped along his body.

"No." Lucas watched him and let the fire burst through his skin. The shift was always red-hot, burning him from the inside out as the beast broke free.

He spared one last glance for Sarah. Her eyes were so wide as she stared at him. Normally, this would be the part where he told her not to be scared. No point in that, though. The woman knew wolves, and as for being scared . . .

Claws hit the outside of the door. Hmmm . . . Good thing Marley had used her power to slam it closed and seal the place. The locked door would buy them a little more time.

"Hide," he managed to snarl the word to Sarah as he fell to the floor. His claws scraped over the wood.

"Lucas . . ."

"Guess . . . you're getting . . ." His spine arched. Fur broke through his skin. "In . . . my . . . mind . . ." Then a howl burst from his mouth as the beast took over.

"Guess I am," her soft whisper seemed too loud in his ears, and when the wolf stared at her, there wasn't just fear in her eyes. There was sadness.

Then she turned and ran, jumping over Marley's body. And he met the dogs at the door.

Chapter 6

No, no, no. This wasn't the way things should have happened. Sarah froze at the sound of Lucas's growl. No way could he and Michael take down that coyote pack out there. He wasn't strong enough for that. Two against ten? Even he wasn't that good.

She glanced over at the demon. Marley was still dead to the world, and the demon's body was about to be slam in the middle of carnage central. Sarah raced forward and grabbed Marley's wrist, then she hauled the demon back, not really caring too much when the chick's head bumped over the floor. She was helping, right?

Growls and howls echoed through the cabin. She could hear the scrape of claws. Those bastards were planning to claw their way inside. Then what? They'd rip Michael and Lucas apart?

She pulled Marley's body behind the couch and let the demon's arm fall.

Stay down. Sarah stiffened at that hard demand. A demand that hadn't been voiced. Lucas. She could finally touch his thoughts now. She closed her eyes a moment and felt that light trail that led back to his mind. Every beast she charmed had a special psychic trail. A trail that she could follow.

Lucas's trail wasn't as bright as others. No, his was dark and twisting. Maybe because the man inside the beast was dark. Twisted? Perhaps. But maybe not.

I've got the bastards that come in through the door. Lucas again. But the words were directed at Michael this time. Shifters could communicate telepathically when they were in animal form. A nice little bonus from Mother Nature that made hunting in packs so much easier, and so much more deadly.

Sarah crouched behind the couch and shook the demon. She hadn't punched *that* hard. Well, maybe she had. Though she'd faked the hand pain after the punch. She knew how to hit hard without bringing pain.

Stay with Sarah. Lucas's order to Michael. *If anyone comes at her, you rip the bastard's throat open.*

Her breath caught at that order. Then a big, black wolf was there. Standing right beside her. Protecting her. But who was protecting Lucas? *Hell, no, Michael. Just haul your ass right back over there. If he falls, I'm dead anyway.*

The black wolf glanced back at her.

He stays. Lucas's snapped command.

Dammit! She poked her head over the couch and got her first clear look at Lucas in wolf form. Unfortunately, that was the same instant that the coyotes burst through the door.

Lucas—a muscled, snarling, teeth snapping mass of black fur—leapt into the air. He caught the neck of the first coyote with his teeth, and, using that hold, he threw the coyote through the air. He swiped the second beast with his claws, cutting him open and the blood sprayed Lucas's fur.

Kill.

Not her thought.

Glass shattered as more coyotes flew through the windows. Two more coyotes attacked Lucas. Snarling, biting.

Kill. Lucas's only thought. No, wait, he was also—

Protect.

She dug her fingers into Michael's fur. His giant body was trembling with the effort of holding back. He wanted into that fray, but he wasn't about to disobey his alpha.

A coyote's body hit the floor. Blood matted his fur. Another coyote launched onto Lucas's back, sinking his teeth into muscle and bone. Lucas rolled over, slamming the coyote into the floor.

Kill.

A howl echoed in the distance, but this howl was deeper than the others. Harder. Darker. Familiar.

Rafe.

The swarm of smaller coyote bodies had almost hidden Lucas now. The coyotes weren't even trying to come for her, they just wanted to take Lucas out. That *had* been the plan, right?

Her fingers were still in Michael's fur. She crouched back behind the couch. *Your alpha needs you. They don't want me, they're going to kill him.* While she hid and watched.

You don't know my alpha. Michael's voice floated in her mind. *He's stronger, he's—*

More snarls and growls. More freaking coyotes. *Help him.* She lunged to her feet even as Michael leapt forward.

"Hey, bastards! How does it feel to be nothing more than freaking pit bulls for—"

Blood. Teeth. Fury. Not from the coyotes. Their bodies littered the floor. From Lucas. The wolf stood poised inside the doorway, blood dripping from his teeth, those blue eyes so bright they hurt to look at.

Oh, damn. He'd taken them all out.

Here's your chance. Run. Get to the car and drive back to base.

Because another attack would be coming.

"They're after you tonight, not me," Sarah said. Michael was sniffing around the coyotes, making sure they didn't rise. "I'm not leaving you."

They'll rip you apart.

Great. Nice visual. Sadly, a true visual. Not like she could fight the coyotes. "Let's *all* get the hell out of here." Before they all died. She knew the wolf waiting out there, he wouldn't be alone. He never was, he—

The wail of sirens echoed in the night. *Sirens?* Oh, crap, yes, the cops had been watching the house. The coyotes would still be in human form when they first arrived. Dozens of men, swarming on a closed crime scene—of course any cop in the area would have called for backup.

Those sirens were getting close now. So close.

And she didn't hear anymore howls. No more snarls.

Some of the coyotes, the dead, had already shifted back to human form. The others were hauling ass out of that cabin.

Run, Lucas. Get out. The cops can't find you here.

His head tilted. She knew he heard the raised voices of the cops. She knew because she was in his head and could pick up his every thought.

His gaze bored into her. "I'll be fine," she promised. Such a lie.

And he knew it.

But what choice was there? Was he really going to face the LAPD in full-on wolf form? Especially when that detective was already gunning for him? A blood-soaked wolf. Right. The cops would shoot instantly when they saw him.

She could already hear the thunder of gunfire. Were the cops firing at the coyotes?

"You've got to run, Lucas. I'll need someone to bail my ass out of jail." Because that's where she was heading.

His blue eyes burned. *Tell them nothing.*

"You can count on that." Like they'd believe her anyway. "*Go.*"

He whirled away, a dangerous shadow, and he dove through the remains of the broken door. Michael followed on his heels, a slightly smaller, but just as dangerous beast.

Her hands balled into fists even as her gaze darted to the dead men. Men, now, not beasts, and they were men who'd died in a manner that looked too similar to John's death. Ripped throats. Torn bodies. And, of course, there she stood, right in the middle of the bloodbath.

"*Freeze!*" A man's snarl this time, not a wolf's, but she

hadn't been moving anyway. Sarah let her stare dart to the doorway. To the two scared-looking cops. Their eyes weren't on her. They were staring at the bodies. Four bodies. And a hell of a lot of blood.

Lucas was stronger than she'd realized and so much more dangerous. Was she really up for this game?

"Holy fucking shit . . ." One of the uniforms swallowed quickly and it looked like he might be sick.

Now what was she supposed to say? The older cop, the one who'd gone two shades paler, had his gun pointed right at her. "I didn't do this," she finally managed. Yes, that sounded good. "There's no blood on me, I don't have a weapon—*I didn't do this.*"

"Then who the hell did?" The older cop barked.

"You wouldn't believe me."

"*Who did this?*"

Her mouth snapped closed. She wouldn't trade Lucas's secrets for her life.

A groan had her attention shifting to that blood-soaked floor. Marley blinked up at her. "Wh—"

"*Is someone else there?*" The cop yelled, and the guy's partner finally seemed to get control of himself. Now two guns were pointed right at her.

"Look, officers—"

"Cops?" Marley's whisper. "*No.*" She sprang to her feet, and then the fire erupted. A line of flames snaked across the cabin, burning the dead shifters as the fire crackled and spread—and those flames, they headed right for the cops.

"Sonofabitch!"

Bullets blasted. Pain burned across Sarah's arm. From the fire? From the bullets? The flames raged higher. The demon vanished in the growing smoke, and Sarah was left to face the fire alone.

The echo of gunfire reverberated in Lucas's ears even as the scent of smoke burned his nose. He froze in the woods, his head tilting back. His body still had the form of a wolf, but the man inside was all too aware of the dangers around him. *Bullets and smoke.* His head turned . . .

The old cabin.

He lunged forward, but Michael plowed into his side, knocking him back.

Have to get away. Michael's desperate thought, one that was reflected in the eyes of the wolf. *We left too many dead back there. Can't let the cops get us.*

Like he fucking cared about the cops. *Sarah.* She couldn't handle fire and if one of those idiots so much as scratched her—

You can't help her as a wolf. Michael's fierce reminder.

No, the wolf couldn't help her.

The cops will take her in, Michael continued, panting from the run they'd made. *We'll get her out. We'll do whatever we have to do, but we'll get her out.*

He spun away, a howl ripping from his throat as he let the hot pain of the shift sweep through his body.

He'd promised to protect Sarah, and he damn well planned to keep his part of the deal.

Dane slowly opened his eyes, aware that something wet was dripping down his face. His nostrils flared—shit, that something wet was *blood*. That scent was undeniable, and so was the scent of . . . coyote.

Fuck. He was sitting down, his body slumped in a chair, and his arms were behind his back. He tried lifting his hands, but metal bit into his wrists. Hard, burning metal.

"It's silver," a soft voice told him.

His gaze flew to the left. There she was. The pretty little thing who'd screwed his concentration in the woods. A weakness for women—when the hell would he learn?

"Sorry about that," she said, not sounding sorry. "But I didn't have a lot of choice."

His lips stretched in a mirthless grin. "I'm sure you didn't." He made *sure* she saw his lengthening fangs.

"We needed you." One shoulder lifted in a shrug that had her red hair sliding back over her shirt. "At least you're still alive."

Why was he still alive? Coyotes didn't usually let their prey survive.

Her gaze tracked to the blood sliding down his face. "Shouldn't you have healed from that?"

And shouldn't she know that not all shifters healed at the same rate? "Silver's slowing me down," he muttered.

A fast blink from her. "Right."

Bullshit. "What's the plan? You gonna let the dogs in so they can take turns swiping at me?" Or was she going to save all the torturing fun for herself?

Now her eyes darted to the window on the left. The only window in the room. He jerked against the cuffs once more. No damn give at all. But . . . he let his claws break through the skin.

"They're not here right now," she whispered.

His brows snapped up, and he felt the faint pull from the torn skin on his forehead. He vaguely remembered slamming into the rocks when the asshole behind him attacked. "Where are they?"

"You don't really want to know."

The claw on his left index finger slipped inside the lock. "*Where?*" His voice was loud, the better to cover the scratch of his claws as he worked on the cuffs. The silver burned, but he was used to pain. Pain had been his intimate friend since before he could even shift, and he had the criss-cross of scars on his body to prove it.

"Why do you think you're still alive?" she asked instead.

Fine, he'd keep her talking. "You want to use me." He let his gaze rake her. "Can't say that I'll mind *you* using me."

She blushed. What the fuck? Since when did coyote women blush? Sex was as natural to them as breathing—and killing. His nostrils flared again. The scent of coyote was everywhere and it was strongest around the woman.

"If they don't succeed, we'll trade you."

The claw snagged on the locking mechanism. "For the charmer?"

He caught the faint widening of her eyes. "She told you what she could do?"

"Even gave us a little demo." He kept his smile in place. "So what does a bunch of dogs want with a little lady who only works with wolves?"

"You know the bounty on her."

He whistled just as the lock popped open. "Can't say I wasn't tempted to take that myself."

"You'd turn on your alpha?" No missing the doubt heavy in her voice. "Don't lie to me."

He wouldn't.

"He should have just turned her over. Now there will be no chance for him."

Tension had his body tight. "Your dogs went after Lucas?"

"The truce is over. They're going to drag his body back."

Pretty face, bitch beneath the surface. "If you really think they're strong enough to take him down, then why am I still breathing?"

"Told you . . ." She paced to the window, peered outside, and made the mistake of giving him her back. Bad mistake. "You're the backup plan. If Lucas manages to get away, then—"

He pounced. He jumped from the chair and had his claws at her throat in less than a second's time. "Then nothing, sweetheart, because your plan has just changed."

She stiffened against him, her smaller body going taut. Her gaze still focused out the window, and, over her shoulder, he saw the trucks spinning into the drive. The dogs were back.

"No, it hasn't," she told him quietly. "But it looks like your time has run out." Then she turned toward him. His claws pressed over her throat. "Kill me." Another shrug. "They'll still kill you as soon as they come inside."

But he could see the limping, bleeding bodies as the coyotes tumbled out of the trucks. She hadn't actually looked at the coyotes before she'd spun away. "Guess again."

Her delicate nostrils flared and her eyes—so gold and wide—searched his. Then she opened her mouth to scream.

Too late.

When Detective Bruce Langston shoved open the door of the small interrogation room, Sarah straightened in the too-hard and wobbly chair.

One black brow lifted. "Back so soon, Ms. King?"

She flattened her hands on the table. "I need to be at a hospital." She coughed, a hard, heaving cough that was only half-pretend. Damn demon—*she'd* gotten away in the smoke while Sarah had needed the cops to pull her out of the flames. "I . . . shouldn't be here . . . I need a doctor."

"And I need a damn wolf in a cage."

Her body stiffened.

He kicked the door closed. "Yeah, you heard me."

She licked her lips. "I heard you . . . I just don't know what the hell you're talking about."

"Bullshit." He paced around the wooden table, his gaze raking her. "Lover-boy blew his hand. I saw his eyes glow. I saw the claws. *I know.*"

"Well, *I don't.*" Her eyes slanted to the left, to the window that lined the wall. Was someone watching in there? "And if you're not careful, your cop buddies are going to think . . ." another cough, this one completely real, "you're crazy."

He stopped in front of her and slammed his fists down onto the table. Sarah flinched.

"Don't fucking lie to me!" He snarled, face far too close to hers. "We both know what Lucas Simone is!"

"I don't even understand what you're yelling about!" So the cop knew the deal. Maybe he'd known all along. Was he working with the other paranormals in the city? Or, hell, no, could he be working with Rafe? So many cops were on the take . . . she knew that better than others.

But if he were working with Rafe, she wouldn't be in interrogation—she'd be in a body bag.

"He left you to burn." Bruce's hands lifted and his finger

traced over the back of her ash stained hand. "You saved his ass, but he left you."

One way of looking at it. She snatched her hand back.

"You don't owe him anything," the detective said, voice a little too smooth now. What? Where was all that fiery rage he'd just shown? Was he a one-man good cop/bad cop routine?

"Maybe I don't," she said, wondering where this was going and also wondering—where the hell was Lucas? Spending the night in a cage didn't exactly appeal to her.

Bruce nodded. "Good girl. Think about yourself."

"That's all I ever think about."

His gaze searched hers. "I want Simone. He's an animal, and he needs to be taken down before he kills again."

"Lucas Simone isn't a killer."

He laughed at her.

"Lucas wasn't anywhere near that house tonight." She exhaled. "Ask the cops. No one saw him. *Because he wasn't there.*"

Bruce's fingers closed around her hands in a grip that was *almost* painful. *Walking the line.* "Officer Meadows told me about the bodies, how they'd been slashed, throats ripped, guts torn open."

Right. Like she needed another visual. *Been there.* "He was wrong." And she owed the demon for this, at least. "And if the fire hadn't burned so fast, you'd see the truth for yourself." But there'd be no seeing for anyone. That demon's fire had burned right through flesh and taken all the evidence away. By the time the firefighters had arrived on the scene, nothing had been left.

The detective's scent—sweat and cheap cologne—clogged the air around her. "You don't want me for an enemy."

"What I want . . . is a lawyer." She tore her hands away from his and turned her head to glare at the mirror. "And I want one *now.*"

Silence.

"No one's in there."

Figured.

"And no lawyer is coming for you."

That didn't sound good.

He pulled away from the table and rolled his shoulders. "I've got a daughter," he told her as he began to pace the small room.

Uh, what? How had they gone from dead bodies to his personal life?

"She's real sick." He paused and his gaze went distant. "Cancer. Eight years old . . . *and she has cancer.*"

What was happening here? "I'm . . . sorry." And she was. No child should ever have to suffer such pain.

"Cops don't make much."

A chill iced her skin. *No, don't say—*

He rubbed a hand over his face. "You're going to try and escape custody in a few minutes."

Rafe.

His right hand brushed back the edge of his jacket, and she saw the butt of his gun. "You're going to try to get away, but you're going to fail."

Her mouth had gone bone dry. "Let me guess . . ." Her hands curled under the edge of the table. "You'll have to shoot me, right?"

"Kelly's *real* sick." His eyes glittered at her. "She's a little girl. She deserves to live. And you—you're a killer, just like Simone. I saw the file on you. I know what you've done."

So she wasn't perfect. "What file? Who told you about me?"

"Jess Ortez."

Damn him. "Jess doesn't know everything." Her left arm still stung from the bullet that had clipped her. The EMTs on the scene had bandaged her up, but she knew the next wound wouldn't be one that a bandage could easily fix. Trapped in this ten-by-twelve-foot room, the cop wouldn't exactly have a hard target.

"I'm sorry, lady, but you're worth more dead than you are alive."

"No, I'm not." Her hands tightened on the table. She could heave it at him, but then what? He was blocking the door and she wasn't armed. "I'm actually worth even more if you can bring me in alive."

He blinked and his hand stopped inching toward the holster.

She almost took a deep breath then.

But old Bruce just shook his head. "Bullshit, but nice try." Then his hand went to his hip.

Her body tensed in anticipation of the bullet, but he just grabbed the cuffs on his waist. " 'Fraid you'll be coming with me."

Because he wasn't going to shoot her there. Relief had her face flushing. So she had a few more minutes to live. A good thing, right? *Where was Lucas?* Bruce crept close to her, nice and slow. "Hold out your hands."

She put them out but said, "If you cuff me, won't that mess up your whole she-was-running-story?"

"Nah, you'll lose the cuffs before you die." He kicked the chair out of the way and snapped the cold metal cuff around her wrist. "But if I get blood all over this room, the captain will freak."

She wasn't stupid. This was a game she *knew.* "He'll also want to know why the hell you were in here alone with a suspect. He'll want to know why no one was observing the interrogation, he'll want to know where my lawyer—" She broke off, her breath hissing out as the second cuff snapped too tightly around her wrist, digging deep into the flesh.

"We can do this two ways." His mouth was at her ear. "A quick bullet in the head so you don't feel any pain . . ."

She could barely feel her fingers now thanks to those cuffs.

"Or we can do this long and slow . . . I'll make sure you die, but I can make sure you suffer, too."

Wasn't he a prince? She swallowed and wrenched back a step, the better to see into his eyes. "I'm someone's daughter, too, you know, asshole."

His eyes widened just a bit at that.

A rap sounded at the door. "Hey, Langston!" The door swung open and a red-haired female cop poked her head inside. "You ready to transfer her to the safe house?"

The safe house? What? Was that a fun new euphemism for the cemetery?

Bruce the Bastard shook his head. "She doesn't want to come willingly, Shirley. I'm putting her in protective custody."

Shirley shoved the door all the way open. "What?" Her gaze raked Sarah. "You barely survived this attack, and you don't want the cops to help you?"

"Two ways," Bruce whispered, far too quietly for Shirley to hear.

Shirley shook her head. "You're so addicted to Simone that you'd let him kill you?"

Now this was a question she could handle. "I don't have to worry about Lucas hurting me." Her head turned and her gaze zeroed in on Bruce. "I'm not the one he'd come after."

His Adam's apple bobbed, and he grabbed her elbow. "Come on. This is for your own protection." He dragged her toward the door, right past Shirley.

Help me, Sarah mouthed and the female cop nodded. "We will, ma'am. We'll help you, if you just give us the chance."

Shit.

Bruce's fingers bit into her flesh. Guess that meant she'd be dying by option number two. The slow, painful death he'd promised.

So what did she have to lose? "He's going to kill me, Shirley."

Bruce double-timed his pace.

"No, he won't, Ms. King! We'll keep you safe!" Shirley called out, voice like some chirpy bird. "You don't have to worry about Simone!"

If only.

"One more word," Bruce muttered in her ear, "and I'll break every bone in your body before you die."

Nice. Her mouth snapped shut, and her eyes rose to the crest hanging just above the exit door: *To Serve and Protect.*

Probably should have read to maim and kill.

Then they were outside. She tripped once on the steps. When she fell, Sarah managed to rip open the knee of her jeans and she felt the wet warmth of her blood. Lucky for her, Bruce was there to haul her back up—and then after a few more stumbling steps, he shoved her into the back of a patrol car.

But, right before he slammed the door, Sarah heard the sweetest sound in the world.

The howl of a wolf.

Bruce heard it, too, because she saw the cop stiffen. Then he rushed forward and jumped into the front of the patrol car.

She slammed her cuffed hands on the dividing screen that separated them. "You heard the howl, didn't you, asshole?"

He revved the engine, and the motor growled.

"Know what it means?" she gritted. "It means you're the one who needs to worry about dying tonight."

The car raced onto the road. Bruce drove way too fast, weaving in and out of traffic.

"You don't know what you're talking about!" But an edge of fear had snaked into his words. "That howl could have been from the wolf who's coming to collect your body."

Rafe was coming? "That wasn't Rafe's howl." But what about one of his men? No, he wouldn't risk sending one of them. Not to her. Rafe wouldn't come close to her and neither would his wolves. But Lucas . . .

Bruce turned off the main road with a squeal of his tires. They were in a long, dark alley now. The perfect place to die. He was still driving too fast. Way too fast.

She slammed her fists into the screen once more. "That howl meant the wolves are coming after you!"

And she saw it then, the fast, dark streak of an animal running in front of the squad car. *A wolf.*

"Shit!" Bruce's yell, and he yanked the wheel to the right.

The car's fender slammed into a big, green dumpster and Sarah's head smacked into the screen.

The world went a quick shade of gray as pain blasted through her head. She blinked a few times, and touched her head—no blood. Well, that was something.

"*Get out!*"

Her head craned to the right. Bruce had her door open. His gun pointed right at her. "*Get out!*" He yelled again.

He thought he'd pull her out and kill her? Because it had to look like she'd run, right? "Make me, asshole," she dared.

He lunged forward and grabbed her arm.

A low, fierce growl vibrated in the air. Then . . .

"You don't want to do that," Lucas said. "Because if you hurt her, I'll have to rip you open."

Chapter 7

The cop froze, then spun to face him. Good old Bruce had his gun up, and Lucas really wasn't surprised when the asshole fired at him. Not surprised, but really pissed off.

Lucas moved, fast—*not fast enough*—and the first bullet blazed a path across the side of his shoulder. The second bullet missed, and the cop didn't get a chance to shoot the third one. Lucas caught him and slammed Bruce's back into the side of the patrol car. The cop's gun clattered to the ground.

Sarah scrambled out of the car. "Get the keys to the cuffs!"

Sure, right after he sliced—

"Lucas, he's working with Jess and Rafe!"

That froze his claws. "Is he now." He smiled down at the cop. Bruce's eyes were bulging.

Sarah shoved in close and ripped the keys from Bruce's belt. She fumbled a bit, swearing, as she fought the lock. He heard the soft snick, then she said, "He was going to deliver my body to them—"

Lucas's teeth snapped together and his fingers squeezed that fat neck. Bruce's face went that fast, deep purple.

"D-daugh . . . ter . . ." The gasped word huffed from Bruce's lips.

Sarah's hand brushed over Lucas's arm. "We all have our reasons for making deals with the devil, don't we?"

What? He glanced at her, but never eased his grip. Her

gaze was on him, not the cop. She seemed even paler, and the scent of smoke clung to her.

"Trust me on this, Lucas," she said. "You don't want to kill a cop."

Actually, he did. Very much so.

She rolled her shoulders and winced a bit. "If he dies right now, guess who this will be pinned on?"

It would be—

"Me," she muttered, not giving him a chance to answer. "Now ease up on him, okay? The guy's gonna black out any second."

For her, he eased his grip. Bruce sucked in a deep gulp of air.

A snarl broke from the shadows. Piers, still in wolf form.

"You stay back, too," Sarah called, huffing out a breath. "We can't kill him," she said. "We need him."

"I don't need the dickhead." Bruce had been going to trade Sarah?

No, he'd been ready to dump her body into the hands of the highest bidder. Fuck that. Lucas lifted the guy up and rammed him back against the patrol car. Bruce's head hit the top of the car and his eyes rolled back in his head. Lucas let the bastard drop to the ground.

Then he turned on Sarah. "What the hell happened to you?" His nostrils flared. "*Why do I smell your blood?*" And the scent was driving him crazy. The beast inside loved the smell of blood. Went wild when prey bled, but . . .

But Sarah wasn't prey, and the beast was having a whole different reaction to her blood. *Kill. Punish. Destroy.*

Sarah blinked at him. "Ah, Lucas . . ."

But he'd already pinpointed the blood. A wound on her arm. A white bandage that was already coming loose and he could still smell—"You were shot."

"Yes, well, when all hell broke loose at that place, I got caught in the cross-fire."

Because he'd left her. His fingers brushed lightly down her

arm, careful to avoid the wound. "You won't get caught again."

She laughed at that. A bitter, mocking laugh. "Dude, getting caught is the story of my life."

His back teeth clenched.

Sarah glanced over her shoulder. "And if we don't get out of here soon, more cops will be on the scene and we'll both get tossed in cages."

Not gonna happen. "You smell like ash."

Her chin shot up. "Well, I guess that's better than smelling like shit."

What? A quick laugh broke from him.

Sarah's eyes widened.

Oh, damn, but she was dangerous.

"Don't do it, Sarah," he warned her, as the laughter faded as quickly as it had come.

She eased away from him. Was she afraid? Finally. She should be afraid. If she knew everything he wanted to do to her, she'd be fucking terrified.

"D-do what?" She almost tripped over the gun Bruce had dropped. She bent and scooped it up with fingers that shook. "I'm not doing anything to you."

She was, even if she didn't realize it. If he wanted a woman too much—*the way I want Sarah*—that lust could become dangerous. To her and to him.

But I already want her too much. So much that I can taste her on my tongue. Not ash and blood. Sweet candy.

Her gaze searched the darkness of the alley. "Tell me you have a car around here."

Even better, he'd stashed his motorcycle. He'd followed her from the station, taken a shortcut and managed to head them off.

He held out his hand to her. "Let's go."

Her eyes dropped to the hand. "I knew you'd be coming for me."

Trust? From her? Her fingers rose and curled around his

offered hand. Her touch was soft, warm. *The cop would have killed her.*

He slanted a glance toward the shadows, where he knew Piers waited for orders. "I'm getting her back to the main house. You take care of him."

Piers would understand.

Lucas caught the slight relaxing of Sarah's shoulders. "There's just some blood you don't want on your hands," she said.

They walked away from the cop. Lucas steered her to the left, toward his motorcycle and away from Piers.

They'd taken about five steps when he heard the soft rustle of clothes, then a soft *click*. Fuck. *Every cop had a backup weapon.*

"I'm gettin' that damn money!" Bruce shouted. "I *need* it—"

Lucas shoved Sarah to the ground and whirled with claws up. Piers snarled as he lunged from the shadows.

Bruce crouched on the ground, the weapon aimed, a twisted smile on his face. "*I'm takin' that bounty—*"

A bullet slammed into Bruce's chest just as the cop fired his gun. Bruce blinked, once, twice, and a gurgle rolled in his throat. His body slumped, and he managed, "Kel . . ."

"L-Lucas?" Sarah grabbed him and spun him to face her. "Are you all right?"

He'd been shot. He glanced down. Blood stained his shirt but he hadn't even felt the hit. After so many bullets, sometimes you didn't feel the pain. "I'm fine," he told her and then he realized—

Sarah had the cop's gun in her right hand. *She'd* taken out the bastard.

Her gaze met his. "I didn't want to kill him." Tears misted her eyes. "I didn't want—"

"If it makes you feel better . . ." He took the gun from her and tucked it in the back of his jeans. He'd get rid of that for her soon enough and make sure that it never surfaced again.

"There was never any chance the guy was making it out of this alley alive."

They had to hurry. The sun would be up soon. More eyes would be on the streets. And there was always the chance someone had heard that gunshot.

He glanced toward the wolf. The order to Piers still stood. *Take care of him.* That body wouldn't be found, and they'd make sure the patrol car was stripped down to nothing.

"He had a daughter," sadness softened Sarah's voice. "A family . . ."

Lucas pulled her through the alley. "His daughter died a year ago."

"Wh-what?"

He jumped onto the motorcycle. "Climb on, and hold tight." He could feel the wound now, a dull throb in his gut, but he wasn't looking at the damage. Not now. *Get her to safety.* Sarah had been in danger enough for one night. "His daughter Kelly died a year ago."

"You're sure of that?"

Lucas grunted as he shoved back the kickstand. "I make it my business to know everything about my enemies." All their strengths and all their weak spots. Little Kelly Langston had died almost twelve months ago, then her mother had packed up and left Bruce.

The cop had already been on the take then. From what Lucas had learned, Bruce had first started taking the bribes to pay for the girl's medical bills. That's how it had started but once you started down that road . . .

There was no going back.

The engine roared to life. Her fingers wrapped around his waist, her thighs pressed into his hips.

He turned to look at her once more. Their faces were close, just inches apart. A tear had slid down her cheek and that made the rage inside pulse harder. "You should be harder than you are."

Her brow furrowed.

"He would have blown us both to hell in an instant." And Lucas was furious—at the cop, at himself, at *her*. He didn't like seeing pain in her eyes. Didn't fucking like it at all—and that just made him angrier. "Don't waste tears on him. Don't waste a fucking moment of your life on him."

He grabbed the helmet and shoved it onto her head. "Hold on." He turned away from her, his fingers gripping the handlebars too tightly. The motorcycle jumped forward, and they roared through the night.

Now she had blood on her hands, too. But was it her first kill? *I make it a point to know my enemies.* Sarah wasn't an enemy, but he still needed to know everything about her. And soon, he would know . . . *everything.*

There was no room for secrets between lovers.

Rafael Santiago watched as the motorcycle streaked through the streets. Sarah was clutching tightly to the wolf, holding him as if her life depended on him. In a way, it did.

The cop was dead. Taken down by her hand. Not surprising. Sarah knew how to eliminate threats to herself. He'd seen the hit as he watched carefully through the binoculars. No point in getting too close and letting the others catch his scent. The game shouldn't end too soon.

All the players weren't even in place yet.

He turned away from the edge of the roof. People were wrong about wolf shifters. They weren't all psychotic, wild beasts driven by instinct. Wolves were smart, and they could also be very patient . . . particularly when it came to hunting. Some prey took time and skill to catch. But that was part of the thrill of the hunt. Easy prey didn't make for a good game.

A few more days, then all would be ready. Lucas had almost revealed a weak spot. Perfect.

Rafe already knew Sarah's weakness. Knew it, accepted it, but still loved her. After all, wolves mated for life. You didn't turn away from a lover just because of a weakness.

He took his time heading down the stairs. He'd pay a visit to the coyotes soon. Ortez had promised him that the cop would handle Sarah, but that asshole human had tried to kill her.

Rafe didn't want Sarah dead. Punished, not dead.

Coyotes. They had their uses. Greedy, strong . . . but they had their weaknesses. And Jess Ortez—the shifter was a wannabe, playing far out of his league.

Rafe had planned to use Ortez as a distraction, and so far, that plan was working fucking beautifully. Ortez actually thought he'd get this land for his coyotes when the battle was over.

Damn fool.

Good thing Rafe hadn't aligned with just one coyote group. But then, he'd formed a pact with Hayden O'Connor years ago. And if he wanted Hayden to keep helping him, then he had to give the bastard what he wanted.

Sorry, Ortez, you're about to visit hell.

The coyote would never even see the danger coming.

It was often hard to see it—especially when your own kind was the one doing the killing.

Steam rose from the bath water, swirling in the air around her. Sarah had her knees drawn up in the water, her arms wrapped tightly around them.

Killed a man.

Not the first time. Not even the second, but unlike Rafe, she'd never been able to turn off her emotions after a kill.

Rafe.

She'd almost felt him tonight. Had he been there? Ready to slice her open?

Her eyes squeezed shut. *You had to kill the cop.*

Right. No choice. *Kill or be killed.* That was the way of the wolf, right?

"But I'm not a fucking wolf," she rasped, and in her mind, she could still see that bloom of red on the cop's chest.

"No, you're not."

Lucas's hard voice had her eyes flashing open as she shot

up in the tub. Water jostled over the side of the old-fashioned bear-claw bathtub. A big tub. Big enough for . . .

Lucas wasn't wearing a shirt. A white bandage lined his left side. Faded jeans hung low on his hips.

"What are you doing here?" She squeezed her knees tighter.

His gaze raked her. "Don't you know?"

Her belly clenched. "You're hurt, you should be . . ."

A shrug. "I don't even feel it. I dug the bullet out, slapped a bandage on it." His lips quirked. "The wound will be healed in no time."

Because blood, pain, and bullets were nothing to a wolf. What was the little matter of death to a beast?

His eyes narrowed on her and Lucas crossed the room in long, slow strides. *Stalking me.* Goosebumps rose on the flesh of her arms. "Lucas . . ."

He knelt beside the tub. His fingers dipped into the warm water, his knuckles so close to her thigh.

She hunched her shoulders. "I didn't . . ." *Invite you here.* "You shouldn't be here."

"You're here. Where else should I be?" His fingers trailed in the water and slid over her thigh. "Don't you want me here?"

Yes, dammit. She did. She'd wanted him, secretly, desperately, and quite stupidly, for a long time now. *Before they'd ever met.*

She stared at his hand in the water. There was no point lying to him. He'd smell her arousal anyway.

Just the touch of his fingers and she was almost trembling.

"I came in just to make sure you were all right." His voice seemed so deep and dark.

"I'm all right." Hers was a whisper.

"That's why I came in . . ." His fingers curled over her thigh. Her nipples tightened. The warm water was no longer soothing. Nothing could soothe her then. "But I'm here now," he said, "because I fucking want you."

Sarah swallowed.

His hand tightened on her. She wanted him to move those fingers, to slide them deeper under the water, to press them against her sex, *into* her.

He released her. "But you're the one who has to say—"

Her hand flew up and she grabbed his wrist, held on way too tight. "I don't want you to leave." Right then, being alone was the last thing she wanted. Remembering blood, pain, death—*no, thank you.*

She wanted passion. She wanted pleasure. She wanted him.

A muscle flexed in his jaw. "What *do* you want?"

She rose from the tub, slowly, and the water slid down her body even as the steam drifted around her head. "I want you." Admissions didn't get more stark than that.

His lips lifted in a half-smile that revealed the sharp points of his teeth. "Then that's what you're getting."

He pounced. No other word for it. Lucas moved in a blur, grabbing her and lifting her out of the tub. Her hands flew out and clutched his shoulders as she tried to balance herself.

"I've got you," he said and he lifted her higher. Strong wolf. He took her breast in his mouth, licking the moisture away, sucking the aching nipple.

Liquid heat shot straight to her sex. His jeans rubbed against her legs, and she wanted to spread her thighs. Wanted to wrap them around his hips and hold on tight as he thrust deep inside. As deep as he could go.

His tongue worked her nipple, making her twist against him, making her pant, making her *want.*

His breath blew over her skin as his head lifted. "So fucking sweet . . ." His gaze burned into hers. "Are you like that everywhere?"

"I—"

In four strides, he had her at the bed. He spun, dropping her lightly on the mattress, and then came down on top of her as he caged her against the bed. The mattress dipped beneath their weight and Sarah lifted her hands, wanting to touch him so badly that her fingers shook.

His smile flashed again. "Do anything you want, Sarah. I sure will." And he licked her other breast. Licked and sucked and when she felt the light edge of his teeth, Sarah bucked off the bed.

Her hips slammed up against his, and there was no mistaking the thick bulge of his arousal. Long and hard. She wanted him inside her. "Lucas!" Her hands buried in the thick darkness of his hair.

The water was drying fast from her skin. Thanks to the thick comforter, his mouth, and his hot flesh. She seemed to burn everywhere she touched him, her body so sensitive, too ready.

Then he started to lick his way down her body . . .

Her eyes squeezed closed and her breath came faster. She heard an eager moan fill the air—*me, that's me.* Because the need inside her was blazing out of control. Burning so hot— burning just like Lucas.

She didn't wait for him to ask . . . when his mouth pressed a kiss to her stomach, she parted her thighs wider. Why pretend? She *wanted* his mouth on her. No, right then, she needed it. Because her whole body was coiled tight, her sex so eager and hungry, and the pleasure he promised was so close.

How long had it been? How long since she'd just let go with a lover? Trusting him to give her the pleasure she needed? With Rafe, she'd never been able to let go. Not fully.

Lucas's fingers touched her first. Strong, rough fingertips that parted the folds between her legs and found the center of her need. His lips touched her next, pressing against her clit, sending a fierce, sensual jolt through her body that was so strong that she would have flinched away . . . but his hands were on her wrists—when had he grabbed her?—holding her tight.

Then came his tongue. Wet and warm. Licking. Caressing. Sliding against flesh and then thrusting inside her core.

Her hips arched toward him. *More.* The whisper in her mind. So close, she was so close and she just needed—

"Even sweeter," he growled the words against her. Then his tongue plunged deep, his fingers stroked her, and Sarah came against his mouth.

When he growled, a long, ragged rumble, the vibration trembled against her sex and the wave of pleasure lashed through her body.

Then he was moving, shoving off the jeans, jerking on a condom, and coming back to her with eyes that were far too bright for a human's. But then, she'd known he was more than just a man from the beginning.

He pushed her legs farther apart. The tip of his thick cock pressed against her sensitive flesh, flesh that was still ready and eager for more.

But . . .

But she could see the edge of his teeth. So sharp. And those eyes were more wolf than man.

A shiver slipped over her as the past whispered around her.

Her hands flew up and pushed against his shoulders. Lucas froze.

Pleasure still hummed through her body. Lust had her aching, but—*but . . .*

"Now you're scared." Gravel-rough. He shook his head and leaned in close to her, so close those glowing eyes bored into hers. His lips were just a few inches away from her mouth. All the while, his cock lodged right at the entrance of her body. Not thrusting inside, not yet, and not withdrawing.

Her nails bit into the hard muscles of his chest.

"You want me," he said, voice dark and dangerous, "but deep down, you're scared as hell of me."

Not deep down. Right then, the fear was on the surface, fighting her need. "It's not you I'm afraid of." The damn memories. Her own past.

Not Lucas—not the man anyway, but the wolf she could see gazing back from the man's eyes. If a wolf got too strong, grew too wild during sex, the man would lose control, he would—

"That fucking bastard hurt you."

She flinched. He already knew Rafe had tried to kill her but . . .

Lucas's mouth pressed against her cheek. A light touch when she'd expected force and fire. "How many times," he gritted, "do I have to tell you? All fucking wolves aren't the same in the dark. We're not all psychotic bastards."

His lips trailed down her cheek. Under the line of her jaw. Just lips and tongue, kissing, licking, caressing. No teeth. No pain.

"Trust me," he breathed the words against her and the fear began to give way once more to the need and the lust that tightened her body. "Let me show you what *I'm* like."

Her nails stopped digging into his chest. Her fingers curled over his shoulders, the better to pull closer, not to push away.

His head lifted and those blazing blue eyes stared into hers. "Trust me," he said again.

His mouth took hers. A hot, open-mouthed kiss of hunger and lust. Of need and—

His cock pushed into her. Not a hard, slamming thrust. A gentle drive of thick, strong flesh, a glide that sent his cock sliding over her clit, making her arch and gasp beneath him.

"Better," he whispered against her lips.

And it was. He was. The past disappeared as he withdrew. His fingers pushed between them, found the center of her desire, teased, pressed—

He thrust. A little harder this time, a little deeper.

Just right.

Again. Again.

His fingers touched, stroked, knew just where she needed him. His cock filled her, so heavy and thick, and her sex clamped greedily around him as the lust built and built.

His mouth was on hers again. Tongue thrusting. Tasting, taking, even as his body took hers.

He was all she could see, everything she felt. Her sex strained around him, the pleasure pressing close again, and

when his cock drove into her, a plunge that stole her breath—
Sarah came, gasping, body shuddering, as the release blasted
through her.

He kept thrusting. Faster now, deeper. Harder. The pleasure shook her body, had her heart racing as the drumming
filled her ears.

She stared up at him, the taut lines of his face, those eyes . . .
His jaw was clenched, his muscles bulging.

Sarah wrapped her legs around him and held him tighter.

Then she saw the wild rush of pleasure in his eyes as he
came. Lucas thrust deep and stiffened against her. His hands
caught hers. His cock jerked inside her with the hard jet of
his release.

And he never looked away from her gaze.

Man, not beast.

No, *both*. But with Lucas, the man was in control.

His lips brushed hers. She kissed him, closing her eyes.
Dammit, why did it have to be like this? A man of power, a
man that she *might* truly be able to trust, and a man that she
was deceiving.

What would happen when he found out the truth?

His lips broke from hers, and he searched her gaze.

There'd be no running from him.

"You trust me." No question from Lucas. Just a statement
now.

"Yes." And it was the truth. *But please, don't trust me.*
Whatever you do . . . don't trust me.

Because sooner or later, she'd have to betray him. Life
could be such a bitch sometimes.

Chapter 8

Lucas's eyes opened the instant he heard the light scratch on the door. He turned at once, and his gaze landed on Sarah.

Sarah.

What in the hell was he going to do with her? Careless, mind-numbing sex was one thing—but not what he'd had with her.

She'd been afraid. He'd had other lovers who were afraid. Others who sensed the beast he kept chained, but had still wanted the wild ride in the darkness.

Sarah had been different. Wanting him *despite* the fear. And the damn thing was . . . of all his lovers, he'd expected her to fear the least.

The woman talked to wolves. She *knew* them. Maybe that was the problem. Maybe she knew just how strong the beast inside could be, particularly when he wanted something.

Rafe had hurt her. He'd seen that truth in her gaze. *I've only had one wolf lover.*

One who'd taught her to fear a shifter's touch.

The scratch at the door came again. Shit. Caleb. He'd sent the shifter to make contact with Dane and to get a report on the coyotes.

He needed to go, but . . . his gaze turned to Sarah once more, just as she rolled onto her stomach. Her sheet dipped with her movement, and he saw the sexy curve of her spine, and the long, still-pink scars that marred the flesh on her lower back.

Lucas didn't make a sound. Didn't snarl. Didn't howl with the sudden fury inside him. His hand reached toward her, his claws springing forth, and he didn't feel the tear of his flesh.

His hand hovered over those lines. A perfect match. But then, there really was no mistaking clawmarks on a woman's body.

No fucking wonder she feared me.

He leaned in close to her. Didn't touch her. Couldn't, not then, because the beast was far too angry then. "He's dead," he whispered the words in her ear.

Sarah stiffened. "Wh—"

"And I'm gonna make damn sure the bastard suffers before I put him out of his misery."

She glanced back at him, her eyes wide, her lips still red from his kiss. "Lucas, I need to—"

He rolled away from her. "Get some sleep." If he stayed . . . *no*. Fuck, *no*. "I'm going for a run." Because the beast *was* howling inside.

The bedcovers rustled behind him. "No! Wait, Lucas! We've got to talk."

"Not now." No time. He glanced down and saw that his claws were still out. Claws just like the ones that had ripped into her skin.

I'll rip him open.

Her hand grabbed his arm. "Oh, what, you got what you wanted, so now you're—"

Her touch burned through him. "I'm in the mood to fuck or kill."

Silence.

He glanced back at her. "I don't think you want to be touching me now." The beast would be staring at her from his eyes, he knew that. And she feared the beast.

Sarah swallowed, but she didn't drop her hand. "It's because of the scars."

The wolf clawed inside, desperate to be free.

Her gaze dropped to his hands, yeah, right to those claws. Razor-sharp. Perfect for tearing flesh.

"Were your claws out during sex?" She shook her head, a frown between her eyes. "I didn't even notice. I should have, but . . ." Her gaze rose back to his. "*I didn't notice.*" There was shock in her voice.

Should he tell her the truth? Lie? Fuck it. "They were out." It had taken all his damn strength to keep a stranglehold on the beast. Fighting or fucking—the wolf liked both. Sarah would know that, though.

She had the marks to prove it.

Her lips parted.

He stepped away from her, breaking her hold. The wolf wanted *out*.

"We have to talk," she told him again. "There are things you don't know about me."

He laughed at that. "Babe, tell me something I *don't* know." But now wasn't the time for talking. The wolf wanted to run. No, he wanted to kill, and maybe Caleb had news on those coyotes that would let him do just that.

Rip. Claw. Blood.

A fist shook the door. "Lucas! I know you can hear me!" Caleb. But with an edge to his voice. Guess the guy's patience had run out. Not that the Texan ever really had much patience.

Lucas yanked open the door. Caleb's narrowed eyes met his. "I can't make contact with Dane."

Shit.

"We sent scouts to the area. There were signs of a fight, and the coyotes are locked down tight now."

Caleb's gaze drifted to Sarah. Widened a bit.

Because Sarah was only wearing a sheet. Lucas stepped to the left, blocking the view. "Did the scouts catch Dane's scent?"

Caleb's gaze snapped back to him. "They . . . thought they picked up his scent in one of the houses but—"

"Then we're going to fucking get our man back." The

wolf howled inside. Just what he needed. Blood and death and fury. "I'm tired of screwing with the coyotes. Time to break that pack."

Caleb's lips twisted into a savage grin. "I was hoping you'd say that."

"Tell the wolves it's time to hunt."

"Lucas," Sarah touched him again. Dammit. He knew Caleb noticed the slight jerk of his body. *Toward her.* "You're hurt," she said, "you can't—"

He laughed at that. "Babe, I can do anything." She looked so delicate, so sexy with her hair mussed and his scent on her. His scent, not his mark.

Already been marked by that fucking bastard.

Rip. Him. Apart.

"You're afraid of the wolf in me." He didn't bother to keep his voice low. Caleb would hear no matter what with his shifter ears. "Fair warning, that wolf is hungry, and he's about to come out."

She didn't let him go. Surprising. "Be careful."

He knew his smile held a razor's edge. "I'm not the one who has to worry." No more playing nice with the coyotes. They'd come at him . . . *my turn.*

The idiots probably thought he'd wait until the cover of darkness to attack. The better to not be seen by humans. What they didn't understand . . . he didn't give a fuck about the humans. They had Dane, the wolf who'd stood by him in hell, and in order to get his friend back, Lucas would cut through anyone who got in his way.

Sarah's gaze held his. After a moment, her hand fell away, and he went to hunt.

With her scent on him.

Sarah watched him leave through the window. Lucas had to know she was there, but he didn't glance up at her, not even once. He left as a man, loading into the SUV with the others, but she knew he'd soon be shedding the cover of flesh for the power of fur and fangs and claws.

The sheet felt cool around her body, and damn if she didn't still feel the press of his hands and lips on her.

What was happening? She'd thought sex might be a possibility, but . . .

But she was weakening with the wolf. She'd almost told him the truth before he left. Talk about crap timing. With his wolf so close—that would have been a nightmare.

The sun beamed down from overhead. Attacking in daylight. Figured that would be something Lucas would do.

The SUVs disappeared along the winding road.

Her gaze darted to the left. To the phone that waited on the nightstand. Should she call and give a warning?

She was at the phone before she gave herself time for second thoughts. One ring. Two. *Answer.* Lucas knew exactly where the coyotes were hiding. The bloodbath would be brutal. She'd seen what he could do when he was the only one fighting.

How fast would they all die when the wolf pack attacked? Another ring. *Not answering.*

She slammed the phone down. Dressed as fast as she could. Then Sarah ran for the door. She wrenched it open—

And found herself staring up into a pair of golden eyes. She stumbled to a stop right before she slammed into the human wall.

"Going somewhere?" he asked, crossing his arms over his chest and thoroughly blocking her way. He was young, probably barely in his early twenties—*not much younger than me*—but his face . . . *like Lucas's.* The same hard chin. The same cheeks. His eyes held the same hard edge, even though the color was different. But then, she'd seen those eyes before.

The wolf who came to greet Lucas the first day. Sarah forced her shoulders to relax. "You're Jordan."

His dark brows rose. "Lucas told you about me?" He even had the same thick, dark hair that Lucas had.

No. "I've heard about you." About the young wolf who'd once been taken by a band of vamps. Lucas had become legend when he'd gone after them and destroyed the bloodsuckers. *Don't fuck with the LA pack.*

That message had been loud and clear for years. Until Rafe's patience had worn too thin. *He'd* wanted to be the legend.

Jordan's gaze searched her face. "You're my brother's lover." Said without inflection.

Her shoulders stiffened. So much for relaxing. "I'm sure you brother has plenty of lovers." Okay, now why did that actually hurt? Wolves were sexual, she knew that. Fucking was sometimes as necessary as breathing.

"None that he ever brings around the pack."

Oh.

His head cocked. "You going somewhere?" Now an edge of steel had crept into his voice. "I don't think Lucas would like to come back and find you missing."

There was a reason the wolf had survived capture by the vamps. He had a core of fire inside. Strength that was apparent in the hard stare of his eyes.

Not a kid. She'd been foolish to make that mistake when he was in wolf form. She'd been nervous because of Lucas, and hadn't been focusing enough. This wasn't a kid. This was definitely a grown man. A very dangerous man.

"I didn't think Lucas wanted you . . ." *Near me.* Ah, how could she put this delicately? "I thought you were out—"

"He told me to keep an eye on you."

While the others hunted.

His gaze dropped to rake her body. "So here I am."

Right.

His stance widened, and the smile he gave her wasn't pretty. "And trust me on this, you're not going anywhere. Not until the pack is back, safe and sound."

She recognized the look in his eyes. She'd seen it plenty of times. "You don't trust me?"

"I don't trust anyone who isn't pack."

While similar to Lucas, she realized that Jordan's face wasn't as hard. More handsome, less dangerous. But the threat was still in him.

"I was just going down to the kitchen." She put her hand on her stomach. "I skipped a meal last night. What with the fire and attempted murder and everything."

No smile curved his lips, but he did step back, giving her space to cross over the threshold.

Guess that meant she got to eat.

Sarah had taken five steps down the hallway when she heard the smash of glass. Jordan lunged in front of her, and she saw the deadly flash of his claws.

The scent of blood filled the air. The wolves growled behind Lucas, their instinct to lunge forward and attack. Blood always drew them in . . .

Lucas let the shift sweep over him, barely feeling the burn of the change. The crack and snap of bones filled his ears, drowning out those growls as the wolf inside was—fucking finally—free.

He sprang forward, his paws slamming down on the earth and the others were right on his heels, racing forward toward the line of buildings nestled near the woods.

No mercy. He sent out the order, knowing the others would understand. If they showed mercy now, word would spread that their pack was weak. Too many bastards were already trying to come after them. Too many enemies needed to learn to stay away.

The coyotes deserved what was coming for them with hungry jaws and sharpened claws.

He burst through the window, and the glass shattered around him.

"Get back in your room!" Jordan ordered, never glancing back. "Lock the door and stay there!"

He raced for the stairs.

Because she wasn't a fool, she raced back for her room.

She hurried inside. Slammed the door shut. Clicked the lock, thought about hauling the dresser over in front of the door and—

"You're a hard woman to catch, Sarah King." A low, taunting growl.

She froze, her eyes on the closed, *bolted* door. If she'd been a shifter, she probably would have caught his scent in time, but . . .

But he'd known she wouldn't sense him.

The floor creaked as he came closer. "Watching you run was fun, but the chase is coming to an end now."

"Not yet," she whispered, then she screamed, *"Jordan, help me!"*

The bastard slammed her head into the door.

Bodies littered the floor. Coyote shifters who'd been slaughtered. The wolves sniffed the air, moving carefully now.

Someone had beaten them to the kill.

When he'd landed on the floor, he'd landed in the middle of the bodies.

Dead.

Jess lay with his head twisted, his eyes open, and his throat gone.

Looked like the coyote leader wasn't going to be a threat to him anymore. Not to him, not to anyone.

Dane. His only concern then. The wolves broke up into groups and began searching. The scent of coyote was all over the place. Coyote . . . and wolf. Blood and death.

More bodies littered the floor as they tracked through the house. *No survivors.*

The killers had been fast and brutal. The dead were still fresh. They must have missed the slaughter by minutes.

They searched all the houses, every room. He caught the wolf's scent, but *Dane was gone.*

Not dead, maybe, but gone.

Piers snarled as he crouched over a pair of handcuffs. *Silver.*

The coyotes had been prepared for Dane, but not for whoever had ripped through them.

Lucas's gaze swept the house once more, the fury building
in the wolf as the scent of blood filled his nose.

I don't like this. From Caleb.

He didn't like it a damn bit, either. Whoever had attacked
the coyotes—someone strong. Damn strong.

Coyote and wolf scents were all over the fucking place.

The coyotes had been caught unprepared because they'd
thought they were letting in an ally. An ally who'd sliced
them apart.

Shit. He whirled away and ran back for the darkness.
Someone else was hunting out there. Someone strong—a lot
of fucking someones. He'd find them.

The world dimmed when her head rammed into the wood,
but Sarah didn't pass out. No, that would have been too easy.

The bastard grabbed her and picked her up, forcing her to
face him as he smiled down at her.

"It's been too long, Sarah."

She blinked and stared up into his squinty brown eyes. She
knew those eyes, they were very distinct with that faint yellow that circled his pupil. Oh, yeah, she knew him. Knew
that thick blond hair, that deceptively handsome face. Those
too-sharp teeth. *Hayden.* The coyote who'd started this hell
with Rafe. "Hayden, how did you—"

"Sarah!" Jordan's fists pounded into the door and the
whole room seemed to shake.

Hayden smiled. "Do you think he's strong enough to get
in . . ." That smile widened as his claws rose to her throat.
"Before I slit your pretty, lying throat?"

No.

The room shook again.

Hayden's lips came close, feathering over her ear. "Don't
worry, Sarah, I'm not going to kill you . . . yet," he whispered. "Someone wants to see you first."

Her heart seemed to stop. *Rafe.*

"But I did kill all the bastards in my way." He caught her chin and forced her head toward him. "Guess who's the king coyote now?"

"Not you, asshole."

Those claws pressed into her throat. Sarah gasped, ready to—

The door exploded behind them, the wood shattering and hitting Sarah and Hayden. She stumbled and grabbed tight to the coyote—and took him down with her.

They rolled, twisting and jerking, and Jordan attacked. He grabbed Hayden, slicing with his claws, and Sarah scrambled back.

The shift started then. A fierce, hard explosion of bones and flesh. The men fought as they shifted, and it was the most savage thing she'd ever seen. Claws buried into flesh, fur exploded. Spines snapped.

She backed away, crawling fast. Her gaze darted toward the door. Now was her chance. She could run through that door and get away.

Sarah started to inch forward.

Kill the bastard. Kill the assholes waiting . . .

Jordan's thoughts, slipping so easily into her mind. Hold on—whoa—the assholes waiting? There were more?

She stopped inching anywhere. Her gaze darted to the window. Open—had Hayden climbed up to get to her? That would have been easy enough for a shifter.

Dammit, Lucas—come back.

Sarah's heartbeat shook her chest. Two choices—run and face who the hell knew what below . . .

Or help Jordan and face 'em together.

Not really a choice.

She grabbed the lamp, and when the two beasts broke apart, she threw it at the coyote's head. It shattered, but didn't seem to hurt Hayden at all. Then those brown eyes locked on her. Fury and hate blazed in his gaze.

Hayden lunged for her.

Sarah jumped away, narrowly missing a swipe of those claws.

Jordan leapt onto the back of the coyote. The two spun, slamming around the room, crashing into furniture, breaking the bed, knocking over the bookshelf. Howls and snarls filled the room. And as they fought, the scent of blood grew thicker.

Hayden tossed Jordan off him. The coyote stood in front of the windows, his lips stained red with blood. The fur on his back was up, his eyes glinting as he prepared for another charge.

Jordan, take that bastard out!

The wolf leapt forward, colliding hard with the coyote, but the wolf was stronger—and he pushed the coyote back, back—

And glass exploded as they both tumbled through the window.

Oh, shit. She jumped to her feet and ran forward. *"Jordan!"* If that wolf had been killed defending her . . . Lucas would go crazy.

She didn't touch the jagged glass as she bent forward and peered below. The wolf had landed on top of the coyote. Neither were moving, and she could see the dark circles of blood blooming beneath their bodies.

"Jordan," whispered now.

More growls sounded then. Big gray and tan coyotes crept from the edge of the house and circled the fallen shifters. As Sarah watched, the fur began to melt from Jordan's body. If he was still alive, he'd be helpless in human form. Easy prey for the coyotes.

She couldn't let that happen. *My fault.* "Up here!" She screamed and the three coyotes turned their bright eyes on her. "I'm the one you want!" *So come and get me, assholes.*

Then they spun around and raced back to the house. Back to her.

Sarah grabbed a chunk of broken glass and went to meet them.

*   *   *

Lucas knew something was wrong even before he smelled the blood drifting in the air. The shifters were quiet in the SUV. No one speaking, all too aware of what the heavy smell meant.

Death.

"Drive fucking faster," he snarled as his hands clamped around the console. His claws burst out and ripped through the leather. *A trick.* They'd gone after the coyotes, found nothing but a slaughter, and someone had gone to his house while it was undefended.

My fault. Should have left more men.

But he'd thought he was eliminating the threat against Sarah.

Should have fucking known better.

The fury had just been riding him too hard.

Clawmarks on pale white skin.

Sarah.

The SUV's motor growled with him, a long, horrible snarl as it raced forward. If Sarah had been hurt . . .

He saw the broken window first, because his eyes went instantly to her room. Saw the broken window, the jagged glass—then his eyes fell below as he sprang from the vehicle.

Nothing.

A stain of blood. No bodies.

"Coyote," Piers muttered, sniffing. "Fucking everywhere."

He knew that, he also knew . . . "*Jordan.*" He'd never forget the scent of his brother's blood. For months, he'd only had that scent to track as he fought to rescue Jordan from the vamp bastards who'd taken him, the bastards who'd planned to use his brother as food for a Born Master, a damn all-powerful vampire asshole.

But even all-powerful vamps can burn.

So where the hell was his brother? And where was Sarah?

The windows on the first floor had also been shattered, the glass knocked inward, not outward, and the alarm blared constantly, a shrill buzz that drove him insane as he raced toward the house.

"Get the hell back!" Sarah's scream. Fear and fury burned in her voice.

He ran faster, shoving open the door and hurrying into the den—

Three bleeding coyotes circled Sarah. She had a bloody chunk of glass in her hand and she had that weapon up, ready to strike again, but then all three coyotes lunged at her, attacking at once.

Hell, no.

Lucas roared and jumped forward. His claws buried into the side of one coyote as he ripped the bastard back. Sarah swiped out at another, cutting deep and hard near his eye. The third bastard drove into her, slamming her back against the wall.

Lucas grabbed him, held tight when the coyote snapped back his head and bit him. *Bastard.* He'd shift and take the asshole out, he'd—

A gunshot thundered.

One. Two. Three.

The coyotes fell to the floor. The fur began to melt from their bodies.

Sarah's gaze widened as she looked first at the fallen men, then at—

Lucas spun around, putting his body in front of hers.

Jordan.

His brother stood in the doorway, naked, blood covering his body, his hand still aiming the gun he held. Piers and Caleb crowded in behind him, their faces tense.

"Couldn't . . . shift . . . went to help her . . ." Jordan's eyes narrowed on the coyote shifters. "Took . . . longer than I—"

Caleb grabbed him under the arms when Jordan started to slip. Piers snatched the gun away.

His brother was a damn fine shot, but then, Lucas had taught him to be. Lucas's gaze dropped to the shifters. One head shot, one heart shot . . . and one lucky-ass survivor who was groaning and twitching as the blood pumped out of his chest.

"Piers, get this bastard contained!" He grabbed Sarah's hand and pulled her forward. *So much blood.* "Jordan?"

His brother's eyes lifted. "Need to . . . shift . . ."

Because shifting sped up their healing process.

"He went through the window," Sarah whispered. "He took out Hayden—they both crashed through and hit the ground."

Hayden. That coyote bastard had been there?

"Hell, boy, you're playin' hard these days," Caleb muttered. "Just like your brother."

Piers brushed by them, going for the surviving coyote.

"I thought—I thought Jordan was dead," Sarah said softly.

Lucas reached for his brother. Jordan's body was jerking, twisting, but the shift wasn't coming. *Too weak.* "He may be," he growled and the fury ate his heart. "*Fucking shift, Jordan.*"

But Jordan's eyes didn't glow. His face stayed human. "C-can't . . ."

He grabbed his brother's hand. Held tight. The past flashed before him. Another blood-soaked day. Another shifter who couldn't change.

His father had died the same way. Was he just supposed to sit and watch Jordan slip away, too?

Hayden, you're dead.

Sarah brushed against him. She caught Jordan's chin in her hand and forced him to look at her. "You saved my life."

Jordan's eyes seemed to dim a bit.

"*Shift.*" She ordered him, the fear and fury in her voice again.

A ripple shook Jordan's body. Fur rose along his arms. But he couldn't change, not all the way.

"Let the wolf out," Sarah whispered. "I just need the wolf, for a minute . . ."

His teeth lengthened. His claws bit into Lucas's hand.

"More," Sarah whispered, her stare locking on Jordan's.

His eyes began to glow.

"Shift."

Bones snapped. He shuddered, convulsing. Sarah stumbled back as the beast took shape before them.

Lucas took a breath. Fuck, yes.

The shift didn't last long, but when Jordan's human form appeared again, his brother wasn't chalky-white. Some of the deeper wounds had healed.

He'd live.

Which was more than he could say for the others.

He grabbed Sarah's hand, tugging her close. "You okay?"

Pale, trembling, with blood on her cheeks, she nodded.

"Where's Hayden? Where did the bastard go?"

"I-I don't know. They went through the window and—"

"I'm the one you want . . ." Lucas's stare drifted back to his brother as Jordan's lips twisted.

His gaze slammed right back to Sarah. She swallowed. "I was . . . a bit busy . . ."

Trying to fight three coyotes? When one slash of their claws could kill her?

"I'm stronger than I look," she whispered.

So he was learning.

"This coyote doesn't have much time, Lucas!" Piers called out. "Jordan blasted one real fine hole in his chest. He lost his beast, and he's bleeding out fast."

He didn't look at Piers. Right then, he couldn't look away from Sarah. Such deep, green eyes.

Jordan groaned.

"Get Jordan out of here, Caleb." Lucas's head cocked as he studied Sarah. "You need to go, too."

Her eyes darted back to the coyote shifter. "What are you going to do?"

Whatever I have to do. "You need to go." Caleb had already started hauling Jordan out of the room.

Sarah's eyes held his a moment longer, then she nodded

and turned away, her shoulders hunched. She walked to the door, but glanced back. "I never meant for Jordan to get hurt. Everything happened so fast, I didn't mean—"

"*Go.*" Because he could hear the ragged tear of the coyote shifter's breath. *Not much longer.*

She went.

He turned back to Piers and the dying shifter. Three steps and he had the bastard's neck in his hand. Wild brown eyes met his. "How much do you want to suffer before you die?" Lucas asked.

The man smiled. "That . . . bitch . . . gonna beg . . ."

Lucas's claws dug into skin. "Where's Hayden?"

"Can't . . . won't . . ." Blood flew from the shifter's lips.

Time to skip the preliminaries. "No time to play," Lucas muttered and drove his claws in deep.

The coyote's screams filled the air. One minute later, he started talking—and two minutes later, he died.

Sarah stood outside the doorway, her heart slamming into her chest. She wanted to cover her ears. Wanted to run as fast and as far as she could.

Running hadn't worked out so well for her, though, so she forced herself to stay. She heard the coyote shifter's confession. Heard the location of their leader. She knew Hayden would be heading back to lick his wounds. She also knew he'd be meeting up with Rafe.

After all, Hayden was Rafe's guard dog. The leash didn't stretch too far.

Rafe had sent Hayden after her. Bastard. Rafe would have known that she couldn't fight the coyotes. He'd wanted her to suffer.

The shifter's screams echoed in her ears.

But she hadn't been hurt. Jordan had. Though that, too, must have been part of Rafe's plan.

The dead coyotes wouldn't matter to Rafe. He'd always thought coyotes were expendable. Weaker physically and intellectually than the wolves, he'd said they hadn't showed much promise.

Other than as freaking attack dogs.

She glanced down at the blood on her fingers. Those coyotes had come too close. If Lucas hadn't been there . . .

She would have been the one screaming, then dying.

Just like the coyote shifter.

"I told you to go." Lucas's low, gravelly voice.

Sarah straightened fast. "Is he—" Lucas's gaze held hers. Right. Stupid question. Coyotes didn't have a healing capacity anywhere close to a wolf's. Different shifters could heal at different rates. Wolves were some of the strongest, and because of that, they could survive almost anything.

"You heard it all?"

She managed a nod.

He turned away from her. "Jess and his coyote pack were dead when we got there."

I killed all the bastards in my way. She tried to speak, couldn't. *Guess who's the king coyote now?* "H-Hayden killed them." Because he wanted more power, more territory, just like Rafe did.

No wonder the two had aligned, but did Hayden know that he was as disposable as the others?

Lucas glanced back at her.

"Hayden told me." She just hadn't understood.

His hands were fisted. "What else did he tell you?"

I did my part.

"H-he's working with Rafe." And if Hayden was there, "Rafe's close."

Lucas grabbed her hand and hauled her away from the wall, and he pulled her down the long, twisting corridor and finally, outside, into the clear air where she could *breathe* and not smell death.

He didn't let her go when they made it outside. Just held her hand tighter. She saw the flare of his nostrils. "I'm going after Hayden," he said, voice grim. "I know where his coyote pack has been hiding."

Because Lucas had made the coyote shifter reveal their location before he died. "Hayden's not going to be alone. Didn't you hear me? Rafe's close. You can't just walk in—"

"Piers will have my back. The others will stay here with you." His eyes glittered down at her. "I won't leave you and Jordan undefended again."

"You can't go." Her hand twisted so that she clung tightly to him.

"I'm not gonna sit back and wait for the bastards to come at me again." His jaw clenched. "And they've got Dane," he gritted.

Her heart seemed to stop. "What?"

"We found his blood at Jess's, but he wasn't among the dead. *They've got him.*"

And Lucas wouldn't leave a packmate to die. Rafe would be counting on that.

He'd walk right into a trap. "No, you can't go after him."

"The hell I can't." Fury had never sounded so cold. "According to you, Rafe's gunning for me. That means he'll do anything he can to take me down, including hurting my pack."

No, Rafe wouldn't hesitate to kill.

Lucas pulled away and began stalking toward the SUV.

"Do you know why he wants you dead so badly?" She called out. *Tell him.*

Lucas froze.

"It's not just about territory." Not just about wolves being possessive bastards who wanted to control as many people and as much land as possible. She took a deep breath. "When you came back to LA, you had to fight to reclaim your pack, didn't you?"

"There wasn't a whole fucking lot left of my pack," he said, throwing a hard glare over his shoulder. The sunlight caught the savaged edge of his ear. "But I didn't come back just for the pack."

No, he'd come back for vengeance. She knew the story, thanks to Rafe. "You came back and killed Kaber." Kaber

Gentry, the lone wolf who'd come into the pack—and killed Lucas's father. Then attacked a ten-year-old boy. She knew exactly how Lucas had gotten that torn ear. Kaber had bit off part of Lucas's ear when the two fought. Kaber hadn't exactly believed in showing mercy to a child.

To anyone.

Lucas growled, "The fucking bastard deserved everything he got."

And Kaber had gotten a lot of pain. The final battle between Kaber and Lucas had lasted for hours and ended with Kaber missing more than just half an ear. Lucas had taken his head.

"You went after him because he killed your father." She sucked in a quick breath. "That's why Rafe is coming after you."

His expression didn't change. Not by so much as a flicker of his eyelashes. "Kaber Gentry had no sons. No daughters. He was Lone, a wolf that had been kicked out of his pack because he was fucking psychotic."

She was aware of the door opening behind her. Sarah looked back and found Piers gazing at them with a shuttered stare. She remembered the touch of his mind. The chaos inside. *Psychotic.* She cleared her throat. "Lone or not, he took the pack from your father."

"He destroyed the damn pack!" Lucas came back to her, fast. "He turned 'em into killers. They hunted humans, attacked at will, made a bloodbath—"

"He mated with a human, and they had a son. Kaber didn't think the boy could shift, so he left them behind." His mistake. His hybrid son could definitely shift into the form of a wolf.

"What the fuck are you saying? That Rafe is coming after me—"

"Because he wants your land, and your pack, just like his father did." She lifted her chin. "But more than that, he wants revenge, and he's not going to stop until he gets his pound of flesh from you."

His broad shoulders seemed to block the light. "I'm not giving his family any more flesh."

She didn't let her gaze drift to his ear. She never had. "If you give him the chance, he'll take it. He's going after everything you care about. Everyone."

He caught her arms and yanked her against his chest. "The whole time, you *knew* it was personal." His breath feathered over her face. "Why didn't you tell me?"

"It's always personal," she said sadly. "Don't you know that?" No kill in the *Other* world was ever just business.

"Is there anything you don't know about me?" he muttered, gaze hard on her face.

She knew the big details . . .

The battle when he'd been a child.

The fight to take his pack back.

The hunt for the vampires.

But there was still so much she didn't know. Sure, she knew the blood and gore parts. Nothing about the man. "A lot," she managed to whisper, but she was trying to know everything, struggling to learn as much as she could.

"*Lucas!*" Caleb's voice cut through the air.

They glanced back. He stood just behind Piers.

"Dane's on the line." He shook his head. "Sounds damn weak . . . and he said—he said he had to talk to *you.*"

Dane. Sarah's shoulders sagged. If he was calling back to base, then he was safe.

They rushed back toward the house. Caleb tossed Lucas the cell phone.

"Dane, where the hell are—" Lucas began, but he broke off, eyes narrowing. "Who the fuck is this?"

Goosebumps rose on her arms and she knew even before Lucas snarled, "*Rafe.*"

Chapter 9

Low laughter filled Lucas's ears. "I've got something you want."

He almost shattered the cell phone. "Put Dane on the line."

"Sorry, no can do. But your boy heard him—he knows I've got the lost wolf."

Fuck.

"I've got something you want," Rafe said again, his voice light, mocking, "but . . ." And now his voice changed. Grew harder. Angrier. "You've got something I fucking need."

Lucas's stare jumped to Sarah. She watched him with wide eyes, biting her lower lip.

"Pretty isn't she?" Rafe murmured. "But be careful, her looks are deceiving."

"You're dead." His promise.

More laughter. "No, but unless I get what I need, Dane will be."

"I'm not making a trade with you." *Pale flesh scarred with clawmarks.* "So fuck off."

"I know how Dane got all those marks on his body."

Lucas's back teeth clenched so hard his jaw ached.

"I'll be adding a few more," Rafe told him. "You have an hour to make the trade."

"How do I even know where you are?"

"Because I *know* you. You made the coyotes talk before you killed them." A brief pause. "It's what I would've done."

Shit. Now the bastard thought Lucas was like him? *"You're not getting her."*

"Don't be a dumbass." Disdain now, no, disgust. "You don't know her, and you'd be a fool to trust her."

Sarah's gaze still held his.

"What, Simone? You think you can fuck her?" Rafe's breath rasped over the line. "You can't. She wouldn't let you touch her. Wouldn't let anyone but me come close." Absolute confidence.

Think again. But he bit back the words. They'd just piss off Rafe, and he didn't want the bastard taking out his rage on Dane.

"One hour," Rafe said again. "Bring her. Bring two men as backup. We switch, and you walk away clean."

"While you kill her?"

Sarah's body tensed.

"I won't kill Sarah." Surprise there. "Hasn't she told you? *I can't.*"

"But you can slash her, can't you, asshole? Can dig those claws into her and—"

"How the fuck do you know?"

Because I saw her. Every damn inch. Touched and tasted.

Lucas didn't say a word.

Sarah came closer, her footsteps silent. She touched his hand. "Make the trade," she whispered.

His breath caught in his throat.

"Make it, or he dies." Sarah's voice was stronger, but fear showed in her eyes.

"*Sarah.*" Rafe's low growl. Hungry, almost desperate. "See, she wants to come back to me."

Like hell.

"Two men come with you," Rafe said again. "You stay in human form, and you bring Sarah to me."

The wind lifted her hair, tossing it lightly against her cheek.

"If I don't get my mate back, then you'll get your wolf in pieces. Very, very small pieces."

The line died.

At first, Lucas didn't move. Couldn't. Rage pumped through his body. A fury that was all too familiar.

The fury he'd felt when his father died . . .

When Kaber had defeated him so easily and tossed his broken body into the dirt . . .

When the vamps took Jordan . . . When he'd tracked the scent of his brother's blood to that hellhole in Vegas . . .

My mate.

Sarah licked her lips.

"Lucas?" Caleb asked. "What's the plan?"

He didn't look away from Sarah. He heard a crunch and realized he'd crushed the phone. "Get ready," he said to Caleb. "You and Piers are coming with me." Michael would stay and protect the house.

"Where are we go—"

"To get Dane back."

Her gaze fell. Lucas caught her chin and forced her stare back to him. "You've been holding out on me." He barely bit out the words. His claws wanted to burst from his skin. His teeth were burning, lengthening.

Caleb's footsteps thundered away. Lucas took Sarah's hand and pulled her around the side of the house. He pressed her against the rough brick walls.

"I-I know . . . there's no choice . . . you have to—"

His mouth took hers in a hot, hard kiss, swallowing the words. She gasped against his lips, and he took her breath, too. Took everything.

The kiss wasn't gentle. Wasn't easy. He was way past that point. The blood pounded in his veins, and he heard the bastard's voice echoing in his mind.

His mouth wrenched away from hers. "Why the hell . . ." He sucked in a breath, tasted her. Wanted more. *Needed* more. Just like that bastard Rafe seemed to need her. "Does that asshole think you're his mate?"

Sarah flinched. "You know . . . you know we were lovers, I told you that."

Yeah, and how the hell that had happened, he didn't know. "What is it, babe? You got a thing for badasses?" First Rafe. *Now me.*

She pressed back harder against the wall, as if she were trying to put space between them. "He wasn't like . . . that at first." The words came slowly. "He understood me, made me feel like I fit in. Finally, I *fit* someplace. I was wanted."

Still was wanted. The guy was willing to kill in order to get her back—and Lucas was ready to kill to keep her. After only a few days . . .

Her lashes lowered. "I didn't realize he was playing me until it was too late. I'd already slept with him."

"How many times?"

Her lashes flew back up. "*What?*"

Don't want to know. Don't want to think about—"How many fucking times did you screw him?"

She shoved against him. "None of your damn business!"

Yeah, it is. His hands curled around her shoulders. "He thinks you're his mate."

Her mouth popped open in shock. "What? No, no, he just wants to kill me—"

"He called you *his mate.*" A wolf wouldn't make a mistake like that.

"Then he was lying or jerking you around or—" She broke off, shaking her head. "I'm *not* his mate."

"Shifters know their mates." Not some predestined oursouls-are-meant-as-one bullshit. He didn't buy that crap. But shifters could recognize those who were the best compatible genetic matches. Survival of the fucking fittest. Not everyone could produce a shifter's offspring. It took a real special match, or else the world would have been exploding with shifters by now.

Some shifters recognized their mates by scent. An instinctive reaction. Some recognized them during the sex act—couldn't get more instinctive than that.

"How many times?" he gritted again.

She shook her head. "I'm not telling you, okay? Like I said, that's none of your business!"

"Babe, your ex-lover is gunning for my pack, he says he's mated to you, that I can't trust you—"

If he hadn't been watching so closely, he might have missed that small widening of her eyes. But he had been watching her. Very closely.

Can't trust you, can I?

"I don't care what he thinks," she said quietly. "I'm not his mate. I'm not planning to spend the rest of my life—however long or short that may be—with him. We're done."

"Damn straight you are." His hand dove into the thickness of her hair. He caught the nape of her neck and pulled her closer.

"He's trying to kill me," she told him, voice husky. "Isn't that proof enough that we're not mated? Would a shifter kill his mate?"

It had happened before. Too many times. The animal was too close and jealousy was a primal emotion. An emotion that had roused his own beast.

"I'm not turning you over to him." Their mouths were so close. He could already taste her.

And since they were so close, there was no missing the flash of sadness in her eyes. "Yes, you are." She kissed him then. A light, open-mouthed kiss that just stirred the animal all the more. "Because there isn't a choice."

Screw that. His lips took hers. Hard. Wild. He thrust his tongue inside her mouth, tasted her deep and long because that was what he needed.

There was always a choice. He might not like the options but . . . *there was always a choice.*

His cock shoved against the front of his jeans. Rage and lust fired his blood. She was all he could feel. All he could smell. Everything he needed right then.

His left hand snaked between them. He found the soft curve of her breast. The nipple was hard, already pebbled against his fingers, and the scent of her arousal deepened around him.

Aroused, yes, but . . . afraid?

His head shot up. No way to do slow and easy now. They were outside. Time was against them, but . . .

Fucking need her.

Because death pressed close. He could feel the cold bastard all around him.

"If you don't want me," he said deliberately, "say it now." Because five more seconds . . .

She blinked. He didn't see the fear in her eyes then. Did she know that his canines were growing? She had to see the beast's glow in his eyes.

But her hands went to the waist of his jeans. She jerked open the snap, slid down the zipper. *Hell, yes.*

Right then, right there. Death could wait. He was taking life then.

Her fingers curled around his cock. Cool, silken hands that tightened as they pumped and worked his flesh. Long, sensual strokes from root to tip. Strokes that had his body tensing as the need built and the lust just burned hotter.

A snarl broke from his lips. *Can't . . . control . . .*

He yanked open her jeans. Shoved them to the ground. Tore away her panties. She stumbled, trying to kick out of her jeans. He caught her, lifted her up high in his arms, and pushed her back against the wall.

He held her up easily. Her legs were parted, open to him, as they cradled his hips. No fear flickered in her eyes. That green seemed so deep. Then she whispered his name.

His cock shoved into her, a long, driving thrust that left them both gasping. Her legs pressed against his hips, her sex clamped around him—tight, hot, wet and—

No condom.

Lucas froze.

Sarah's breath heaved out and her nails dug into his shoulders. "*Lucas.*"

His teeth clenched. *Thrust.* The command was snarled from inside, but he didn't move. "You . . . protected?"

A thin line appeared between her eyes. Her hips arched against him. "Wha—"

Thrust. "I'm clean." A shifter's natural healing ability protected him from just about every disease or illness out there.

Her delicate, inner muscles squeezed him. "Me too, don't worry—"

And he'd only be able to get her pregnant if she were his mate. If she was . . .

He withdrew.

"*I want you,*" she whispered and broke his control.

Lucas drove balls-deep into her, again and again. His hands dug into her hips as he held her tighter, positioning her so that he could plunge deeper into her creamy warmth. Deeper, harder, and with every thrust, she welcomed him with her hot, wet sex, holding tight, so fucking tight.

The base of his spine taunted as the need mounted. Harder, deeper. The sound of her gasps filled his ears. Her body slickened more for him, the flesh plumping as she strained against him.

Harder, deeper. Not him this time . . . that was her whispered command.

And he gave the lady just what she wanted.

His mouth took hers, his tongue drove deep, and she came around his cock. A wild squeeze that had his own climax erupting. He came inside her on a long, shuddering wave of pleasure that racked his body.

When the haze cleared from his eyes, Lucas realized that he had Sarah pinned to the wall. Her body seemed limp against his, her hands now light on his shoulders.

Carefully, he pulled away from her, a slow glide of his flesh, but she gasped at that friction. His gaze flew to hers. He didn't see pain or fear in her stare. Just a little flash of pleasure.

Sarah.

The lady was much stronger than she looked. She'd be able to take all that he could give her. He had plans to give her one hell of a lot.

He eased her legs down. When her knees trembled, he steadied her, and helped her to right her clothes. Her lips were dark, her cheeks flushed, her eyes glittering. Sexy enough to tempt the devil.

Want her again.

He yanked up his jeans. "I shouldn't have . . ." Oh, fuck that. He'd done just what he wanted. Lucas cleared his throat. "You okay?"

A slow nod. "Better than okay." She smiled at him, a ghost of a smile that lifted her lips and chased a few of the shadows from his eyes.

"Next time," he told her quietly, his gaze raking her. "I taste every inch of you." The words were a promise.

Her smile dimmed. "You sure there'll be a next time?" She brushed by him, heading back toward the blood and the scent of death.

"Count on it."

She glanced back at him. "You sound awful sure of yourself. Especially when we've got the devil pounding at the door."

"Let him pound," Lucas said. "I'm not afraid of the asshole." He looked forward to going fang-to-claw with the bastard.

Sarah turned away and hurried inside. "I wish I could say the same thing." Her whisper drifted back on the wind.

His gaze slid to the left. To the rolling hills and the trees that bordered his land. So many places to hide. So many places to watch.

Lucas let a smile curve his lips as he stared at the hills. *My mate.* Hell, no, she wasn't Rafe's.

She wouldn't let you touch her. Wouldn't let anyone but me come close.

"Wrong again, asshole," he murmured and turned slowly

toward the house. When he went to kill Rafe, Sarah's scent would be on his body. And when Rafe died, Lucas would make sure *he* was the last sight the bastard ever saw.

The binoculars shattered in Rafe's hands.

"We need to get out of here," Hayden said, voice shaking with nerves and pain.

Rafe didn't look at the coyote. They'd met at their rendezvous point, just like they'd planned. With one not-so-minor glitch. *No Sarah.*

He didn't have Sarah because she was busy *fucking Lucas Simone.* He threw the shattered remains to the ground and jumped back inside the jeep.

Hayden groaned next to him. The scent of the coyote's blood was growing stronger. The guy had barely dragged himself out of the battle. Guess the stories about the younger wolf were true. Jordan wouldn't be as easy to kill as they'd thought. Good.

"He . . . bringing her?" Hayden rasped.

Rafe slammed his foot on the gas and the jeep lunged forward. He glanced to the right and saw that blood had trickled from Hayden's nose. "He'll bring her." It wouldn't really be the wolf's choice. The deal hadn't been for Lucas. It had been for Sarah.

Because he knew all of her weak points, too. Knew them very, very well. Deep inside, Sarah was soft. Pity. If she'd been harder . . .

But, no, she'd showed her true colors. "Sarah won't leave Dane to die." Even if Lucas would. "She'll come with him or she'll sneak away and come on her own. Either way . . ." His fingers tightened around the wheel. *She'd let him fuck her.* "Either way, we'll have her."

"And Lucas?"

His claws burst through his fingertips. "I've been waiting years for that bastard to beg." The time for waiting was over. "Simone and his brother—and any wolf who stands with him—will die." He'd make sure that death was as painful as possible. After all, that's just what Lucas had done to his father, he'd made sure Kaber suffered.

Blood for blood.

Get ready to beg, Simone.

"Are you going to trade her?" Sarah held her breath when she heard Caleb's voice. She couldn't see the wolves, but—

"Hell, no," came Lucas's instant response. His feet thudded on the floor. "How's Jordan?"

"Still out." A sigh. Had to be from Caleb. "He's gonna be all right, though. Dane's the one we need to worry about. We can't just leave him. You know what happened before—"

"I know." Growled.

Sarah turned away from the room and tried to creep quietly away. Probably didn't matter how quiet she was, though, the wolves would know she was in the hall. She'd just wanted to peek at Jordan before she left, but there was no chance for that now.

He'd almost died for her. When she'd first planned to come after Lucas, she hadn't thought about the risks she'd bring to his pack. She'd just thought—

Hell. *About myself.*

Jordan had nearly died, and if she didn't do something, Dane *would* die.

The weight of her knife seemed to burn her ankle. She'd taken the liberty of retrieving her knife from Lucas's room moments before. She'd changed her clothes, tried to ignore the imprint of Lucas's body on hers, and gotten her weapon back. Because there was no way she'd face Rafe unarmed.

And I am facing him.

Too many bodies were piling up. If Lucas wouldn't make the trade, she'd make it herself.

Sarah slipped through the open front door, and ran for the SUV. No wolves were out there, and no one called out to stop her.

Fate was finally on her side. The keys were still inside the vehicle. The wolves must have been too distracted when they pulled up, and they'd forgotten to take the keys out. Their mistake.

She hopped inside. She'd heard enough from the coyote during that brutal pre-death interrogation. She knew where to go. And if she could just get close enough to Rafe . . .

This time, I won't miss your heart.

Lucas's head snapped toward the window when he heard the growl of the engine. Piers wouldn't go to the meeting without him—

He lunged for the window, saw the flash of red tail-lights, and *knew.* "Sarah!"

Going after the bastard.

Lucas spun around and almost slammed into Caleb.

"Wait, Lucas, what's—"

"*Rafe.*" He didn't need to say more. Lucas shoved past the other shifter and bounded down the stairs. *She'd left. Gone out on her own.*

"Dammit, I'm comin' with you!" Caleb yelled.

Piers stepped from the kitchen, blocking his way. "So am I."

Lucas didn't slow down, he just pushed the wolf out of his way. "Why the fuck didn't you stop her?" Piers had been downstairs. He would have caught her scent, heard Sarah as she fled.

"Because someone needed to make the trade."

Lucas froze and fired a deadly stare over his shoulder. "That's not your call to make."

Piers swallowed, his Adam's apple bobbing. "It was hers. She made the call. I just . . ."

"Let her walk to her own death." He wanted to rip Piers apart. Piers had been his friend for years, but right then, he wanted to hurt the bastard. "If she dies . . ." *So do you.* The words wanted to come, but he bit them back.

Piers's lips parted in surprise. Yeah, the wolf understood.

Wasting time. He whirled around and raced for the other

SUV. Sarah must have overheard the location of the drop site. He'd been aware of her while he questioned the coyote. Her scent had been strong, too strong—because she was close.

He jumped into the SUV and gunned the engine. Piers and Caleb were right with him.

"Michael will guard Jordan," Caleb told him. "He saw us go, he—"

Lucas spun out of the graveled drive. *She came to me for help, so why is she running back to the bastard now?*

"What's the plan?" Caleb asked from the backseat. "I mean, our first priority is Dane, right? He's pack, he's—"

Lucas spared him a glance in the rearview mirror. "The plan is that we get Dane back, we get Sarah, and we kill Rafe." Simple enough to him.

"We should bring more men," Piers growled.

"The deal was I bring two men." His fingers whitened around the wheel. "I bring two men. He gets Sarah, I get Dane." Only Lucas planned to get them both. "If he catches the scent of more than two . . ." The bastard might kill Dane.

Silence. They all knew what could happen.

The SUV hit one hundred and ten miles per hour as it flew down the winding road.

"Do you really trust her?" Caleb asked quietly. "What if this is just part of a setup?"

Lucas didn't answer him.

But Caleb kept pushing. "If you find out that she's tricking you, what will you—"

"Lucas would do anything to protect the pack," Piers snapped, voice gruff. "You know that."

Would he? He'd spent so many years fighting for the pack—maybe it was time he got something for himself. Someone. *Sarah.*

If Rafe had touched her, he'd tear the bastard's fingers right off his hand.

The warehouse was boarded up, the windows covered, the main entrance blocked with a thick chain. Sarah climbed out of the vehicle, her movements slow, too stiff. She could feel eyes on her, watching her every move. She lifted her hands up high. "I'm not armed!" She could lie, too.

No one called back to her.

Sarah glanced around. All the buildings on this stretch of road had been abandoned. One looked like it had barely survived a blaze. Two others were boarded up, just like the warehouse. She caught the furtive stare of a homeless man and heard the squeak of rats.

But didn't hear the voice of a wolf shifter.

Sarah crept away from the SUV. "I'm here! Isn't that what you wanted? Dammit, Rafe, I know you're watching! Isn't this what you—"

"Hello, Sarah." He said her name softly, and she spun around. He stood less than five feet away, dark hair tousled, one brow raised, and his lips twisted in that familiar smile.

"*Rafe.*"

"Good to see you again, sweetheart."

She flinched at the endearment. Rafe sidled closer, that smile still on his lips. His face was deceptively handsome— strong angles, high cheeks, a square jaw. And his body was still as strong and powerful as ever. "Wh-where's Dane?" she demanded, her gaze trying to search the growing shadows. "I'm here, so let him go."

"No." He stood less than a foot away now, staring at her, his nostrils flaring.

Oh, shit. That damn keen wolf sense of smell. He'd know—

"You really shouldn't have fucked him, Sarah." His brown eyes slit.

An engine roared. Her head swung to the side and she saw another dark SUV hurtle down the road. *Lucas.*

Rafe's fingers locked around her throat. Her heart froze as he leaned in close to her. "Don't worry. I'm not going to kill him," he whispered.

Lucas leapt from the vehicle, with Piers and Caleb at his heels. "Sarah!" Lucas charged forward, his eyes already lit with the glow of the beast. His claws were out, up, ready to rip and tear. "Get the fuck away from her, Santiago!"

But Rafe just pulled her closer. He spun her, so that her back was pressed to his chest and his hand still circled her throat. "Sarah's used to having me near her."

Lucas snarled and charged at them.

Rafe's claws cut into her skin. "Another step and I'll cut her throat wide open." A rough laugh. "She won't be any use to either of us then, will she? So I'd suggest you *stand down!*"

Lucas threw out his hand and caught Piers just as the guy ran by him. Caleb waited a few paces behind them. All three men seemed to vibrate with fury.

"Where's Dane?" Lucas's hands were at his sides.

"All in good time." Rafe's muscles were rock-hard behind her. "You only brought two men. Good."

Lucas didn't speak.

"You know I could kill her before you so much as touched me, don't you, Alpha?" Now Rafe was taunting. "Charmers are no different than humans. One slice—and she's gone."

Lucas wasn't looking at her. The fury of his stare was directed fully at Rafe.

"You fucked my mate, Simone," Rafe snarled, "and that really, really pisses me off!"

"I'm not your—" Sarah began but his claws dug deeper and her words ended in a gasp.

Lucas looked at her then, burned her with his blazing blue eyes. There was death in those eyes. The savage promise of hell coming. "She's not yours," Lucas told him, his voice quiet, a hard contrast to the fury of his stare.

"Do you think she's yours?" Laughter. "She's playing you, the same way she played me."

Oh, hell. "Lucas—" Damn, those claws *hurt*.

One hand smoothed back her hair. "Did you tell him, sweetheart? Does he know about your little secrets?"

No, he didn't.

Lucas was still looking at her, and she knew he'd seen the flicker of her eyelashes. Too telling for someone as observant as he was.

"Did you really think she was just some innocent charmer who'd stumbled into your path?"

No one's innocent.

Sarah licked her lips.

"She killed a cop last night," Rafe murmured. "But her face hasn't been splashed all over the TV. In fact, no reports of that cop bastard dying have even made the news."

Lucas glanced back at Rafe.

"Why do you think that is?" Rafe asked.

Lucas kept his hands at his sides. Caleb stalked closer to him.

"Did you even wonder why the story didn't spread like fucking fire?" Rafe hauled her closer. "I bet Sarah knows why she's safe from scrutiny. I bet she knows why the cops aren't chasing her, why they have *never* chased her."

Her body trembled. She hadn't expected this. She'd thought Rafe would fight her, that Dane would escape. *Why is he doing this?*

What had he told her about Lucas? *I'm not going to kill him.* Then what was his plan?

"You fucked her, and you may have trusted her." Rafe's fingers tightened on her throat. "I made the same mistakes."

"Let her go." Finally, Lucas spoke.

She felt Rafe tense. "Do you know what she is?"

"A charmer."

True enough.

"That's not all," Rafe told him, voice cutting like the claws on her neck. "She came to me for a reason, came to you—for the same damn reason."

Now he was hitting too close to the truth.

"The cops aren't after her," Rafe said, "because she's got someone covering her back."

Sarah tried to crane her neck away from those claws.

"I'll give you a chance, Simone." She knew Rafe was bullshitting. He wouldn't really give Lucas anything. "You can walk away from her. Go back to your pack—"

"What about Dane?" Piers wanted to know.

Rafe didn't acknowledge him. "You can go back, leave her with me, and life can just . . . go on."

Everyone else's life.

"I'm not leaving her," Lucas told him.

If claws hadn't been digging into her skin, she would have relaxed.

"She's here to destroy me." Rafe was adamant on that. He was also right.

"No," Lucas smiled now. "I'm here to do that, asshole."

Chapter 10

Thin trickles of blood ran down Sarah's throat, and the sight had rage boiling within Lucas. "Let her go," he snapped, the beast inside howling for freedom.

Rafe narrowed his eyes. "Did Sarah tell you why she first came to me?"

Don't want to know. His nostrils twitched. He couldn't detect Dane's scent. There were coyotes around, close, hiding in the shadows, and the thick odor of blood hung in the air, but—*no Dane.*

"I thought she was innocent the first time I met her, too, then I found out the truth." Rafe's mouth was too close to Sarah's ear.

Sarah's head twisted to the side. "You don't know what you're—"

"She's FBI, Alpha. She came into my pack, seduced me, used me, because her mission was to take down my wolves."

What? Lucas's gaze flew back to Sarah.

"Didn't mention that, did she?"

Hell, no, she hadn't.

"She's the bait they used, to get into the pack. To get to me." Rafe's lips curled back in a snarl. "To get to you."

"Sarah." Lucas said her name flatly, not letting the fury tightening his gut to be voiced. "Is he lying?"

He saw her throat work as she swallowed, a delicate movement against the claws. "No," she murmured and her lashes lowered. Then . . . "He's not lying. I-I was with the FBI."

Every muscle in his body locked. He knew there was a division in the FBI that followed *Other*. A division that even had a so-called "extermination list" for the paranormals that the Bureau felt should be put down.

He'd known about that group, but he just hadn't particularly given a damn about them. Until now.

"You can't trust her," Rafe murmured, and his hold eased a bit as a satisfied smirk curled his lips. "Bait, that's all she is."

Maybe. Maybe not.

"How'd she get those scars on her back?" he demanded.

That smirk slipped away. "I found out who she really was."

"Um . . . was that before or after she went for your heart with her silver knife?"

Rafe's teeth snapped together. The light dimmed more as dusk swept toward them. "She told you about that?"

"She told me a lot of things." *Like the fact that you want me dead because I took out your asshole of a father.*

"Don't believe her." The claws lifted a bit, but they were still killing-close. "She's good at lying."

He'd figured that out. So when Sarah said she worked for the FBI, was that a lie? Or the truth? "If she's such a damn liar, why the hell do you want her back so badly?"

"Because she's mine." Rafe spoke the words in a tone that said the answer should be obvious.

Sarah's head slammed into his. Rafe swore and blood spurted from his nose. He stumbled back, and she tore free as the claws raked across her flesh. "No," Sarah shouted, "I'm not yours!"

Around him, Lucas heard the howl of the coyotes. So they were finally coming out to play. The waning sunlight bled across the sky. The sky wouldn't be the only place filled with blood soon.

Bones crunched behind him. Caleb would be shifting, getting ready to attack. Lucas would change, too. The better to rip Rafe's throat right out.

"No!" Sarah's scream. "Don't shift, Lucas!"

His muscles locked, and he fought the change. Sweat broke over his body as he held back the beast.

Rafe laughed as the blood poured from his nose. "Too late," he murmured.

Lucas leapt forward and caught the bastard around the throat. "Where's Dane?"

Rafe spat blood. "How the fuck should I know?"

Now *that* he hadn't expected.

Rafe started laughing then, loud, wild laughter. "So fucking easy. And here I thought you'd be a challenge to take down."

Lucas lifted the bastard up, letting Rafe's feet dangle above the ground. "*Dane.*" The coyotes were closing in. Piers was shifting, the man disappearing as the wolf howled and broke free of his leash.

Rafe's laughter slowly faded. The guy could have broken away. Could have shifted. But he hadn't.

"Lucas . . ." Sarah grabbed his hand. "I don't—"

"*Where the fuck is he?*" Lucas shook Rafe.

"Don't know." He smiled, and the blood smeared his teeth. "I never had the asshole."

But, wait, no, he'd wanted a trade. Caleb had said—

Howls filled the air. Lower, harder cries from the two wolves behind him, and the higher-pitched howls from the swarming coyotes.

Then a bus hit Lucas, slamming him to the ground as Sarah screamed.

No, not a bus. He'd been taken down by . . . a wolf.

Dane knew there was trouble at the wolf compound long before the big house came into sight. The scent of fresh blood hung in the air, a silent call to his beast.

He stayed low, going in carefully when he wanted to run flat-out and storm the place.

Quiet. The whole damn area was too quiet. And the lingering scent of coyote teased his nose.

Not those bastards again.

He pressed a hand to his side. Most of his wounds had healed. *Most.* He needed to shift again, but wouldn't, not until he found out what the hell was going on.

"Dane?" Michael's shocked voice.

Next to Dane, Michael's nose was the strongest of the pack. Dane gave up the shadows and charged forward.

Michael shook his head, his brows high above his dark eyes. "They got you back already? But—"

"Got me back? Wait, you *knew* the coyotes had me?"

Michael came away from the doorway with slow, measured strides. "The coyotes . . . they're working with Rafe. He was going to trade you—"

"Rafe? That bastard hasn't been anywhere near me." Just coyotes. *Dead coyotes.*

"—for Sarah," Michael finished.

A fist punched Dane in the gut. "I wasn't part of any damn trade."

"But . . . Caleb heard your voice. *You* were with Rafe. The bastard said he'd kill you if Sarah wasn't brought in as a trade."

The compound was tomb-silent. "Where's Lucas?" But he already knew.

"Gone to make the trade."

Dane's hands fisted. "There was no fucking trade."

"Caleb—"

Dane's snarl stopped him. "Where are they?" Lucas was walking right into a trap. Dammit, a trap. *For me.*

Michael's gaze swept down his body. "Why do I smell human blood on you?" Suspicion had him tensing.

Don't think about her. "Caleb never heard my voice. If he said he did, he was . . ." *Lying.* No, Caleb was pack. He wouldn't lie. "Mistaken." And shit, they didn't have time to kill. "*Where are they?*"

"Monclave and Grant. Sarah went first, she took one of the SUVs and—"

Dane turned away and ran back toward the van he'd stolen a few hours before. *Hold on, Lucas. I'm coming to cover your back.*

He owed the alpha everything, and he damn sure wouldn't stand back while Lucas was slaughtered.

Mistake . . . or fucking lie?

Lucas spun around and barely caught the muzzle that came at him. The wolf's teeth were dripping saliva, the beast ready to bite, to rip him open. And the damn bastard was one of his own.

Caleb.

"Guess Sarah didn't tell you about her other talents." Rafe's voice drifted in the air.

Caleb's claws dug into Lucas's chest.

A wolf's snarl of fury reached his ears. *Piers.* Lucas craned his head, just a bit, that was all he could manage. Piers stood in front of Sarah, his back up, his teeth snapping. Attacking her?

"Stand down!" Lucas roared.

But Piers didn't move. Lucas could barely see him and Sarah. Caleb's body blocked his line of sight.

"Good job, Sarah," Rafe told her, his voice oozing satisfaction. Lucas clamped down tighter on Caleb's muzzle. The bastard had almost bitten his fingers with that head twist. "You did real good with him."

Betrayal burned in Lucas's gut.

Rafe crouched close to Lucas. Not too close. Out of grabbing reach. "She can't just read the minds of wolves, you know." He said the words like he was revealing a big secret. Maybe he was.

"Fuck off!"

Caleb jerked his muzzle free. He came in for a bite—

Lucas shoved his forearm between the wolf's teeth. When

Caleb bit down, sinking his teeth through muscle and bone, Lucas didn't make a sound. *Betrayal. From my own damn pack.* Like this was the first time.

"She can control the wolves, too," Rafe murmured. "In wolf form, your men are helpless against her. Whatever she thinks, whatever she wants, they'll do."

Shock froze him for a moment.

Caleb jumped back, then came in for another bite—

"*No!*" Sarah's scream. Rage and terror. "Leave him alone! Don't!"

The change swept over Lucas then. Uncontrollable. Instinctive.

"Hell, yes . . ." Rafe said. "Finally."

Lucas shoved his claws into Caleb's chest. The wolf bursting from within gave him power, and he lifted Caleb, tossing the wolf into the air and right at Rafe.

"*Shit!*" Rafe scrambled back, too late.

Lucas's hands hit the ground. His fingers curved. His back arched as the bones snapped. Fur burst over his skin.

"No, Lucas! That's when you're—"

His head rose and he saw Sarah. The coyotes had surrounded her and Piers. Piers was trying to hold them off, trying to protect her, and Sarah was swiping out with a knife. But she'd turned away from the coyotes, turned to shout to him—

And a coyote caught her, locking his teeth around her arm and the knife clattered to the ground as she stumbled.

No!

A soft snick reached his ears. His head whipped back around. Rafe smiled at him. The asshole stood less than two feet away, and his right hand curled around a gun—a gun that was aimed straight at Lucas.

"I think what Sarah was trying to say . . ." Rafe began.

Lucas's body bucked, his hands vanished, paws appeared.

". . . is that you're helpless when you change."

"*Lucas!*" Sarah's scream of pain and fury.

"The bullet's made of silver, Simone." Rafe pointed the gun at Lucas's head. "And there's no way I'm missing when I'm this close."

Lucas tried to leap forward, but his legs were useless, the bones reshaping, too weak now to—

"When you get to hell, tell my old man I said hello." Rafe pulled the trigger.

Sarah barreled into Rafe just as he fired. Lucas lurched to the side. The bullet missed his head but plowed into his exposed stomach, burning through muscle and lodging deep in his gut. The silver was molten, frying him from the inside out, and Lucas opened his mouth to yell—

And the wolf's cry of pain rang into the night.

"The hero's going to die."

Lucas lifted his head and narrowed his eyes. Sarah and Rafe were in a tangle of limbs, fighting for the gun. Sarah was no match for the bastard.

I am.

He pushed back the fire, bunched his legs and—

Two coyotes sprang at him. Lucas swiped at them, catching one on the back and breaking another's leg. They kept fighting him, snapping, clawing.

Get out of here, Lucas! Sarah's cry but . . . only in his mind.

He could feel her then, the warmth of her touch, her scent. Inside, though, not out.

What the hell is happening? Lucas pushed the question through their link. *Why did Caleb attack me?*

She cried out then and his head snapped toward her. Sarah was on the ground, not moving. Rafe rose beside her, the gun still in his hand. He pointed the gun at her.

No! Piers stop him!

Piers bolted past Lucas.

Don't let him kill her!

Lucas sank his teeth into the nearest coyote. The asshole screamed, a high, keening cry.

Piers slammed into Rafe. Rafe staggered, fell, but before Piers could close in for the kill, the coyotes attacked, immediately surrounding him.

They swarmed. Slashing. Biting. Piers's white coat turned red as he went down.

Piers! For a moment, Lucas's vision went gray as fury churned his blood.

They're all gonna die.

Lucas swung his head to the left. Caleb stalked toward him, his white coat gleaming. *They're all gonna die and the blood will be on your hands, Alpha.* Caleb's taunt.

The psychic link between him and Caleb was sharp, perfectly focused. The way it was supposed to be between packmates.

Why the hell are you doing this? Lucas wanted his blood. *Why are you turning on me?*

He hadn't seen this coming. He'd fought side-by-side with Caleb for so long, and he'd never seen—

Caleb's teeth snapped closed as the two wolves circled each other. *What makes you think I was ever with you?*

Fucking bastard.

Lucas attacked. Caleb's wolf was just as big as his, but not nearly as strong—and not nearly as fucking pissed.

Lucas raked his claws down Caleb's side. Caleb snarled but backed away.

The guy didn't try to fight at all—just *backed away.*

Lucas slammed his front paws onto Caleb. The other wolf fell. Lucas locked his teeth around Caleb's throat.

The bastard still wasn't fighting back. *Why aren't you fighting? You want to take me out? Then fight!*

But Caleb wasn't fighting or answering. Caleb wasn't—

Watch out! Sarah's voice in his mind. Weaker than before.

Lucas jumped back instinctively, but the bullet still hit him; this time, it lodged in his back. *Fuck.* Fire burned near his spine. Lucas's claws dug into the earth. The coyotes were coming back, closing in, but screw them.

He took the pain that blazed through his body. Took it,

used it, and Lucas launched into the air. His paws crashed into Rafe, and the asshole fell. The gun flew from his fingers and hit the ground. Rafe fought him, catching his claws, holding tight with both hands. Lucas's blood dripped on the bastard.

A coyote locked his teeth around Lucas's right hind leg. Another dog caught the left. They dragged him off as he howled his rage.

Rafe laughed. "Guess the mighty have fucking fallen, huh?"

The other coyotes attacked.

The last thing Lucas saw was Sarah's face. She'd staggered to her feet. Blood dripped down her cheek and terror filled her eyes.

Lucas. Her desperate fear filled his mind.

Don't worry, babe. I got this.

Maybe. Maybe not.

Then he couldn't see anything but teeth and claws.

"Stay here," Dane ordered as the van squealed to a stop. "You try to break free, you so much as make a single sound . . ."

The woman with the golden eyes blinked at him. She lifted her bound hands and pointed to her gag.

"You try to escape, I'll have to knock you out again." Right, he was bullshitting there. He wouldn't be around to knock her out. Because the blood was flowing close by and the fight called. He grabbed her arms and jerked her up toward him. "*Stay here.*"

She blinked and then gave a slow nod.

He sprang from the van, ran, and knew that she'd be long gone when he came back.

If he came back.

He rushed down the dark road. He hadn't parked too close, that would have been dangerous. But he could hear the fight, the snarls and the growls, and when he rounded the corner, he knew he'd see—

Caleb jumped at him and took his ass down to the pavement.

*   *   *

"You bitch," Rafe snarled, whirling on Sarah. "I was going to let you live, I was going to—"

Bullshit. He'd already sent his attack dogs after her. Hayden had been ready to slice her open.

Piers had finally shaken free of the coyotes who'd attacked him. The big white wolf stalked toward the group attacking Lucas. His movements were slow, and blood soaked his right side.

"For old times' sake," Rafe told her with the grin that had once made her heart race faster, "I'll make it quick."

She kept her gaze on him, but she let her thoughts shoot out, let her mind connect with the wolf. *Piers.*

His rage hit her first. The wild fury of the wolf. *Destroy. Attack. Protect Alpha.*

"Our old times are over," Sarah said, lifting her chin. She could feel the wetness of blood on her cheek. "And they were never that good."

Rafe's eyes narrowed with a flare of rage.

Piers, come to me.

The white wolf froze. She swallowed and kept her gaze on Rafe. He could strike at any moment. She didn't have time for . . .

"You're right," Rafe said. "They weren't that good." His gaze dismissed her. "So maybe I will make this *hurt.*"

Great. She should have kept her mouth shut.

Piers, here. Attack!

The white wolf's body shuddered and he began running toward her. Fast, faster . . . "There's something you should know," Sarah told Rafe quietly.

One brow rose.

"I definitely plan to make your death *hurt.*" *Attack him Piers!* The white wolf hit Rafe, and they both barreled to the ground.

She muttered, "Guess you didn't see him coming," and her shoulders sagged.

Go for the throat, Piers. Go for—

Rafe shoved off the white wolf as he screamed in agony. Piers had bitten him. Not a death bite, not deep enough but—

Rafe tossed the white wolf into the side of the warehouse. Piers was so weak he wasn't fighting back.

"No!"

Rafe spun back to her. "You—"

Get back, Sarah. Lucas's order, drifting in her mind. *Run.*

She stumbled, nearly fell in the blood on the ground, but then she turned and ran as fast as she could.

"Come back, damn you!" Rafe's scream. He'd be running after her. He'd be—

She risked a glance over her shoulder. Lucas had him. They were fighting, man versus wolf. Rafe wouldn't be able to defeat Lucas, not while Lucas was in wolf form. But . . .

But Lucas was hurt. He'd taken two silver hits. His pain beat at her, steady, burning, a fire that churned from the inside of his body. *In the blood.*

Lucas?

Rafe lifted something, metal glinted. No, not just metal. Silver. *Her knife.* Sarah tripped and hit the cement. Her hand went to her ankle sheath. Gone. Hell, no, she'd lost her knife.

She whipped her head back to the fight. The coyotes were down or limping away, Piers wasn't moving, but Rafe was still up, and slashing out with that knife.

She couldn't run and leave Lucas. If Rafe killed him . . .

Snarls reached her ears. Angry, fierce. Sarah barely had time to stagger to her feet when two more wolves burst onto the scene.

A white wolf with a pelt already stained red. A black wolf with teeth dripping blood. Caleb and Dane.

She tried to reach their minds, but found only a tangle of fury and desperation.

Sarah sucked in a deep breath. She could do this. Rafe had been right about one thing. She had her secrets. *Not weak.* At least, not now she couldn't be weak. Her heart pounded so hard her chest shook but she advanced on Caleb and Dane.

Dane, break away. Go help Lucas.

Dane's big body shuddered. He glanced up at her. Caleb swiped his claws down Dane's right side. Sarah winced, feeling the pain herself. *Dane, go.*

He wouldn't be able to resist her order. In wolf form, he'd be helpless.

Because Sarah couldn't just talk to the wolves. Rafe had actually spoken the truth. She could control the wolves.

A rare charmer—and a dangerous one. As Rafe had come to learn.

Dane bounded away from Caleb. The white wolf shook his head, frowning. She caught Caleb's thoughts, heard the—

Come back and fight, bastard—

"No." She stepped forward. Caleb growled at her as his head lowered toward the ground. He arched, bending low, getting ready to attack. *Stand down, Caleb.*

A tremor shook his body.

"I don't know what the hell is happening here, but you need to *stand down.*"

Caleb's smoky eyes were locked on her. She pressed deeper into his mind. There was a shield there, one she hadn't noticed before during her little "test," because she hadn't probed deep enough. If she could just—

Don't remember inviting you inside.

Her knees locked. If a wolf could smile, well, Caleb would be grinning right then.

Think you can control me?

"Stand down." Her whisper held a tremble of fear.

Think again.

He leapt at her. Sarah didn't even have time to scream before he had her on the ground. His weight suffocated her, taking all her breath away.

All wolves aren't the same. His snarl.

Caleb, no! She pressed her power at him, shoving with all she was worth. *Go, run away! You don't want to kill me!*

The scent of blood and wolf filled her nostrils. *Yes, I do.*

His head lowered. His teeth hovered over her throat. *Call them.* His taunt echoed in her mind. *Tell them to come and save you.*

Lucas and Dane.

His teeth scraped her throat. *Call them,* he ordered.

Sarah swallowed. *Lucas! Dane!*

Caleb nuzzled her throat. *Good girl.*

The earth shook around her. The wolves were racing to her rescue. And Rafe? What was he—

A motor gunned to life.

Escaping.

Dane growled. *Get the fuck away from her.*

Lucas didn't bother with an order. He just plowed right into Caleb. They rolled off her, twisting and turning, banging into the concrete.

Sarah scrambled off the ground and ran a hand over her throat. Caleb could have killed her in an instant, but he hadn't.

Why?

Now Caleb lay on the ground, Lucas at *his* throat, and the white wolf wasn't fighting. Wasn't moving at all. Just waiting for death.

And death was coming. Lucas snarled and went in for the kill.

"Stop!" She jumped to her feet. Dane raced in front of her. She wasn't sure if Dane was trying to protect her or tying to keep her from stopping Lucas. Either way, she didn't have time to touch his mind and find out. "Stop, Lucas!"

Lucas's teeth snapped together. He swung his head toward her.

"He's not fighting anymore," she whispered. "Don't kill him." *Not until we can figure out what's happening. Why he betrayed you.*

The black wolf's head jerked, but then Lucas surged forward and caught Caleb's neck between his teeth.

No, I told you not to kill him!

With his jaws closed around Caleb's neck, Lucas lifted the

white wolf, then slammed Caleb's head down into the concrete. Caleb's eyes fell closed, but his chest kept rising and falling. Still alive.

Her breath rushed out. Lucas loped back toward her, his sides heaving, his gait slower now. How much silver was inside him? Eating at him?

"Lucas?" She held her hands out to him. His head butted against her palm. His eyes closed.

Then he fell at her feet.

Chapter 11

Dane drove the van at breakneck speed. He'd pulled on a pair of jeans—Sarah didn't know where the hell he'd gotten those—and the van careened down the road. There was a woman in the back of the van with them. A *familiar,* bound woman who stared at her with wide eyes and kept trying to choke out something behind her gag.

Sarah knew she should probably try to help her, but the woman wasn't in any immediate danger then and—

And she wasn't about to let go of Lucas. He'd shifted after he'd collapsed, and Dane had carried him into the van. His blood was everywhere, his breath rasping out, and Sarah was . . . scared. No, terrified.

They'd left a pile of dead coyotes behind them. Left Caleb. Sarah didn't know what would happen to the white wolf, and right then, she didn't care. All that mattered was Lucas.

"Got to . . . get the bullets . . . out . . ." His voice was so weak.

She stared down at the mess that was his stomach and didn't know where to start.

His head lay in her lap. He tried to heave up to check out the damage.

"No." Her hands tightened on him. She couldn't control him anymore, but she damn sure didn't want him to see the damage. "Don't look."

His blue eyes weren't so bright anymore. "Been . . . shot . . . before."

"He got you with silver." She would *not* cry. But . . . this was her fault. The whole thing had been a trap. Rafe hadn't been holding Dane. If she hadn't gone out on her own, *this never would have happened.*

"Been . . . hit . . . with silver . . . too . . ." The words seemed softer. "Can dig it . . ." His claws ripped through the tops of his fingers. "Out . . ."

Her nails dug into his skin. "They were some kind of—of exploding bullets." Had to be based on the damage. They'd shattered on impact. She'd seen something like this once before, and that poor bastard hadn't survived. *Lucas will.* "You can't just dig them out. They're in pieces, fragmented." Smart asshole. Rafe had known exactly what he was doing.

"Let me see him."

Her gaze flew up. Piers was awake. His eyes were narrowed, and dried blood marked his face. He'd shifted twice already in the van. Shifted twice, then passed out. But he seemed to be back with them now, and most of his wounds had healed.

He reached for Lucas.

She bit her lip.

His fingers skated over the wounds, and his breath hissed out when he saw the full extent of the injuries. "Can you shift, man?"

The lines on Lucas's face had deepened. If I could . . . I . . . would . . . have . . ."

But he'd wasted all his energy, fighting for her.

"We need to get him to a hospital," Piers yelled to Dane. The woman with the gag froze, her eyes huge.

Sarah slid her fingers down the side of Lucas's cheek. "A hospital isn't going to work."

"We have to get the silver out!" Piers snapped. "Either we dig it out or—"

She grabbed his hand, held tight. "It's in his blood." Her

voice was low, but she knew Lucas still heard her. "Don't you understand? It's fragmented, in his organs, in his blood—*in him.*" Burning him alive, from the inside out. The legends about wolves and silver had been so true. Some called it an allergy. A genetic quirk.

But silver could truly kill a wolf shifter. The more intense the exposure, the quicker the death. *And you didn't get more intense than a blood exposure.* "We need more than a doctor," she whispered and felt just as she'd felt months before. Helpless. Because Sarah was very afraid that Lucas would be dying in her arms.

Not what I planned.

"What the hell?" Came Dane's snarl. "He's *not* dying!"

Lucas's gaze was on Sarah. She knew he saw the knowledge there. "I . . . am," he said. Soft. Not sad. Not afraid. Not Lucas.

Her cheek was wet. Blood or tears? Or both?

"Who can help him?" Piers asked, voice breaking.

Sarah couldn't look away from Lucas.

Piers grabbed her upper arm. Shook her. "*Who can help him?*"

She pressed her lips together to control the tremble. The van hit a pothole and they all lurched, but Piers's grip never wavered. "You know any witches?" she whispered, and she wasn't kidding. "Because that's what it's going to take. Medicine won't work. We need magic." *So much blood.* Soon he'd bleed silver. "One hell of a lot of magic."

She took a breath and smelled death. "You know anyone with that kind of power, Piers?"

His hold eased on her. "Yeah, yeah, I do."

Her gaze flew up and a rush of wild hope had her choking on her breath.

"Dane . . ." Piers's face could have been cut from rock. "Turn this bitch around and get us to Gaines and Hillray."

Lucas stiffened against her. "Piers . . ."

"If Marie Dusean can't help you, no one can," Piers said.

"Look, I been keeping track of her group since that vampire hell, I know where they are. Believe me, if anyone can help, *she can.*"

"If she will," Dane called from the front, and the van swerved as he turned the vehicle around.

Marie?

A hard curl lifted Piers's lips. "Tell me, charmer, have you ever heard of the *mambo?*"

Mambo. The hair on her arms rose. *Mambo* . . . voodoo priestess.

He nodded. "If anyone has power in LA, it's her." His stare dropped to Lucas. The alpha's eyes had drifted closed. "You hold on, dammit! We got some power coming."

It had just better be enough.

Because if it wasn't, Lucas would die.

The sun had set when they reached the house on Gaines and Hillray. Men and women in white stood along the porch of the long, rambling house, and when the van squealed to a stop, they didn't race forward, but they didn't run away, either. They just turned toward the road. Watched. Waited.

Dane spun in his seat. "You think she'll see us?"

Piers shoved open the back doors. "I'm not giving her a choice."

"There's always a choice, wolf," a deep, masculine voice said. The voice rose and fell with the musical cadence of a Haitian accent.

The owner of that voice—a tall, dark-skinned man—stood just beyond the van. His arms were crossed over his chest. His head was cocked, and his too-knowing eyes were on Lucas. Like the others, he wore white. Loose white pants, white shirt, and even some kind of long, white scarf that had been wound around his neck.

Piers jumped from the van. "We need to see Marie."

The man's gaze drifted to him. "*Mambo* don't want to see you, wolf. After the way you disrespected her last home . . ."

He shrugged. "Take your dead and go. You're not gettin' help here."

But they had to get help. There wasn't another option.

"We were looking for our pack member." It sounded like the words were gritted from between Piers's teeth. "We weren't after the *mambo*, just the vampires."

"But you came on the *mambo*'s land. You came as animals and you attacked when the *mambo* was near."

"Fine. I'm fucking *sorry*, okay? But we need—"

"Please," Sarah whispered because Lucas wasn't moving anymore. Didn't seem to be breathing. "If she can help him— *please.*"

Silence.

Sarah lowered her lips to Lucas's. She pressed her mouth to his. *You're supposed to be the strongest, the most bad-ass. You can't go out like this.*

Anger had her blood heating and her body shaking.

I won't let you go out like this.

She kissed him again. Tasted salt and blood. Then she eased him carefully off her lap. His blood smeared across her clothes, but she didn't care. She held his head carefully, easing him down to the bed of the van. Then Sarah hurried forward, her eyes going to the big brick wall of a Haitian who was between her and—

Marie Dusean. Voodoo priestess extraordinaire. Oh, damn but the stories she'd heard about ladies with power like Marie's . . .

She jumped from the van, and would have fallen, if Piers hadn't caught her so quickly. "Please," she said again, looking up, way up, at the man's face. Now that they were closer, she could see the scars that criss-crossed the right side of his face. "We need her help."

His gaze narrowed on her. "You smell like wolf."

"His blood's on me." Literally, figuratively, every way.

The Haitian's nostrils flared. "Charmer." He sighed out the word and his mouth curved. "Lost little charmer out among the wolves."

"I'm not lost." Not anymore. "I—"

A woman walked up behind the brick wall. A woman with long, braided black hair and skin that seemed to shine under the moon's light. The woman wore white, too. A light, gauzy top and a skirt that barely skimmed the tops of her long legs. And a thin white scarf circled her neck—just like the Haitian's. The woman pointed one slender finger at Sarah. "Marie wants to see her." No Haitian accent from her. Just the soft rolls of the south.

Sarah's shoulders slumped with relief. Okay, seeing Marie was something. If she could see her, talk to her, Sarah was sure she'd get the *mambo* to help.

Sarah brushed by Piers. The woman's fingers wrapped around her wrist. Piers tried to step forward and go with her.

The Haitian shoved a hand against Piers's chest. "Not you, wolf."

Sarah kept her head up as she followed the woman in white. The wooden porch steps creaked beneath her feet, and the light from inside the house—soft, flickering light—seemed to beckon her closer. *Candlelight.* The whole place was lit with—

Sarah almost tripped as she headed into the house. She glanced down quickly at the doorway. Some kind of dark red dirt lined the entranceway.

"The wolf would never have made it past the door," her guide said, her voice soft, but she didn't glance back.

Sarah kept following the other woman, aware of the fierce tension in her shoulders and the blood that was literally on her hands. *Have to hurry.* Because Lucas didn't have much time. Not much time at all.

"Go in there." The woman freed Sarah's wrist and pointed to the white door on the left.

Sarah lifted her hand to knock.

"No, just go in. She's waiting for you."

Sarah's fingers shook a bit when she grasped the doorknob. She twisted it and the door swung inward with a groan.

More candles. Flickering. The scents of jasmine and vanilla hung in the air. And in the far right corner, a woman leaned over an old wooden table. Her long hair—a shade of smoke between black and pure gray—cloaked her features.

"Come in, child," she murmured, her voice rising and falling in the same rhythm as the man. Her native accent. Haiti. Marie Dusean lifted her head and her hair slipped back, revealing a face lined with knowledge and time, a face that was strangely beautiful. Otherworldly. But Marie's eyes . . . those blue eyes were cloudy. Far too cloudy to see.

Cataracts? Was that—

"I can see everything I need to see," Marie told her. "Far more than you." Her gnarled fingers lifted and she beckoned Sarah closer. An empty seat waited on the other side of the table.

Sarah walked forward slowly as her gaze searched the shadows. The wooden floor creaked beneath her.

"Only us," Marie told her. "No more eyes . . . no more ears . . ."

Sarah's fingers slid over the back of the chair. "I have a friend outside. He needs your help."

Those blank eyes stared up at her and a faint smile curved Marie's lips. A smile that was the faintest bit cruel. "What makes you think I'd want to help the wolf?"

Her palms were sweating. "Because he'll die if you don't."

Marie's hands slapped against the wooden table top. "Might anyway."

No.

Marie leaned forward. "Matters so much to you, does he?"

Sarah eased around the chair and sat, hard, her knees weak. Was Marie reading her mind? "He saved me. I can't let him die."

"Can't stop Death." A shrug. "Not when he's coming." Those eyes were just eerie as they locked on her. "He's coming for you, charmer."

First the Haitian, now the *mambo*. "How did you know I was—"

"Special . . . aren't you?" The thin shawl around Marie's shoulders slipped a bit. "Better be careful. Some would kill for a little power."

"I'm just here about Lucas." She reached forward, scared but determined, and caught the *mambo*'s hands in hers. *"Please. I'll do anything."*

Marie laughed and the hollow sound chilled Sarah. "How badly do you want him?"

The hair on her nape rose.

"What would you trade?" Marie pressed.

Sarah hesitated.

"Um . . . what I thought. Not yet ready to give your life for his, are you?"

The woman was jerking her around. Ancient or not, this Marie was as sharp as they came. "*Can* you save him?" Maybe she hadn't been asking the right questions.

"I can do anything." Not boasting. Sounded just like Marie was stating a fact.

"Can you—"

"Two ways . . . Stop him before Death comes . . ." Her eyes slit a bit. "Drag him back after. But, you might not like how he comes back."

Oh, hell, no, the woman had not just offered to make Lucas into what—a freaking zombie?

"Don't look so shocked, child. Wouldn't be the first time, wouldn't be the last." Her gaze trekked to the window on the right. "Sometimes folks can't let go." A hint of sadness colored the words.

"I don't want him dead. I want you to *save him.*"

Marie's stare turned back to her. "What will you give?"

Dammit. Time was running out. *For Lucas? "Everything."*

A small nod and some of the lines smoothed from Marie's forehead. The woman almost looked . . . satisfied. "Good. But it won't take all that."

Sarah didn't believe her.

"I'll have Maxime bring in your man."

Sarah leapt to her feet. "And you'll really be able to save him? He's got silver in his blood. The bullets fragmented and—"

"Already know that." The thin shawl slipped down her shoulders another few inches. "If your man didn't have such a strong spirit, Death would already have him." Those cloudy eyes closed. "Felt his spirit long ago, when he came after my Maya. Knew he was coming, long before he set foot on my land."

Maya. The name clicked. Maya Black was a vampire in LA. Powerful, kick-ass, and rumored to be mated to an equally powerful shifter.

"Strong spirit," the mambo whispered again. "Spirit wants you, charmer. He's not making this easy."

No, Lucas wouldn't.

Marie's eyes opened and fixed unerringly on her. "If Death takes him, you want me to bring him back?"

Her breath caught in her throat, almost choking her.

"How bad you want him to stay with you?" Marie pressed, blind eyes watching too closely.

"I don't—" Back from the dead? This was too beyond her experience. *You can't do that.* That was her instinctual response. No, that was the way she'd been raised to think. But the truth was . . . vampires bit their prey, demons played with fire, and she controlled wolves. "I just want him to live," she whispered.

"Maybe he will." Marie rose, her long hair fluttering around her. "Maybe he won't." Her smile was gone. "Either way, I'll be collecting what's owed to me."

A chill slipped down Sarah's spine. "Save him."

Marie's head inclined. "But there's no saving everyone. No matter how you fight, Death will still be there." The candles flickered. Marie's hands fisted. "When the time comes, tell her to let go."

What? "Um, tell who?"

But Marie just smiled her small, tight smile.

The candles flickered again, a wild, desperate dance, and the shadows in the room lengthened as Marie began to chant.

"This is a bad idea," Dane said, his shoulders brushing Piers's as they faced off against the men and women blocking the entrance to Marie Dusean's house.

"It's the only idea I had," Piers growled back at him.

Their claws were out. Claws and teeth were the only weapons they had. Normally, that would be enough, but with Marie—

If half the stories floating around about her were true, claws and teeth wouldn't even scratch her skin.

Dane threw a glance over his shoulder. Lucas barely seemed to breathe. The stench of silver burned Dane's nose. Dammit, this was *not* the way the alpha should have been taken out. Not for—

Me.

His breath hissed out. "He shouldn't have made the trade."

"Wasn't him," Piers said, not looking his way. Piers had locked his gaze on the big Haitian with the seen-the-devil eyes. "Sarah went for the trade."

Grunts reached his ears. Frantic, wild. Muffled. He turned his head and caught the golden gaze glaring at him. *Her.* Hell. He couldn't just leave her bound and gagged. Not forever.

When hell had come calling at that coyote slaughterhouse, he'd grabbed the woman. *Human.* As far as he could figure, anyway. He'd heard the screams of the coyotes, smelled the blood, and knew that a war had broken out. He'd tossed the blonde over his shoulder and held tight as he fought his way out of that nightmare. He'd gotten away, mostly in one piece. And he'd taken her with him.

He'd thought they might get information from her. Thought they might be able to use her.

Her head twisted toward the line of men and women in white, and she mumbled something behind the gag.

Hell. He leaned into the van and yanked out her gag.

"Are you crazy?" she whispered. "Do you know where we are?"

"He's dying." That was all that needed to be said. If they had to trade with the devil, so be it.

She gulped. "Marie won't help you for free. There's *always* a price."

"Then we'll pay it."

"Even if she wants wolf pelts?"

His fingers brushed her delicate jaw. "He's not dying."

Her gaze seemed to bore into him. "You're playing with some serious fire."

"For a human, you are, too."

He caught the flicker of her lashes. Ah . . .

"Bring the wolf." The voice boomed into the night.

Dane spun back around. The big Haitian had stepped forward. "Marie will take him."

He caught sight of Sarah's hair then, blowing in the breeze. A breeze, shit—where had that come from?

Sarah ran toward him, her face stark white. "She'll help us!"

Hot damn.

"Piers, Dane, bring him in!"

Carefully, he and Piers lifted Lucas. The alpha's head hung limply and his eyes never opened.

They'd taken four steps when he heard the crunch of gravel. Dane glanced back. The woman—still didn't know her name—was outside of the van, and the ropes were at her feet.

"Don't go in there!" She stared at the line of white with narrowed eyes. "Don't trade with her—just let him go!"

She meant let him die.

No.

She shook her head and backed away slowly. "You already have enough enemies after you. Do you really need more?"

"Get out of here, Karen," Sarah said. "This call isn't yours to make."

What the hell? Sarah *knew* her?

Karen turned around and ran into the night.

Dane's shoulders stiffened as they approached the house. Piers was heading in first, his hold on Lucas's feet and—

Piers froze. No, not just froze. The guy seemed to slam into some kind of brick wall.

"He can't enter." The Haitian. He pushed Piers out of the way and grabbed Lucas's feet. "Too much of the beast inside. Wanting to break free, is he?"

Piers growled. "I'm not letting you take—"

"You know you're losing control." A woman's voice rang out, lifting and rolling like the man's. "How long will it be . . ." A small woman appeared, skin dark, her eyes blue—blind. *Marie Dusean.* "Before you lose yourself?"

The breeze was back, stronger now.

Marie turned her stare onto Dane. "You like the pain too much now." She shook her head. "You won't make it inside either. Not with the demon on your back."

What the hell?

"You'll have a choice," she whispered to him. "Go back to the shadows and the screams, Dane, or—"

Another man tried to shoulder him out of the way. His hold tightened on Lucas.

"He's dying," Sarah whispered, her hands wrapping around his. "Just let her take him."

That blind stare of Marie's was still on him. "Screams or sacrifice, Dane. Choose."

He let Lucas go.

Marie's men took Lucas inside. Sarah hurried after them. Fuck this, he was going, too. Dane barreled forward—

And seemed to slam into the same invisible wall that Piers had hit.

"Evil can't cross my line," Marie's voice floated back to him.

Line? He looked up, down—and saw the line of red dust. And wait—had she said evil? Dane glanced at Piers. Since when in the hell were they evil?

Too much of the beast inside.

His fist slammed into nothing, but it sure as shit felt like he'd just punched a solid wall.

They lowered Lucas onto a table. Candles were placed at his feet, his head, and near his bound hands.

"Why are you tying him down?" Sarah asked.

"So he doesn't kill us," the Haitian—Maxime—said quietly.

"He can barely move." Wasn't moving, "Why would you need to—"

Marie threw a gray liquid onto Lucas. Her chants filled the room. The clouds left her eyes and the blue sharpened, too bright, glittering . . .

A howl tore from Lucas. He arched up, nearly ripping his binds apart. Silver began to leak from the deep wounds on his body.

"Hold him," Maxime ordered.

Sarah jumped forward. Her hands pressed down on Lucas's chest. His eyes opened, burning as brightly as Marie's, and they locked on her. "*Sarah . . .*" The broken rasp of his voice.

"You're okay," she told him, talking quickly, babbling. "She's getting the silver out, you're going to be fine, you're—"

He sagged back against the table. His eyes still stared up at her, but he—he was gone.

Dead?

"Lucas?"

He didn't move.

Sarah's gaze flew up. Marie had her hands in the air, her chants came now, fast, but low. "What's happening?" Sarah demanded.

Marie kept chanting.

"Dammit!" Sarah tore her hands away from Lucas. "What's—"

The binds snapped, and he surged off the table.

"*Hold him!*" Maxime yelled.

She turned back to him, but Lucas was already changing. The snap and crunch of bones filled her ears. His body convulsed, twisting, heaving, as fur burst over his skin.

"Reach for the beast," Marie said. "Control him."

Sarah took a breath and tried to find a psychic link with his wolf. *Lucas?*

Pain hit her, tearing apart her insides, ripping, burning . . . Sarah fell to the floor.

"Hold him," Marie murmured. "Hold the spirits close, don't let them go."

Spirits. The pain had tears leaking from her eyes. Shifters had two souls, two spirits inside of them. Man and beast. She could feel them both right then. The savage pain of the beast. The fury of the man. Both buffeting her.

Lucas, stay with me.

A small cloud appeared before her mouth, as if she were cold, and suddenly Sarah was shuddering because the temperature in the room seemed to have dropped about fifty degrees.

"*Hold him tighter,*" Marie's voice rose. "*Don't let go!*"

Did she mean hold him psychically? Hold him physically? Sarah forced herself to move, to crawl back to the table. The psychic link had broken because the wolf was gone and only the man remained. She grabbed his arm. Ice cold.

Sarah tried to find his mind, but with the wolf gone, she couldn't connect with him.

"Will you bind to him?" Marie's whisper floated to her.

Sarah glanced up. Maxime was at her side. "What does that mean?"

"If you want him to live, you bind." Marie grabbed her left hand. Stretched it out and turned her wrist up. "Do you bind?"

If it meant Lucas lived, then . . . "Y-yes."

Maxime yanked out a knife and slashed her exposed flesh. Sarah didn't even have enough breath to scream right then.

"He lives . . . that's what you want?"

Why the hell was Marie asking that? Wasn't it obvious? "Yes!"

"You live, he lives . . ."

Marie's fingers smeared the blood over Sarah's arm. Then the *mambo* lifted her blood-stained fingers into the air and seemed to paint letters. "He dies . . ."

No!

The bright blue of Marie's eyes began to fade. "Then you die."

All of the candles sputtered out. The darkness swept over her, and the last sound Sarah heard was the growl of a wolf.

The figures in white slowly filed out of the dark house. Marie led the line, her hair a veil around her face. Dane tensed when he saw her. He could almost feel the power crackling in the air around her.

"Did he make it?" Piers voiced his obvious fear.

Marie stopped and spared him a glance. "Death wanted him."

Fuck. Lucas had pulled his ass right out of hell before and he'd let the alpha . . .

"But your wolf fought back." Her eyes looked right through them. "Had to bind the souls. Life and death will follow, but for now . . . they live."

They? The wolf and the man?

Marie shook her head. "He has a weakness. One that could destroy him. Sometimes . . ." She waved her hand in the air, and the big Haitian at her back stumbled, then seemed to topple onto the porch. "We just delay Death. We don't stop him."

The Haitian was on the ground now. Not moving. Eyes wide open.

"What the hell did you do to him?" Dane asked, voice tight.

The delicate woman that he'd seen before hit the ground next. Her braided hair spread behind her like a halo.

Shit. It looked like the *mambo* was killing her own people. Dane's claws burst through his skin.

"Easy, wolf." Marie's head lowered as she stared at the man. Then the woman. "They did their service to me, so I was keeping my end of the deal." Her hand hovered over the Haitian. "I didn't raise them, but I am setting them free."

The Haitian's body stiffened as a fast rigor set in, the way it usually did when a vampire got staked. But wait, this guy wasn't a vamp. Dane hadn't caught the vamp scent on him.

But now the scent of death and decay—several days old— hung in the air.

Marie's head lifted. "You'll find them inside. Watch over them until dawn. Be ready for the betrayal and the choice, Dane."

Piers was staring at the woman with the braided hair. Her body had tensed with rigor as well. The woman who'd been walking around seconds ago now looked like a corpse. "*Sonofabitch,*" Piers whispered. "What was she? A damn zombie?"

Marie didn't look at Piers. "Remember what I say," she told Dane. "*Screams and pain or sacrifice.*"

Hell of a choice.

"And you're not the only one who'll make it." She turned away. Walked slowly down the porch and across the yard. Her attendants—the ones still alive, anyway—followed close behind her.

Dane didn't speak until the group had cleared the porch.

"*What the fuck?*" Piers grabbed his arm. "Is Lucas alive or—" His hand jerked toward the dead bodies. "Or is he like these poor bastards?"

Like puppets on a string—with a string that could be cut any moment. Because he'd heard about cases like this, and Piers had been right . . . *zombies.* Or, as close as reality could come to the zombie nightmare.

Dane sucked in a breath and tasted death. "He's alive." Because he had a sick feeling in his gut. One that told him ex- actly what Marie had done to Lucas.

Weakness.

He crept toward the Haitian's body. Other than his skin already taking on a chalky appearance, he *looked* unharmed. How had he died? How had—

Dane's eye narrowed on the white scarf around his neck. Both the Haitian and the woman had the scarves. Dane's fingers lifted and latched onto the soft fabric of the scarf. He tugged lightly . . . *shit.*

The man's throat had been ripped open. The scarf had hid the wound, but—*ripped open.*

"One of ours?" Piers asked from behind him.

Dane's claws hovered over the wounds. "Shifter . . . can't say for sure if it was wolf." But his gut told him it was. He glanced up at Piers. "If a wolf killed her man, why would she—"

"You sure she saved him?" Piers charged for the door. Dane expected him to slam into that invisible wall again, but Piers ran right inside. Dane followed him, rushing forward. His shoes brushed against the loose dirt near the door. The line he'd noticed before. But now, a huge chunk of that dirt had been cleared away. Like a path had been opened.

The hair on his nape rose but Dane kept going. Lucas was in there, and he'd damn well better not be the living dead.

"Here!" Piers's shout had him turning to the left. The candles were sputtering out, but his shifter vision let him see clearly. He hurried down the hallway, darted into the room, and saw them on the table.

Blood pooled beneath them. Lucas was on the table, Sarah on top of him. Her hair covered his face, and her arms hung limply, her fingertips nearly brushing that pool of blood.

They looked dead but he could hear—

Thump. Thump.

Their hearts. Beating in near perfect time with each other. *He has a weakness.*

"Let's get them out of here," Piers muttered. "This place, man, it's creeping me out."

Dane hurried forward and reached for Sarah. He pulled

her up against him, and her head sagged forward. The woman was *out*. Lucas was in no better shape. His eyes didn't open when Piers shook him. His slow breathing didn't change. But the gaping wounds on his stomach appeared smaller.

Piers inhaled. "You smell that?" He looked down at the bloody floor. "*Silver.*"

No mistaking that metallic scent. "Looks like Marie got it out of him." The relief was obvious in his voice. He hefted Sarah higher against his chest. They needed to leave. Marie had said Lucas and Sarah would be weak until dawn.

Piers wrapped one of Lucas's arms around his neck and lifted the alpha.

"I can . . . walk . . ." Lucas's faint growl, but he didn't open his eyes.

Piers froze. "Alpha, you back?"

A grim nod. His eyes were still closed.

"Damn man!" Piers burst out. "You scared the hell out of us! We thought you were dead when that silver got—"

"I was." His eyes opened now, faded blue. For an instant, his eyes looked just like Marie's. Then he blinked and the color deepened a bit. Became more like Lucas.

Piers's eyes widened. "You . . . what?"

"Ask me . . . about it . . . another time . . ." His eyelids began to sag. "Now let's get . . . out . . ."

That sounded like one fine plan to Dane. He tightened his hold on Sarah—her eyes were still closed, her heart still drumming slowly—and hurried out of that dark room. When they hit the porch, the two bodies were gone, as if they'd never been there.

The night was quiet. Too quiet. They climbed into the van. Lucas looked pale, but he was *with* them, dammit. And as soon as the alpha got settled into the back of the van, Lucas reached for Sarah.

"What are we going to do with her?" Piers wanted to know.

Dane gunned the engine.

"Keep her." Lucas's quiet response. Dane glanced in the

mirror and saw Lucas gently brushing back Sarah's hair. The alpha? Gentle? What. The. Hell.

"But we can't trust her. After tonight, after what happened . . ." Piers heaved out a breath. "Man, I've got to tell you what she—"

"Later . . . Everything . . . later."

Piers's teeth snapped together but he gave a fast nod. A nod Lucas didn't see. The alpha's eyes had closed again.

Dane shoved the gas pedal down to the floor as he raced away from the *mambo*'s house. He didn't think they'd be followed by Marie's men, but he didn't want to take any chances.

They'd have to watch out for the *mambo* until she collected her pound of flesh. Spells never came cheap. He knew. He'd sure bled for plenty over the years.

"Caleb." Lucas's voice rasped and Dane realized the alpha wasn't out completely, not yet.

Dane's gaze met Piers's in the rearview mirror.

"He's . . . dead," Lucas said.

Maybe. "We don't know for sure what happened to him. Our priority was gettin' you out, we didn't—"

"*No.*" Said with more heat. "To us, *dead*. If you see him . . . again . . ."

Caleb. A man who'd been like a brother to him for ten years. A wolf who'd attacked their alpha with fangs and claws.

Dane's fingers squeezed the steering wheel so tightly his knuckles turned white.

"Send someone . . . back for his body . . ." The alpha's breath heaved out. "If he . . . lives . . . I want him brought to the pack." A growl built in his throat. "Trial by pack."

Oh, shit. That meant a fight to the death.

How the hell had this happened? Dane's jaw locked. All these years, and he'd never known a traitor stood right next to him.

Chapter 12

Sarah awoke to the feel of rough fingertips sliding down her arm. She gasped, jerked, and a hand closed over her wrist. A light pain hit her at the touch—the flesh sensitive— and her eyes flew open.

She found herself staring into intense blue eyes. *Lucas.*

Sarah didn't realize she'd murmured his name until his lips kicked up in a faint smile. The light of dawn surrounded him. "Not dead yet, babe."

And she was so very grateful for that fact.

His fingers slid over the inside of her wrist. Her breath hissed out.

His gaze dropped to the jagged wound, a wound that had healed so much. Too much. "What happened?"

She sat up, and when the cold air hit her chest, she realized she was naked. Sarah snatched up the sheet with her right hand, feeling vulnerable. Nervous. Time for him to know everything. "I-I made a trade with a voodoo priestess."

He didn't blink. "What did you trade?"

Everything. "I don't really know . . . Marie will—"

"How'd you know to visit Marie Dusean?" he asked, his thumb still caressing her flesh.

Sarah bit her lip. "*I* didn't know—we just needed magic. It was the only thing that would save you. Piers—*he* knew how to find her."

"*Sonofabitch.*"

"You were dying! There wasn't a choice." Her gaze dropped to his stomach. He was fully healed. The only sign of his ordeal was a raised line on his stomach. Shifter healing, got to love it. "The silver was destroying you."

"No, it was burning me. Fucking burning me alive." His fingers fell away. "You don't know what you've done, do you?"

Saved your ass.

"If Marie cut you, she used your blood in a spell. She *did* something to you, Sarah." He shook his head. "I don't know what. I can't remember a damn thing, but she's got power over you now. Power over you and power over me." His eyes narrowed. "Marie is a very dangerous woman."

"She's also the woman who saved your life." The sheet seemed cool against her flesh. Lucas's touch had been red-hot. "When she calls me, I'll pay my debt."

"No matter what? Marie's a woman used to the shadows. Life and death . . ." A rough laugh broke from him. "They don't always have meaning for her."

She stared at him. Bright eyes. Strong body. *Alive.* "They do for me."

The mattress dipped beneath his weight as he closed in on her. His hands came down on either side of Sarah, caging her. "You've been keeping secrets, sweet Sarah."

Oh, crap, this was it. "Lucas . . ."

His lips brushed hers, stealing her breath. She wanted to press into him. To take his mouth, to take the pleasure.

But he'd already pulled away. "How many lies have you told me?"

The warmth chased from her skin. "I've told you the truth about myself. I'm a charmer, just like I said, I'm—"

"Fuck." Bit off. His eyes glittered at her. "Right now I don't give a shit what you are or who you work for." His hands caught her shoulders. "I should . . . but now, I just want you." Then his mouth took hers, hard and deep, the way she'd wanted.

Sarah gasped into his mouth, her heart thundering. Her

tongue met his and the need, that reckless want built in her. A fierce desire to match his.

They were both already naked. The sheet was a thin barrier, one that he yanked out of the way, then his hot flesh was on hers. Strong, muscled. She wanted to touch him, wanted to make certain he was alive and safe—

But he pushed her back, easing her down onto the mattress. His mouth tore from hers and he licked his way down her throat.

He'd almost died.

He bit her collarbone. A light nip. "That bastard was gunning for us both." His tongue caressed her wound. His hands traced down her body. Lucas's fingers cupped her breasts, made the nipples ache for his touch. His tongue.

"The last thing I saw . . ." Now his mouth was near her breast, and his breath feathered over the sensitive flesh. "Was you."

Her hands caught his shoulders. Her nails dug into the skin. "You were leaving me." The accusation slipped from her.

He pushed her legs apart. Settled his hips against her. "No damn chance."

He took her breast into his mouth. Sucked and licked and the need heated her blood.

"You . . . ah, Lucas!" She was wet for him, already. And he was hard for her. The length of his cock pushed against her sex, not entering her, not yet. "You . . . scared me." An admission that cost her, but the words were true. When he'd been slipping away, she'd been terrified. Not because her protector was gone. Not because she'd have to face Rafe alone. *But because I was losing Lucas.*

He pressed a hot kiss to the curve of her belly. "I heard you." He glanced up at her, his dark hair tousled, lines of lust etched on his face. Lust and . . . fury? "I heard you calling me in hell."

His fingers curled over her thighs. "Don't worry. I'm not leaving you."

Then he put his mouth on her sex. His tongue brushed over her folds, tasted her, then drove deep. Sarah's body jolted as pleasure flooded through her. His thumb pressed on her clit, thrumming the nub, and she buried her fingers in his thick hair. "*Lucas!*"

He didn't ease up. Just kept taking and stroking and—*oh, damn his tongue*—she came against his mouth.

He licked her while she came. Then he rose above her. His eyes watched her every move.

One thrust sent him balls-deep into her. The ripples from her climax still shivered through her and her sex squeezed him.

Then he withdrew. Drove deep. She wrapped her legs around him and let her nails sink into his skin.

Her hips arched toward him. Faster, faster. Harder. His gaze burned into hers. Strength and fury. Life. Not the cold whisper of death she'd felt in the dark hours of night.

Life.

Lucas.

The climax hit her, stealing her breath, and Sarah opened her mouth to scream. Lucas kissed her, thrusting his tongue into her mouth just as he plunged into her body. He erupted inside of her, his body shuddering against hers. She held him as tight as she could with arms, hands, and legs, not wanting to let him go. Not wanting the pleasure to end.

The rasps of their breath filled the air. His heartbeat drummed against her, and the beat as fast and wild as her own. After a moment, his head lifted slowly, and he stared down at her with a gaze she couldn't read.

Sarah licked her lips and tasted him. "Lucas . . ."

"Are you FBI?"

Not the sweet, after-sex words she'd hoped to hear.

He withdrew from her body, a long, sensual glide of flesh that had aftershocks trembling through her.

"Are you FBI, Sarah?"

No way this was going to end well. Naked, sated, she stared up at Lucas and gave him the truth. "I was."

*   *   *

Marie Dusean stared out of her window, watching the sun rise over the sky, its fingers already like blood on the day. Her body ached. Too many years. Too many lost lives. Too many souls that called to her.

She stared at the sun and knew what would come for her. But it was okay. Marie feared no man. She didn't fear Death, either. Why fear what you controlled?

But she would regret. She would miss.

Belle fille. She'd miss the girl so.

Her guards were leaving. Drifting away with the daylight. What was the point in them staying? More bloodshed? No. Enough of hers had died already. She wouldn't lose more souls.

She stared at the sun and waited.

"Fuck." Lucas rolled out of the bed. He stalked forward and grabbed a pair of jeans. "You *were* playing me. You think I don't know about the Feds and their damn extermination list?" He shook his head. "I've been on that list since I was sixteen."

"You're not on the list anymore." She could give him that, at least.

He whirled on her.

Okay, maybe that hadn't been the right thing to say.

"You were sent to take down the wolves." Not a question. His hands clenched into fists. The jeans hung low on his hips. His body tightened with fury. "That bastard was right, you were sent—"

"A year ago, we found the first body." She wouldn't talk about death and hell while she was naked. Sarah didn't know where her clothes were or who'd taken them, so she rose from the bed slowly, trying to hide the quiver in her knees. Her body still ached from the sex, but she wouldn't show that, either. She grabbed the sheet, wrapped it around her, toga-style, then faced him.

His brows had shot down low. "Body?"

"In Arizona. A man. The poor guy's throat had been ripped out. At first, we thought it was just a random killing, but then the other body turned up. A month later, just when the full moon rose again." Maybe the words came out too fast, but she needed to tell him everything. If he told her to walk, she would, but it was time she revealed all the secrets she'd been carrying. "The local papers started dubbing the killer as The Werewolf."

"Shit."

Right. "The *Other* world doesn't need attention like that." Her job had been to make sure no paranormals attracted that kind of heat. A low profile equaled humans and paranormals who continued to exist semi-peacefully together. A big supernatural coming out party—well, that equaled hell. Humans were too biased against their own kind. No way would they all take to monsters with open arms.

His shoulders rolled. "A shifter was killing?"

"Killing *only* humans. Every month, he left another body." Those dead haunted her. "Our crime-scene guys measured the cuts, found trace evidence on the victims and we *knew* we were after a wolf shifter." At first, the crime-scene guy had thought he'd found dog hair on one of the vics. That had been the evidence they needed. Not dog hair. Close, but . . . "We thought a Lone was hunting."

Lones were the wolves who'd been forced out of the relative safety of the pack. The wolves who'd be most likely to have a psychotic breakdown. They were the ones with the sharpest blood hunger, the fiercest rage. Their beasts were too strong, they needed—

"I was Lone for six years."

She knew that. "But now you're alpha." The only Lone who'd ever come back. That was one of the many reasons he'd been watched by the FBI.

"I'm alpha only because I clawed and bit my way through the bodies to claim the pack."

And he had killed. She knew that. Pack justice. Pack was brutal. Wild. But for the wolves, it could be all that kept them sane.

She cleared her throat. *Finish it.* "There weren't any Lones in the area near the kills. There was a pack, but . . . no Lones. So I was sent in." Because she hadn't believed they were truly looking for a Lone. The prey was always different—men, women, all races, all ages. But the location had been centered around Fallen, Arizona. Right around the home of Rafe's pack.

He laughed. A rough, bitter sound. "Let me guess. When you went into the pack, no one knew you were a charmer. You went in, spied in their minds, and tried to find your killer."

That had been what Rafe wanted him to believe. *She came into my pack, seduced me, used me, because her mission was to take down my wolves.*

Rafe was a very good liar.

"Rafe knew exactly who and what I was." How else would she have gotten into the pack? "Rafe knew that I was a charmer, and he wanted to use my power. He came to me." And she'd been so stupid. "He found *me* at the FBI. He knew about the killings and he said he wanted them stopped before his pack was forced to leave the area."

The tension in the room was so thick it seemed to suffocate her. Sarah tried to suck in a deep breath of air.

Lucas just watched her. "I'm guessing Rafe wasn't on the extermination list? Not if he just waltzed into the FBI office."

She shook her head. "He'd—he'd never hurt anyone. Always kept a low profile. He'd pulled together his own pack, and he—"

Lucas lifted a hand, stopping her. "Right. Got it. The fucking upstanding citizen came to you because he wanted the killings stopped."

He really had seemed upstanding, at first.

"How long was it," Lucas asked. "Before you found out Rafe was behind the kills?"

Too long.

* * *

The wild, musky scent of the wolf teased Marie's nose. She pulled her shawl closer. She was always cold, even in the summer. Death stood too close to her.

She didn't look back over her shoulder. Just kept staring at the sun. Not so bloody anymore. Almost . . . beautiful. Parts of the world were rather nice to look at.

Others weren't. She'd seen it all in her ninety-three years. War. Famine. Hope.

Horror.

Time to let it all go.

She began to chant softly, whispering so carefully. She'd learned the words at her mother's knee. Had passed them down to her darling Carline, only to see her only daughter die at the hands of a vampire.

Vengeance had come.

Vengeance always came.

"Rafe had taken a new wolf into his pack. A guy, barely eighteen, named Sean Walker." Wide smile, dark eyes—his image flashed before her. He'd seemed so nice, so *normal*, then he'd shifted into a wolf and she'd caught the darkness in his mind. Seen the flash of bodies and the pool of red. "He'd been making the kills."

"The guy *knew* you were a charmer and he let you close enough to see his thoughts?" Doubt hung heavy in Lucas's voice.

"Rafe—Rafe brought me in as his companion, he didn't tell the others—"

His eyes glittered. "That was your cover?"

Being Rafe's lover. A lie that had become truth. Her chin lifted. She wouldn't apologize. She'd made a mistake—like Lucas's hands were lily-white. "Sean didn't know," she said instead. "All of the pack changed around me at some point. Sean—when he shifted, *I knew.*"

"And what did you do?"

Her lashes lowered. "I reported to my boss at the FBI. Special Agent Anthony Miller is the leader of our task force. I told him, and then he told Rafe." She'd followed the chain of command, thinking it meant something.

But Miller had already known how Rafe would deal with Sean . . .

"Pack justice."

"Yes." She hadn't realized how brutal or how swift it would be. Two wolves, fighting to the death. But no news coverage. No nosey reporters to deal with. Just a quiet end for a murderer—at least, that's what Anthony had thought he'd get. "Rafe . . . Rafe killed Sean."

The FBI had believed the murders were over then. Six dead. Peace for the victims, finally.

"Then you and Rafe got close." She could easily hear the fury underscoring Lucas's words.

Fury and . . . jealousy.

For a moment, her lashes lowered. Rafe had understood her. Seemed to, anyway. After years of being on the outside, not having anyone who understood other than her grandmother, he'd been a temptation for her.

Sarah forced herself to meet Lucas's gaze. She'd kept a lot from him, afraid he wouldn't help her fight Rafe. *Trust has to start somewhere.*

She was already in too deep with Lucas. She'd realized that when his blood covered her and his eyes wouldn't open. The terror had almost choked her.

No going back now. "I never knew my father. He cut out of town long before I was born. And my mother wasn't a charmer. Or, if she was, she never found an animal that connected with her. She didn't like—"

Monsters.

Sarah cleared her throat. She wouldn't say that because Lucas *wasn't* a monster. "My mother wanted me to be normal." Her shoulders lifted, then fell. "The problem was that I never felt normal." The little house in suburbia hadn't been her.

"When I was six," she told him, her voice quiet, "I took a

field trip to the zoo." It had been her first visit to see the animals. So many animals. So many cages. "When the wolves started talking to me, I thought everyone could hear them." But her friends had laughed at her. Her teacher just said she had a vivid imagination.

And the wolves had kept talking.

Sarah swallowed. "As soon as I got off the bus that afternoon, I told my mom. The wolves had made me feel so good—like they *knew* me. I told my mom," she said again, "because I was sure she'd believe me." *The wolves liked me, mommy. I could hear them whispering in my head. They'd—*

Her mom had paled as she yanked Sarah away from the bus and away from the other laughing kids.

Don't ever talk about the wolves again, Sarah! Do you hear me? Don't mention them, and Dear God, stay away from them.

The floor groaned beneath his feet. "I'm guessing she didn't believe you."

"Belief wasn't the problem. My mom knew about the *Other*, she just wanted her daughter to be normal." And really, she knew now that her mother hadn't been asking for so much.

"Normal's over-rated," he said, watching her closely. Did he realize how important this was? She'd never told anyone else about her past.

Just Lucas.

You can trust me.

"I couldn't stay away from the wolves. No, I didn't *want* to stay away. I snuck back to see them. Stole money from my mom and took one of the city buses back to the zoo." She'd been terrified the whole trip, but she'd needed to see the wolves once more because echoes of their voices kept playing in her head. They'd been magic, and she'd wanted that magic so badly.

"What did your mother do?"

She blew out a hard sigh. "I scared her to death. I know I did." *Now.* "She found me there. I was standing in front of the wolves." She could still remember the cold steel of the metal railing. Her fingers had wrapped around it so tightly as she stared at the three wolves who'd come to talk to her.

Mommy, the wolves like me! They don't like being here, though, but they like me! She'd turned to her mom, smiling, not even worrying that her mother would be angry with her for sneaking away. *They say they want to leave. They don't like it when the people come and watch, they want to run, to—*

"When she pulled me away from the wolves, she was crying." It had been the first time she'd ever seen her mother cry. "Then the wolves started howling, snarling, trying to get out—"

Lucas pulled her against his chest. Just . . . held her and it felt so good. But, then, Lucas had seemed right from that first moment, even when *he* was the one in the cage. "They were trying to defend you."

"They got tranqed." She'd never forget their cries as the darts hit them. *Please, mom, stop them! Don't let the men hurt the wolves. The wolves need me—*

Never say that again, Sarah Belle King! Never! Her mother had run faster. Run so fast as she yanked Sarah away from the wolves.

Screams and howls had followed them as Sarah and her mother ran from the zoo. For months after that, those same screams and howls had filled her nightmares.

Her mother had still been crying when they finally made it out to their old station wagon.

I want the wolves. She'd whispered that as her mom buckled her into the car with shaking hands.

"After we left . . ." She lifted her head and looked into his eyes. "She said that if I told anyone the wolves talked to me, then someone would come and take me away. She said people would think that I was crazy and that I'd be locked up." *I've seen it before. It's not happening again.* Her mother's tearful words. *Stay away from the wolves.*

"You weren't the first charmer in the family," he guessed, voice gruff, but the hands that held her were so gentle.

"No." Her lips twisted into a wan smile. "A week later, she took me to visit my grandmother." Her visit to see Grandma Belle. "Grandma Belle lived in a big hospital. There were bars on all the windows, and guards who watched everyone too closely."

Do you want to live here? Her mother's question. Sarah had been scared of the men in white uniforms. The men who watched Grandma Belle and the others every moment.

Needles, screams—they'd followed her out of the hospital just like the howls of the wolves had followed her from the zoo.

She pulled away from him. Faced Lucas with her chin up. "After that, I didn't mention wolves to my mother again."

"The world can be too damn hard on those who are different."

He would know.

"I pretended to be normal for years." But she'd never really fit in. "When I was seventeen, my mom died in a car accident. A head-on collision." So fast, so brutal. The other driver had been drinking. He'd slammed into her mother's car when she was driving home from work at the diner.

The normal life she'd wanted so badly had killed her—and Sarah had been left alone.

"Is that when you stopped pretending to be normal?"

She gave a brief nod. "A few years after that . . ." After bouncing around, living on the streets, struggling to survive, "I was arrested for shoplifting." The luckiest break she'd ever caught. "But it turns out the cop who caught me wasn't *normal* either." That had been the beginning. "He got me straight. Gave me direction, told me that I could make a difference in the world."

And then he'd introduced her to Anthony Miller, the FBI's go-to guy for the paranormal.

She licked her lips. *Slipping into the past just sucked.* Too much pain waited there. "When I worked with Rafe . . ." Hell, this had been why she dragged up her past, to make him understand about the other wolf, so there was no stopping now. "He made me feel like I belonged. For the first time, I wasn't an outsider." She'd been weak. Ready to fall. "You know what happened after that."

"When did it end?" he asked, eyes narrowed. "When did you find out—"

"That Rafe was a lying killer?" she finished. "More dead bodies turned up. Only they weren't found near Fallen. They were discovered one state over. And Rafe made a mistake." A deadly one. "He shifted in front of me."

Just once. Rafe learned from his mistakes.

"He shifted and when I touched his mind, I saw the blood." The man she'd been sleeping with—he was the killer she'd sought. "He ordered Sean and the others to attack humans. It was all his idea. His plan. His big game."

That's all it had been. Just a game. A hunting game.

"I think he planned to kill me. I know he did." Those brown eyes had locked on her and a growl broke from his lips. "He charged at me, but—" She stopped, body tensing.

Lucas caught her chin and tipped her head back. "This where you make your other big confession? Where you tell me that you can't just read the minds of wolves, but you can control us, too?"

"No need to confess, is there?" He'd had first-hand experience. "Not when you already know."

"I sure as fuck do." His jaw clenched. "If it hadn't been for your little command in my head, Caleb would be dead."

Because he'd gone right for the other wolf's throat. "We needed to find out why." Was Caleb even still alive? "He was so close to you, we needed—"

"*You controlled me.*" He cut across her words. "Controlled Piers."

Yes.

"Dane?"

She nodded.

His hand fell away. "And what about my brother? He told me he didn't remember launching at Hayden, just flying through the fucking window."

She forced her stare to hold his. "I wanted him to take the coyote out." *Her fault.* She hadn't thought past the fear. "I didn't mean . . . Hayden was coming at me, and I just wanted Jordan to help me."

"To help you," he repeated, the words a dark rumble of sound. "You traded my brother's life for yours?"

"No, I—" Hell, hadn't she? "I'm still not used to it," she whispered. "I didn't even know I could control wolves, not until I stopped Rafe from sinking his teeth into me." *Stop! Get the hell away!* Her wild psychic shout. Rafe had frozen, his eyes wide and startled. Then he'd flown back across the room, like a puppet on a string, snarling and growling the whole time. But he hadn't been able to attack her.

That had been the first time she'd used her power, but not the last. Once she'd realized what she could do, she'd started to practice. To try and control her newfound strength by working on the wolf shifters who crossed her path.

I didn't practice hard enough.

"I never meant to hurt Jordan." Her shoulders sagged. "I didn't mean to hurt anyone."

"I wish I could believe you." His drawl was mocking. "But, babe, you've been lying to me since day one."

Half-truths. White lies. Lies of omission. When had she become so good at deceit? Before or after she joined the FBI? *Before. I lied for years, pretending to be normal. Lying was all I knew.* "I'm a charmer. Rafe wants me dead. He wants you dead. All of that is true. I left the FBI shortly after Sean was killed. I'm not an agent anymore."

"Then why are they covering your ass?"

She knew he was talking about the detective's death. *Damn Rafe.* Sarah exhaled. "I suspect they're covering because they want me back. My ex-boss made contact with me right before I got into town." That was why she'd been late. Miller had held her up when he'd caught her at that gas station. Of course, he'd known exactly where to find her. He'd probably tracked the GPS on her phone.

But Miller hadn't offered protection. Oh, no, because there wasn't a human safe house strong enough to protect her, not from a whole wolf pack. But the FBI had wanted something . . .

"What does he want?" Lucas turned away.

"He wants the killings to stop. Rafe has plans—he's attracting attention, a national manhunt is going to be launched soon if we don't stop him. Everyone will know about The Werewolf. The kills will come faster, the coyotes he has in his pocket will help him. The dead will fill every airwave, every newspaper—"

He glanced back over his shoulder.

"He has plans," she said again softly. "And it doesn't matter what the FBI's motives are, *we* have to stop him. If we don't, he'll just keep killing. He'll come after me, after you, and he'll keep killing."

The floorboards creaked behind Marie. Those soft creaks were the only sounds that the wolf shifter made. Marie didn't jump. She was far too old and experienced for that. Her fingers smoothed over her necklace. The delicate ruby ring hung on the thick chain, always resting close to her heart. "You came faster than I thought," she softly said.

Silence.

She wouldn't look at him. Her eyes were going hazy again, the sun blurring and she liked that. But if she looked at him—she'd see the evil too clearly. And that would *not* be the last sight she had.

"You saved the fucking bastard," he snarled.

"Yes, Rafael, I did." She'd helped him once. Her mistake. But he'd been young, grieving, his father lost to fangs and claws. *Her mistake.*

But he'd crossed her line then. Meant no harm.

It wasn't until after she'd helped him, after she'd given the wolf within strength, that she'd seen the glimmer of darkness. Darkness could hide easily inside a child. She hadn't possessed the will to kill him, not when he was so young.

What if she'd been wrong? Her vision had failed twice in her life.

Once with her daughter, Carline.

She began to rock slowly, back and forth. The cold whispered over her skin. "I know why you killed Maxime and Helene." The poor souls that had come to her. Lost, forced back from the grave. Only dark magic could pull the souls back.

Should have been left at peace. Some people had a hard time letting go.

Carline. Hadn't she been tempted to raise her baby? But her strength lay in another area.

Whereas her belle fille . . . Her grand-daughter Josette had surprised her. Saddened her.

"Good fucking deal for you." More creaks filled the air as he stalked closer. "You couldn't keep me out this time, could you? Guess I'm stronger than your red dust now."

No, not stronger. She'd left the line open. He wouldn't come away from this deed unscathed. Fool.

"You should have let the wolf die, *mambo.*"

That wouldn't have served her purposes. If Simone had died, then the charmer wouldn't owe her.

His fingers rose, and his claws curled over her shoulder. *I won't see him.* But she could feel the press of darkness, those same whispers that had been in the boy, only they were screams now. Screams from all the dead he'd taken.

"Tell me how you brought Simone back. You don't touch the Dark. He should have been a rotting corpse. *Tell me.*"

"I used something you can't understand." Something he'd never grasp. "Sacrifice."

"What? Did you kill a fucking chicken?" His rough laughter grated in her ears.

He dared to mock her? Her faith? Her power?

No one mocked Marie Dusean.

See him.

She turned in his grasp. The fog parted for her, and she saw the monster staring down at her. "Death's comin' for you, boy." Her voice rolled with the promise. "You can beg, you can plead, but in the end . . . he'll have you."

His claws sliced across her throat. Marie didn't feel the pain. She was already gone. Gone into the fog that waited. Welcomed.

He'll have you.

Her necklace fell to the floor, severed by a wolf's claws. The ruby ring slipped off the chain, then became lost in the blood.

Chapter 13

"**W**ill you still help me?" Sarah whispered. "Now that you know I'm—"

"Bait from the Feds?" Lucas finished, voice biting, and he saw her flinch. Dammit, he didn't want to attack her. He wanted to yank her back into his arms, hold her tight but—

Pack law. She'd deceived not just him, but his whole pack. Controlled them. Wolves didn't like being controlled by others.

Might as well be a fucking mental cage to them.

"I told you," Sarah said, voice tight. "I don't work for them anymore."

But he didn't believe her. Sarah's ex-boss had contacted her right before she came to LA, and he was supposed to buy that the guy hadn't brought her back into the fold?

Lucas knew he was on the FBI's extermination list—and he didn't trust those Bureau bastards not to set him up . . . and not to use their perfect bait to do it.

Shit. From the beginning, he'd known she'd held back. He'd known better than to trust her, but damn if he hadn't started to let his guard down for her.

Now that he knew about her past, it made him want her all the more. She'd been so strong, keeping her talents hidden from the world, then struggling through life on her own.

But the pack . . .

Sarah came closer to him. Her hands pressed to his chest. "We want the same thing. To stop Rafe. Once he's dead . . ."

What? She'd slip away? Get out of his life? *No.*

One delicate shoulder lifted. "Then you can tell me to hit the road, okay?"

But what if he couldn't let her go? The woman didn't realize just how thin his control was with her. "You're a dangerous weapon, Sarah King."

Her eyes widened a bit. Such green eyes.

"Tell me . . ." He breathed in her scent. "Are you still lying?"

"No!"

"If you wanted, could you control me right now? Get me to do anything you wanted?"

She licked her lips, a quick flash of pink tongue that made his idiotic cock twitch. *Always want her.* "N-no . . . I told you before. I can't read your thoughts when you're in human form—"

"That's not really the same thing, is it?" He broke through her words. His heart thundered too fast and he knew she felt the wild beat. But when he was close to her, he was wild. *Need more.* "Not talking about reading thoughts. I'm talking about *control.*" He waited a beat. "Can you control me now?"

She shook her head. "No."

"You sure about that, babe? Wouldn't be the first time you were . . . ah . . . a bit unclear with me."

Her hands dropped. "I tried to control Rafe when he was in human form. It didn't work." Anger fueled her own words. "And it's not working now with you, or else you'd be on your knees in front of me, telling me how sorry you are for being a jerk."

One brow lifted. "A jerk?" He'd been called much worse. But the word still drove into his gut. "I'm not the one who's been lying." Odd, that. He usually lied one hell of a lot, but . . . *not to her.*

While she spent all her time lying to him.

"I stayed with you." She spun around, giving him her back. "I made the deal with Marie. I was willing to trade everything—"

His body tensed at that. "Tell me you didn't." He remembered the fire in his gut. The burn that lashed through his organs. *"Tell me you didn't."* He could still feel it—the whisper of cold, of death, sinking into his body.

She threw a glance back over her shoulder. "I agreed to her trade." A rough laugh. "Hell, I don't even know what was happening. You were dying. She was chanting, asking me about binding with you."

No, hell, *no.* "Sarah, did you—"

Her body swung toward him. "Did I what? Fight for your ungrateful self? Yes, I did. I'm not all bad, you know, Lucas. I don't want you dead. I don't want Jordan dead. I just want—"

He lunged forward and grabbed her arms. "Did she bind us?"

Her lips parted. "I—"

A hard rap shook the door.

"Did she?" He gritted, his eyes only on her.

Sarah nodded. "Yes."

And he knew he was fucked.

The door swung open. "Alpha, Caleb's up."

He didn't glance at Dane. He'd known the pack had recovered the wolf. Severely injured, barely alive.

But barely was all they needed.

"He's awake. I don't know how long he's got, though." No emotion filtered through Dane's voice. Not like he was talking about a friend, a pack brother. Oh, yeah, *he damn well was.* The betrayal ate at Lucas.

Dane exhaled on a hard sigh. "He won't make it through the trial by pack."

Lucas was still staring at Sarah. He saw her pale. "You— you would force him to face that?"

A trial by pack. The same method Rafe had used to "eliminate" the threat of Sean. When the pack was attacked, when a wolf crossed the line, the trial was to a wolf's surrender or to his death. If the wolf surrendered—he lived, but would be banished from the pack.

If he fought to the end, either he killed the alpha . . . or died trying.

"Does she go up, too?" Dane asked, voice still flat.

Sarah tried to jerk back. "What? I'm not pack. I get that you guys are pissed over the control thing—but, dammit, I'm not pack!"

"But you came to us for protection. We took you *in*." He didn't let her go. Couldn't. Because she hadn't just deceived him, she'd used, *controlled* the whole pack. And the pack wanted their justice.

He had to give it to them.

"Does she go up?" Dane repeated.

Lucas nodded. The man couldn't make this choice. The alpha had to lead the pack. Protect the pack from all enemies.

Even those from within.

"I'm sorry, Sarah." He was.

"They'll kill me." Were those tears in her eyes? "You'd really let them—" She broke off, shaking her head, sending that thick mane flying. "You'd make love to me and then, not ten minutes later, you'd let them *kill* me?"

Dane's footsteps thudded down the hallway as he left. But he was still close enough to hear every word they said.

Who could he trust these days? Suddenly, Lucas just wasn't sure.

So he didn't speak. A teardrop streaked down Sarah's right cheek. Just one drop because she didn't let the other tears swimming in her eyes fall. "You're really not so different from Rafe, are you?" she whispered.

The fuck he wasn't.

Her shoulders straightened. Her eyes narrowed. "*Your* mistake. You'll regret this, Lucas Simone."

Maybe.

She brushed by him.

When he was sure Sarah was gone, he finally unclenched his fists. His claws were out. They'd dug into his flesh. His blood dripped on the floor.

That wasn't the only blood that would spill. Not even close.

Pack law. It was the only law they had. Human rules didn't mean a shit. They were too easy to break. But pack . . . it was more than skin deep. They all had to follow the law. *All.*

Even the alpha.

She wouldn't let them see her fear. Sarah went into the back courtyard, her steps slow but sure. She kept her chin up and her gaze focused straight ahead. Those wolves wearing the bodies of men wouldn't see how scared she was.

Sure, they could probably *smell* the fear. Sweat trickled down her back as the group closed around her. And she was sure they could hear the frantic beat of her heart.

Didn't matter. She'd stare them down. She'd be ready for what came.

"Easy." Dane's whisper in her ear. His shoulder bumped against her. He was on her right. Piers on her left. Jordan stood in front of her. Two more wolves, she didn't even know who the hell they were, had come up behind her.

"I hear that you've got some secrets," Jordan murmured. The sun beat down on them. They were protected from prying eyes by the thick walls that surrounded the back of the compound. So if they wanted to shift and attack out there as wolves, no one would see.

No one would stop them.

Did I really think I'd be safer here?

"I didn't mean for you to get hurt." Sarah's voice was clear. "I sent the order out to stop him, but I didn't consider the risk to you." She hadn't anticipated the guy would fly through a freaking window. The power of suggestion. Too strong. She'd remember that.

For next time.

Warm, hard fingers curled around her shoulder. Sarah didn't look back. No need. She'd know Lucas's touch anywhere. The bastard.

"Caleb first." His command.

The other wolves eased back.

What? A reprieve for her?

Jordan turned and stalked toward the small guardhouse in the back. The guy didn't even seem to be limping from his injuries today. The power of the wolf. If only she had some of that power right then.

Jordan shoved open the door. Piers went in first. Then Dane. Sarah hung back. Tried to, anyway, but Lucas pushed her forward.

Caleb was on a bed. Michael stood guard near him. Caleb's eyes were open, the smoky stare on her. Blood had dried on his chest and near his mouth. "Little . . . charmer . . ." He murmured. "Still . . . alive, too?"

His voice rasped at her, so weak. But his injuries didn't look that bad. And as a shifter, he should have healed by now.

Lucas stepped in front of her. "Why." An order.

She tried to slide around Lucas. He shoved her back, keeping her away from the injured shifter.

"I fucking trusted you, Caleb. I brought you in when you had *nothing*." Lucas lunged forward and grabbed Caleb, jerking him out of the bed. "Then you turn on me. Try to *kill* me." He shook Caleb, hard. "*Why?*"

Caleb laughed, but Sarah heard the edge of desperation in the sound.

"Why didn't you stop him?" Piers asked her, his breath blowing against her ear. "You can control us—why the hell didn't you just stop him?"

She saw Lucas freeze. He dropped the still-laughing Caleb and turned to lock his glittered eyes on her. "Yes, Sarah . . ." He drew out her name slowly. "Why didn't you stop him?"

"You controlled me easily enough," Piers said.

"Me, too." Disgusted, from Dane.

What? Now they thought she was working with Caleb? With Rafe? Jerks. What did a woman have to do to prove her loyalty? Other than risking her life for them. *Been there, done that.* So she'd lied, more than once. But she'd also fought for their sorry asses, and she'd gone to the damn edge to save Lucas in the *mambo*'s house. "He has a shield," she gritted from between clenched teeth. "I couldn't get past it. I couldn't get to *him.*"

"But you could get to all of us?" Piers pressed.

Now she was getting scared *and* pissed. "With barely a thought."

His eyes slit at that. What? What was he going to do? Force her to face the pack in a life-or-death battle? Already doing that.

Caleb had finally stopped laughing. Now he was wheezing. Wheezing?

"Something's different about him," she said, voice thoughtful, her eyes drifting to Lucas. "I couldn't control his beast."

"Caleb's a hybrid," he said.

"Like Rafe?"

"Not quite." Lucas's gaze watched her so carefully. "Half wolf," Lucas murmured, "and half demon."

Wow.

Silence. The thick, hard silence that pressed down on a woman.

"You . . . knew?" Whispered from Caleb.

"What the fuck?" Snarled from Piers as he lunged forward.

Lucas's hand shoved against Piers's chest as he held him back. "What?" His hand was on Piers but his stare had turned to Caleb. "Did you really think you were so damn special? That you were the only hybrid wolf running around out there?"

No, Sarah had learned of others like him while she'd been at the FBI. There had been one incredibly powerful wolf/demon hybrid in Atlanta who'd almost taken the city to hell a while back.

Caleb's skin paled even more. As she watched, the gray bled away from his eyes until only demon black remained. No more pretending. No more glamour. "You . . . let me in . . . pack . . ."

"So you had demon blood." Lucas shrugged. "At the core, you're wolf." A pause. "Or you were."

Until he'd betrayed the pack.

A demon. That would explain why she hadn't been able to get into Caleb's head. Demons, even the low-level ones, had psychic powers. In the *Other* world, demons were gifted with many powers. Low-level demons, those who ranged on the scale from one to three, could barely work most magic. They could do glamour spells, but little else. But the higher end demons, those with a power scale of seven or higher, those were the guys that humans truly needed to fear. They could make the phrase, "hell on earth" come true.

But was Caleb a low-level demon? Or was he something much, much more powerful?

"Why would you help Rafe?" Sarah asked. "What did he have on you?" Because she knew the way Rafe worked. He loved to go after his prey's weaknesses.

"Not a . . . damn . . . thing . . ." Blood spilled from his lips.

"Why hasn't he shifted?" Sarah pushed back her hair as she glanced at Lucas. "Why hasn't he healed by now?"

"He can't shift," Michael said, stepping forward. "He's tried. Several damn times, but he can't get a full shift."

Caleb screamed them, bucking in the bed as his body twisted and the veins bulged on his arms and chest.

Lucas braced his legs apart. "You're dying."

Caleb's face contorted. "Fucking . . . *know* . . ." Caleb's claws burst from his fingertips, then vanished in an instant, leaving only bloody fingers behind.

"What the hell is this?" Michael grabbed him and pinned him against the bed. Caleb was thrashing, screaming, snarling as he kicked out and arched on the bed.

The guy was acting like he was possessed. Just like she'd seen in an old movie once with . . .

Oh, shit.

"Poison." Her whisper had all eyes on her. All eyes but Caleb's. His black eyes had squeezed closed and bloody tears leaked down his cheeks.

"What?" Lucas crossed to her. "You know what's happening?"

Sarah swallowed. Thanks to the extermination list, she had a very good idea. "He dosed you, didn't he?" There'd been rumors about this particular mix back at the Bureau. And as she'd learned, every rumor held some truth.

Caleb didn't answer. At this point, she wasn't sure he could. His vocal cords would be closing soon. "Body control, vision, speech . . ." That was the order of loss. If the dose was in his body too long . . .

"What the hell is happening, Sarah?" Lucas caught her arms and pulled her close.

"He's dying." That was obvious enough.

"How?"

"Poison. I-I think a special batch made just for demons." All the supernaturals turned on each other at some point. Some feuds went past the skin, down through the bone and the magic. "At the Bureau, there was talk . . . an agent heard that some shifters created a brew a few years back. A mix that could destroy a demon," she swallowed, "from the inside out."

But each demon reacted a little differently to the drug. Demons *always* reacted differently to drugs. With this brew, *if the story was true,* some had died instantly. Some had become comatose. Some had hung on, fighting for weeks, slowly wasting away. Others . . .

They'd just had a few days.

"What is it?"

She licked her lips. "I think it's Angel's Dust."

"Angel Dust?" Piers echoed. "What—PCP? You're telling us that Caleb's strung out on—"

"Here's a little demon lesson for you." Her gaze darted down Caleb's twisting body. His skin was mottling, flashing bright red, then turning pale white. "Demons don't react so well to drugs. Some of them get hooked with one taste, others can OD immediately. Demons and drugs *don't mix.*" Which is why drugs were their deadliest weakness.

Some smart shifters had known that.

"He's not strung out on PCP," she told them slowly, clearly. "It's Angel's Dust, a poison made for demons. The first batch . . . I heard it came from the blood of an angel."

"Bullshit," Dane said instantly.

"Right, werewolf." She didn't glance at him. "Talk about angels and demons has to be bullshit, right? I mean, it's not like you're staring *at* a demon or that you're a *werewolf.*"

Lucas curled his fingers around her arms and lifted her onto her toes. "How do I fix him?"

Here was the tricky part. "Is that what you want? I thought you were going to let him die. Pack justice and all." Yes, her words had bite. Couldn't control that—not when she was so scared and so damn angry. *He'd really let his pack turn on me?*

Lucas's hold tightened a bit. Not enough to hurt. Just enough to let her know his control was thinner than it looked.

"If he dies, he can't tell me what I need to know."

No, and the guy was beyond talking right then. No words were coming from his lips, just blood.

"If it's poison, then there's an antidote, right?" Michael asked, his body rocking forward.

Not always. "He doesn't have a lot of time left."

"Then I need the cure right now."

She shook her head. "It's not that easy. If it's Angel's Dust—"

"You just said it was," Piers fired, voice rough.

Sarah glanced over her shoulder at him. "I said I *thought* it was. It looks like what I've heard about an Angel's Dust poisoning." She didn't want to look back at Caleb, but she forced herself to. *Damn.* Agony etched deep lines into his face. "Never seen a poisoning up close," she admitted.

"Sarah."

She blinked and her gaze zeroed back in on Lucas.

"I need that cure."

If only she had a cure to give him.

"How'd you find out about the Dust?" Dane wanted to know.

"There was an agent . . . he'd been following a series of demon deaths. I saw some of his files at the FBI. Some demons who'd been . . ." *On the list for death.* "They were taken out before the Bureau got to them. The agent on the cases suspected Dust was used. The demons . . . they'd attacked some bear shifters near Yosemite, took their pelts . . ."

"Fuck," Piers snarled.

The absolute insult to a dead shifter—take the pelt before the body shifted back to human form. That left the dead body twisted, malformed. A monster at death's gate.

"He heard about the Dust then, from some warlock named Skye." She'd remembered the warlock. She always remembered names that could help her. But this part . . . "The agent also wrote that once ingested, he didn't know if there *was* a cure for a demon."

No cure, just death.

"But Caleb's not just a demon." Lucas's fingers eased their hold. Caressed with a soft touch. A hard smile curved his lips. "He's also wolf." He turned away from her and stalked toward Caleb's heaving body. "At the core," he said again, "he's wolf."

But the wolf wasn't fighting then, and the demon was dying.

"Time to let the wolf out to play," Lucas announced with a nod. "Get it, Jordan."

Jordan. She'd forgotten he was even there, but when she looked back, Jordan stood in the doorway, a silent shadow. "What do you want him to get?" she asked.

But Jordan was already leaving.

"Shit," Dane whispered. "You're not giving him the Balkans?"

"Damn right."

"He won't be in control!" Dane argued. "He'll just be wolf, he won't—"

"He'll be wolf," Lucas said, "and the wolf can heal."

Balkans. Yes, okay, she knew the geographical area, but what did that have to do with saving the man's life?

"Will he even be able to ingest it?" Piers asked.

"He'll take it," Lucas promised. "Even if I have to shove it down his throat." His blazing eyes turned back to Sarah. "Take her out, Dane."

Her knees locked. "I thought you—"

"You can't control him, Sarah. You said so yourself." Lucas's mouth tightened. "When the shift comes, the beast is going to take over."

"And humans, charmers—they all smell like prey to us," Dane told her quietly.

Prey. Was that really what she was to them? To Lucas?

Jordan came back, shoving open the door. He had a small vial in his hand. Some kind of clear liquid.

"There's a white flower in the Balkans," Dane told her as he guided her back toward the door. "About five hundred years ago, folks believed if you ate that flower, you'd become a werewolf."

Piers and Michael hauled Caleb up. Lucas caught his chin and pried open Caleb's bloody mouth. Then the alpha shoved the open vial past the snarling man's lips.

"They were half-right." Dane's breath blew against her ear. "The flower forced an instant shift in those who carried an animal inside. No stopping it, just fast, full on—"

Lucas threw the vial to the floor. It shattered. "Get her out!"

Caleb's wasn't jerking anymore. He'd gone still. Dead?

Then his bones began to snap. A howl tore from his throat.

"*Get her out!*" Lucas yelled again.

You all smell like prey.

Dane pulled her outside just as another howl shook the small guardhouse.

* * *

"No matter what happens," Lucas snarled, his voice roughening as the beast fought for control of his body. "Caleb doesn't leave this room. He *doesn't* get near Sarah."

Piers still stood as a man, by Lucas's order. Lucas knew how delicate that shifter's control was. Now wasn't the time to test him.

"He won't get by me," Piers vowed.

"Or me." From Jordan.

Good to know, but Lucas didn't plan on letting Caleb get past *him*.

Already, the man's body was gone. The white wolf crouched on the bed, his eyes wild, his fangs bared. Ready to rip and attack at any moment.

Lucas let the change sweep over him. It was such a beautiful pain, savage and brutal, but the power of the beast was a heady addiction. One that had long ago worked under his skin.

He expected an attack from Caleb. It would have been smart for the other wolf to attack while he shifted. But Caleb just stood, body trembling, and watched. Waited.

The fire of the shift began to cool. Lucas stretched in his new body, feeling the pull of muscles, the tensile strength.

He stalked toward the bed—and toward the waiting wolf.

You in there? He sent the question out, searching.

A breeze teased his nose. The scent of grass, of ocean, of . . . Sarah.

The white wolf's nostrils flared and he launched off the bed, heading right for Lucas. Lucas twisted, but didn't let his claws touch Caleb. Not yet.

Poison.

Caleb had been loyal once. Lucas had called him friend. But if he had to, Lucas would kill him. He'd killed other friends before.

But Caleb . . .

Get control, wolf. He snapped out the command in his

mind. There was no mental link that he could find with Caleb. He just touched rage, fear, pain.

Get control, he fired again but the white wolf attacked him. This time, Lucas had to use his teeth. He caught the beast around the neck, held tight, then tossed Caleb across the room.

Not a good fucking way to heal.

The white wolf's ears flattened.

"Lucas, I sure as shit hope you know what you're doing," Piers muttered.

Yeah, he did, too.

The white wolf attacked once more, a hard, driving attack. Lucas met him head on, jaw snapping. He didn't want to kill the other wolf. He needed Caleb to heal. He needed to find out what the hell was happening, but—

They rolled, twisted, and Caleb's claws dug into Lucas's side. He growled at the fiery burst of pain. *Get control, Caleb.* The shift should have pushed some of the poison out of his system, and if the man could just get control of the beast—

Caleb broke away from him and sprang for the door.

" 'Fraid not." Jordan stood before the door, arms crossed. "You're not getting by me."

Lucas jumped onto the white wolf's back and as the snarls and growls burst from them both, the wolves crashed onto the floor.

Dane's shoulders were tense, his attention focused on the guardhouse. Sarah stood behind him, the sounds of battle seeming to echo in her mind. Her body ached because her muscles were locked so tight.

She swallowed and forced herself to speak. "How'd you all find out about the Balkans?" She'd never heard of the plant, and if it could do what they said . . .

Dane didn't glance back at her. "We have our sources, too, Sarah." He exhaled. "We would have tried it on Lucas last night, but he had too much silver in him for it to work. The Balkans can't fight silver."

Her hands fisted.

"You should trust him," Dane said, his voice barely more than a whisper.

Sarah's breath stuck in her throat. "Lucas?" Her brittle laugh blended with the snarls in the air. "He wants to put me up for a pack trial! You both do!"

He still didn't look at her. "You sacrificed for me."

She edged back a step.

"And you could have let Lucas die at Marie's. I know how she works. You didn't have to agree to her trade. You could have just let him die."

"That's not who I am."

Glass shattered. Her gaze flew back to the small, two-room building. Through the broken window, she caught sight of the white wolf, jaws snapping as his eyes blazed at her.

Her left foot lifted.

"Don't back away," Dane snapped. "You know wolves like to chase their prey."

Oh, crap.

She held herself perfectly still.

The wolf vanished.

Silence. Sarah didn't make the mistake of thinking the battle was over. Silence had lied to her too many times before.

So they waited, not moving, as the minutes ticked by. Her heart pounded, her muscles ached, and she waited.

When the door finally opened, and Lucas stood in the entranceway, a pair of faded jeans hanging low on his hips, her breath heaved out.

But she knew the real battle, for her, wasn't over yet.

He came toward her, that bright blue stare on her. Piers and Jordan were at his back.

"Caleb?" Dane called out.

Lucas's head moved in a jerky nod. "He'll make it. He's

out now, but when he comes back to us . . ." A smile, cruel, deadly, lifted his lips. "He'll tell us all we need to know."

She knew the words were a promise.

She also knew the pack was now coming for her. Closing in. *Trial by pack.*

There wasn't any place to run. Like she could run. Dane had been right. The wolves enjoyed the chase far too much.

No, there was nowhere to run. *Surrounded.* The wolves had her trapped.

Dane slipped away, no longer protecting her. He'd left her open to attack. Fine. Not like she'd really expected anything else.

She faced Lucas with her shoulders back and her chin up. "I know how this works."

One black brow rose. "Do you?"

When it came to pack, there might be a few surprises still out there—like the Balkans—but some things, a girl knew. "Trial by pack. Two fight. The alpha and the accused."

The one accused of betrayal. Because only a betrayal could open a pack trial. The alpha was the judge. Death could be the verdict or . . .

He could spare his prey.

"You can't shift." Lucas's voice held an edge of anger.

"Not like that's my fault!" Her head cocked to the right and she gave a shrug. "I guess you'll just have to take me as I am."

"I intend to," he murmured.

Her eyes narrowed.

"If I shift, you'll just control me," he told her.

Damn straight she would. Not like she'd *let* any wolf come for her throat. "Then what do we do?" she demanded. "You don't trust me, you want my blood—"

He moved then, in a flash, catching her arms and hauling her up against him. "Your blood's not what I want," he growled.

Her hands caught his shoulders. Curled over the hot, hard

skin. "Lucas?" She saw the fury in his eyes, but . . . more. Need. Hunger. *For me.*

"You lied to the pack." His voice rang out. Loud and strong. "Controlled us. Risked us."

"I helped you!" She yelled right back. "Doesn't that matter? I went to trade myself for Dane. I fought for you! I didn't—"

"We're not fucking puppets," Piers snapped.

Her gaze collided with his.

"No," Lucas said softly. "We're not."

Sarah swallowed.

"You don't control us," Piers said. "You don't come into our minds, see the hell we carry—"

Because she had seen the darkness there.

"—and control us!"

Dane's shoulders rolled, a fast ripple of movement.

Sarah's gaze darted to the left. Jordan watched her with narrowed eyes.

Oh hell. This wasn't going to end well. Not at all.

"The fight will be in human form," Lucas said, his fingers easing their tight hold on her.

Sarah's heart slammed into her chest. She'd never have a chance if they stayed human. Guess he'd learned from Rafe. Staying human had been Rafe's technique, too. No, he'd like to change a little, to let his claws out.

The better to attack.

Her scars seemed to burn.

Lucas turned his back on her. She felt the move like a slap right in the face.

"The fight's in human form." His voice was flat. "For pack justice." His hands were at his sides now, loose. But those claws were coming out.

She backed up a step.

The hiss of her name had Sarah's head shooting up. Dane stared at her, giving a small negative shake of his head. She froze.

"Wolves want justice. A challenge has been issued." Lucas lifted his hands, those claws gleaming now. "So if you want your justice, *come and fucking get some.*"

What?

His hand flew out, caught hers. Held tight. His stare stayed on the others. "Because no one is gonna touch her, you understand? You want justice, then challenge *me.* I brought her in, and I'm keeping her in." His voice deepened with every word, became more guttural. Hardly man, more animal. "She's pack. And she's *mine.*"

Sarah couldn't move right then. Hell, she could barely breathe. Because what Lucas was doing, for an alpha to declare an outsider to be pack, for him to say—

Mine.

—yeah, it was possessive, barbaric, but . . .

In the wolf world, it was also the equivalent of a marriage ceremony.

"You want justice . . ." His dark voice sent a shiver down her spine. "Dane, Piers, Jordan, and any other wolf lurking in the shadows . . . you want your justice, then you come at me for your pound of flesh."

For an instant, just one tense moment, his gaze locked on her. She saw the wolf looking back at her from the man's eyes. "You come at me," he said again. "Because from now on, I'm standing between her and everyone else."

That was . . . Sarah swallowed. Sweet. Okay, not really sweet, a little brutal and stark but—

"So come on." He pushed her behind him, shielding Sarah with his body. "Let's see which of you gets to bleed first tonight."

Right. Sarah peered around his side. Now he was just talking big. Because the wolves wouldn't actually attack their alpha. They wouldn't—

Piers came at him first. His claws were out, his canines lengthening, and he lunged right for Lucas.

Sarah didn't even have time to scream. Because about two seconds later, Piers was on the ground.

"Next."

She stood on her toes now and glanced over his shoulder.

Dane just smiled. "Alpha, I don't have a problem with your mate."

Wait. Mate. Crap, that's exactly what Lucas had done, though, he'd claimed her in front of his pack.

"She was willing to trade her life for mine." Dane sauntered around Lucas. Came to stand beside Sarah. "I stand where I always stand. With you and now, with her."

That lump in her throat was getting pretty big. So one guy had still wanted her hide. One stood by her side, and her lover—

He was ready to take 'em all down for her.

It looked like her taste in men was definitely improving.

"Jordan?" Lucas still had his claws out.

Piers had risen from the ground. He could charge again, but Lucas didn't seem too worried about that.

What would Jordan do? She'd almost killed him. He would be the one with the most cause for an attack.

"Jordan, I never meant—" She began.

Dane grabbed her arm. "Not right now. Really, *not right now.*"

Lucas's head whipped toward her.

Then she saw Piers and Jordan both spring forward. Both were attacking.

Jordan was coming after his own brother. She'd done this, she'd messed things up, and he was—

Lucas's leg kicked, slamming into Piers's stomach, and just that fast, Piers crashed back to the ground. The alpha's hand flew out, and he caught Jordan right around the throat.

Jordan stared back at him. An almost mirror-image. But . . . less fury on the younger man's face.

"She almost killed me," Jordan said.

Sarah flinched.

Lucas dropped his hand. "Challenge me, but you're not getting to her."

Jordan's gaze turned to her. Gold, deep. "I remember what you said."

She shook her head. She couldn't speak, because right then, she didn't know what to say.

"I was lying in a pool of blood, my bones bursting through my skin, and those coyotes were coming to rip me apart."

Lucas's shoulders stiffened.

But Jordan smiled. "That wasn't the first time Death tried to come for me, but I was sure wondering how the hell I'd get away from him then."

"You nearly didn't." The words slipped out. But she knew just how close he'd come. She could still see those coyotes closing in for the kill.

"I'm the one you want," he said. Voice so quiet she had to strain to hear him.

Lucas stepped forward, his hand rising once again.

"That's what you said." Jordan's lips curved in a crooked grin. "Even as I was bleeding out, I heard you. *'Up here. I'm the one you want.'* And those bastards turned away from me, and they went after you."

Now all eyes were on her. She shoved her hair back. "They *were* after me." He was trying to make it sound like she'd saved him. She'd been the one to make him do the header through the window.

"One human, at least three coyotes." Jordan whistled. "Them aren't very good odds, lady."

"No," Lucas growled. "They're not."

She forced one shoulder to lift and hoped the shrug looked careless. "I like to gamble."

She hated gambling.

"And I was FBI. It's not like I was some kind of defenseless human." She'd had training. Hand-to-hand, weapons—

"When you're a human fighting a shifter, you *are* defenseless." This came from Dane.

But obviously, the guy didn't realize just how devious humans could be. He'd have to watch that weakness.

"You challenged the coyotes and you saved my ass," Jordan drawled. "Not quite even, not yet, but I have a feeling we will be. One day." That grin stretched a bit. "Especially since it looks like you'll be staying with us. Permanently."

Um, now about that—

"*Piers.*" Lucas's voice snapped out. "You gonna keep dicking around or are you gonna attack like you mean it?"

Piers was up again. His green eyes gleamed. "What's the point? We both know you can kick my ass even when you're loaded with silver." His teeth snapped together. Such sharp teeth. "I just wanted to get in a few swings." Then his gaze turned to Sarah and his head inclined. "If she stays out of my head, and I mean *out*, then we have no problem."

"If you shift around me, I'm in." Sarah spoke quickly, because she didn't want any more lies or half-truths with the pack. Not when they were offering her . . . everything.

Home. Safety. Pack.

Pack was forever.

"I get a loud broadcast unless you're shielding, and Caleb's the only wolf who's ever shielded with me." Probably not the best guy to bring up right then.

Piers's eyes narrowed.

"If you shift, I'll be in your head." She glanced around at the men. "This goes for all of you. It will be just like—"

"You're one of us," Lucas finished. "It will be just damn like you're a wolf. So think of her that way because she *is* one of us now." His gaze didn't leave her. "But you don't control us. You don't push your compulsions on my men or me."

Now this she could do. *Try* to do. "Okay."

"Okay?" Piers repeated. "Hell, man, I was hoping for more of an I-swear-on-my-life—"

"I won't push, I won't try to—" Sarah stopped talking because, quite suddenly, the wolves weren't focused on her anymore. They'd turned as one toward the main house, faces intent, noses—twitching?

"*Vampire,*" Jordan breathed and there was hate in the word. Yeah, with his particular history, who could blame the guy?

But wait, *vampire*. Sarah's mouth got very dry, very fast. Vamps were her least favorite of all the supernaturals. They liked to play with their food way too much for her taste.

"Sulfur," Piers muttered. "It's in the air . . . *shit*. It's them."

"Camellia?" Jordan asked, and he lunged forward, racing toward the house.

Wait, Camellia . . . that name was familiar. It clicked in her mind. When Jordan had been taken by the vamps, he hadn't been their only prisoner, they'd also taken a girl. A shifter. Of course, Sarah had thought some of the rumors about the girl were bullshit because those stories had said the girl wasn't your run-of-the-mill two-spirit shifter.

The stories claimed she was a dragon.

Lucas ran after Jordan, roaring his name. The other wolves followed, quickly closing rank, and Sarah, well, she wasn't about to be left behind.

After all, pack stayed together.

She rushed after them, wishing she had a weapon. It was daytime, and any vamp would be a fool to attack now. All vamps were at their weakest during the day, even those born to the blood.

Lucas tackled Jordan. "*She's not with them*. Her scent's on him, but she's not here."

Sarah saw the woman then. A small, dark-haired woman vaulted over the outer wall and began to stalk toward them. A man was at her side, tall, his blond hair gleaming. His body stayed close to the woman's as their steps shadowed each other.

"Thanks for that open invitation, wolf," the woman called out, her voice carrying easily. "It was nice not to have to fight my way past that new security of yours."

Security Sarah knew he'd put out to protect them from Rafe.

The woman didn't really look like a vamp. Other than the paleness. She looked . . . pretty. Actually, the chick was freaking beautiful. High cheeks. Heart-shaped face. Not a blemish, wrinkle, or scar anywhere on her.

Vampire? Really?

Then Sarah caught sight of her fangs.

Vampire.

"Maya." Lucas rose slowly and she noticed that he kept his body in front of Jordan's. And she also noticed the way he said the woman's name. With affection.

So those tales were true, too. Lucas did have a soft spot for the vamp who'd hauled his brother out of hell one night. Sarah knew that hard kick in her gut was jealousy.

Maya lifted her right hand. Her fingers were curled in a fist.

"Easy," the man next to Maya said, his shoulder brushing hers.

"Wanna tell me . . ." Maya bit out. "Why your scent was all over Marie Dusean?"

Lucas just shrugged.

The vamp lunged forward.

But her man was faster. He grabbed her arms, yanking her back. Maya's hand opened, though, and she threw something at Lucas. Something small and hard, something that hit him in the chest and fell to the ground.

"You shouldn't be out when you're weak, Maya," Lucas said mildly.

She growled at him. Pretty good growl for a vamp.

Sarah's eyes narrowed as she stared at the ground near his feet. What was—

A ring.

Not just any ring.

She hurried forward.

"Sarah!" Lucas caught her arm. But it was too late. She was in front of him, scooping up the familiar ring. Marie's ring.

Now it was time for her fingers to curl around the precious ruby. "Why do you have this?" she asked, meeting the vampire's stare. Right then, they were a perfect fighting match. Almost human-to-human. She didn't need to be scared of Maya Black.

No matter what the whispers on the streets said.

One tough bitch to stake.

"You know that ring?" Maya's attention sharpened on her.

Sarah nodded. "Did she send you?" And her palm was sweating around the ring. "Is it time for me to—"

The laughter stopped her. The hard, rolling laughter. Laughter edged with a fine coat of rage. "Marie didn't send me," Maya said. "Marie can't do anything right now."

The blond beside her dropped his hold.

Maya stepped forward. "The *mambo*'s dead. I found her less than thirty minutes ago." Her gaze drifted past Sarah. "Her throat had been slashed. That ring—she wore it on her neck, *always*. But the bastard who killed her, his claws were so strong he cut through the gold chain, through the flesh, and he took her life away."

Another step forward. The man came with her, and the same rage was reflected on his face.

"She sent for me, but I got to her too late," Maya said, and there was pain in her voice. "All these years, and I got there too late."

The ring seemed heavy in Sarah's hand.

"I found her dead, lying in a pool of blood, and the stench of wolf was all around her." Maya shook her head. "We all know there's only one alpha in LA. One alpha, a bastard that I know saw Marie last night. And now she's gone, killed by a wolf's claws."

Sarah braced her body in front of Lucas. "It wasn't him."

Maya smiled at her with a flash of vampire fangs. "Of course. Let me guess, he was screwing you last night, right, human? Screwing you . . . so he couldn't have been killing her."

Half-right. The sex hadn't started until morning, and it hadn't been screwing. "Marie helped us last night. I owe her." She opened her hand and glanced down at the ring. "Lucas wasn't in any condition to deal a killing blow when we were at her place."

More laughter, only this time, it came from the big blond and the scent in the air—yeah, it did kinda smell like sulfur—deepened. "Lady, trust me," he said, "Lucas Simone is always up for a killing blow."

Maybe. "He didn't kill her," she said, her own voice fierce.

Maya's gaze darted to the men who'd gathered. When she looked at Jordan, her stare seemed to warm a bit. Only semi-arctic. "Then which of these wolves," she wanted to know, "is the one who's gonna bleed for attacking my *mambo?*"

Chapter 14

"You're looking at the wrong wolves," Sarah said.

Maya's gaze turned measuring. "Sorry if I don't believe you, but his scent..." Her index finger pointed at Lucas. "Is all over you. So I'm guessing that makes you not exactly unbiased when it comes to the pack."

Sarah's back teeth clenched. "They aren't the only wolves in town."

"Oh?" One black brow rose. "Got a Lone on the loose? Then how come I haven't heard about him?" Her legs braced apart, and, quick as a flash, she drew out a gun, one that was aimed right at Sarah. "Silver bullets kill humans and wolf shifters real easy."

Sarah stared at the gun and didn't blink.

"Get that fucking weapon off her!" Lucas snarled.

But Maya shook her head. "Like I said before, your scent's all over her." Her gaze tracked to the alpha. "That means you give a shit what happens to her, right?"

"You don't want me as your enemy, Maya," he told her quietly. "You truly don't."

The blond's fingers touched Maya's shoulder. "You were supposed to go easy," he murmured.

"And Marie was supposed to be damn well alive! She wasn't supposed to get slashed up by some mangy wolf!"

At that, Lucas flew forward and shoved Sarah to the side. Dane instantly covered her, using his body to shield her.

Sarah twisted, glanced back, and saw that Lucas stood right in front of Maya. The gun pressed into his chest.

"You think I killed her?" His arms were up, his claws out. "Then shoot. But then you . . . and the winged asshole . . . had better get the hell out of LA because my pack will be out for your blood."

She didn't squeeze the trigger. "Why was your scent on Marie?"

"Because she saved my life last night." A pause, then . . . "And that's probably why she's dead today."

That gun shoved harder against his chest. "Wolf . . ."

"There's another alpha in town. One who's gunning for me."

"I think he's telling the truth," the vamp's guy said, head cocked.

"He is." Jordan stepped forward. Maya's attention swung to him. Sarah saw the vamp's eyes narrow. "Lucas isn't lying to you. A bastard named Rafael Santiago is here, hunting him."

"Hunting *us*," Piers added.

Jordan took another slow, gliding step toward the vampire. "Believe me if you believe no one else, Maya. It's not us you're after. It's him."

But the gun wasn't dropping. "I'd like to believe you," Maya said and almost sounded like she did. "But no one would have crept up on Marie. She saw *everything*." Was that an echo of pain in her voice? "She wouldn't have let a wolf she didn't know get to her, she wouldn't—"

"Then she knew him," Sarah yelled out the obvious, still covered by Dane. "She knew Rafe, and if she's as strong as I think, she knew he'd be the one to kill her."

Maya's hold on the gun finally eased, and in that second, Lucas's hand flew up and snatched the weapon away. Maya didn't spare him a glance. Her focus was fully on Sarah. "Who are you?"

Lucas moved again, a gliding step, and blocked Maya's view of Sarah. "Consider your entrance pass to my place revoked."

The blond man's shoulders tensed. "I think she's *Other*."

"She smells human," the vamp muttered.

Dane lifted Sarah back to her feet, but he stayed close.

"Not a witch," the man said. "Not a shifter . . ."

"Brody, you don't need to know a damn thing about her!" Lucas glared at the vamp's companion.

The guy, Brody, kept talking. "Demon? I can never smell them and if she's using glamour . . ."

She wasn't.

"Get off my land," Lucas ordered, voice flat. "And don't come back." Then he turned away and strode to Sarah's side.

"You owe me, wolf." Brody's hands were on his hips when he threw this out.

Sarah caught the narrowing of Lucas's eyes. Saw his lips move when he growled out, "Shifter bastard."

"If you didn't kill Marie," this came from Maya, "if there's really another wolf in town . . ."

He glanced back over his shoulder. "There is."

Maya edged forward. "Then I want him."

"Get in line. *I'm* taking that bastard out."

"If he killed her, then I'm—"

"I think he's killed some of her followers." Dane was the one who dropped this bombshell. "He knew the *mambo*, and he's killed at least two of her people."

Sarah's eyes widened. Why hadn't Dane said something sooner?

"We saw 'em last night." Now it was Piers who spoke up. "A woman from the South, and a Haitian male. Their throats had been ripped open." His lips tightened. "I know a wolf's work when I see it."

The Haitian? But . . . he'd been with her, he'd talked to her. "When?" Sarah asked. "Did he kill them while we were inside—"

Dane shook his head. "No, they were dead long before that." His dark eyes met hers. "*Long* before that."

Two ways. The memory of the *mambo's* voice drifted through her mind. *Stop him before Death comes.*

Oh, damn.

Or bring him back after.

Maxime.

"She had 'em under some kind of spell," Dane said. "She let 'em go right before we found the two of you on that table."

Sarah didn't remember that part of the night. She didn't remember anything after the slash of the knife and Marie's dark promise.

He dies . . .

Then you die.

With those words, everything had gone straight to black.

Sarah glanced at her arm. The wound was gone now. She didn't have any enhanced healing powers, but the wound had vanished far too quickly.

"Marie said she didn't 'raise them' but that she was letting them go free." The words had Sarah's eyes lifting back to Dane. His jaw locked. "One minute, they were walking around, talking, the next—we were staring at corpses that had been dead for days."

"Fucking zombies," Piers growled. "Hell, of all the *Other* . . . the dead belong in the ground."

Brody's hands fisted. "*Watch it.*"

Ah, right. Technically, Maya was dead. Well, undead. She would have died briefly before she was reborn as a vamp.

"Marie never raised the dead. She didn't like to touch that power," Maya spoke softly, as if mostly to herself. "She said you never knew what you'd bring back if you tried to raise the bodies of humans."

Lucas didn't seem fazed to hear that zombies had been around them the night before.

Piers ran a quick hand over his face. "There's another who can raise them."

Maya's chin jerked up a notch. "No."

"She can do it. You know she can."

"Just because you *can* do something, it doesn't mean you will. Josette doesn't use the power, she doesn't—"

Piers started laughing then, but there was no humor in that hard, mocking sound. "Maya, you been playing house with your shifter too long, staying gone out of LA . . . you're missing some news, baby." He put his hands on his hips. "Guess life in . . . where is it—Maine?—has made you soft."

The woman just looked angrier. "Nothing makes me soft. Don't make that mistake."

A faint grin still rode his lips. "Little Josie . . . she's been playing with power. Not keeping those hands of hers clean anymore."

Brody swore and Maya gave a hard shake of her head. "You're wrong."

"Am I?"

Maya spun away, her hand automatically reaching for Brody's. "We have to go."

Now she was running away?

No, not away. Running *to* something.

Probably to wherever this Josette/Josie was.

"The wolf is mine!" Lucas shouted after them. "Do you hear me, Maya? That kill is mine!"

It was Brody who stopped and looked back. "I let you have the last kill." Suddenly, his teeth looked longer, the skin on his arms darker. "This one's for Maya."

"Not if I get to him first!"

But Brody had spun away. He and the vamp disappeared, no, not disappeared, they just moved *fast*.

"Shit." Lucas's eyes fixed on Sarah. "You okay?"

She nodded. Other than an aching knee from where she'd plowed into the ground, yes, she was fine.

She also still had Marie's ring. Sarah's fingers unfurled. The red of the ruby seemed so dark.

"Josette." Lucas repeated the name, as if tasting it. "She's Marie's granddaughter. How the hell do you know anything about her and her power, Piers?"

"Cause the lady is sexy as sin, and she's also taken to hanging out in the darker part of town." Piers flashed a wolf's grin. Too many teeth. Too sharp. Too much challenge. "How wouldn't I know her?"

But Lucas stared at him and didn't seem to buy that grin.

"You're the one who knew where Marie was last night," Dane spoke slowly, as if thinking his way through something.

Piers slanted him a measuring glance. "Because Lucas wants us to keep tabs on her. I do what the alpha wants."

"You're not looking into the Dark, are you, Piers?" The question was Lucas's.

The Dark—dark magic.

But Piers just lifted one shoulder. "The Dark's been looking at me for years. We all know it." His grin faded. "There's only so much time until it takes over."

Because he thought he'd be one of the wolf shifters who crossed the line and became psychotic. She'd touched his mind, she knew the potential was there. But, then again, it was always there.

With man and beast.

"You been looking for a magic cure?" Lucas pressed.

There was no cure. Not unless . . .

"I've just been looking at a pretty lady. Where's the crime in that?"

But Sarah was sure he was lying then, and she knew the others realized it, too.

Piers's spine straightened. "Do you want me to take you to Josie or do you want to let the vamp get to her first?"

"Josette isn't my prey. Her fight isn't mine."

The ring seemed heavier in Sarah's hands. "I promised a trade to Marie."

Was this the debt she'd pay? Marie had saved Lucas, now . . .

"Someone gave Caleb the Angel Dust." Piers huffed out a hard breath. "And Josie . . . hell, if anyone knows how to make it in this town, it would be her."

Sarah saw Lucas's claws burst from his skin. "Why the hell didn't you say so sooner?"

"Cause I didn't want her marked for death." Lines bracketed his mouth. "Cause I'm a selfish bastard, and, hell, yeah, I was hoping to use her." Pain hollowed his eyes. "Every time I shift, I want the blood, I want it so bad . . ."

Lucas grabbed his shirt front and hauled Piers closer. "Then, from here on out, you don't shift without me by your side, got it? Because I'm not losing another packmate."

Piers's gaze fell.

"Where is she?" Lucas barked. "Shit, if Maya and her man get to her first, they'll take her away and we won't find out a damn thing about the Dust."

"They won't get there first." Piers swallowed. "Maya doesn't know how far the angel fell, not yet."

Lucas's stare bored into him. "But you do?"

"Let's just say I know what it's like to fall, and I know where the Fallen go."

Yes, Sarah bet he did.

At a little past noon, the bar on Brinks Street should have been empty. And if it had been a regular joint, the place probably would have been closed up tight.

But it wasn't your typical hole-in-the-wall bar. Not by a long shot.

Lucas eyed the entrance, noting the two men who slouched just outside the doors. He'd bet those guys were a lot more aware than they pretended to be.

"You sure she's here?" he asked.

From what he remembered about Josette, the lady was pure class. She owned an art gallery, a real fancy place that he'd never even gotten within a mile of—except for the few times he'd been tracking her.

Josette had cut off contact with Marie a while back. It had looked like the woman had gone no-magic and hadn't looked back.

So he'd stopped watching her.

And hadn't seen her fall.

"She's there." Piers was certain. "She comes here for the blood."

"Uh, the blood?" Sarah repeated, and there wasn't really any fear in her voice. No, it sounded more like morbid curiosity.

"There's a lot you can do with the blood of *Others*," Piers said. "If you have the right magic."

Lucas grunted. Piers was the only shifter he'd brought with him. He hadn't wanted to attract too much attention.

But with Rafe out there, he also hadn't wanted to risk being separated from Sarah—so he'd made certain she stayed at his side.

I'll keep her safe. From now on, where he went, so did she.

He'd claimed her, right in front of the pack. Been ready to fight for her. Hell, had the woman really thought he'd let any of his wolves hurt her? No matter how pissed . . . hell, *no,* he'd never let anyone so much as scratch her.

He'd wanted his intent to be clear. So he'd challenged the others, and claimed her.

Mine.

And she hadn't refused the claim. Hadn't told him to shut the hell up. She'd . . . accepted him.

"So what's the plan here?" Sarah wanted to know. "We go in, you guys with claws up and blazing . . ."

Blazing? Lucas shook his head. "Let's try charm first."

She smiled at him then. A real smile. One that lit her face and had his cock rising.

Later.

He might want to shield her and cover her twenty-four/seven, but the woman was ex-FBI.

That meant cosseting her wasn't gonna fly. Besides, he'd already noticed that Sarah seemed to like the action.

Good, so did he.

"Let's take it easy," he said, rolling his shoulders to push the tension away. " 'Til we find our prey." Then the claws could come out.

Angel's Dust. If Josette really had made the drug and given it to Caleb . . .

Even being Marie's granddaughter wouldn't save her ass.

"I'm guessing the guys at the front will let you in," he said to Piers and wondered just how close to the edge his friend truly was. Close enough to trade in the Dark.

Hell. That was too close. Because no trade was ever as simple as it looked on the surface. Magic always took so much more.

And you didn't realize it, not until the trade was made, and your soul was gone.

"They'll let me in." Grim words.

So they went straight for the door. The guards glanced at Piers and eased back. Their stares tensed a bit on Sarah, but they didn't try to stop her or Lucas from entering the bar.

Silence greeted them inside, but then, it would. In a place like this, the first thing you saw would always be a lie. Usually a scene set to fool humans.

Piers went straight for the staircase on the left side. A staircase that led down, not up. A gnarled old man sat there. The guy motioned with a roll of his hand for Piers to go forward, but when Lucas approached, the guy's hand rose and pushed against his chest.

"Don't have what you need," the old man said.

Sarah's arm brushed Lucas's.

"Not for either of you."

Piers glanced back at the guy. "They're with me."

The man studied them with sharp, pitch-black eyes. Demon eyes. Lucas's nostrils flared. *That scent . . .*

"No," the demon said definitely. "They're not with you. Don't make that mistake, wolf."

Lucas brought his claws up and let the tips hover just over the bastard's carotid. "I don't really care what shit you try to sell to the other fools who come in, but don't jerk around my pack." And that's exactly what the asshole was doing. Trying to make Piers doubt their alliance.

The old demon grinned, showing off a gold front tooth.

"Now get your hand off me, or my claws will go deeper."

The hand dropped.

Lucas grabbed Sarah's wrist and followed Piers.

"I know your weakness, alpha!" The bastard called after him. "Damn foolish to show us all."

Lucas froze. Then he turned his head, very slowly, and met that black stare. "Demon, if you think you can take me, come on and try."

Sarah's fingers curled around his arm. "Lucas . . . remember why we're here."

The demon's gaze dropped to that touch. Studied it. "Does your charmer know how many you've killed, Alpha?"

He wouldn't look at Sarah. "You seem to know," he said instead. "And yet you're still stupid enough to keep talking right now?"

And that shut up the little bastard. The demon turned and scurried away.

Lucas growled and when he glanced back at Piers, he found the other guy watching him, too closely. "Don't believe any shit they tell you here," he ordered Piers, but really, the guy should have enough sense to know that. "They try to break you so they can use you."

A fucking Magic Hole. That's what this place was. He could feel the edge of the dark magic pulling at him. Some places were thought of as hotspots for the supernaturals. Places where power could peak. Yeah, this wasn't a place like that. It was a place that would suck you dry and here, only those who bled the others—only those would get stronger.

Get out.

As soon as he could, they'd be leaving and not coming back. Because a place like this, where the power was so close, so close and all you had to do was—

Reach out and kill for it.

—it was tempting him.

So he knew the magic was calling to Piers.

Sarah's hold tightened. "Let's find this Josette and get out of here."

Right.

They climbed down the stairs. Eyes watched them. Whispers followed. Almost every kind of paranormal out there liked to set up a safe house of sorts. Vamps created feeding rooms, bars that lured in unsuspecting human prey. Demons who were addicted to drugs flocked to their damn dens.

And then places like this . . . holes for the darkest of the *Other* . . . lurked in the big cities.

Lucas kept his claws out. He figured he'd be fighting his way out soon enough.

But no one approached them, not yet. A makeshift bar was set up near the foot of the stairs. Piers headed to it and slapped his hands on the surface. "*Josette.*"

The bartender stared back at him.

"I know she's here." Piers glared back. "Do you really want me to claw the truth out of you again?"

And Lucas saw the healing scratches on the bartender's muscled arms.

The guy grunted and pointed to the left. Another door.

A trap?

Probably.

But they went toward that door anyway. And with every step they took, the scent of death deepened around them.

He risked a quick glance at Sarah. She hadn't caught the scent. Wouldn't for a while yet. But . . .

Death waited behind that door.

Piers reached for the knob. Lucas got ready for the battle that was coming. So much death, the scent clogged his nose and he wondered what he'd find, how many bodies, how much blood, how—

The door swung open. Candles sputtered in the room, the only light that glowed, and illuminated the kneeling woman. A white circle had been drawn on the floor, it surrounded her. Her long black hair hid her face.

But he didn't need to see her face in order to recognize Josette. And, damn, what had happened to her? Because that scent of death was coming *from* her.

She didn't look up. Not when they came inside and not when the door shut behind them. She knelt there, frozen like a statue, and waited.

It was Sarah who moved first. She pulled free of Lucas and walked across the room. She bent, coming close to Josette, but Lucas noticed she was very careful not to touch that white circle. Smart.

Sarah put the ring on the wooden floor. Sat it down and . . .

Josette's head snapped up. She was just as beautiful, her face just as perfect as it had always been, her skin still a sweet dark cream but her eyes . . . they were different. The darkness of her eyes just looked . . . empty.

"I know she's gone." Josette's voice was perfectly modulated. No whisper of Louisiana, though Lucas knew that had been her home for many years. "You didn't have to bring me proof."

She didn't reach for the ring. Just stared at it.

Then her gaze lifted to Lucas. "You came to kill me."

"I came to find out what the hell you're doing." That scent was clogging his nostrils. Since when did a human smell like death?

Her gaze dropped to the ring. "Vampires killed my mother. I thought—for years I thought they were the ones I should hate."

"Most vamps are bastards that need hating," Piers said, edging around behind Josette.

"Most," she whispered. "But they aren't the only monsters out there."

"No," Lucas agreed. "You're surrounded by monsters right now, aren't you?"

Her gaze rose once more and tears glistened in her eyes. "I let the monster in. *I'm* the one."

Sarah still knelt near the other woman. "You know Rafe, don't you?"

"*Rafael.*" Whispered with emotion. Love. Pain. Hate. "I knew him when we were children. My *grand-mère* took him in. I thought he was safe. I-I didn't know . . ." She swallowed. "This time, *I* took him in. *I* let him in." Her hands turned over and she stared at her smooth palms. "All the blood is on me."

"There's nothing on you," Sarah told her. "Have you been taking something? You could be hallucinating. Nothing's there, it's—"

A choked laugh interrupted her words. "The blood is always there now. Never thought I had much power, thought I was safe. *Normal.* I tried to be for so long . . ." Her shoulders fell. "But I guess I was good at one thing."

Lucas glanced around the room, searching for more threats, but he saw nothing. Just the small woman.

"He killed Maxime and Helene. He killed them when I wouldn't give him the Dust. I told him I didn't work the magic. That *grand-mère* had all the power, but he said she wouldn't see him." Soft, slow. "I said I wouldn't help him, *I said I wanted to be normal.*"

Sarah's hand lifted, as if she were going to reach over the circle and touch Josette. "Don't," he growled because he knew just how powerful those magical circles could be.

Sarah's hand froze in mid-air.

"He killed Maxime and Helene because they blocked him from getting to *grand-mère*, and then he went after my Martin." She breathed the other man's name on a sigh.

"I would have done anything for Martin." Her eyes rose to Sarah's. "You'll know what that's like soon."

The hair rose on Lucas's nape.

"I got the Dust. *Grand-mère* gave it to me. She didn't like it, but—she gave it to me. She would've given me anything. I always knew that." Such aching sadness. "Then I gave it to the bastard . . . *but he still took my Martin.*"

"I'm sorry," Sarah whispered.

Josette kept talking. The words tumbled from her lips. "Martin was going to marry me. He was going to make sure I never had to face the Darkness again. He was going to be mine!"

That was when Lucas noticed the other ring. A diamond ring, resting in that cast circle.

"I wasn't ready to let him go." She reached for the diamond ring and traced it with a loving fingertip. "*Grand-mère* said I should, but I just wasn't ready. You see, I'd waited for him my whole life." Her eyes squeezed closed and a tear tracked down her cheek as she whispered, "Death wasn't going to take him away from me."

Chapter 15

Hell. "We can't always stop death," Lucas told her, but the words were a reminder the woman shouldn't need. She'd lost both her parents long ago. She knew what a fickle bitch death could be.

At that, Josette's lashes lifted and her dark eyes met his. "It turns out I can." The ghost of a smile curved her full lips. "Seems I do have a bit of power after all."

"What did you do?" Sarah asked her, and Piers just stood, watching. "You didn't . . ."

"I wasn't letting him go!" Josette jumped to her feet, but stayed inside that circle. Sarah rose, too. "He was mine. I tried to get him back. How is that wrong? I tried . . . and he came."

Because little Josette had raised the dead. Oh, she hadn't made a zombie the way Hollywood portrayed them to be. No mindless monster that had to eat brains. No, the Raised didn't feed on humans. Didn't feed on anyone; well, not unless the person who'd raised them gave that order.

"You crossed the line, Josette." He kept his voice firm because to raise the dead, hell, that took some very dark magic.

Bokor. That was the name for the one who used the Dark powers. But there was a price for that magic, there always was.

"I brought him back. He didn't have to die! I brought him back and—"

"And you brought the Haitian back, too, didn't you?" Piers narrowed his eyes on her. "Him and the woman."

Her lips trembled. "They didn't deserve to die."

"But they *did* die," Lucas pointed out. "You're not the one who gets to yank them back, you're not—"

"Fucking vampires cheat death! They come back, they live forever! They feed on humans and they kill and destroy." Josette's chest heaved. "Martin, Maxime, and Helene—they were good people. They should have gotten to keep living." She shoved back her hair. "So I gave them a chance."

No, because he knew how this worked. Josette wasn't the only one who'd ever been tempted. "They don't come back the same. You know that."

Her bottom lip still trembled but she caught it, biting it with her top teeth.

"They don't have a will of their own." Piers spoke now. Yeah, figured he'd know all about the Raised, too. Because that was what they were called in the right circles. *Raised.* "They're puppets. They have to do whatever you command."

Her hair flew back as she shook her head, hard. "I commanded them to live, that was all. They had choices. They had free will!"

Had. Interesting word choice. Lucas let his gaze rake her. "You know Maxime and Helene are back in the grave, don't you?"

Her eyelids flickered. "*Grand-mère* released them." Flat.

"And what about Martin? Did she release Martin, too?"

Her gaze dropped to the diamond ring. "I did that." She swallowed and the painful click was too loud. "He . . . asked . . . he didn't want to stay with me. He knew what . . . he was and he didn't want to stay with me. He said—he said I'd made him into a monster." A tear tracked down her cheek. "I just wanted to save him!" Her eyes looked as dark as a demon's. "But he said *I* was the one who'd turned him into a nightmare. Me!"

Sarah's gaze cut toward Lucas. Her expression was so

stark—but then she glanced back at Josette. "He didn't realize what you'd done for him."

Her shoulders fell. "I traded everything for him. There's
no going back now. Once the Dark gets you . . ." Her hand
lifted and her fingers curled into a fist. "There's no fighting."

The hair on his nape was still up. Lucas looked at the sym-
bols she'd written so carefully around her circle. Some signs
he recognized. Some had him worried as hell. And some . . .
some he didn't understand at all. "What's the circle for,
Josette?"

"I can hear the dead," she said, speaking quietly. "They
call to me now. Some are stronger than others, and some
want to rise."

Fuck. "Who are you bringing back?"

"*Grand-mère.*" Whispered.

"No!" Sarah's voice snapped out, fueled with an angry
heat. "No, she doesn't want to come back. I don't know
what you *think* you're hearing, but Marie wouldn't want to
be pulled from the grave."

"She's not in the grave yet . . ."

"She wouldn't want this!" Sarah's cheeks flushed.

Josette's head whipped toward her. "How would you
know? You know nothing about her, you don't know—"

"Marie could see the future, couldn't she?"

"She could see everything."

Lucas knew that was true.

"Then she knew Death was coming," Sarah said, and Lucas
saw her shoes edge closer to that line. *No.* "She didn't fight her
attacker. She let him in, let him get close enough to kill."

"Damn you!" Josette lunged forward. Her hand flew out
of the circle and caught Sarah's arm.

A hiss of sound filled the room, just like a snake's hiss.

The candles flickered.

"Marie knew." Sarah kept talking. Her body was still out
of the circle, and Josette was trapped inside. "She said—she
told me, *'There's no saving everyone. No matter how you
fight, Death will still be there.'*"

Josette swayed.

"She wants you to let her go. She told me, I didn't understand then, but she said—"

"I won't be alone, I won't!" Josette screamed.

Then Sarah lunged forward, slamming her body into Josette's, and the two women pitched back, falling right out of that circle.

The hiss died away. The candles stopped flickering.

"She's gone." Sarah crouched over Josette. "*Let her go.*"

Josette started to cry, not just silent trickles of tears. Deep, gulping sobs.

The door shattered, sending wood flying into the room. Lucas spun around, claws up, and saw Maya and her shifter shoving through the wood.

Ah, figured they'd be here now. Always a little late to the party.

But Maya froze after taking just a step. "Why the hell does this place smell . . ." Her nostrils flared a bit and he knew she'd caught the stench of death. "Josie, what have you done?"

"Just raised a little dead," Lucas muttered, rubbing the back of his neck and wondering what would have happened if Sarah hadn't gotten Josette out of that circle. "Just a little dead."

Josette cried harder and he heard her choke out, "Martin."

"Oh, damn." Understanding filled Maya's voice. She crept forward, but Josette immediately flinched. Josette's hands curled tight around Sarah.

"Josette." Lucas said her name, deliberately making it snap like a whip.

Her head jerked up.

He knew grief was ripping her apart, but time was his enemy right then. He didn't want any more dead on the streets. "You know Rafe killed Marie, don't you?"

A slow nod.

He growled, satisfied. "So that means you stay the hell off my back, vampire."

"He's still *mine*." Figured Maya wouldn't back off that easily.

Josette's gaze darted between them.

Maya tried taking another step forward. "Josette, let me help you."

"No one can help me." But she kept holding onto Sarah.

Lucas unclenched his teeth. "You have a cure for the Dust?"

"There is no cure." No more tears. Flat, emotionless. Like the woman had totally shut down now, her fight gone.

Fucking fantastic. "Where's Rafe?"

She just stared up at him.

His teeth were clenching again. "Where. Is. He?" He stalked toward her. "You want vengeance for what he's done? I'll give you vengeance. I'll rip his head off and I'll bring it to you and you can make sure no one ever lets that bastard rise." His breath heaved out. "Just tell me where he is."

"I don't know."

Maya took a few more steps. "That's a circle for protection, Josie. Did you think he was coming after you?"

"I know he is." A sad smile. "Rafe always likes to—"

"Tie up loose ends," Sarah finished.

Josette looked at Sarah then, a deep, probing look. "He told me about you."

Oh, this wasn't going to be good. Lucas reached for Sarah's hand and closed his fingers around hers. "We can't stay here." There was nothing more to learn. If Josette wasn't—

"He thought you were his mate," she told Sarah.

"He thought wrong," was her immediate answer.

"Rafael thought you'd be the one to give him the thing he desired most." Her dark gaze slid to Lucas. "For wolves, it's always about the base needs, isn't it? Lust, hunger, vengeance."

Lucas held her stare. "I didn't start the war. He came gunning for me." Not like he'd just stand there and become the asshole's bitch. "No one makes that mistake and lives."

Her stare slipped to his savaged ear. "Wound for wound," she whispered. "The way of the beast."

No, the way of the beast was tooth and claw until death. Fight and kill. Or damn well be killed.

"He knows your weakness, Lucas Simone." She rose with Sarah, her body shaking just a bit. "That's how he works. He knew my weakness, and he used it against me. Knew mine, knew *grand-mère's*."

The *mambo* had a weakness?

Her breath whispered out. "Rafael always knows how to hurt his prey the most."

Good damn deal for him. "I'm not afraid of pain."

For just an instant, her dark gaze seemed to fog, the way he'd seen Marie's do once. "Very soon, you will be."

Not likely. "I can handle any pain the bastard throws at me."

"I never said it would be your pain." Her gaze drifted over Maya.

"Now you sound like Marie," Maya said.

Josette's face tightened.

"Piers, take Josette back to the compound." His gaze met the other shifter's. *Don't let her out of your sight.* There was much more to learn from Josette, he knew it. He just didn't want to question her more with the vamp and her body-guard/mate there.

Sure, they had an alliance, of sorts, and he was in the un-fortunate situation of actually owing Brody, but he made it a policy not to trust vamps too far. Or at all, really.

At his words, Maya shook her head. "Josette's coming with me." She offered her hand, palm up, to the other woman. "You know I'll keep you safe."

Josette didn't take the offered hand. "The Dust . . ." She cleared her throat. "Why did you ask about it, Lucas? It wouldn't hurt wolves, just demons."

"Rafe used it to infect a demon I know." That's all he'd say. Josette and the others didn't need to know about the hy-brid in his pack.

Secrets stayed in the pack.

"Is he . . . is he dead?"

"Not yet."

"I only gave Rafael one batch."

Maya and Brody were watching with narrowed eyes. Both of them hearing everything that was said, and what wasn't.

Her palm brushed at the tear tracks on her cheeks.

"I wasn't even sure it would work."

Oh, it had worked.

"I couldn't make it. But *grand-mère* . . . could do anything."

But she'd still died. No matter how powerful, everyone could still die.

"All kinds came to see *grand-mère*." Her lips curved down. "When you traded . . . even angels had to fall."

Almost helplessly then, his stare slid back to Sarah. Just because Marie was dead, it didn't mean she still wouldn't claim her payment. No, a payment was always due.

"Come with me, Josie," Maya said again. "You know I can keep you safe. If you don't want to stay with me, I've got some cops who will—"

"I wouldn't trust the cops in this town if I were you," Lucas advised.

"No," Sarah echoed him. "I wouldn't either."

Indecision flashed across Josette's face.

"*Josette.*" Intensity fired Maya's voice. "You trusted me once. Trust me again. I *will* keep you safe." Her gaze zeroed in on Lucas. "He just wants to use you."

True enough. He didn't exactly trust Josette. That circle hadn't been all about protection—Maya was wrong. Josette had been set to raise the dead again. Marie, or . . .

No, he didn't trust her. And he wanted her where he could keep a guard on her.

But Josette reached for Maya's hand.

Lucas growled. "Wrong choice."

Maya pulled the woman closer.

And he had to give a warning. Because . . . once, he'd seen

past the vampire and glimpsed the woman inside. "Don't trust her."

Maya's jaw dropped. "You bastard! I'd never hurt her, I'd—"

"I was talking to *you*, Maya." He caught Sarah's hand and pulled her toward the door.

"She's not the good little Josie anymore," Piers said.

The candles flickered.

Lucas wondered . . . had she ever been that Josie? Or had she been tricking them all along?

Death teased his nostrils.

A strong hand grabbed his shoulder. Ah, now Brody was trying to get a piece of him. Wrong move. Lucas didn't care how old or strong that shifter was; even legends could die.

"If I find him first," Adam Brody's mouth hitched into a hard grin—one that promised pain. "They'll be nothing left for you to see but ash."

Promises, promises.

"I gave you a kill once," Brody said. "This one's personal."

"You're damn right it is." He knew Maya had been close with the *mambo*, but her revenge would have to wait. "He's after me. After my pack." Lucas let the wolf off his leash, and he knew his eyes would glow with the power of the beast. "He'll be dead by my hand."

"Not if I find him first, wolf."

Asshole. Brody wasn't backing down. But Brody also didn't know this town, not like Lucas did. "You won't." He pushed through the broken door, aware of the silence behind him, ahead of him. Everyone in the bar was straining to hear. Not that hearing would be so hard for most of the bastards. Not with their *Other* senses.

He stalked to the center of the bar. Sarah was at his side. Piers at his back. All the eyes were on him, the silence even thicker now.

He waited, letting his gaze sweep the place. Maya guided Josette up the stairs, glancing back at him only once. He caught the black flash of her eyes.

Brody stayed below, taking up a position right at the foot of the stairs. The blond crossed his arms over his chest and waited, watching Lucas.

"I'm looking for a wolf shifter." Lucas let his voice ring out. Loud and clear.

No one moved.

"Rafael Santiago. The bastard came to town, started killing in *my* area, and I want him found."

"Dead . . ." A woman's voice called out. "Or alive?"

"Alive." Because the kill would be his.

He saw a few gazes slide away from him. Two men sidled toward another door on the right-hand side of the room.

The woman who'd questioned him pushed through the crowd. Her hair was red as fire and her mouth was stained with blood. "How much?" *Vampire.*

He heard Sarah's quick, indrawn breath. He brushed his fingers lightly over the inside of her wrist.

"Yeah, wolf . . . how much?" Now a big, burly bastard was next to the woman. A bear shifter. McKennis. Their paths had crossed more than a few times. "What will you pay if we bring him to you?"

Lucas smiled at him. "I don't pay you a damn thing."

Mutters in the crowd then. Growls. A snarl.

He saw Brody raise a brow.

"Then why the fuck should we tell you anything?" McKennis demanded.

"Because . . ." Lucas strode toward him and in a flash, he had his claws right over the bear's heart. Dumb asshole. For all his size, he was always too slow to defend. "If I find out someone in this shithole knows where Rafe is or has been helping him hide . . ." His claws sliced right through McKennis's shirt. The bear didn't even seem to breathe. "Guess who'll be next on my hit list?"

That shut 'em up.

He let his gaze scan the room once more. He memorized every face. Because he would be seeing them all. Sooner or later.

No one spoke as he turned and followed Sarah and Piers back to the stairs. He stayed in the rear, deliberately, hoping someone would try to attack.

But they all stood frozen.

"Don't have a lot of charm, do you?" Brody murmured when Lucas reached the stairs.

Lucas froze. Actually, he had all the charm he needed.

Sarah glanced back. "Lucas?"

"Keep going, Sarah. You and Piers wait outside." Because he knew what was coming. There was only one reason Brody would have stayed behind.

"Lucas . . ." Now Piers sounded worried.

Lucas inclined his head. "Don't worry. It won't touch me." His gaze was on Brody.

"It?" Sarah repeated. "What's—"

"*We need to go*," Piers growled and pulled her up the stairs. "Trust me. Shit, I've seen his work before."

A faint smile curved Brody's lips. "You really should just let me handle this. I can take Rafe out, nice and neat."

Neat? Since when was fire and singed flesh neat?

"You do it your way." His claws dug into the wooden banister. "I'll do it mine."

Brody nodded. "Fine. If that's what you want."

Then the guy was moving. Stalking back toward the death room that Josette had used. Figured. Maya would want that place destroyed.

And Brody had a thing about making Maya happy.

Lucas's feet pounded up the stairs. He'd just reached the top when the scent of smoke teased his nostrils. Yeah, just what he'd thought.

Lucas shoved open the door. He spared a glance for the old demon. "Better get a head start on running. The stampede will be coming up soon." Once they realized there was no stopping Brody's fire.

Because Adam Brody wasn't your run-of-the-mill shifter. In fact, Lucas had never met anyone quite like him.

Got to find Rafe first. Pack business. The kill wasn't for an outsider.

The demon turned and scrambled, rushing for a side door. Screams drifted up from below. Voices rose and fell.

Lucas kept walking. He could have barred the door behind him. Made the monsters who liked the dark suffer more, but then, that wasn't the point, was it?

No, his job now was to wait and watch. To see just who crawled free and scrambled for safety.

And who went running to Rafe.

The heat from the sun hit him when he stalked outside, but it was nothing compared to the fire igniting in the bar. The dragon knew how to burn. Others ran out behind him. The female vamp. Figured she'd escape first. Vamps didn't get along so well with fire.

Sarah waited for him with her hands on her slender hips. "What the hell was that? Did you want to piss off every paranormal in the place?"

"Yeah, I did." A group of demons flew past him. McKennis rushed into the parking lot. Looked like the back of the bear's shirt was smoking.

Sarah marched toward him. "You succeeded then. They'll be gunning for you, they'll be—"

He covered her body with his, pulling her close and kissing her just as he heard the explosion behind him. Glass shards rained onto his back, some breaking through the skin. He didn't let her go. His lips opened over hers and his tongue thrust inside her mouth.

She breathed his name and the lust surged through him. *Dangerous.* No, those jerks running away weren't the ones he needed to worry about. They wouldn't hurt him.

But Sarah . . . yeah, she just might be able to.

He eased back and gazed down at her. "Lucas . . ." She looked over his shoulder and her eyes widened. The growing fire was reflected in her gaze. "What happened in there?"

"I think Maya and Brody wanted to make sure Josette didn't try casting her circles there again." He threw a fast glance back at the bar. Now the place was really burning. Those orange and red flames stretched straight to the sky.

Sarah's breasts brushed against him. "But how'd the fire start?"

He pressed another kiss to her lips. "Babe, you don't want to know." From the corner of his eye, he saw McKennis and the female vamp. The vamp jumped into a pickup while McKennis fled the scene on foot.

And he also saw the old demon. Not running, just staring at the fire, watching the place burn, and there was fury on his face.

"Who do we follow?" Piers asked, coming up beside him.

"You go after Maya. Make sure that Josette keeps her nose clean." Like that was going to happen. Playing with dark magic was like taking crack. Or so a witch had told him once. Just a few hits were all you needed to get hooked, and that was one addiction you couldn't beat.

He stepped away from Sarah. "We're following the demon." Because the guy had whirled away from the building and was now rushing down the alley. Moving fast for someone so old. But then, Lucas didn't really think the guy *was* old. A demon didn't just use glamour to disguise the true color of his eyes. If the demon had enough power, glamour could be used to hide anything . . . or to transform the demon into just about anyone.

A lesson Marley had taught him.

"Stay close," he said.

"Try to keep me away," she told him and then they were running, heading right for that alley, sticking close to the old building's walls. The stench of garbage hit him and old alcohol burned his nose.

The demon was moving fast. Didn't really matter how fast he ran, though, Lucas had the scent now.

Sarah kept pace easily, rushing just as quickly as he did through the narrow alley. In the distance, a fire truck's alarm screamed. Lucas knew that by the time the truck got to the scene, the building would be too far gone to save.

Brody didn't screw around.

Neither did he.

The demon burst from the alley. Lucas froze, and threw up a hand, blocking Sarah. That demon wasn't just running blind. He was heading for a black van, one with a familiar cable company's logo on the side.

His gut twisted. The van didn't fit with Rafe's setup. No way, but . . .

The door flew open as the demon approached and the guy jumped inside. The van's motor snarled to life. Lucas's eyes slit.

"No, wait, Lucas, I think—"

Too late. He raced forward just as the tail-lights flashed on. They weren't getting away from him that easily.

Once again, the back doors of that van flew open. Only Rafe wasn't the one glaring down at him.

A woman stood there. A woman with long red hair and golden eyes. The demon was right behind her, gripping her shoulder.

"Told you he was comin'!" the demon cried. "We need to go, we need—"

The woman smiled at him.

"No, Karen! Don't!" Sarah's scream of fury.

But the woman lifted her hand and tazed him. Fucking *tazed* him.

The electrodes shot right into his chest. His body jerked, shuddered, and the shock rode hard through his system. The tremors didn't stop after a few moments, they just continued, shaking his whole body—she must have amped up the tazer.

Growling, his hands flew up and he yanked out the electrodes even as the electricity still pumped through him.

The redhead's lips parted.

"That all you got?" he asked, his claws ripping out. "Not good enough." Then he attacked.

Chapter 16

Lucas leapt up and landed in the van, tackling both Karen and the demon. Sarah jumped up behind him, ramming her knee on the bumper. She ignored the stab of pain and focused on the danger.

"A tazer?" Lucas laughed at that. "Did you really think that shit was going to work on me?"

Sarah scrambled closer, her breath panting out from the run and the adrenaline that spiked her blood. "Lucas, she's FBI, she's—"

"Tazers work well enough on coyotes," Karen Phillips said, her voice calm, as if a wolf shifter didn't have his claws very near her throat. "I figured it was worth a shot." Her gaze darted to Sarah. "Besides, if I'd shot you, I knew she'd be seriously pissed."

The demon made a sound somewhere between a whimper and a moan.

Then there was a click. A very soft, very dangerous click of sound. Sarah glanced up and found herself staring down the barrel of a gun. One that a guy—a young guy with dirty blond hair but one very steady hand—had aimed on her.

The driver. No wonder the van wasn't flying down the road. The driver had stopped to get in on the action in the back.

"Tell the wolf to back off," the blond ordered.

Lucas didn't look away from Karen. "Tell the dumb asshole to drop his gun or I'll start slashing his partner."

Ah, yeah. Sounded like a Mexican standoff to Sarah. "You heard the man." Sarah extended her hand toward the driver. "But don't drop it, just give it to me." Because she'd been itching to get her hands on a weapon. *Tired of being defenseless.*

The guy didn't move for ten seconds. Then Lucas's fingers drew closer to Karen's chest.

"You're FBI!" The blond yelled at Sarah, veins bulging in his neck. "You're supposed to be on our side! You can't just stand there and let—"

"She's not FBI anymore." Lucas's glittering eyes lifted. "She's pack."

Suddenly, the agent's hold wasn't so steady.

The demon tried to sidle toward the still-open back doors. *Not going to happen.* Sarah moved slightly, putting her body between the demon and freedom.

"Curtis, give her the gun!" Karen yelled. "I know shifters. He'll slice me before you can even fire."

"Yes," Lucas said softly. "I will." He smiled. "Then I'll come after you, Curtis."

Curtis swore and turned his hand, offering the gun to Sarah. She reached for the weapon, wrapped her fingers around the butt of the gun—

The demon tried to jump out of the van. Right. She'd expected that. One fast elbow jab and she had him slamming into the side of the van. Still holding the gun, Sarah yanked the back doors closed, one at a time.

Then her gaze swept the small scene.

"You can . . . get off me now . . ." Karen glared up at Lucas.

He shook his head and leaned in closer. "Wanna tell me why the hell you smell like coyote . . ." He inhaled and Sarah saw a muscle jerk in his jaw. "And *wolf?*"

Uh, oh. Sarah pointed the gun at Curtis. "Drive. Get us out of here." They'd wasted too much time. Left those back doors open too long. There were too many other eyes out there, watching.

"Drive?" The guy parroted. "To where?"

"My place," Lucas said. "And, yeah, I'm sure you know

exactly where that is, right?" His right hand waved toward the row of surveillance equipment that lined the interior of the van. "You bastards have fun watching?"

Curtis didn't answer, but he did crawl back toward the front of the van.

Lucas rose slowly and Sarah could see the leashed tension in his body. "Who is she, Sarah?"

Sarah licked her lips. "Karen and I worked together, back when I was in the FBI."

"I figured that much."

The demon was on the floor, glaring at them both. Karen sat up, her shoulder brushing against his. The agent wasn't glaring. In fact, she didn't look the least bit pissed.

Odd.

Karen wasn't known for keeping her cool. Sarah's internal alarm went on high alert.

"Is she a charmer, too?" Lucas asked.

"No, I'm human," Karen told him, a little heat finally slipping into her voice. "We do exist too, you know."

The driver shoved down the gas pedal and the van lurched forward.

"Fuck, I need out of here!" the demon yelled.

Lucas shot a piercing gaze at him. "Want me to shut you up?"

The demon's mouth closed.

"You don't smell human." Lucas turned his gaze back to the agent.

"That's because I've been living with the coyotes for the last five months." She pushed her hair out of her face. "Hang around animals enough, and their scent sticks to you."

Half-true. So Sarah called her on the lie. "And it helps if you visit a certain *mambo* in the area and get a special oil that gives off shifter scent, right, K?" Because Karen wasn't the only agent who'd used that trick. Only Sarah hadn't visited Marie. On another mission, she'd used the warlock, Skye, to get the oil.

Karen's head inclined toward her.

"Is that why you smell like wolf, too?" Lucas wanted to know.

"No." Karen's breath eased out. "That would be because one of your precious pack kidnapped me. What you're scenting . . . that's your boy Dane." One red brow quirked. "But I'm guessing you already know that, right? You recognized *his* scent, and I'm sure he would have briefed the big old alpha right away.

Lucas smiled. "Yes, he would have." He leaned in toward her. "He also would have told me that a human woman named Karen helped to get him captured, that she was working with the coyotes."

The van hit a pothole and Sarah grabbed the side of the vehicle to steady herself.

"Not *with* them," Karen said, a faint line appearing between her brows. "Working undercover. You know what that is, right, wolf? When you have to do shit that makes you sick . . . all so you can keep the innocents in the world safe."

"There are no innocents," Sarah whispered. "Not anymore."

Karen's gaze cut to her. "*She* knows. Sarah's worked undercover more times than you can count. She blends. It's what we do. We get in, make 'em—" She shut up, fast, when she caught Sarah's narrowing eyes.

But Lucas would have been an idiot not to realize what Karen had been saying. "You make 'em trust you," he finished. "Then you take the bastards down?" His eyes were on Sarah.

"That's usually the plan," she managed, the gun feeling way too heavy in her hands.

"The bullets are silver," Karen told her. "You didn't check. Bad move there, S. You're losing your touch."

The demon's eyes were bulging, but he wasn't saying a word. Sarah lifted the gun a bit. "I felt the weight difference." Slight, but noticeable. The FBI was so predictable. "I knew what I had."

Lucas's stare dropped to the gun, then slowly rose back up

to her face. Oh, hell, *no*, he'd better not be doubting her. Hadn't they already cleared this up?

"The gun will come in handy," Karen told her. "Because I'm guessing you don't have that knife of yours anymore."

Not anymore. Thanks to Rafe.

"It's about to come in real handy," Sarah said, and adjusted her aim, just enough so that the barrel of the gun pointed at the demon. "Where is he." Not a question.

Damn, but that demon was *sweating*. And, as she watched, his glamour faded away. His hair darkened, lengthened, his chin firmed up, his eyes flashed from weary gray to dark black.

"Did you ever have the chance to meet Agent Greg Dulane?" Karen pursed her lips. "He's pretty good at undercover work, too. Even better than you."

She could see where he would be.

Karen and Greg gazed up at her. "Help us," Karen said quietly. "And we'll help you."

She'd been offered this deal before. Pretty much verbatim from her FBI supervisor.

Lucas's claws gouged into the side of the van. *Damn.*

"Cut through this shit and tell me where the hell Rafe is," Lucas snarled. "Or in a few minutes, you'll both be needing more *help* than anyone can give you."

The demon flinched.

"Rafe isn't working this alone. You *know* that." Karen's face had paled, but she was still fighting. Still Karen. "I spent so long working on getting in with the coyotes, but then Rafe came in—and he took out the whole damn group."

"What a fucking shame." Lucas looked bored.

Karen swallowed. "Rafe didn't kill 'em. He sent more dogs in." Her hands pressed against her jeans. "You know he has Hayden on a tight leash. When Rafe says bite, Hayden rips the throat out of anyone near him."

Like John's throat had been ripped out.

"We've been working on the coyotes for so long, but now John's dead." Karen's hands fisted. "My five months are shot down the drain and Hayden knows who I am. Who I *really* am. He's got me marked."

Sarah knew how that felt.

"The coyotes have been killing with Rafe. They used to stay to the shadows but now—they think it's a whole new game."

"Isn't it?" Lucas growled. "Isn't that what it's fucking become? The Bureau tries to shove the paranormals back, tries to scare us with the threat of extermination." He laughed at that. "But we're not the ones who'll be exterminated."

Karen blanched. "That's wh-what Rafe said, too. You all think that—"

"Right." Disgust had Lucas's mouth tightening. "In the dark, all paranormals are the fucking same, aren't we? We're all big, bad monsters who'll kill humans in a blink."

Some would. But not all. Didn't Karen realize yet? The supernaturals were just like humans. Some good, some very bad.

Karen's chin dropped. "Rafe and the coyotes have a list of undercover agents."

Now Karen had finally surprised Sarah. A fist squeezed her heart. "How the hell did they get that?"

"Because they had someone in the FBI who gave it to them. Someone who hacked the system, got the names, and just handed them right over."

Shit.

"Those men who were murdered in Arizona weren't random. John wasn't random. Everyone they've killed . . . they're taking out our watchers. Our agents."

No, that wasn't possible. They couldn't—

"Rafe thought he could turn you to his side. If he couldn't turn you, he'd kill you." Flat. "John wasn't given the option of turning. The coyotes didn't want a traitor with them."

An image of John's dead body flashed before her eyes.

"Everyone they've killed," Karen said again. "They're working on their own extermination list. Not just humans— they're also taking out charmers and demons, but all their victims are undercover agents."

No. "You're wrong." And she remembered Josette's grief. "There were three others. Here, in LA. They weren't—"

"Maxime and Helene?" A bitter smile tugged at Karen's lips. "They were keeping tabs on the *mambo*. Letting us know who came to visit, and what price they had to pay. The *mambo* saw the most powerful and the weakest supernaturals in the area. Did you really think no one was watching her?"

"But . . ." What had been his name? "Josette's lover, he—"

Sarah caught the fast glance the demon sent Karen. Oh, damn. "Did she know?"

"That he was a demon?" Karen shrugged. "Probably. Marie would have told her that."

"Did she know he was FBI?" No, she hadn't known. Because Josette thought she was responsible for his death. She didn't know he'd been marked, just as they all had been.

"If she knew then she wouldn't be working so hard right now to find and stop his killer, would she?" And Karen's smile stretched, flashing way too many teeth.

Sarah's gut clenched. This wasn't right. "Do you know what she's been doing? She *raised* him, K. The pain was so much that *she raised him*."

Karen's gaze dropped. "I didn't . . . I never thought she'd do that."

"Then you never fucking thought."

Karen flinched at Lucas's disgust.

"She's the granddaughter of a voodoo priestess, and you really believed she wouldn't turn to magic when her lover was killed?" Lucas heaved out a hard breath. "Lady, you were kidding yourself. You knew she'd break, and you and your boss didn't care."

At that, Karen tried to jump up, but he shoved her right back down.

"You don't know me!" she threw at him. "Don't say what—"

Sarah shoved the gun into the back of her jeans. "Who's the leak?"

Her head nearly rapped into the top of the van. She had to crouch to stay upright.

Karen slanted her a fuming stare, but Sarah saw the tears glittering in the agent's eyes.

"*Who's the leak?*" Lucas shouted.

"We—we thought it was Sarah."

Hell. Figured. "Then you never fucking thought," she repeated Lucas's words quietly, aware of the slight tremble in her fingers. She'd bled for the Bureau. Taken so many cases, nearly lost herself. And they really thought she'd sold the agents out? Sent them to their deaths?

"He was *your* lover, Sarah. You got in with him so fast. Some said too fast." Karen glanced at the demon, then back at Sarah. "And you had access to the files on the undercover operatives."

"Me and a dozen other agents." Dammit.

"Then you quit the FBI." Karen sighed. "You *looked* guilty."

"I'm not."

"What Rafe wants, he gets." Karen's voice roughened. "He wanted to turn the tables on the Bureau that was hunting his kind, so now he has the list of names." Her eyes were on Lucas. "He wanted revenge on the man who killed his father, and now he's got you in his sights."

What? Was that supposed to make Lucas suspicious of her? What kind of game was Karen spinning?

Sarah glanced out the back window. No other cars. Just a line of trees. "Stop the damn van!" she yelled.

The van squealed to a halt.

The demon flew forward.

Lucas didn't move. He just watched Sarah.

"What's the trap, Karen?" Sarah demanded. "What's the deal? We're not heading to Lucas's, this isn't the right road."

"No," Lucas said immediately.

The driver shoved open his door and ran.

Sarah surged forward. Lucas caught her hand. "Let him go," he said. "There's nowhere for him to run here."

But where was here?

"Coyote land," Lucas said, as if reading her mind.

What the hell?

He laughed at the expression on Karen's face. "Did you really think I didn't hear the beep of the transmitter beneath the van? I knew where the asshole was taking us. Guess that was the plan, though, right? Lure me in, keep me trapped. Take me to a slaughter." He shoved open the back doors, letting in the setting sun. Soon, darkness would be calling. "The thing is, agent, I *wanted* you to take me to the bastard. Why the hell do you think I followed your bread crumbs? Why do you think I ever got in the van?"

Karen didn't speak.

Lucas pointed one claw at the demon. "By the way, Marley, did you really think I was dumb enough not to spot you on sight?"

Marley.

Once more, the demon's image began to waver.

"Shit!" Now Karen was the one sweating.

"You look different, Marley, but the scent is the same. With you, it always is. Glamour's only skin-deep, right?"

The dark hair lengthened, sliding past the demon's shoulders. The face softened, the hard edges slipping away. The cheekbones stretched higher. The lips plumped. In bare seconds, the man was gone.

And the demon who'd left Sarah to burn was back.

"Demons didn't send you to watch my ass," Lucas said. He grabbed Sarah's hand and they jumped from the van.

Marley sprang after them, with Karen right at her side.

"Lucas!" Now the demon's voice was feminine. So she'd changed that, too? "I wasn't given a choice, I—"

"You wanted someone to keep tabs on my pack, right, Karen?" Lucas drawled. "And like Marley said, she knew my weak spot."

Sarah had read the profile on him, too. Because of his past, Lucas had a protective streak. A soft spot for victims.

A lump rose in her throat. *I used that weakness against him, too.*

Did he realize?

His mocking smile said he did. *Lucas.*

His gaze drifted to the darkening woods. "We're not alone out here, you know."

Sarah already had the gun out and in her hands. This time, she had it aimed at the demon.

"Back away from her, Karen."

But Karen moved closer to Marley. "She's on our side. Dammit, if you'd both just calm down, I could explain! She really is an agent. Marley Dulane is—"

Sarah didn't care to learn anything else about the demon. She already knew what mattered. "She told the coyotes about John. She watched him die."

Karen's lips parted. "But . . . no, that's not—"

"*Back away, Karen!*" Because there was a traitor in the Bureau, all right, and Sarah was looking right at her.

Karen began to edge away from the demon.

Just not fast enough.

Two coyotes sprang from the bushes and launched at Lucas.

The demon bent down low, then rose in a flash, driving her fist right into Karen's stomach.

The agent screamed and punched out, even as Sarah fired the bullet.

But it was too late.

Too damn late.

The demon had already jumped back and Karen fell to the ground, the handle of an all-too-familiar knife buried in her stomach.

My weapon. "Karen!"

Snarls and growls filled the air even as Karen's blood pooled on the ground.

The demon laughed. "When they find the body, they'll know you killed her."

Sarah rushed to Karen. The agent was still alive, but blood trickled from her lips.

"But you'll be dead, too . . ." Marley's voice promised.

Sarah whipped the gun up, ready to fire, but the fast bitch had already run into the woods. Sarah knew the demon was just biding her time. Watching, waiting to attack.

With what? More fire?

Dammit.

The two coyotes circled Lucas, and he slashed out at them with his claws. He hadn't shifted, and she knew he *couldn't* shift. Because in the time it took to shift, they could kill him.

The hell they would.

Smoke began to fill the air. *Bitch.*

Sarah narrowed her eyes as she took aim.

"*Don't hit your lover . . .*" Marley sang out. "*But, of course, you like to hurt your lovers, don't you, Sarah?*"

Karen choked, and her body heaved.

Sarah fired, catching one coyote in the shoulder. The bastard howled and turned his stare on her.

Hayden. Like she'd ever forget those eyes. That bright circle of yellow gleamed in the darkness of his stare.

He growled, then he leapt toward her.

Sarah squeezed the trigger once more. This time, the bullet blasted right between his eyes.

He didn't even have time to whimper.

But the other coyote did. Lucas had driven his claws into the animal's side and now the coyote was down, jerking and heaving and twisting.

"Lucas!" He had to move so she could get a clear shot. "I can't get the—"

A line of fire burst from the woods. Flames that separated her from Lucas.

Damn demon.

"S-Sarah . . ." Karen grabbed her hand. "D-don't let me . . . die out here . . ."

Sarah glanced down at Karen. They'd been friends once. Hadn't they? She'd worked with Karen on three cases. They'd laughed. Traded stories.

But never met outside of work.

Never talked about anything personal.

Hell, she didn't even know if Karen was the woman's real name.

"D-Don't want to d-die . . . out here . . ." Karen's fingers squeezed hers.

The fire closed in.

"Sarah! Fuck, Sarah, jump over the flames! There's time!" Lucas's roar. Her head whipped up. He'd taken out the other coyote.

She shook her head. "I can't—I can't leave her." Because, dammit, she had a weakness, too. They'd probably profiled her at the FBI, just like they had Lucas. If she was really a suspect like Karen had said, the profile would have been one of their first investigative tactics, and Marley would've had access to that profile.

Using my weakness against me.

Sarah stood, trying to drag Karen to her feet.

The other woman groaned, pain heavy in the sound. Sarah started to lift her. She could try a fireman's carry, she could—

Lucas leapt through the flames. The scent of burned flesh rose, clogging her nostrils. *No, Lucas!*

"Get in the damn van."

She jumped inside, pulling Karen with her.

"Stop the fucking fire, Marley!" he shouted.

But Marley didn't stop the fire. The flames just flared higher and they closed in tighter.

Lucas ran to the front of the van. Jumped inside. "The bastard took the keys!"

Shit. Now they were trapped. Sarah covered her mouth and yanked the back doors closed. *So much smoke.*

"Don't worry, babe. I got this." Her head whipped around. He'd bent under the dash.

One moment. Two . . . The motor revved to life. He slammed on the gas and the van lurched forward. Sarah saw a wall of flames waiting on them. Bigger, so big now . . .

They went right through the fire.

Sarah didn't even have time to scream. The van blasted

through the flames. The windshield cracked, rubber burned, and they were free.

Lucas jerked the wheel and the van streaked to the left. "How much longer does she have?"

Karen's eyes were closed. Her blood soaked Sarah's clothing. Sarah touched the wound and Karen didn't wince. Sarah wasn't even sure Karen had felt her touch. *Too far gone.* "She needs a hospital and she needs one *now.*"

No, what she really needed was a miracle.

Lucas's gaze met hers in the rearview mirror.

"I'm trying to stop the blood." Her hands were so red and the blood flow wouldn't stop. "We have to get her to a doctor. She's not going to make it if—"

If he stopped. If he went back for Marley and whoever else waited in the woods. Sarah couldn't get Karen to a hospital on her own. She needed him to drive so she could keep the pressure on the wound.

She needed him.

He needed vengeance.

"*Please,* Lucas. She'll die."

Did he even care? What would a human's death matter to him? Just a human. A dead stranger.

Wasn't that what she could have been?

The van's engine roared. "We'll be at Saints Hospital in ten minutes." His gaze met hers. "Can you keep her alive that long?"

"D-don't let . . ." Karen whispered and a tear streaked from her eye.

Sarah swallowed down the fear that had risen in her throat. "You're going to make it." Not a lie. Not really.

"Sarah?" Lucas's voice growled.

"I can keep her alive." *I hope.* "But, dammit, drive *fast.*"

Because she didn't think she had ten minutes. From the look of things, Karen barely had any time at all.

Don't die on me.

But Karen's eyes were already closed.

Chapter 17

Lucas braked right next to the hospital's emergency-room doors. He jumped out of the van and raced around to the back, shouting for the guard on duty to get help.

Shit, couldn't he tell when there was a damn emergency? *Humans.*

He yanked open the back door and hoisted Karen into his arms. Her head sagged back against him and her blood . . . *so much blood.*

Sarah's gaze met his. "Her heart's barely beating."

Fuck. He spun on his heel and ran for the sliding glass doors. The guard was just coming out of the doors, a gurney beside him, two guys with stethoscopes hauling ass with him.

"She's been stabbed!" He yelled but thought that should be obvious. The stab wound had been perfectly placed for maximum damage.

Lucas put her on the gurney. The agent's eyes never opened. The docs swarmed her.

"Sir, you've got to come inside." The guard grabbed his arm. "We'll have to call the cops, file a report—"

Lucas didn't move. "No."

The doctors had Karen inside now. They'd do what they could for her. If she lived . . . if she died . . .

He turned away, breaking the guard's hold.

"You can't leave!" The guard didn't make the mistake of touching him again. "You can't—"

Sarah had climbed from the van. Blood covered her.

"Oh, shit! Ma'am, hold on!" The guard streaked past Lucas and caught Sarah's hands. "You should've said there were two victims!"

Sarah shook her head. "I'm not hurt." She stared down at her hands. At all the blood.

Not hurt. This time. But next time, she could be.

The wolf inside howled. Not fucking next time. No one would hurt her. *No one.*

"Come inside, ma'am," the guard said, trying to tug her closer. "Come inside, you need to—"

"The woman they took inside is a federal agent." Lucas pulled Sarah away from the man, deliberately keeping his hold gentle with her. Even though she wasn't an average human, she was as weak physically as the agent, he knew that. So why the hell couldn't he be easier with her?

Because I need her. Too much.

The wolf within craved her as much as the man did.

"Call Anthony Miller at the Bureau ... tell him the victim's Karen Phillips." Sarah's voice was whisper-soft.

"The—the FBI?"

Lucas steered Sarah toward the front of the van. She moved quickly, jumping into the passenger seat.

The guard scrambled back. Lucas cast one last glance toward the brightly-lit hospital. That agent had been so far gone. No *mambo* was around to save her. Would the doctors be able to do enough?

He climbed into the van.

"He's going to report the license plate number," Sarah said. "The cops will be after us in no time. Especially if they think we're the ones who stabbed Karen."

"Doesn't matter." He gunned the engine and raced past an ambulance. "We'll ditch the van."

"I can't ... I ..." The rasp of her breath filled the vehicle's interior. "I need to get the blood off, Lucas." A pleading note had entered her voice. "Please ... *I need to get the blood off my hands.*"

Some blood wouldn't wash clean.

But he drove faster, snaking through the lanes. Heading deeper into the heart of the city.

There.

The rundown hotel waited just off the highway. A place where no one asked questions, because the folks damn well knew better than to make that mistake. The owner was a shifter who'd spent years lying to human cops.

"Stay here," he told her, and ran into what counted as the main office of the place. His fist slammed down onto the bell. Shit. He had blood on his hands, too. The scent had been so strong on Sarah, he hadn't even realized . . .

A key was shoved across the scarred desktop. "Twenty for an hour."

He tossed the money onto the countertop and swiped the key. The fox shifter had to see and smell the blood. But in that place, it wouldn't be the first time.

Or the last.

Lucas tossed out an extra hundred. "I've got a van that needs to disappear."

The fox's palm covered the money. "Consider it gone, Alpha."

He spun away and hurried back outside. Room seven. The room the fox always gave him when the pack needed to clean up.

How much blood have I washed away?

But, damn it, he hadn't killed innocents. He'd taken out the bastards who'd come after him. He'd protected his pack. And if he had to . . . hell, yeah, he'd do it again.

Sarah shoved open the door when she saw him. Beautiful Sarah. She could have stayed out of this life. Could have passed for normal.

He glanced toward the side of the building. The fox was already heading for the van. "Come on."

She'd clenched her hands, probably trying to hide the blood. Didn't do much good though, not when her clothes were covered in dark red.

He pushed the key into the lock and the door swung open seconds later. The place was a dump, no getting around it, but it had a shower and soap and he could make certain Sarah got what she wanted.

I need to get the blood off my hands.

Oh, yeah. He understood. *Been there, babe. Done that.*

She brushed by him, stopping only long enough to put her gun on the nightstand before she walked toward the bathroom. Sarah yanked her clothes off as she went, dropping the bloody shirt, kicking out of her shoes and socks, and ditching her jeans.

She disappeared into the small bathroom and the roar of the shower filled the motel room. Lucas's gaze tracked around the area. Sagging bed. Scarred nightstand. Not much else. No TV because the folks who came to this place weren't real big on staying and relaxing.

He glanced at his hands. Would the human agent live? Marley sure wouldn't. Not when he got his hands on her.

He stalked to the phone and dialed quickly. Dane answered on the second ring. "Where the hell are you?" the other shifter asked at once.

His gaze tracked to the peeling ceiling. Hell was a pretty good description. "Langdon's." The name of that cagey fox. Dane would know the place. He'd cleaned up there often enough. No telling how much blood this room had seen. He exhaled. "We need a team on Prentmore."

A low whistle. "That's close to where Jess and his coyotes made their base."

"And it's where you'll find two more dead coyotes. But they're not the priority." His gaze locked on Sarah's gun. "They can fucking rot. I need a nose to search the scene."

"Whose scent are we after?"

"Marley's."

"What? What the hell was she—"

"She's FBI." Who wasn't? "And she's also been the one working with Rafe." The agent who'd flipped. Not Sarah. Not Karen. The demon who'd been right under his nose.

"Find her, follow her scent, and let me know which hole she crawls into."

Because he'd drag her out, and when he did, he'd find Rafe.

Lucas exhaled, feeling the aches in his muscles. "Has Caleb talked yet?"

"No, not yet . . . he's still out."

There is no cure. "Get out to Prentmore." He could count on Dane. He'd track the demon. "But don't take Marley out, got me? No matter what she says or does, she's mine."

Because she'd lead him to Rafe.

He ended the call, his hands yanking at his shirt. The water was still running and he wasn't going to leave Sarah in there alone.

Crave her.

Need her.

He was naked by the time he crossed the threshold into the bathroom. Steam curled in the air, and he could see the outline of Sarah's body behind the thin shower curtain.

For a moment, he just watched her. She had bent her head beneath the spray and her shoulders seemed to shake a little. Fuck. Was she crying?

He yanked the curtain back. She didn't whirl around in surprise. Didn't even look up. Lucas climbed in behind her. When the water hit him, the clear liquid changed to red as the blood washed from his body.

He didn't touch her. Not yet. Lucas didn't want to touch her with the blood still on his hands. He grabbed the soap. Lathered and scrubbed until his flesh was clean.

Sarah moved forward, letting more of the spray hit him. The water stung a bit. She had it on full-blast and it was hot and it was just what he needed.

The red water slowly drained away. His hands looked clean again. What a lie.

But he reached for her anyway now. Lucas wrapped his arms around Sarah and pulled her close.

"Sometimes, it seems like I don't know who to trust anymore." Her whisper.

"You can trust me."

"I *have* to trust you for this to work." She turned in his arms, facing him. Her head tilted back. Her black lashes were wet, spiky. From the shower or tears? Probably from both. "You told me that before."

It was still true now.

"But do you trust me?" She asked him, then shook her head. Her hands curled around his shoulders. "After everything, how could you?"

Her lips trembled. He bent close and brought his mouth over hers. *"Trust me,"* the words probably shouldn't have come out as an order, but they did. His mouth took hers, and his tongue thrust deep.

She moaned in her throat and her nails bit into him.

Trust me.

He yanked tight onto his control. This time, he'd show her that he could be more than just the beast the world thought he was.

For her.

He forced his head to lift. Her eyes were big and deep. Eyes that a man could probably lose his soul in—if he had a soul.

Sold mine long ago.

Blood. Screams. Death. Had the trade been worth it?

He lifted Sarah out of the tub, wrapped one of the threadbare towels around her, and carried her to the bed.

He put her down on the mattress and stepped back. She opened her arms, almost immediately, reaching for him.

Worth it?

He went to her and knew that nothing would keep him away from her. Not now. Not fucking ever.

He didn't touch her with his hands. They could be too hard. The claws could break through flesh too easily. And the damn wolf always wanted her.

He used his mouth. Kissed her lips. Stroked her with his tongue. Then he licked his way down her throat. Her body arched against him, her hips and thighs shifting so that he felt the move right over his swollen cock.

The minute her clothes had hit the floor, he'd gotten hard for her. Blood, death . . . didn't matter. He'd wanted her.

Would have killed to have her.

The thought didn't give him any pause. After all, he'd known for a while now that he'd be killing for Sarah.

The towel had come loose and her nipples—tight, hard peaks that looked like perfect cherries—waited for him. He licked her nipple, the sound of her moans filling his ears.

Gentle.

His claws dug into the sheets.

He took her breast into his mouth. Sucked. Licked. The taste of her spilled onto his tongue. So fucking sweet. So . . . Sarah.

His breath blew over her nipple.

"Lucas . . ."

He turned his attention to the other breast.

The edge of his teeth scraped over her flesh.

She gasped, jerking.

Control.

His mouth left her flesh.

"No! No, Lucas, I liked—"

He kissed her stomach. Worked his way down her body, touching her with his mouth and tongue, caressing. Her legs parted for him and the scent of her arousal filled his nose and drove him wild.

Control.

"Open your legs wider." His voice was a growl. Dammit.

But she opened her legs wider. She brought her hands between their bodies, and she used her fingertips to part her sex for him. "Kiss me, Lucas."

Fuck, yes.

He did. His lips took her. He sucked her clitoris, used his

tongue to taste and to take and her breath came faster, hitching, gasping as her lips lifted and she pressed closer to him.

He drove his tongue inside of her.

Her hands were in his hair now, urging him closer and she was saying . . .

"I want you, Lucas! Oh, yes, now, come on, I need you—"

He was starving for her. So he took more. *More.*

She came against his mouth. Her whole body tensed and a broken scream ripped from her throat. But he didn't stop. Couldn't. Because he had to have—

More.

His claws dug deeper into the mattress.

She trembled, whispering his name, and his mouth pressed against her. He'd take everything she'd give to him. Every damn thing.

So fucking sweet.

He waited until the shudders eased, until her nails pulled free from his flesh, then he rose up. Sweat slickened his back. His muscles were so tight and his cock felt like it was about to burst.

Take her.

The head of his cock lodged at her creamy core. He still had control—barely—he could do this right, he could—

"No."

The word stopped him cold. Every muscle in his body locked and a distant roaring filled his ears. "Sarah?" She was turning him away? Now?

She pushed against his chest. "You're not doing this to me."

He'd tried to be gentle. Tried to show her that he was more than an animal. Couldn't she see that?

"You're not the only one who's giving this time, Lucas." Her eyes sparkled at him. A red flush stained her cheeks and her plump lips firmed. "This time, I'll give to you."

Her hands circled his wrists. His claws were still lodged in the mattress. Right then, he didn't want her to see . . . him.

"It's okay," she whispered and pulled his wrists. She didn't look at his claws.

Sarah pushed him onto the mattress. She rose above him. Her scent surrounded him, and he just wanted to take and take.

But he was more than an animal.

Her hands trailed down his chest and his cock jerked.

More than an animal—right?

Her lips feathered over his jaw. "I want to know everything about you, Lucas. I want to touch everything." She nipped his chin. "I can handle you. I might not be a shifter, but I *can* handle you."

No, she couldn't. If his control shattered, if the wolf ever took over and he became psychotic, there was no way she'd be able handle him. No one could. Wolves that pushed past that boundary were put down. Pack law. The law he'd directed because he'd seen what happened when madness ruled.

"I know so much about you," she told him, her voice like sin in the dark. "More than you realize."

She'd been FBI. Was there anything she didn't know?

Her breasts pressed against his chest, the nipples still tight and hard, and he growled.

She licked the skin just under his jaw. "All your life, you had to be the strong one." Her lips kissed a path up his jaw. She licked his right earlobe.

Lucas tensed. "Sarah, *don't.*" Because she didn't—

Her mouth whispered over the torn remains of his ear, kissing lightly. Such soft, tender kisses.

"You were too young for so much pain."

No. He wouldn't remember. He grabbed her hips and yanked her close.

But she kissed his ear again. "Everything you've done," she told him, the words a breath in his ear. "Just made you stronger."

There was no revulsion from her. Her mouth pressed against the torn edges of flesh. "So strong."

Sarah. "I want you, *now.*" The wolf was fighting free. The man didn't want to hold him back. The hot clasp of her sex was too close, pleasure waiting—within his reach. Release. Hunger. Her.

She pulled back and stared into his eyes. "They whisper about you. In the other packs, they talk about the alpha who should have died years ago. The boy who proved to be stronger than the wolves after him."

He hadn't been strong. He'd been desperate. He'd had to go back and protect his friend. Dane—they'd tortured Dane, sliced him to pieces because he wouldn't betray—

"I don't want you going back to that place right now." Sarah's voice had his eyes rising up to meet hers. She licked her lips. "No pain now, okay? Only pleasure."

Then she eased down his body, her hair sliding over his skin. Just like silk. Soft and sensual and so cool, while her mouth—

Fuck.

Her mouth closed around the tip of his cock. Hot and wet and she took him inside, sucking and licking.

"Sarah!" A roar.

She didn't stop. Her mouth widened and she took him in deeper. Her lips closed around him and her palm curved around the base of his cock. Her hand squeezed him, pumped and her mouth tasted and tasted—

His hips arched up, and his cock drove into her mouth. So damn good. She was taking him in, pulling at his flesh and the pleasure had his spine tightening and his chest burning. He was going to come in her mouth. *Fuck.*

Her tongue swirled over the head of his cock and she swallowed.

He caught her arms—*too rough, slow down, ease up*—and pushed her back. His hands were shaking with a need too strong to ignore. "In you . . . got to be buried in you . . ." He could hardly get the words out. His voice was far more wolf-growl than anything else.

But Sarah understood. She always understood. She smiled

at him and she climbed up his body, straddling his hips. Her creamy flesh teased his cock.

Take it easy, go slow, not too deep—

"Hard, Lucas. Hard and wild and deep."

His control shattered and he surged into her as deeply as he could. His fingers bit into her hips. He lifted her up and down, forcing her to match the speed of his thrusts.

But she was laughing and driving down with her body and meeting him thrust for thrust. Her sex closed around him, so tight, so hot, and she squeezed his cock.

He lowered her onto the bed and caught her hands, pinning them to the bed. Her gaze met his. No fear. Just need. Animal need.

Lust.

But . . .

More. Desire. Hunger. Passion.

Trust?

"More, Lucas." She arched her neck. Her heels dug into his ass. "More!"

He gave her more. The bed squeaked and slammed into the wall. His heart thundered in his chest. He drove into her, again and again, deeper, so deep, and the feel of her sex squeezing him was fucking fantastic. His mouth pressed against her throat. Pressed over the pulse that raced so fast.

He could taste her lust.

He licked her. Let her feel the edge of his teeth.

She shuddered against him, but didn't tell him to stop. Didn't fight—no, she pushed her throat to his mouth. She wanted him.

Everything.

He found her sweet spot, the soft curve where neck and shoulder met. Lucas bit.

She came beneath him, a hard ripple of her sex that stroked every inch of his cock.

She came and he bit her again, and the need broke free. He surged into her, drove deep, and let the pleasure rip through him.

When he climaxed, when his body shook and he pumped into her core, he finally realized the truth.

He wouldn't just kill for Sarah King.

Very slowly, Lucas lifted his head and he stared at the mark he'd made on her flesh. A claiming mark. The way of the wolf. His gaze met hers. Sated green. Wide open, seeing all of him, accepting all.

No, he wouldn't just kill for her.

If he had to, he'd fucking die for her.

After all, it wasn't every day that a wolf found his mate. And when he found her, he knew to hold on tight.

Because if he lost her, only madness would be left.

The scent of blood was like a punch in the face. Dane narrowed his eyes as he studied the bodies still lying on the twisting road. No big surprise that the dead shifters hadn't been found by someone else. Most folks stayed the hell off this road.

It was known to be a hunting ground. Humans who got lost on this trek didn't always make it back out. And the *Other*, they either came there to hunt or to die.

The coyotes had been there to hunt, but the dumb sonsofbitches had wound up prey.

"A silver bullet right between the eyes," Jordan said, staring down at the body. "Yeah, that'll take you out, no matter if you're coyote or wolf." He glanced up at Dane. "Sarah's a good shot."

"And Lucas is a fucking brutal killer." He turned away from the younger shifter and stared at the remains of the other coyote. Rage had been riding Lucas hard when he'd made this kill. Because the assholes had threatened Sarah?

Did the guy even realize how important she'd become to him? Maybe, if he was smart, he did.

"I guess that's from Marley's fire."

Dane's gaze tracked to the right. The demon had sure been burning wild. Those scorchmarks were all over the place. The scent of ash lingered in the air, tangling with the blood.

He inhaled, drawing the scents in deeper. He'd have to get past the blood and fire first, then he'd find Marley. He'd get a lock on her and run the demon down.

His eyes closed and he inhaled.

"Fuck!" Dane's eyes flew open. His heart had kicked hard in his chest and his claws burst out.

"Dane? What is it? What's—"

He grabbed the silver knife that had been tossed onto the side of the road. He barely felt the burn on his hand.

"Drop that, Dane!" Jordan shoved at his hand. "Are you crazy? That's silver!"

"Blood."

"Yeah, there's blood all over the place out here. Now let's get the bodies moved and find that demon."

Dane shook his head. "*Her* blood."

Jordan's eyes widened. "Marley? You've already got a lock on her?"

It wasn't Marley's blood. "Lucas didn't tell me she was here."

Jordan tensed.

"*He didn't tell me.*"

"Dude, he told us to come and get Marley, what the hell are you—"

"*Karen!*" Not Marley. He didn't give a shit about her. "Her blood—it's everywhere." Too much blood. Human blood. He'd never forget her scent.

"Karen?" Jordan grabbed Dane's fist and ripped the knife away. He hissed out a breath at the scorch of the silver and tossed the weapon into the woods. "That woman you found with the coyotes?"

The thunder of his heartbeat filled Dane's ears. "Sarah's knife was used on her."

"On Marley?" Jordan shook his head. "You're losing me here."

Dane's teeth snapped together. "*On Karen.*" She'd been attacked but she was gone now. No body. Just blood. Was she alive? What the hell had happened out there?

Trap.

Karen had worked with the coyotes before. Had she been in on the attack? Had Sarah fought back and stabbed her? Was she dead?

"Dammit, I don't know!" Jordan yelled, grabbing his shoulders and Dane realized he'd been snarling his questions. "We're not here to find her." Jordan shook him. "We're here to find Marley. Dammit, *Mar-ley.* The demon bitch that is after my brother, our pack. Karen . . ." His eyes narrowed. "I don't know her. She doesn't matter."

She does to me. "Only two people really matter to you." The words flew out. "Lucas and Cammie." Oh, he knew all about Jordan. The wolf who'd left them a boy and come back a broken man.

Got to be broken to see it.

He'd seen it. When the vampires had taken Jordan, he'd changed. Lost the light he'd held for years and finally become as dark and dangerous as the rest of his pack.

And as for Camellia, or . . . Cammie as Jordan called her—Dane knew all about her, too. She'd been taken by the vamps just as Jordan had, and during their captivity, Jordan had become the girl's protector. In the years that had passed, Jordan still snuck away to see her, when he didn't think anyone was watching. But Dane was always watching. He knew all about Jordan's little obsession. Still young, but Cammie was growing up fast. Was Jordan counting down the days?

Jordan's eyelids flickered and rage burned bright in his stare. "You don't know what the hell you're talking about. If you're not going to find the demon, I will."

Then he spun away and headed for the woods.

Jordan had a good sense of smell, no doubt, but picking up the demon wasn't gonna be easy.

Then Jordan started running. Maybe it *was* that easy.

Where was Karen's body? No body meant she could still be alive.

And why does it matter? The woman had trapped him, taunted him . . . and—

And I fucking want her alive.

He chased after Jordan. He couldn't leave the other wolf alone. If he did, Lucas would skin him alive.

A burst of speed sent him through the bushes. Branches clawed at him, but he shoved them out of the way. It didn't take him long to catch the scent Jordan was following.

No way to miss the scent of the dead.

He jumped over a fallen tree, snaked to the right and burst into a clearing.

"Didn't have a damn chance," Jordan shook his head and stared at the body.

Not Karen. There wasn't a whole lot that you *could* tell about those burned remains, but the scent was wrong. Whoever had died right there—it hadn't been his redhead.

"Marley's work." Obviously. Dane's gaze lifted and scanned the scene. His nostrils twitched. Marley had made a mistake. Most demons were hard to track, but a demon who'd been playing with fire . . .

He inhaled.

. . . a demon who'd been playing with fire might as well have left a trail of ash to follow.

He and Jordan turned as one and rushed to the left. The demon wouldn't get away from them, and she'd soon find out that wolves weren't afraid of a demon's fire.

Chapter 18

"It's been sixteen years," Lucas's voice rumbled beneath her ear and Sarah slowly lifted her head. "But sometimes I feel like I can still smell my father's blood."

A chill skated over her skin.

"Hell, I didn't even know a rival alpha was in town, not until I came home," he said quietly "and found my father struggling to shift. Kaber had cut his throat open, nearly taken his head, and no matter how hard he tried, my father couldn't shift to heal. Then . . . Kaber came over and finished the job. To make sure my father was good and dead, he took his head."

A sure-fire way to kill just about any paranormal out there. Sarah swallowed and pushed up onto her arms, bracing on his chest as she stared into his eyes. In the darkness, she couldn't see much. But that blue stare seemed to shine. And really, he was all she needed to see.

"The bastard was in my house before my father's body was even cold."

She didn't speak because Sarah wanted to hear this.

"The scent of his blood clogged my nostrils. And that bastard Kaber *laughed* when he saw me."

Her hands began to stroke his chest. She knew this moment was important. Lucas trusted her enough to tell her about his past. *You can trust me. I won't betray you.*

"Something broke in me. Everything was red, just like my father's blood. So much red. So much rage. I . . . attacked."

She wouldn't cry. *Ten. He'd been just ten.*

"Kaber shifted and came after me as a wolf. Hell, I knew I didn't have a chance, but my father's body was there. *Right there*, and I wasn't just gonna let that asshole take over. The wolves from my father's pack—they weren't doing a damn thing. Just standing back, watching Kaber, watching him take everything away."

"No one tried to help you?" Damn them.

"Dane." He exhaled. "After Kaber bit half my ear off, Dane attacked him from behind. Dane was only eight then, but he came out, flying on Kaber's back. He gave me the chance I needed."

His fingers smoothed down her arms. "My claws broke free. They shouldn't . . . it was too early for a full shift but I guess the adrenaline pushed me over the edge. My claws came out, and I slashed the bastard, I dug my claws as deep into his side as they could go." A rough laugh. "That didn't stop him. It barely slowed him down. He tossed Dane aside and came back after me."

Silence. She hated silence. Her hand pressed over his heart. The beat was slow, steady. "How did you get away?"

"I had to fucking run. He would have killed me. I would have died right next to my father, lost my head . . . for a pack that wouldn't stand up for me."

Except for Dane.

"I didn't leave the city right away."

Now this was part of the story that she'd never heard.

"Some demons in the area owed my father, and they paid his debt to me. They gave me shelter and helped to hide my scent." His fingers curled over her shoulder. "And when they got wind of what was happening to Dane, they told me."

She didn't want to know, but she asked anyway. "What did Kaber do to him?" *Those scars . . .*

"He started clawing the flesh off Dane's body."

Her gut clenched. "But he was eight, he couldn't—"

"Kaber knew Dane couldn't heal, that's why he did it. Kaber was sending a message to the pack. Either you were with him or you were one of the assholes he'd torture."

Sarah sat up in bed, dragging the sheet with her, but she kept her hand on Lucas. She needed to keep touching him. "Guess there's no doubt Kaber was crazy."

"Just another psychotic wolf," Lucas murmured.

Okay, *now* she wished she could see more in the darkness because she would've loved to catch his expression. "What did you do?"

"I went back for him." Spoken as if there had been no other option. "Two demons took me up there. They wouldn't go in, but I didn't need them to. I knew every inch of that place. Still do."

Because the wolf compound was his father's old home. She'd known that, but hadn't realized just how much that truly meant . . .

"I found Dane and I carried him out. I got him the hell out of there and we didn't look back."

But, no, wait, he *had* gone back. He'd grown up and then he'd gone after Kaber and—

"I wouldn't have ever gone back, Sarah. Those assholes in the pack turned their backs on me. Together, we could have fought Kaber but . . ." Now he rose, pulling from the bed, leaving her cold and alone with only the too-thin sheet. "Then when I was sixteen, I met a demon named Trace in a shit-forsaken bar in Mexico."

She wasn't even surprised to find out that he'd been in a bar at sixteen. Not like the normal rules of society had ever applied to him.

"Seems this demon had been in LA. He'd seen Kaber's pack, and he'd noticed a kid there—a black-haired, golden-eyed kid who looked, according to Trace, one hell of a lot like me."

Jordan. "You didn't . . . you didn't know about him when you left." Well, hell, wasn't that obvious?

"My mother gave birth to me and then she left the pack."

No emotion there. "At least, I thought she'd left, but it turns out she came back a few times over the years. I just didn't know about her little visits."

She'd come back and she'd gotten pregnant again.

"She dumped Jordan just like she dumped me, only my dad wasn't around to keep him safe. She left the kid with Kaber. *Kaber.*" His fist slammed into the wall and she realized just how fake his calm actually was.

Sarah licked her lips. "You went back for him, too."

"I went back for everything that was mine. My brother, my house, my pack." She saw the big shadow of his body stalk to the window. He peered out between the blinds. "I went back for it all, and I made sure Kaber suffered for everything he'd done to me."

Yes, this part she knew. He'd gone back and given a hard, painful death to Kaber. Everyone at the FBI had known how the story ended, too. That's why he'd been put on the extermination list. A brutal kill at sixteen—they'd just expected more blood and death to keep coming from him. "And what about the wolves?" she asked. "The shifters who'd been part of your father's pack?"

"Only a few were left alive by then." A rough laugh. "Imagine that. Packs are supposed to keep you safe, but with Kaber, just a few were left, and they hauled ass fast enough when I came back on the scene."

Because they probably had expected Lucas to kill them. "So you started a new pack."

The blinds fell back into place. "I started *my* pack. With Jordan and Dane, and when we found others, we brought them in."

Always protecting. Always strong.

"What happened to your mother?" She voiced the question that nagged at her mind.

"I heard she died a few years back."

Sarah slid from the bed. "I'm sorry."

"Don't be. I never knew her. She ditched me as fast as she could because she didn't want to be tied down—"

She hurried around the bed. Hit her shin twice. Managed to find him and grab his hands and she held tight. *"I'm sorry, Lucas."*

That shut him up.

"I'm sorry that you went through hell." Because that's exactly what it had been. While he'd been walking in his father's blood, she'd been rebelling at her *normal* life. Ah, damn. She must have seemed like such a fool to him. "I wish things had been different for you."

"Wishing doesn't change the past."

No, nothing could change the past. "But your future can be different," she whispered. "Your life doesn't have to just be blood and death. It can be more."

His glittering gaze seemed to bore into her. "And what about you, Sarah? What do you want your life to be? You came looking for the death and the action and the monsters. Is that what you want your life to be like? Is it the thrill of the dark that gets to you?"

The words were a dig at her, a swipe that hurt, but she didn't let him go. "It's not the dark I want. It was never that." *Just to fit in.*

"You wanted to belong, sweet Sarah, with the wolves."

"No." Not just with the wolves. There were other packs. Other wolf shifters. Rafe hadn't been the first she'd come across in her time at the Bureau. He'd just the first wolf she'd taken as a lover.

And if that hadn't been enough to scare a girl off shifters . . .

But no, she'd gone right back in. Fallen hard for her legend.

"I wanted to belong with you." The words came out quietly, and she knew there'd be no more hiding. "I knew you'd keep me safe." The profile had been dead on. He protected those weaker, always looked out for them if they were *his.* Did he consider her part of his family? He'd said she was in the pack, but . . . "I think I was a little bit in love with you before I even met you."

He blinked at her. "Sarah . . . ?"

"The big, bad LA wolf. The alpha who took on a den of vampires to get his brother back—took them on and took them out."

"Well, I did have a little help with that," he said, voice dark and rumbling.

The wolfpack rumors didn't care about his help. "You've never killed humans. There's never even been so much as a whisper about you hurting them."

He stared down at her, not saying a word, and she tensed. "I'm not as desperate as you seem to think, Lucas. It's not pack or nothing for me. Hell, it's not even pack. It's just . . ." *You.*

"Be careful," he warned her. "Be very, very careful." And his hands bit into her flesh.

"Why?" She'd turned her back on the careful life years ago.

"Because if you push me too far, I won't ever let you go."

What if that was what she wanted? "Lucas . . ."

His lips brushed over hers. A quick, hard press that had her wanting him back in the bed with her. His body against hers, in her.

But he lifted his head too quickly. "Dane's here."

What?

"You should dress."

She'd rather keep talking to him. Dammit, she'd just said she was in love with the guy. She'd never said words like that to a man before. "We're not done, wolf," she promised him.

"No." Soft. "We're not."

A knock shook the door. Sarah wrapped the sheet around her body, tighter this time. She didn't want it to slip and fall.

Lucas yanked on his pair of jeans and headed for the door. She caught his arm. "I'm going to keep pushing you." She could give warnings, too. She stood on her tiptoes and let her lips tease his savaged ear, then Sarah whispered, "I'll push and push until I get just what I want."

His head turned. His eyes caught hers. "And what is it that you *really* want?"

Couldn't he see? "You. Just you, Lucas."

She stepped away from him. He'd believe her or he wouldn't. This wasn't about protection or the FBI or Rafe or any damn other thing. It was just about them. "And I need you to just want me, too." Not the charmer. Not the woman he could use to spy on enemies or to make sure that his pack was always loyal. "Just want *me*."

"I do." Growled.

Her breath rushed out.

He reached for the door and yanked it open just as a fist slammed into the wood again.

Dane blinked. Faint light spilled on him from the bulb outside. Jordan stood just behind him, his shoulders hunched against the night.

"You were right," Dane told Jordan, slowly lowering his fist. "She needed clothes."

He tossed a bag to Sarah. She caught it, and her sheet didn't slip.

"I know my brother." Jordan's lips curved a bit. "And I saw the way he looked at her."

What? Did they think Lucas had ripped her clothes off? Oh, tempting, but no. "There was blood on my clothes, I—"

"I *know*." And Dane came through the door with narrowed eyes and a tight jaw. "I could smell it outside." He crossed to Sarah's side. "*Her* blood."

Jordan kicked the door closed and flipped on the light. "Here we go."

A muscle flexed in Dane's jaw. "Is Karen dead?"

"I don't know." And why did it matter to him? He'd been the one to gag the agent and stuff her into the back of a van.

Suspicion hit, hard, and she knew Lucas had the same thought because he grabbed Dane and tossed him back against the wall.

"How well do you know the *FBI agent*, Dane?" Lucas's arm was at the other shifter's throat.

Dane blinked. "FBI? I thought—I thought she was working with the coyotes . . ."

"She was," Sarah said, seeing the immediate relaxation of Lucas's shoulders.

Dane had my back.

Always.

"But she was playing them," Lucas told him, dropping his arm and stepping back. "She was undercover."

Dane's gaze tracked to Sarah. "She's like you?"

"No one's like Sarah." Lucas shoved a hand through his hair. "No one."

That was sweet of her wolf to notice.

"What happened to her?" Dane stepped away from the wall, his hands clenched. "Lucas, tell me you didn't hurt her."

Lucas frowned. "I didn't hurt her."

Sarah tightened her grip on the bag. "He may have saved her."

Dane's head whipped toward her.

"It was the demon, Marley." Sarah wet her lips. Ah, how to be delicate?

"Turns out she was an FBI plant, too." Lucas didn't bother with delicate. "They've been watching the paranormals. Keeping tabs on us."

"Figures," Jordan said, slumping against the wall but his sharp gaze belied the relaxed pose. "Big brother does like to watch."

"And exterminate." Dane's eyes were still on Sarah.

"Only this time, the FBI agents are the ones being taken out." She should have been told about the connection between the victims sooner. Without that Intel, she'd been working the case blind. But if Miller thought she was the one who'd turned, dammit, yes, the bastard would have been trying to keep her out of the loop. She sighed. "According to Karen, Rafe's been targeting undercover agents—killing them."

"Huh." Dane's stare tracked to Lucas. "You're not FBI. Why's he so hot for you?"

"I pissed off the asshole because I killed his bastard of a father."

"Kaber." A low whistle. "That piece of shit was Rafe's father?"

"Yes." Sarah saw his sharpening canines.

Dane growled. "Rafe should probably thank you for taking him out."

"Probably."

She could feel the rage in the room. Dark shadows had filled Dane's eyes. Sarah's toes curled into the thin carpet. "Did you—did you find Marley?"

It was Jordan who answered. "We found the burned remains of some poor human in the woods." He crossed his arms over his chest. "Marley didn't leave a lot for us to identify."

"Was it a man?" *Curtis.*

Jordan nodded. "No weapon."

Because she'd taken his gun. Sarah sucked in a deep breath. "It could have been the agent with Karen." Could have—who was she fooling? The odds were sky high that Marley had killed the man, and Sarah had been so intent on getting Karen to safety, she hadn't even thought about him.

"Don't." Lucas's voice snapped like a whip.

Sarah swallowed and glanced at him.

"He left us. He ran into the woods. He knew the coyotes were there, he took us to that trap and *left us.*" The faint lines around his eyes deepened. "His blood's not on you."

"No, it's on Marley." Dane shoved his hands into his pockets. "And that's one of the reasons it was so easy for us to track the bitch."

"Where?"

Sarah tensed at Lucas's stark voice. So much fury.

"208 Mythlin Street." Dane lifted a brow. "Sound familiar?"

"When we were looking for you—when those vamps took you—" He shoved a finger toward Jordan. "That was where we found Marie. That's one of her safe houses."

"No," Jordan said, "it *was* one of Marie's houses, but now

Rafe and Marley are holed up inside, and I think it's past time we went in and hauled their asses out."

"Damn right."

Okay, she needed to get out of the sheet. Sarah whirled around. "I'll change and get my gun." The adrenaline already had her blood pumping faster. The nightmare was ending. If they could take out Rafe . . .

She shut the bathroom door and yanked on the clothes as fast as she could. Hiding out at Marie's—Rafe probably thought that was brilliant.

Sarah grabbed the knob and pulled the door open. "Okay, I'm—"

Lucas was gone. Dane was gone. Jordan still slumped against the wall. One dark brow climbed when he saw her and he shook his head slowly. "Ah, Sarah, did you really think he'd risk you?"

Her heart lurched. "He left me?" But she'd only been in the bathroom for a few moments and she hadn't even heard the creak of the door.

"Like I said . . . I've seen the way he looks at you." Jordan shrugged. "He's not going to put your life on the line."

Damn him. "He needs help."

She caught the slight tightening of Jordan's lips. "He has Dane. And Dane's already arranged for Piers to meet 'em there. Those guys are his backup. Always have been."

"And what about you? What are you, Jordan?"

"Now that's a good question." He smiled, but it was grim.

"You're as strong as they are. I'm not—yes, I get that." Lucas needed more back up. No telling how many of his wolf pack Rafe had brought in. And then there was Marley. "He can't do this with just Dane and Piers backing him." She grabbed the gun from the nightstand.

"He and Dane have experience taking down rogue wolves. I know, I saw the blood firsthand."

"But Kaber didn't know Lucas was coming back for him and that jerk also didn't have a fire-throwing demon on his side." Not good odds. "Rafe will have that house protected.

He's going to do anything and everything he can—he wants Lucas dead."

Jordan caught her shoulders when she tried to go for the door. "You may as well be just human. If you go, you'll just slow him down."

Did everyone have to throw up the human comment to her? "Humans aren't as weak as you think." They all made that mistake. "If Rafe's men shift . . ." Now she smiled and she knew the grin was as grim as his had been. "They're mine."

His golden gaze searched hers. "And if they don't shift? If they attack with claws but still with the bodies of men? What the hell then? You'll distract my brother. If anything happens to you . . ." *His* claws were out. "I'm not going to watch him go over the edge."

"Neither am I." She raised the gun. "It's loaded with silver bullets, and I took backup ammo from the van. If Rafe's men don't shift, then I can still take them out." *Wasting time.* "I'm a good shot, better than good, I—"

"Yeah, I know you are, lady."

"Then why are we just standing here?" Now she was the one nearly growling. *He'd left me.* "Lucas needs us."

The struggle was clear on his face. "He told me to keep you safe."

Fine. "Then stay by my side. Stay with me every step of the way, but come on!" Her gut was twisting, her knees shaking, and she knew that this battle wasn't going to end easily. Rafe wasn't this sloppy. He wouldn't have let the other wolves track him—or even track his demon—unless he'd wanted to be found.

Because he had a backup plan already in place. Yes, she knew him well. Better than Lucas did. And if Lucas had just stayed and given her the chance to explain . . .

"You don't leave my sight," Jordan snapped. "You stay within a foot of me at all times."

Sarah jerked her head in agreement and ripped open the door. "Just don't get between my gun and a target." *Weak.*

Not hardly. It was time to show the wolves how strong their prey could really be.

"Yes, ma'am," Jordan agreed, "but you can't get between my claws and the assholes I'm planning to rip apart."

Fair enough.

Hold on, Lucas. Because from now on, he wouldn't be leaving her behind. In the wolf pack, mates hunted together.

Time for the man to realize he was mated.

Chapter 19

The house at 208 Mythlin hadn't changed much. The sprawling two-story brick house still hid behind the twisting trees at the end of the long, pothole-filled road. The wraparound porch showed no signs of neglect. Unlike the other dumps on the street, this house was perfect . . . because it was hers.

The first time he'd been there, he'd been tracking Maya Black. He'd been so desperate to find his brother, he hadn't cared that he'd courted the *mambo's* wrath by bringing blood and death right to her door. No, he hadn't cared, not until later.

Then he'd had to bleed for the *mambo*. Blood for blood. But he'd set his debt to rights.

"It sure is quiet," came Piers's whisper. "I've been watching the place for the last twenty minutes . . . not a peep."

And he couldn't smell a thing. Literally, not a damn thing. No wolf scent. No telltale ash. Not even sweat. "I thought you followed Marley's scent here."

Dane's eyes were on the house. "I did, but it's—hell, it's different now."

"Magic?" Piers barely breathed the word.

At Marie's? Hell, yeah, magic was a definite possibility. "Time to shift." Because he wasn't gonna waste those precious moments later. Better to shift now, go in strong and take the bastards out. He knew Rafe likely had his coyote dogs and some wolves around. Lucas was ready for the blood and battle. This war was ending tonight.

"We should be able to smell 'em," Piers growled and his bones began to snap. "Should still be able to . . ." Fur covered his flesh.

He was right. Lucas stared at the windows of Marie's house. He could see light flickering. Bright light.

No, not just light. *Fire.*

But he couldn't smell the smoke. *What the fuck?* "Be ready for anything," he ordered, and the burn of the shift swept through him. His bones broke, stretched, his hands vanished and his claws dug into the dirt.

Rafael, I'm coming for you, asshole.

Then he heard it. The faintest sound of laughter drifting in the air.

"About time you showed up, Simone!" Rafe shouted from the recesses of the house. "I was getting bored waiting on you . . . so I had to go ahead and start my party."

Shit.

Then a woman screamed, loud, long, full of pain and fear.

Marley? It figured that Rafe would turn on her. He seemed to turn on everyone.

"And before you go guessing . . ." Came that damn, mocking voice. "Marley's not the one screaming." The laughter filled the night again. "Come and see what I've got in here!"

Not what. Who.

Lucas glanced to the left, then the right. Dane and Piers had shifted, and their eyes were on him. He threw back his head and howled. Forget going in softly. Rafe knew he was there. So Lucas would go in fast—

His legs pumped as he flew over the earth.

—and he'd go in hard—

He dove right through the window, barely feeling the glass slice into his pelt.

—and he'd take that bastard *out.*

* * *

Jordan's motorcycle braked and Sarah jumped off the bike—just in time to see a big, black wolf hurtle through a pane of glass.

Lucas.

A slightly smaller black wolf and a white wolf dove after him.

"Smoke." Jordan climbed off after her. "That demon's burning again!"

Sarah's gun was already out and in her hands. She and Jordan ran together, rushing for the house.

They'd taken about ten steps when the first two coyotes appeared. The coyotes stalked from the bushes, their heads low to the ground, their ears up, and damn if it didn't look like they were smiling.

"Dammit, I could have used a heads-up here!" Sarah said, her shoulders bumping into Jordan's. She lifted her gun, aimed, and got ready to fire. "When you smell them, Jordan, you're supposed to let me know!"

"I don't smell them."

Her gaze flashed to his for just a second, but her gun didn't waver. Those coyotes kept closing in. "What?"

"They're right in front of me, and I don't fucking smell them. I can't smell anything—just that fire. *Only the fire.*"

Oh, hell. Not good.

Two more coyotes jumped from the darkness. Saliva dripped from their sharp teeth.

Sarah braced her legs. "I think now might be a good time for you to think about shifting."

"No." But from the corner of her eye, she saw his claws burst from his fingertips. "If I try a full shift, I'll be dead before the wolf comes out."

Right. Because the coyotes liked to attack when prey was weak. "Then I guess it's my turn." Sarah took a deep breath.

The coyotes attacked.

Blood dripped from Josette Dusean's throat. A long, steady line of blood that trickled down her neck.

Lucas froze when he saw her. She shouldn't have been

there. She should have been with Maya. The vamp and her dragon were supposed to be protecting Josette.

Piers snarled behind him and leapt forward, racing right toward the woman who was tied to a chair and slowly dying in front of them.

Bait? A trap?

Lucas's gaze scanned the room. He couldn't smell anything but the fire. Couldn't even catch the scent of Josette's blood.

She shouldn't be there.

Fuck. A growl built in his throat. *Piers, no!* He snapped out the order in his mind. *Get away from her!*

Piers stopped, his claws digging into the hardwood. *Look at her. She fucking needs help!*

Appearances could be deceiving.

Dane edged around the room. Sniffing. Or rather, trying to sniff.

Lucas advanced on Josette. He could feel the heat from the fire burning in the next room. Josette's eyes were open, glistening with tears, staring right at him.

Go search in the other room. The room that smelled of smoke and hell. *Go, Piers! Go!*

But Piers didn't move.

Shit.

Go! He shoved the command at him once more, but Piers had his entire focus on Josette.

She needs me. Piers advanced toward her. *I won't leave her to die.*

Fuck. He'd suspected this, feared it. Damn well not the time. *Dane—get in the other room!*

Dane raced forward and drove his body into the door. The wood smashed and smoke seeped through that hole.

A faint, weak smile curved Josette's lips and her hands were pulling at the ropes. Only those ropes didn't look that tight.

"Help me," she whispered. "I came . . . I came to kill him . . . to avenge my grandmother, but he caught me—"

Fuck the lying bitch.

Lucas lunged forward, his front legs kicking the other wolf out of the way. She screamed, a high, desperate scream that was Piers's name.

Smart. Damn smart.

No, Lucas! The desperate roar in his mind came from Piers. *Don't hurt her! I think she's my mate!*

The tip of a knife scraped Lucas's side. He stopped wasting time. Lucas attacked. His teeth went for her throat even as a gunshot echoed in his ears.

Then claws sank into his back. *Get away from her!* Piers bit him, digging his teeth into Lucas's flesh.

Snarling, Lucas twisted and shoved back against the other wolf. *What the fuck?*

She's. Mine.

Josette wasn't screaming anymore. Piers blocked her body with his, and the white wolf's eyes blazed with fury. *Mine.*

It really was one hell of a time for Piers to think he'd found a mate. The rich flavor of blood lingered on Lucas's tongue. He stared at the other wolf, sides heaving.

Mine. Piers snarled again.

No, she's not.

Because that wasn't Josette Dusean. The smells might be off thanks to magic or drugs or who-the-hell-knew-what, but Lucas was certain of one thing.

Demon blood always tasted the same. Bitter to the last drop.

Stay away from her!

More gunshots blasted.

Then "Josette" lunged out of the chair, the knife he'd felt before still gripped in her hand—

Piers! He screamed the psychic warning.

—and she sank it hilt-deep in Piers's back.

Fire crackled, greedily eating its way up the walls of the interior room. The red and gold flames twisted and heaved, and in the middle of the hell, Dane saw a woman lying on the ground.

A woman with long black hair. Perfect coffee skin.

He jumped over the fire, feeling the heat lance his fur. He went in carefully, ready for an attack.

But the woman didn't move.

He tried to catch her scent but the smoke seemed to burn the inside of his nose. *Can't smell a thing.*

His muzzle pressed against her back. She coughed then, her body heaving, and he saw her face.

Josette Dusean.

The same face that had stared at him in the other room.

Demons could really piss him off. Dane growled.

She didn't move.

But the fire seemed to tighten around him. Those flames were definitely higher now. Higher, fiercer, stronger. Like a net of fire that was closing in. Fucking magic.

Sonofabitch. He was an idiot. They'd raced right into the bastard's trap. But then, Rafe had used very, very good bait.

Piers howled in agony and twisted, but he didn't hit his attacker with his claws.

Of course not. Piers thought the woman was his mate. Lucas's muscles bunched as he prepared to leap.

She laughed, yanked the knife out and plunged it in again. *Hell, no.*

Lucas flew at her. But instead of catching her flesh, he barreled into Piers. Piers lifted his head and met Lucas's stare. The white wolf's eyes were filled with pain and fury and fear.

Back away. Lucas didn't want to hurt him. *That's not Josette.*

Piers just snarled at him.

And then the bastard came out of hiding. Rafe sauntered into the room as if he didn't have a fucking care in the world.

"I think he's past caring, or maybe even hearing what you say." Rafe smirked at Lucas. "And your boy Dane . . . well . . . the fur's about to burn right off his body. You won't be getting help from him."

Lucas lunged for the asshole.

But Piers caught him, held him tight with claws and teeth.

"Everybody always said Piers was close to the edge," Rafe's smirk turned into a cruel grin. "Good thing they were right, or otherwise, you both might be at my throat right now."

I will get your throat.

Rafe lifted his hand and pointed at the woman. "This time, use the knife on Simone."

The bitch came at him, bloody and strong.

But she didn't stab him. Lucas didn't give her the chance. One swipe of his claws and he ripped open her throat.

The roar of fury that filled his mind told him that Piers had gone over the edge.

And wasn't coming back.

"Bad move, Simone. Very, very bad . . ." Yet Rafe sounded so pleased. "Of course, I was hoping to kill you myself, but getting killed by your own packmate—ah, fitting, isn't it?"

Lucas twisted and barely managed to keep Piers's teeth from biting into his throat. Piers didn't even seem to notice that Josette's image had changed in death. Her skin had lightened, her hair shortened, her face—*not Josette anymore.*

Marley.

A demon's glamour spell ended in death, and the illusion was totally gone now.

If only Piers would fucking look!

"Haven't you learned anything since I've been in town?" Rafe's mocking drawl was really pissing him off. "You can't trust your pack. You thought they had your back, didn't you? Now, well, they're after you. First Caleb. Now Piers."

I don't want to hurt you, Piers. Listen to me, dammit. That wasn't your mate. Look at her!

But Piers was only looking at him and the rage in the other wolf's eyes seared his skin.

Josette. He should have connected the dots sooner. Shit, Piers had even told him that he'd been watching her. How long had the guy known she was his? And why the hell hadn't he tried to claim her? Piers had danced near the edge too long, he should have gone after Josette with everything he had.

Like Lucas would have gone after Sarah.

Piers swiped at him, but Lucas slammed his head into the wolf's side. *I don't want to hurt you.* He blasted out the thought again. His teeth snapped together. *But I will.* He couldn't get past the red wall of rage in the other wolf's mind.

"Caleb turned on you." Rafe's voice droned on. "Sure, it took some poison and the promise of an excruciating death, but I got him to lie and lead you right into my trap."

A trap that hadn't fucking worked.

"He should have killed you." Now Rafe didn't seem quite so pleased. "Caleb had the chance to attack, but . . ."

But he'd pulled back.

Piers tore into Lucas's shoulder.

"This one won't pull back." Ah, now Rafe was happy again.

Sorry, Piers. Lucas leapt up and shoved his claws into the knife wounds on Piers's back. When the wolf howled in agony, Lucas lunged off his body and dove right for Rafe.

Rafe didn't back up. He didn't try to shift. He just stood there and Lucas crashed into him. They slammed into the floor, and he went for Rafe's throat.

"Something you should know . . ." Rafe murmured. He wasn't even *fighting*. "Sarah's dead."

Lying bastard.

His teeth dug into Rafe's skin.

"Or else, she will be, if you don't get the fuck off me." Lucas froze, the taste of the bastard's blood on his tongue, then Rafe said, "My men have her surrounded outside. Her gun—the one you probably heard firing a moment ago—is out of bullets, and as for your little brother . . . well, let's just say he's not quite the scrapper that you are."

Shit, shit, shit . . . Sarah!

She should have been back at the hotel. Safe. Rafe could be lying, but . . .

The gunshots.

"Get off, wolf . . . or you can rip my throat out, like you did to Marley, and then you can go and mourn over your dead lover."

Lucas lifted his head.

"Thought so," Rafe said as Lucas raced back to that broken window. He hurtled past the jagged glass and his paws slammed into the ground. He ran, fast, fast—desperate to get to her side.

He heard the clicks just as he burst onto the sidewalk. The clicks from Sarah's empty gun. Six dead coyotes littered the ground. Sarah and Jordan were standing, back to back. Sarah had her gun up and when she saw him, her eyes widened. "*Lucas!*"

He realized too late that her shout was a warning. He tried to turn and glance back, but the bullet drove into him, and even as he fell, the form of the wolf began to melt away.

The fur melted from Dane's body and the heat singed his flesh. He didn't have a choice. He had to shift. The wolf could escape the fire, but if he did, the woman would die.

Maybe, just maybe, the man could save them both. Besides, what was a little pain?

This what you meant, Marie? Do I have to get ready for the fucking pain again?

He hefted Josette into his arms. Her head lolled against his shoulder. "Baby, this is the part where you're supposed to be holding on," he muttered. He took a breath. No clothes. No cover. The fire would burn right against his flesh.

Her eyelashes began to flutter.

"No." He exhaled. "You don't want to see this."

Then leapt, dove through the fire, but the flames touched her skin and she screamed.

And screamed.

He didn't stop running. The fire ate at him, and he hunched his shoulders, trying to protect her as much as he could. The smoke filled his lungs, choking him, but he kept going and then he was before the door he'd broken. Dane shoved his way past the splintered wood and into the other room.

He fell to the floor, rolling, twisting as he tried to put out the flames.

Josette wasn't screaming anymore. Her eyes were open, wide, and blank with shock.

He caught her chin. His hands were covered with blisters and rough, red flesh. "You're going to be okay." The pain rolled through his body. Pain—that teasing bitch. He knew her so well. He took the pain, pulled it in deep, and let it make him stronger.

A ragged groan reached his ears. He turned his head and saw Piers staring at him. The white wolf's pelt was matted with blood. Piers growled at him, advancing slowly.

Behind him, Dane saw what was left of Marley. Looked like Lucas had kept his word and taken her out.

So where *was* Rafe?

"Ease up, Piers. She'll be all right." He glanced back at Josette.

Piers growled again, and the low, menacing sound had Dane tensing.

Piers leapt toward him, but froze when thunder filled the night. No, not thunder. Gunfire.

The white wolf's head snapped toward the busted window. Seconds later, Piers raced into the night.

The fire slipped into the room then, and the crackles almost sounded like an old woman's laughter. *Not again.* Dane grabbed Josette, didn't even feel the tear of his skin as the burned flesh ripped, and followed that bloody wolf.

"*Lucas!*" Sarah lunged forward, but Jordan grabbed her, hauling her right back to him.

Lucas was on the ground, his body contorting, and the wolf vanishing as his body automatically shifted in a bid to heal and *live.*

Her heart raced in her chest and then . . . then her knees gave way. If Jordan hadn't held her, Sarah would have fallen face-first onto the ground.

A strange cold wrapped around her body, a cold that numbed her legs and arms, even while her back burned—burned and throbbed as if a bullet had lodged near her spine.

Not my spine. Lucas's.

"Sarah? What the hell is happening?"

The gun slipped from her fingers and hit the ground. She opened her mouth, tried to explain to Jordan, but only a ragged moan of pain came from her lips.

"Bastard, you should have died the first time I pumped you full of silver," Rafe snarled and closed in on Lucas. "Fucking magic won't save you now. It can't."

He lives . . . you live.

Sarah's eyes squeezed shut as the fire from her back fought that numbing cold in her limbs.

He dies . . . Marie's voice whispered through her mind. *Then you die.*

Her eyes flew open. "No!"

Lucas was on the ground, on his hands and knees, trying to push up as the blood poured from his back. Behind him, Rafe had a gun up, aimed, ready to blow that silver bullet into him again.

"Don't!" Sarah screamed, pushing through the pain and breaking away from Jordan. "Damn you, Rafe, *don't!*"

But his fingers squeezed the trigger.

Sarah saw the flash of white behind him. Piers. Running fast. Snarling. *Piers!*

A red haze of fury rolled back at her.

She'd promised. Said she wouldn't control—

The hell with that. Lucas's life was on the line. She'd do anything for him.

"I win, Simone," Rafe said, lips raised in a half-grin "*I win.* I'm the legend now."

Attack, Piers! Take Rafe down!

Piers slammed into Rafe. They fell in a tangle of fur and arms. The gun discharged, but the bullet didn't hit Lucas.

Sarah started to breathe again.

Then she realized the bullet *had* struck Piers. The white wolf slumped to the side. His fur began to vanish.

Growls filled the air now. The wolf shifters in Rafe's pack. They'd been lurking in the shadows but now they sprang forward. Still in the form of men, but with claws out and teeth sharp.

Jordan pushed her behind him and when the first man attacked, he sliced the guy from neck to groin.

"*Lucas,*" she whispered. He was on his feet now. His wild eyes focused on her.

"*You should be dead!*" Rafe shoved away from Piers. "You should be fucking dead!" He had his gun pointed at Lucas again.

Lucas turned toward him.

Rafe fired. Once. Twice.

The bullets drove into Lucas's chest.

He didn't stumble. Sarah did. She slipped and fell down behind Jordan. He kept fighting. Slicing and clawing and her chest burned. She touched the skin, expecting to see blood. She felt as if she'd been ripped open.

Not me. Lucas.

What had Marie done?

"You're not killing me . . ." Lucas's voice rumbled in the night. "But I am taking you . . . to hell, asshole." She pushed to her knees. Tried to see—

Rafe fired again. The gun clicked then, the chamber jamming. *Yes.* Lucas swiped with his claws and cut Rafe's wrist open. The gun fell from his slack fingers.

Rafe's eyes flew to her. He saw her on the ground, struggling to rise, and he smiled. "*Shift!*" He roared the order to his men. "*The bitch is weak. She can't do anything but die!*"

Lucas's head whipped toward her. "Sarah!"

"*Shift!*" Rafe screamed. "And we kill 'em all!"

"Screw the shift." Lucas's claws drove into Rafe's chest. "You're fucking dying . . . now."

But it was too late. The men were already shifting around her. Curses turned to snarls and growls and Jordan fought, taking out three men while they were vulnerable during the change. But it wasn't enough. Not nearly enough. The wolves closed in on Sarah and Jordan.

Chapter 20

The bitch is weak. Rafe's taunt echoed in her ears. Sarah rose slowly, the fire in her chest and back pulsing and sending waves of nausea through her body.

Not my pain. Not my wound. Though it sure felt like it was.

Jordan slashed with his claws, fighting, struggling for all he was worth. Determined to protect her.

Sarah's focus narrowed. She stared at the snapping wolves and a slow smile curved her lips. "Guess what, assholes?" She sucked in a deep breath and tasted blood. "I'm not weak."

Rafe was still alive. Still fighting with Lucas. Swiping with his claws even as Lucas carved a hole in the bastard's chest. Some people just weren't easy to kill.

Some were.

Attack Rafe. She ordered his wolves. *Kill.*

The wolves around her froze.

"Please tell me you're doing that," Jordan said. "Please."

"I am." She fought to inhale another deep breath. She was in so much pain she could barely stand on her feet. But she didn't need physical strength. The *Other* should start understanding that it wasn't always about physical power.

Attack Rafe.

The wolves spun away and charged at Lucas and Rafe.

Lucas looked up. She saw his eyes widen.

"Back the hell away, Lucas!" Jordan shouted.

Lucas yanked his claws out of Rafe's chest. Rafe staggered. Blood dripped from his mouth.

The bastard fell.

The wolves swarmed him, attacking their leader at her command.

Sarah's eyes closed. *Kill him . . . then get the hell out of here. Never come back.*

Yelps and whimpers had her eyes opening. Looked like the wolves weren't going to get the chance to run. Lucas was slicing, clawing them, and Dane was at his side. Taking the wolves out. The ones who weren't already dead turned tail and ran as fast as they could.

Over. Finally, it was over.

Sarah's shoulders sagged and the last of her energy slipped away. Jordan ran forward, chasing after the fleeing wolves and she fell, her side slamming into the ground. *Lucas.*

She was so cold. Her body was shaking and her throat—it seemed like she was drowning. She couldn't suck in enough air. Couldn't . . .

Sarah saw Lucas fall. He went down, his knees crashing into the earth. Blood soaked his chest. The burning glow in his eyes began to fade.

Rafe had used silver bullets on him. Had they exploded on impact like the others? Three shots.

"Sarah." She saw his lips move as he whispered her name, and she wanted to go to him. To touch him. To hold him once more.

But she couldn't move. Rafe was dead, the coyotes were dead, the rival wolves were running—the nightmare was over.

And she was scared. Because Sarah knew that she couldn't fight anymore. Lucas couldn't fight. Her heartbeat was slowing, and even though she didn't have an injury on her body, she knew she was dying.

He lives . . . you live.

She could taste blood on her tongue and see the precious liquid drip past Lucas's lips.

He dies . . .

Her hand lifted toward him. Just one more touch.

He stretched out his hands, trying to crawl to her side. But Lucas was too far away.

Her legs weren't working. That meant his weren't.

"Lucas?" Jordan grabbed him, hauling him up, and swearing when he saw the full damage to his brother's body. "It's all right. You're going to be fine!"

Such a liar.

The fire in her chest wasn't as strong anymore. Sarah kept her eyes on Lucas. She wouldn't look away from him. If she was dying, he'd be the last thing she saw in this world.

"Now you understand."

Sarah didn't look away at the woman's soft voice. She *couldn't* look away. She'd never seen Lucas's eyes so pale before. They'd always blazed with life and power. Jordan was trying to stop the blood now, screaming at his brother to *"Shift!"* But Lucas wasn't changing.

Sarah swallowed twice and finally managed to speak. "I understood . . ." she whispered, "Long before now . . . Jo-Josette . . ."

The woman bent toward her and cool fingers slid over Sarah's cheeks. "Was the extra time worth the pain you have? Just a few days, that's all you got . . . and now you share his agony and soon, his death."

Was it worth it? "I'd do . . . anything." Everything. The trade was fair.

Josette leaned in close. "You've already done everything," she whispered, her breath light at Sarah's ear. "Don't be afraid."

She wasn't. Just . . . sad. There was so much she'd hoped to do. Wanted to do. All with Lucas. "Does he . . . have to die?"

"Wrong question." A slight wind rustled Sarah's hair. Josette murmured, "You should ask, 'Do I have to die?' "

"Sometimes . . ." So hard to talk now. She licked her lips and tasted more blood. Lucas still hadn't shifted. *Shift.* "Others are worth . . . more."

"Lucas is worth more to you than your own life?"

Shift. If he'd just shift, he might survive.

"Sarah King . . ." Josette's hand brushed back her hair. "Do you even know when you gave your heart to the wolf?"

Did it matter when? He had it, just as he had her. *Mate.* Beyond life. Beyond death.

If only she could touch him one more time.

"You're going to be fine! Lucas, are you hearing me? You're going to be fine!" Jordan yelled at him.

His brother had flipped him over and now Jordan's hands were shoving at his chest, quickly becoming soaked in Lucas's blood.

"Fine," Jordan snapped out. "You're going to be—"

Bullshit. His chest was on fire, burning from the inside out. Damn silver bullets. Blood was rising in his throat, trying to choke him, and the air around him seemed colder. So cold. He wanted to close his eyes and let the pain sweep over him, but . . .

Sarah.

What was wrong with her? Her face had been too white. Her eyes not the dark green he knew. Instead, lighter, strained. Weak. And she'd fallen to the ground. Her hand had reached for his, and she'd fallen.

Lucas swallowed. Choked, but gasped, "Sarah . . ."

"She's okay, man. I swear, I didn't let them so much as touch her." Clawmarks littered his brother's chest and arms. "We had to come. Sarah said it was a trap, that Rafe would be ready for you and that he'd have his wolves waiting."

She'd been right. But . . . if she wasn't hurt, then why was she on the ground? And why was fear twisting his insides, even as that pain blasted him? Not fear for himself.

For her.

"Shift." Jordan glared down at him. "You have to shift, and you have to shift *now.*"

He couldn't even feel the wolf inside. The transformation back to man had been too brutal, fueled by pain and the silver burning his body.

"Sarah . . ." She was his focus. Maybe if he could get to her . . .

"She's dying."

His head turned slowly to the right and he saw Dane. The guy's body was covered in blisters and angry red burns.

"Sarah's not dying!" Jordan immediately yelled. "Fuck, Dane, why the hell would you say that *now?* She's fine, Lucas. Fine. Just shift and everything will be—"

Fine? No.

"You still don't understand what happened, do you?" Dane asked, and his eyes narrowed on Lucas's face. "I thought you understood magic better than this."

Jordan swore. "Dammit Dane, you're not helping—"

"The first time Rafe shot you full of silver, you were dead. No, you *should* have been dead, but your Sarah made a trade for you."

No trades would be made tonight. No more magic. Just death.

"Marie said she bound your souls . . ."

A tremor shook Lucas's body.

"And the minute I saw Sarah sprawled on top of you, hell, I knew she wasn't just yanking our chains. She did it, Lucas. Marie kept you alive, but the price for that life was a bonding with Sarah. Man and wolf. Hell, if she hadn't been a wolf charmer, I don't even know if it would have worked . . ."

Jordan's hand gabbed Lucas's chin. "We don't have time for this. *Shift.*"

But Dane kept talking. "You're linked, Alpha. You lived before because Sarah lived. Her soul pulled you back. That was the only free ride you two got. From now on, if you live, she keeps living."

No, *no*. Because he knew what was coming. Knew—
"And if you die, then she dies too."

He wrenched his head and managed to look at Sarah. His damn legs weren't working or he would have gone to her. He'd already tried to crawl once. *Must get . . .*

"So listen to your brother," Dane snarled. "You want to live, you want her to live, then you fucking find the strength to *shift*. There's no *mambo* to bring you back tonight."

Maybe that had been part of Rafe's master plan all along. He'd taken out the *mambo* so magic couldn't aid Lucas. Dominos, all falling down . . .

"So you save yourself and you save your mate," Dane ordered. "Because otherwise, she's dying for you."

Sarah wasn't supposed to die. Sarah wasn't supposed to hurt. Sarah was supposed to be safe, happy. Free.

Fuck, no!

His claws dug into the earth and he fought to pull the wolf back, to raise him through the fire and agony that burned his body.

Sarah wasn't dying. He wouldn't let her.

"I can't help you." Josette's hand fell away from Sarah. "I wish I could, but I'm not . . . strong enough." Tears thickened her voice. "I'm so sorry."

"Just . . ." Was that really her talking? The voice was so weak, so broken. "Just . . . get me to h-him . . ." Could Josette even understand her?

Touching Lucas once more was all that mattered. Her entire focus had centered on him. She *needed* him. And she wasn't dying without telling him the truth.

Because she'd been lying to her wolf. She wouldn't die with that lie and she wouldn't let *him* die without knowing the truth.

Josette lifted Sarah's arm. Sarah didn't wince. Didn't gasp. She just took the wave of pain that came when Josette pulled her up. Josette eased her shoulders under Sarah's arm and the

other woman wrapped her hands around Sarah's stomach.
"Easy . . ." Josette whispered. "Go slow."

When you didn't have a lot of time, slow wasn't really an
option.

A chorus of high-pitched howls split the night. She heard
the fear in those howls.

Sarah's head lifted and she saw an explosion of fire light
the night. Fire that had come from behind the line of trees
to the right. Rafe's wolves had fled that way, disappearing
into the trees. But it looked like those bastards might not
have gotten away after all.

A woman walked from the woods. Her dark hair brushed
past her shoulders. Her steps were sure, certain, and her fingers curled around a gun. The full moon also revealed that
her nails had sharpened into claws and her teeth—*vampire.*

"Maya!" Josette yelled. "Help me, *please!*"

Maya's eyes widened and then she raced forward. "Josie,
dammit! Why the hell did you run from me? I lost your
scent—it just disappeared and—"

"They're dying," Josette said, her soft voice cutting through
the fury of Maya's.

The vampire kept running toward them. The scent of fire
came with her. "I don't see any blood on her." Maya took her
away from Josette. Sarah's hand slipped into her back pocket,
searching . . . *there.* Her fingers curled around the treasure
and she whispered, "Lucas . . ."

"He's the one with the blood," Josette said.

"Yeah, *that* I can smell. The blood and the silver. Not anything else, though, why—"

"*Lucas* . . ." Sarah dug her nails into the vampire's arm.

"Ouch! Shit, okay, you want him, you got him." Maya
scooped her up, even though the vamp was smaller than
her—gotta love that enhanced vampire strength—and carried her to Lucas. He was on the ground, body twisting, his
bones snapping, but he wasn't shifting. Just . . . trapped. In
pain.

Maya eased her onto the ground. "Someone tell me what the hell is happening here. Ah, Rafael's dead, that's good. Guess Lucas beat me this time . . ."

Sarah ignored her and reached for Lucas's hand. His fingers curled around hers.

"When he killed *grand-mère*, Rafe stole a brew of hell-fire from her," Josette said. "It burns, fills the air, and the scent covers nearly everything else."

Lucas's hand was cold. No, she was cold. Sarah wet her lips. He was close. Everything should be better now. "Need to tell . . ."

The others fell silent. They didn't matter then anyway. Only he mattered.

His claws were out, but he still had the body of a man. Still had those too light blue eyes.

Her fingers squeezed his. "I . . . lied." But what else was new, right?

If he were in wolf form, she could think all this instead of struggling to speak. But then, if he were in wolf form, he might have a fighting chance.

"*Do something, Josette.*" Dane growled. "Dammit, your grandmother was the *mambo.*"

"And I'm a dead-raiser. I can't do anything unless he—" She muffled a sob. "You don't want my help. Trust me."

Sarah kept her eyes on Lucas. "I made . . . deal . . . with FBI . . ."

Lucas didn't speak. Maybe he couldn't. His mouth was blood-red. No, that was blood dripping from his lips.

"Miller . . . w-wanted me to take out Rafe . . ." He'd stopped her outside of LA. Given her orders, even though she didn't even work for the jerk anymore.

Sarah realized her heart wasn't beating just right. Far too slow.

"If . . . if I . . . d-did . . . you'd be o-ff . . ." *Off the extermination list.* His pack would be clear. They wouldn't be watched. Wouldn't be targeted for death. But she couldn't say any of that. *Couldn't.*

A growl built in Lucas's chest.

"Shift!" Dane snarled.

But he had too much silver in him. She knew it.

"Get the silver out!" Maya shouted. "Cut him open and get it *out!*"

"It shattered," Josette said. "Exploded on impact. Rafe said it—"

"He's not dying!" The furious determination was Jordan's. His claws sliced into Lucas's chest.

Sarah felt the rip of her own flesh.

Tell him.

"M-mate . . ." He was hers. She'd known it the first time he kissed her. More than a legend. The man who'd offered her protection. Passion. Life. And . . . "Love." Her chest rattled. "Love . . . Lucas."

She wouldn't die without telling him.

He wouldn't die without knowing.

For him, she'd trade anything, do anything.

And it sure looked like she'd be dying for him.

"*Love . . .*"

His eyes glittered. Her heart lurched. Lucas's fingers opened and Marie's ring, the ring Sarah had kept close, lay nestled between their hands.

Josette gasped. "*Grand-mère . . .*"

Not ready to give your life for his, are you?

Marie's voice. The *mambo* had asked her that and Sarah had been afraid. She wasn't afraid anymore. "I . . . will . . ."

The ring began to slip from their hands.

Josette dove for them. Her fingers wrapped around theirs, and she held tight. "*No!*"

Thunder rumbled. A whisper of a thousand voices filled the air. Hands reached for Sarah, cold, greedy hands.

"*No!*" Josette tightened her hold and heat, fiery heat, exploded in Sarah's palm. "Death, you can piss off!" Josette screamed. "I'm taking my *grand-mère's* power!"

Then an electric current ripped through Sarah's body. She jerked, heaved, and saw Lucas do the same. But Josette took the hardest hit. She cried out, and her body flew back through the air. Sarah saw her slam into the ground and crumple near Piers.

Then she didn't see anything else but darkness.

Love . . .

If you were gonna die, Sarah figured there were worse things to die for.

The change poured over Lucas, his blood seemed to boil, his body contorted, and he roared Sarah's name.

But she didn't move.

Jordan stumbled back, his hands bloody. "Got some, I got—"

Fur burst over Lucas's skin.

"Hell, yes," Dane shouted.

The wolf within scratched and clawed his way to the surface. The silver still inside burned like a bitch, but something was different now. Maybe his brother *had* managed to get out enough silver, maybe Josette had worked some of her *grand-mère*'s magic. Either way, the wolf was coming out.

Sarah.

She'd be able to link with him now. She had to hear him. *Sarah.*

But when he reached for her mind, he only touched darkness. No, not just darkness . . .

Love . . . Lucas . . . The faintest trace of her voice. It seemed almost like a muted echo, as if he were catching a whisper she'd already voiced.

Free . . . no extermination list . . . free.

Sarah was leaving him. The wolf felt it with absolute certainty. He rushed to her, his muzzle pressing against her throat.

No, stay with me. The man's order. She was supposed to stay. He'd claimed her in front of the pack. That meant they were mates. Together always.

Stay. He was desperate now.

He howled, fear and fury building.

"The wolf's spirit is strong." That was Josette, and when his head whipped toward her, he saw her sitting on the ground—her eyes were cloudy, a glazed blue. *Just like Marie's.* "But what will you give, wolf? To fight Death, what will you give?"

Everything. His muzzle pressed against Sarah once more. *Stay with me.* Not an order. Not anymore. He couldn't hold the shift, already the wolf's body was trembling, weakening, and the muscle and flesh of man would be back soon.

Sarah.

"Are you strong enough to fight for her?" Josette asked.

Fur disappeared. The wounds on his chest weren't as bad. Healing, slowly. Lucas coughed, choked, and rasped, "I'll do . . . any . . . thing for her . . . ."

Because *she* was in him. In the heart that others thought he didn't have. She'd worked her way inside, slipped right past his guard, and he wasn't about to go back to the emptiness he'd known before her.

With Sarah, it wasn't about pack and responsibility. It wasn't about the wolves and their safety.

Just a man and a woman.

Just . . . life.

If only she wouldn't die on him.

His hand touched her chest. Her heart pounded beneath his touch. Growing stronger, stronger . . .

"Sarah? Come back . . . to me."

"She can't ever leave you." Josette. Still with the blind eyes and faraway voice. "Bound—spirits, minds, hearts. If you live . . ."

Sarah's eyes opened.

"She lives."

His arms curled around her and he yanked Sarah against him, holding her tight. "You scared the hell out of me." Still *was* scaring him.

"The battle isn't over . . . more to come . . . so many years . . . so much blood . . ." Josette's voice drifted in the air, slurring a bit.

Lucas eased back and stared into Sarah's eyes. Such a deep, beautiful green.

"Give everything . . ." Josette was almost whispering now, "you'll survive all that comes, give nothing . . ."

"Josette?" Maya sounded worried. "Dammit, Josie, what the hell is happening? You can't do this stuff—"

"I'll give you everything I have," Sarah whispered. "I love you, Lucas."

Love.

He hadn't really been given a lot of that in his life. Didn't understand it. Didn't know . . .

Her lips brushed his jaw. "I . . . should have told you sooner . . . I don't really understand what . . . the hell happened here tonight . . ." With every word, her voice grew stronger. *He* grew stronger. "But we're okay, right? We're . . . gonna make it?"

He nodded and held her tighter. Death had been too close. Life and death—the line between them was so very fragile. And humans weren't the only ones weak enough to fall over that line.

Linked. Bound. When she left this world, he'd leave, too.

Her lashes brushed against his cheek. "I don't want to lose you."

"You won't." Not in life and not in death.

Sarah looked up at him. "Promise me."

He'd do more than that. "Sarah . . ."

Josette gasped, her breath wheezing. Lucas glanced over as her eyelids fell closed. Maya grabbed her, holding tight. Brody ran from the woods, heading toward them. "Maya!"

"Help me!" She yelled to him. "I don't know what's happening to her!"

A shudder rippled over Josette's body. Her palm opened, revealing Marie's ring.

Behind Josette, Lucas saw Piers's body. Josette's left hand was touching his side.

A groan broke from the man's lips. He rose, blinking. "L-Lucas?" His gaze swept the scene. Saw the remains of

Rafe. Saw Lucas holding Sarah tight. Saw the limp arm of the woman who'd been touching him. *"Josette."* Need and raw hunger shook his voice.

But Maya came at him with her own claws. "Don't even think about hurting her, wolf."

Lucas knew he wouldn't. Piers looked at him, shaking his head, his eyes wide and horrified. "Alpha . . . I—"

Sirens wailed in the distance. Not like the humans would have been able to overlook Brody's fire and the fire from Marie's house. Even in this part of town, two blazes wouldn't go unnoticed.

"We have to get out of here," Jordan said, grabbing Lucas's arm. Dane took Sarah's. *"Now."*

He knew they had to flee because he wasn't healed. Wasn't ready to bullshit an explanation about the savaged bodies there and the dead demon inside.

Maya's gaze raked them. "Go. I can handle the cops."

Probably, since she'd been a cop . . . once upon a time. Before a vamp's bite had changed her life and taken her from that world.

Piers reached for Josette. "No damn way, wolf," Maya snapped and Brody pressed closer to her. "You're not taking her."

Piers growled.

"Piers!"

The blond wolf shifter's head snapped toward him. Right then, he understood. Oh, did Lucas fucking understand. His mate was against him, her body trembling, and there was no way he'd separate from her.

But . . .

Josette didn't know what was happening. "Heal first, then claim her." An order from the alpha.

And Piers had damn well better obey. Lucas could understand the guy going bat shit crazy because he thought his mate was dead—*if Sarah had died*—no. He *could* understand. So Piers wouldn't be punished, but he would obey now or hell would come.

Piers lowered his head. His fingers curled into a fist, never touching Josette.

"He needs her," Sarah whispered.

Just like I need you.

Piers could fight his battle for Josette. But right then, the priority was getting Sarah and the rest of the pack to safety.

He stood, would have stumbled, but Jordan was there. Watching his back now, the way Lucas had once watched his brother's.

Lucas didn't let go of Sarah. He didn't look back at the house or at the torn body of his nemesis. It was over.

"Another part of the legend," Sarah murmured.

Lucas frowned down at her.

"You took out Rafe, his pack is destroyed, and you walk away, cheating death again."

Not cheating death. Telling the bastard to wait. *Wait—I'm living with her.* And that cold asshole wasn't getting either one of them for a long time.

He planned for them both to have very, very long lives.

"Tell Josette I'm coming for her!" Piers yelled, turning back once. "I waited . . . years, but I'll be coming for her now."

"You won't hurt her." From Brody. Always so protective of Maya and those close to her.

"No, but I'll have her."

Did Piers understand just what he'd be getting? Because Lucas suspected that Josette wasn't the same woman she'd been before. He knew power when he smelled it.

A new *mambo* seemed to have taken over.

Dane had hot-wired a truck. Jordan leapt on his bike. The other vehicles couldn't be traced to them.

Lucas eased Sarah inside the truck. Her eyes had closed again. Fear pumped through him. "Sarah?"

Her eyes didn't open. "Relax, Lucas . . . can't go anywhere . . . without you." The faintest of smiles curved her lips.

He climbed in and pulled her close. "No, babe, you can't." From here on out, they'd be together.

And if anyone tried to come between them, he'd slaughter the dumbass.

Because Sarah King was his. He'd bled for her, killed for her, nearly died for her . . . and he'd never give her up. *Never.*

When Sarah opened her eyes, she was in a bedroom. Lucas's bedroom. The window's broken glass had been repaired. The room was cleaned up and no signs of the old battle remained.

The mattress was soft beneath her, and Lucas's hand was a warm weight on her stomach. She stared up at the ceiling, not daring to look at him yet.

Last night they'd almost died. Somehow, they'd made it through. Rafe hadn't. One less crazy jerk in the world. One less nightmare to haunt her.

They'd made it, and she'd told Lucas—*I love you.*

But he hadn't said a word back to her. If she hadn't been barely clinging to consciousness, that would probably have hurt her more then.

Since she was fully awake and aware now, it hurt like a bitch.

She tried to ease away from him, but his hand slipped down and curled around her waist, holding her in place. "Thought we covered this," his voice rumbled. "You don't get away from me."

Yes, she vaguely remembered something about that. But, what was crystal clear in her head . . . *He didn't say he loved me. We almost died and he never said* . . . She swallowed. "I just . . . I—" Great. She didn't know what to say. What to do.

"While you were sleeping, you called my name."

That wasn't going to embarrass her. She'd already said she loved the guy. So she whispered his name in her sleep. So what?

"I don't know if anyone has ever *dreamed* about me before." His lips pressed against the curve of her shoulder. "Had nightmares, yeah, but not *dreamed* about me."

"Well, if you want the truth . . ." She turned her head and

met his bright stare. "I've been dreaming about you for months."

He blinked.

What did she have to lose? "I wasn't out of my head last night. It wasn't pain talking. I meant what I said." *Did you mean what you didn't say?* "I'm in love with you, Lucas."

No more blinks. His gaze bored into hers. "What do you want from me?"

Not that response. "I want everything that you can give me. You said we're mates. Okay, I don't know what makes someone a mate or—"

"You can have my children. Your genetics balance with mine. I knew the first time we had sex that we were compatible."

Compatible? She didn't want compatible. Sarah rolled away from him.

He caught her arm and rolled her right back. "Dammit, I'm messing this up!"

"Yes, you are." Gritted.

His eyes blazed down at her. "I'm not sure I know what love is."

Her lips parted.

He kissed her. Hard and deep and his taste was right, just what she wanted, and her sex began to moisten. *For him. Only him.* The guy had ruined her for other men. And not because they were *compatible* or had a good *genetic* match.

His head lifted. "In case you haven't noticed, my life hasn't exactly been easy."

She'd noticed.

"Women in my life have been around for a few days. I just took the pleasure and walked away. No attachments."

She didn't want to hear about his pleasure with other women. The guy was really lucky she didn't have claws.

"Jordan's my only family. The pack—hell, we don't know about love. None of us. Obsession. Need. Hunger. Lust. Yeah, we got that."

Wolves always understood the darker drives. Animal instinct.

But it was the man who could love. Didn't he realize that?

"I want you, Sarah. I need you. Hell, sometimes I feel like I need you more than I need my next breath."

That was . . . oh.

"I knew you were dying last night. I could see it, and I just wanted—"

"I wanted to touch you," she whispered, cutting across his words. "Just one more time."

"That was some powerful touch." His lips skimmed hers. "I think you pushed death back for us again."

How many more chances would they have?

"You know how it works now, don't you? Whatever magic Marie wove, it can't be broken," he said. "Our lives are linked, everything tied together. When one of us dies . . ."

"I—I know."

His gaze dropped to her mouth. "You could do better than me." Said gruffly. "We're bound, but you don't have to spend your days with—"

"Watch it, wolf," she warned, her own voice sharp. "You're talking about my mate."

His jaw clenched. "Mating doesn't equal love."

Okay, why didn't he just claw her heart out? "With you, for me, it does."

Lucas stared at her, then his eyelids squeezed shut. "I'm going to fuck this up. I'm not easy to live with, hell, nothing about pack is easy."

Her fingers curled over his broad shoulders. "What makes you think life with me is easy?" She paused. "What makes you think I *want* easy?" Maybe she should have been trying to spare her pride and pull back from him, but her confession was out there, and she wasn't going to slink away in shame.

His eyes open. Burned with so much intensity. "I'm a possessive bastard. I'm wild. The animal inside is too strong. I can't always control him."

Bull. "You have more control than anyone I've ever met."

His legs eased between hers. She could feel his arousal, thick and hard and so long. Aroused, but . . . he wasn't pushing his flesh against her.

Sex wasn't going to solve this. They both seemed to understand that.

"I'll lie for you, Sarah. Kill for you."

He already had.

"I'd turn my back on the pack for you . . ."

Now he had her tensing because that was more of a sacrifice than she'd ever ask of him.

"And I will *never* want anyone as much as I want you." He shook his head. "But I don't know that I can give you what you need."

And he was breaking her heart. Her hand slid down his chest. Pressed once more over the heart that raced so fast. "What do you want for me?"

His brows furrowed.

"What do you want my life to be like?"

A muscle flexed in his jaw. "I want you . . . happy."

Promising. Maybe he really didn't know. "When you're with me, how do you feel?"

His breath hissed out. "Like I've finally found home."

The wolf was going to make her cry. "That's how I feel when I'm with you. Like I belong. Like I found a part of myself that was missing . . . I didn't even know it was missing. . . ." Not until she'd walked into a jail and peered at a wolf caged behind the bars. *Mine.* "I love you, Lucas, and I'm not going to walk away. I won't give up on us." Whatever came their way—wolves, wars, pack—she'd stay by his side.

"Love." He said the word as if he were tasting it. "You're the first thing I think about when I open my eyes. The last damn thing at night. And when I dream . . ." He swallowed. "It's of you. Sarah, is that close to love?"

So lost. Her big, bad wolf was strong in so many ways. She'd teach him this. Show him the way. "Yes, Lucas, it's close." No, better than close.

"I'd rip apart anyone who hurt you, and damn, woman, I feel like I'd give my soul—or whatever the hell is left of it—just to see you smile."

Better than close. "That's love," she whispered.

His brows smoothed. His lips began to curl. "Then Sarah King . . . I love you."

She was pretty sure her fast heartbeat shook her chest. Maybe even the whole bed.

"I won't let you go," he told her, his mouth so close to hers that she could taste him. *Would* taste him, very soon.

"Good. Because I'd hate to hunt you down." She nipped at his lip and felt the tightening of his body.

"Forever, Sarah?"

"Forever, Lucas," she promised.

Bound, linked, always—with her big, bad wolf.

Epilogue

"Caleb's gone." Dane spun around as soon as he made the announcement. Shit, okay, he *should* not have busted into the alpha's room. But, wow, Sarah had one fine ass.

Lucas's growl filled the bedroom. "*Don't* look back, Dane."

Yeah, he knew a death threat when he heard one. Dane stared into the hallway. "He slipped away while we were fighting Rafe." His gut tightened. "Do we hunt him?"

"Lucas . . ." Sarah's soft voice. Husky. Sounded like pleasure and sex.

Lucky bastard.

But maybe, just maybe, he could have the devil's luck, too. *Karen had survived the attack.* He'd already checked the hospital. *Had* to check. She'd survived.

Now what would he do with her? To her?

If Caleb hadn't pulled this vanishing crap, he'd be at Karen's side right then.

"He didn't kill when he had the chance. He never went for your throat," Sarah told Lucas.

Sheets rustled. Dane still didn't look back as he asked, "Is he Lone?" Cast out. Left to fight and struggle on his own.

"No."

Dane's head jerked but he managed—barely—not to glance over his shoulder.

"Not yet. The pack will judge. All of the pack. Once we find him."

Dane stepped into the hallway. "Do we start the hunt now?"

"No need." More sheets rustled. Dane heard Sarah sigh softly. "I know where he's going," Lucas said. "There's only one person in town that might be able to help him, and she's already being watched by pack."

"Then what are the orders?"

"Stand down—and wait. Our lost wolf will be back. One way or another . . ."

Josette slipped the ruby ring onto her finger. A perfect fit. Her mother's ring. Taken when Carline was slaughtered in a dirty alley by a vamp.

Taken, but then retrieved by another. Maya had recovered the ring when she'd killed the vampire who'd drained Josette's mother.

We're not all monsters. Maya's words, spoken years ago. Josette just hadn't wanted to believe her then.

Now, she knew the truth.

"What's happened to you, Josie?" Maya asked quietly. They'd washed away the blood. Bandaged the wounds. Now Josette stood, waiting.

Because she knew what was coming.

Thanks to her *grand-mère,* she wasn't weak anymore. Wouldn't ever be weak again, and now, she knew *everything.*

Not all monsters. No, some paranormals were good, some were bad. Just like humans.

And they would be coming to her. Over and over. Seeking help. Seeking power. Seeking life.

Perhaps finding death.

"I didn't want this," she whispered to the vampire who'd once been her only friend. In another life . . . so long ago.

Maya's hand brushed her shoulder. "Let me help you."

Josette shook her head. "You can't." No one could.

She lifted her chin when she heard the creak of the floor-board. The first. Far from the last.

Not the wolf she'd wanted to see, though, not him. Not yet.

Caleb McKenzie paused just outside of her doorway. "I-I need your help."

She'd seen *grand-mère* do this so many times. "And what will you give me?"

"Anything."

So desperate. That would make him dangerous. The world began to fog around Josette as power fueled her blood. *Anything.*

If he wasn't careful, the wolf would end up trading every-thing.

After all, magic demanded a high price.

It was a lesson Sarah King had learned. She'd paid, she'd loved, and by a trick of fate, she'd lived.

Not everyone could be so lucky.

But then, Sarah King truly lived a charmed life.

If you liked this book, try Dani Harper's
CHANGELING DREAM,
in stores now . . .

What kind of woman runs after a wolf?

James was no closer to answering that question than he had been many hours before when he had paused in the clinic loft, two bounds away from the open window, and listened to the human calling after the white wolf. He had been startled to find the woman up and around so close to dawn, but more surprised by her reaction when she spotted him. She should have been terrified, should have been screaming. Instead she had stopped still, remaining quiet until he melted back into the darkness—then had plunged forward in a vain attempt to follow him. She acted as if she knew the wolf, but how could that be? There was something else too; something in her voice had almost compelled him to—what? Answer her? Reveal himself? He didn't know. The woman had gone from room to room then, switching on every light, searching.

He wasn't surprised when she didn't check the loft. After all, it was fifteen feet above the ground floor and accessible only by a vertical ladder. A wolf couldn't climb it, and she had no way of knowing that what she pursued was not a wolf and that the ladder was no impediment to him at all. The stack of bales outside, from which he had initially leapt, was more than thirty feet from the loading door of the loft. Only a very large tiger might cross such a span. Or a Changeling.

James felt a strange disappointment tugging at his senses,

almost a regret that the woman had not found him. *Who are you? Why do I know you?* Within his lupine body, James chuffed out a breath in frustration. *And why do I care?* The angle of the fading light told him it was time to hunt, that deer would be on the move. Weary of human thoughts and human concerns, he relaxed into his wolf nature and disappeared beneath it.

"What a tourist I am!" Jillian berated herself for not bringing a cell phone, for not paying more attention to the time, for traveling in the bush alone, for not packing at least a chocolate bar. Two chocolate bars. Maybe three. The energy bars she'd brought tasted like wet cardboard. She made a long mental list of the things she was going to do to be more prepared for the next hike, because as difficult as the trail was, she simply had to go back to that rocky plateau, had to see if the wolves would return. Was it part of their territory or were they just passing through?

The sun was long gone. Stars were pinning a deep indigo sky, and a full moon was floating just above the horizon. It had climbed enough to glimmer through the trees and lay a broad swath of light over the surface of the river when Jillian finally found the marked hiking trail. Compared to the goat path she'd been traveling, the graveled corridor was like a wide paved highway, level and free of overhanging brush and fallen logs. It promised easier, faster travel in spite of the darkness. She was still two and a half, maybe three, miles from the truck she had borrowed from the clinic, but at least now she had a direct route.

The flashback broadsided her without warning.

It might have been the crunch of gravel beneath her feet, the rustle of leaves in the trees, or the scent of the river, but whatever the trigger, she was suddenly on another trail by another river. Phantom images, sounds, even smells burst vividly upon her senses. Jillian stumbled forward and fell to her knees, skinning them both right through her jeans. She rolled and sat, but clasped her hands to her head rather than to her wounds. "Don't close your eyes, don't close your eyes. You're not there, it's not real, it's over. Jesus, it's over, it's over and you're okay. You're okay." She spoke slowly, deliberately, coaching herself until the shaking stopped. "It's a different place and a different time. I'm not back there, I'm here. I'm here and I'm okay." *I'm okay, I'm okay.*

But she wasn't, not yet. She rocked back and forth in the gravel. "My name is Jillian Descharme and I'm a licensed veterinarian and I'm okay. I'm thirty-two years old and I'm in Dunvegan, Alberta, and I'm okay. Nothing is threatening me, nothing is wrong, I'm okay." She drew a long shaky breath and rubbed her runny nose with her sleeve like a child. "I'm okay. Jeez! Jeez goddamn Louise!" She was cold, freezing cold, her clothes soaked with sweat and her skin clammy, but the fear had her by the throat and she couldn't move. She had to think of something fast, something to help her break away from this terror, break out of this inertia or she'd be here all night. And then it came. The image of the white wolf—the memory, the dream, flowed into her, warmed her like brandy. Jillian clung to that mental picture like a life preserver in rough seas, let the wolf's unspoken words fill her mind and calm it. *Not alone. Here with you.*

She rose at last on trembling legs and cursed as her knees made their condition known. The sharp stinging cleared the last of the flashback from her head however, banished the nausea from her stomach. She stood for several moments, hugging herself, rubbing her hands over her upper arms. She sucked in great lungfuls of the cool moist air until she felt steady again, and took a few tentative steps along the dark path—but had to resist the impulse to run. If she ran, she might never stop.

"Think of the white wolf, think of the white wolf." Calm, she had to be calm. Take big breaths. "Walk like a normal person. It's okay to walk fast because I'm busy, got things to do, places to go, people to see, but I don't have to run. I can walk because nothing's wrong, I'm okay." She was in control, she would stay in control. As she walked, however, she couldn't stop her senses from being on hyper-alert. Jillian's eyes flicked rapidly from side to side, searching the darkness, her ears straining to hear any rustle of leaf or snap of twig. She noticed the tiny brown bats that dipped and whirled in the air above her. She noted the calls of night birds, of loons settling and owls hunting. A mouse hurried in front of her, crossing and re-crossing the path. A few moments later, a weasel followed it, in a slinky rolling motion. Jillian was keenly aware of everything—the blood pounding in her ears, the sound of her footsteps in the gravel, the liquid sounds of the nearby river—but not the tree root bulging up through the path.

She yelled in surprise, then in pain as her knees hit the gravel again. She rolled to a sitting position, cursing the sharp stinging and her own clumsiness—hadn't she *just* successfully negotiated a rugged game trail down a steep hillside for heaven's sake? She couldn't see much even with the moon's light, but a quick examination showed both knees were bleeding, her jeans in shreds. She cursed even more as she picked out a few obvious shards of gravel, but cleaning and bandaging were just going to have to wait until she reached the truck. At least it wasn't anything worse. Annoying, damn painful and embarrassing, but not a broken ankle or snakebite. Her eyes strayed to the underbrush in spite of herself—there weren't any poisonous snakes this far north, were there? "Good grief!" Jillian yanked her mind firmly away from *that* train of thought and was pondering whether it was possible to stand without bending her knees when she heard the howl.

She sat bolt upright as if an electric current had suddenly passed through her, every hair on end, every sense alert. The call came again, closer. Deep, primal, long and low. Drawn out and out and out, an ancient song, mournful yet somehow sweet. When it fell silent, Jillian felt as if time itself had stopped. And she found herself straining to hear the song again, fascinated, even as her brain told her to run and instinct told her to freeze.

The moon was higher now. The pale light filtered down through the trees and laid a dappled carpet of silver on the stony path. There was no wind, no breeze. Jillian held her breath, listening, watching, but all was still. Her heart was pounding hard with both excitement and fear. Normally she would have loved to get a glimpse of a wolf in the wild, but the idea was a lot less attractive when she was alone in the dark. There were few recorded incidents of wolves attacking or killing humans, but all the data in the world wasn't very reassuring when she was sitting there bleeding. Immediately she wished she hadn't thought of that. It was just a little blood, but she struggled to get the image of a wounded fish in a shark tank out of her head.

A movement at the edge of the path beyond seized her attention. A pale shape emerged from the shadows, seemed to coalesce in the moonlight and grow larger until it was a vivid white creature of impossible size. Jillian's heart stuck in her throat as the great wolf slowly turned its massive head and stared directly at her.

Oh, Jesus. She had studied wolves more than any other wildlife, but only from books and captive specimens. Wolves don't attack humans, she reminded herself. Wolves don't attack humans—but there had been cases in Alaska. She gritted her teeth and sat perfectly still, afraid to breathe as the wolf began to slowly move in her direction. The creature approached within ten feet, then abruptly sat on its haunches and stared at her.

It was enormous. She swallowed hard, realizing if the wolf attacked there would be nothing she could do. Nothing. She wouldn't even manage a scream before it was on her. Not one bit of her martial arts training would help, especially when she was sitting on the ground. Nevertheless she scanned the ground with her peripheral vision for anything she might use as a weapon. Her fingers inched toward a rock, closed around it as the wolf rose, took a slow step toward her, into a pool of moonlight. Instantly its snowy fur gleamed and its eyes were . . . its eyes were. . . .

Blue.

Jillian felt as if the air had been knocked from her body. The rock rolled out of her palm. Trembling, shaking, she reached a tentative hand toward the animal. "You. It's you," she choked out. "Oh, my God, it's you, isn't it? You're real."

The wolf closed the gap between them and licked her out-stretched fingers. *Omigod, omigod.* She couldn't move at first, both enthralled and terrified—until the animal nudged its head under her hand like a dog asking to be petted. Jillian moved her fingers lightly across the broad skull, scratching hesitantly at first. Then fear fell away, and she worked both hands behind the sensitive ears, into the glossy ruff. The wolf stood panting mildly, the immense jaws slack and the great pink tongue lolling out in apparent pleasure. Jillian had no illusions about the animal's power—it might behave like a big dog but those jaws could easily crack the leg bones of a moose, those teeth could tear out the throat of a bull elk in full flight. And as surely as she knew those facts, she knew the wolf would not hurt her. It wasn't sensible, it wasn't logical, but the certainty was core-deep. Instinct? Intuition? Insanity? She didn't know and didn't care. The wolf held steady as Jillian wrapped her arms around its great neck and buried her face in its thick white fur. "I thought I dreamed you. You came to me. You came when no one would come, but they all told me I dreamed you because no one saw you but me. And I looked and looked for you, but I couldn't find you."

Here now. Found you.

Try MISTRESS OF THE STORM,
the third in Terri Brisbin's sensual trilogy, out now!

Every possible space in the hall of Duntulm Keep was filled. Many of those who owned land in the surrounding areas attended the early autumn feast hosted by Davin to meet the men from Orkney and take their measure. Though invited to sit at table with him, Duncan declined Davin's invitation, choosing to sit away from the guests so he could observe them. It seemed the fires of hell had left his sense of curiosity intact when they burned away all the rest, so he listened and learned much about the visitors from the north.

Greeted as cousins, they were related to Davin through the marriage of their grandparents or some other ancestor, and the welcome he gave was warm. Foodstuffs and ale were plentiful and everyone ate and drank their fill. Ornolf placed a bowl and cup before Duncan, bothering him every so often so he would eat and drink. The smoke grew thick as the fires burned lower, offering heat but not much light. The torches and rushlights added what they could, but Duncan could see clearly through the dimness and the haze.

It was a strange effect he'd noticed the last few months, and it served him well in his attempts to watch and learn. He was studying the similarities in appearance between Davin and the one called Ragnar when the woman arrived. The room suddenly grew brighter and the chatter lessened as though everyone wanted to see her at once.

Nothing she wore was ostentatious, but the cut of her

gown drew every man's eyes to her body. He could not identify the material of it, but it draped her curves as though painted over her flesh instead of being a garment. Duncan noticed the tightened nipples of her very full breasts as the gown molded to them and the way it fell into the juncture of her thighs. When she turned to sit down, he and every other man noted the way it hugged her arse, flowing into the indentation of the cleft and outlining her strong legs. Watching her move in it, he did not have to imagine what her body was like—he could see it.

He let his gaze wander over her, waiting for her to be seated so he could see her face.

Something he had not felt in months coursed through him in the moment their eyes met. A heat, a need, a wanting made him ache. Her eyes widened as though she knew her effect, but she looked away when someone spoke her name.

Isabel.

Who was she?

What was she?

How could she cause him to feel the blood heating and rushing through his body when he'd thought himself empty of such things? Duncan shifted in his chair and continued to watch as the attention of those gathered began to drift back to the honored guests. But he realized every man eventually turned back to watch Isabel.

She'd gathered and arranged her hair in a way that made her look well bedded. Its black waves accentuated every move she made and framed the creaminess of her skin perfectly. It was her mouth that sent waves of heat through him; her lips were bow-shaped and red as though well kissed. The blush in her cheeks added to the display—one he could tell was orchestrated carefully for its effect. Tearing his gaze from her, Duncan looked at the people she had followed into the feast.

Strange.

The man and younger woman she'd walked behind had taken seats much closer to their host, while she remained farther away. Was she the girl's maid? Neither of the women resembled the man in any way for he was as light as they were dark in hair and eye coloring. Duncan thought the women might be related based on the frequent glances they shared, cousins probably, though mayhap even sisters.

But, if sisters, why did they so clearly separate themselves at table?

The meal continued and Duncan resumed his perusal, watching her as she ate the food placed before her, and as she spoke to others, seeming to watch every move made by the man with whom she'd entered. It was only when she lifted her chin, gazed up at the ceiling of the chamber and closed her eyes that Duncan realized he'd seen her before. Searching his memory, he finally remembered where and when.

In the early hours just as the sun rose, when unable to sleep, he would walk the battlements of the keep, gazing down at the sea and the village outside the walls. Several times in the last months he'd noticed her leaving the keep just before dawn, and walking to the south beach.

With nothing more than curiosity to keep his attention, Duncan would watch as she took off her clothes and flung herself into the water. Her practice was the same each time he'd watched—dipping twice under the surface of the water and scrubbing her skin as she did. Then she would plunge down and remain in the freezing waters until he thought she'd perished. He remembered several times when he began counting how long she stayed under the water, wondering if she would rise from it at all.

Over the months he'd witnessed her behavior, the changes within him making any tension he felt as he counted out the seconds lessen until he'd watched in complete disinterest, no matter how much he knew he should be concerned.

Watching the way she tilted her head, he was reminded of the way she looked up at the sun as she walked, sometimes struggling, out of the waves. In the earlier times he'd seen her, he'd thought she might be a selkie or water spirit. But, lately, he observed her actions from an emotional and physical distance—until she lowered her head and gazed at him through her lashes.

That heat seared him again, letting him feel things he'd not felt in months. Was she a selkie risen from the sea or some otherworldly creature capable of giving him back all he'd lost? His moments of disinterested watchfulness were over, for his body and his soul knew she was more than she appeared, and his mind knew he must discover her secrets and their link to his own. Standing, his feet moved before he could think on what words to say or what he wanted. All he knew was that he wanted . . . her.

Don't miss DEAD ALERT by Bianca D'Arc,
coming next month . . .

Fort Bragg, North Carolina

"I've got a special project for you, Sam." The commander, a former Navy SEAL named Matt Sykes, began talking before Sam was through the door to Matt's private office. "Sit down and shut the door."

Sam sat in a wooden chair across the cluttered desk from his commanding officer. Lt. Sam Archer, US Army Green Berct, was currently assigned to a top secret, mixed team of Special Forces soldiers and elite scientists. There were also a few others from different organizations, including one former cop and a CIA black ops guy. It was an extremely specialized group, recruited to work on a classified project of the highest order.

"I understand you're a pilot." Matt flipped through a file as he spoke.

"Yes, sir." Sam could have said more but he didn't doubt Matt had access to every last bit of Sam's file, even the top secret parts. He had probably known before even sending for him that Sam could fly anything with wings. Another member of his old unit was a blade pilot who flew all kinds of choppers, but fixed wing aircraft were Sam's specialty.

"How do you like the idea of going undercover as a charter pilot?"

"Sir?" Sam sat forward in the chair, intrigued.

"The name of a certain charter airline keeps popping up."
Matt put down the file and faced Sam as his gaze hardened.
"Too often for my comfort. Ever heard of a company called
Praxis Air?"

"Can't say that I have."

"It's a small outfit, based out of Wichita—at least that's
where they repair and maintain their aircraft in a company-
owned hangar. They have branch offices at most of the major
airports and cater mostly to an elite business clientele. They
do the odd private cargo flight and who knows what else.
They keep their business very hush-hush, *providing the ulti-
mate in privacy for their corporate clients,* or so their brochure advertises." Matt pushed a glossy tri-fold across the
desk toward Sam.

"Looks pretty slick."

"That they are," Matt agreed. "So slick that even John
Petit, with his multitude of CIA connections, can't get a bead
on exactly what they've been up to of late. I've been piecing
together bits here and there. Admiral Chester, the traitor, accepted more than a few free flights from them in the past few
months, as did Ensign Bartles, who it turns out, was killed in
a Praxis Air jet that crashed the night we took down Dr. Ro-
driguez and his friends. She wasn't listed on the manifest and
only the pilot was claimed by the company, but on a hunch I
asked a friend on the National Transportation Safety Board
to allow us to do some DNA testing. Sure enough, we found
remnants of Beverly Bartles' DNA at the crash site, though
her body had to have been moved sometime prior to the
NTSB getting there. The locals were either paid off or pre-
empted. Either option is troubling, to say the least."

"You think they're mixed up with our undead friends?"
They were still seeking members of the science team that had
created the formula that killed and then turned its victims
into the walking dead. Nobody had figured out exactly how
they were traveling so freely around the country when they
were on every watch list possible.

"It's a very real possibility. Which is why I want to send

you in undercover. I don't need to remind you, time is of the essence. We have a narrow window to stuff this genie back into its bottle. The longer this goes on, the more likely it is the technology will be sold to the highest bidder and then, God help us."

Sam shivered. The idea of the zombie technology in the hands of a hostile government or psycho terrorists—especially after seeing what he'd seen of these past months—was unthinkable.

"If my going undercover will help end this, I'm your man." He'd do anything to stop the contagion from killing any more people.

Sam opened the flyer and noted the different kinds of jets the company offered. The majority of the planes looked like Lear 35's in different configurations. Some were equipped for cargo. Some had all the bells and whistles any corporate executive could wish for and a few were basically miniature luxury liners set up for spoiled celebrities and their friends.

"I'd hoped you'd say that. I've arranged a little extra training for you at Flight Safety in Houston. They've got Level D flight simulators that have full motion and full visual. They can give you the Type Rating you'll need on your license to work for Praxis Air legitimately."

"I've been to Flight Safety before. It's a good outfit." Sam put the brochure back on Matt's desk.

"We'll give you a suitable job history and cover, which you will commit to memory. You'll also have regular check-ins while in the field, but for the most part you'll be on your own. I want you to discover who, if any, of their personnel are involved and to what extent." Matt paused briefly before continuing. "Just to be clear, this isn't a regular job I'm asking you to do, Sam. It's not even close to what you signed on for when we were assigned as zombie hunters. I won't order you to do this. It's a total immersion mission. Chances are, there will be no immediate backup if you get into trouble. You'll be completely on your own most of the time."

"Understood, sir. I'm still up for it. I like a challenge."